SANDS OF RECKONING

JANEAL FALOR

Sands of Reckoning
Janeal Falor

To learn more about this author, please visit: www.janealfalor.com
Print Book ISBN: 978-1946860101
Cover by Miblart

To Erik

Always & Forever

CHAPTER ONE

The grains of sand slopped beneath my feet, leaving me feeling as though I had trekked for ages, and I wished for nothing but water. Then again, the river was tainted, if we'd interpreted the plans Nikon stole from the Reding right.

The Reding—Nikon's brother. It was still impossible to believe. As was finally having my parents with me.

The heat continued to press heavy on my shoulders, as a murmur of voices grew louder. I hoped this meant we were almost to the marauder camp. Moments later, my hopes were realized when the slap of sand shifted to the sound of someone running toward me.

I stiffened, until Zoe called out, "You're back."

Next thing I knew, she wrapped her arms around me, embracing me as tightly as I did her. I clamped down my jaw to keep from crying. I needed this—someone to care about me in a time when I wasn't sure what to think or feel. Nikon or my parents should have been the ones comforting me, but I'd pushed Nikon away, and Mom and Dad were too tired to do anything but sludge forward—much like my thoughts.

"What's wrong?" Zoe's tone was nothing but concern, as she pulled back. "Everyone's here. Tewy's scrambling toward us, and Nikon is heading toward Na'eehma. The man and woman at your side look like you. Are they your parents?" Her anticipation and excitement carried to me.

"They are." I forced a grin, trying to feel the full joy of being reunited with them but struggling.

She squealed. "I can't believe it. Will you introduce me?"

"I would like to. It's just..." I trailed off. As much as I wanted to shout and dance with happiness, the need to tell her who Nikon really was dampened my exuberance.

"I'm her mother, Edita Palmira. I'm afraid I had news that upset my daughter." Mom's voice was dry. She probably needed liquid, despite all we'd been giving her to drink on our journey here. She and Dad had been through far too much, and here I was, dragging them through the desert. At least they might be safe here, which could change how they felt.

"We'll talk more." Zoe moved to my side, and I rested my hand on her arm. Dad had been helping me, but she was steadier. "Why don't you come into camp, and we'll get some supplies?" she asked.

"That would be most good of you," Dad said.

I was grateful for her insight. As much as I'd leaned on my parents off and on throughout the trip, they'd leaned on me more. They tried to take care of me as much as I tried to take care of them. They hadn't said much about the dungeons after being locked up there for... well, years. The betrayal I dealt with was nothing compared to that.

I let Zoe lead me forward, without worrying about the growing hints of camp—the clang of pots, murmured voices... and a littler chirp, familiar and heartening. I bent down, and Tewy jumped on my arm and scurried up my shoulder. The excited-monkey noises that followed gave way to distress every few squawks.

I rubbed his chest, cooing at him while keeping myself together. "Missed you as well, Tewy."

He yanked on my hair, before simmering down.

"Some refreshment," Zoe said, and a water skin brushed against my hand. As I sipped, she asked, "What happened?"

No sense delaying it, but I did keep my voice to a whisper. "Nikon is Reding Theodore's brother."

She gasped. "No."

At least I wasn't the only one shocked by the reality. The numbness that'd been spreading in my chest receded enough for me to figure out what it meant for us. For him. For me.

"It changes everything," I said.

She didn't respond. Tewy's shifting on my shoulder was the only indication it was a lot to process. *Sand it all*, I was trying.

"I can't believe it," she finally said.

All I could do was nod. Being the Reding's brother was beyond what I'd expected of Nikon as well.

Zoe said with a touch of hesitancy, "It is concerning that he could keep so much from us, but I can understand why he did so. That's a heavy burden for one to carry, when he's so against what the Reding and Vading stand for."

I squeezed the water so hard, it spilled a bit onto my lap. Throwing the flask to the ground beside me, I struggled to keep my voice low. "You're siding with him?"

"I wouldn't say that. More that I can see where he's coming from. Can you imagine being a sibling to the Reding or Vading? What would you do?"

She almost had a point, but Vading Antonia had been like an older sister to me, and yet I told Nikon about it as soon as I knew.

Then again, I hadn't told Zoe and Kaius right away. I kept things from others, just like they kept things from me. Zoe and Kaius didn't tell Nikon they were married, and not siblings, as we all thought. There'd been much deception going around.

The rebellion had attempted to kill the Reding and Vading.

They didn't listen to Nikon and me when we disagreed. He and I had decided to do what we could to save the Reding and Vading, even though we wanted them to be punished for their actions. It'd be difficult, but neither of us wanted their deaths on our hands. It made more sense now why Nikon would have hesitated to share. All the hate toward the Reding might have made him worry the animosity had spilled out to him. I shook my head, thinking of how it affected me.

I relented. "It's hard to say what I would do, without being in his position."

"Maybe it'd be best to remember that," Zoe said.

I nodded, trying to imprint it on my mind, but it would likely take some work. "You are going to tell him about you and Kaius, yes?"

"When the time is right."

I didn't like the sound of that, but there was little I could do about it, unless I was to tell him myself. It was their news to share, so I'd leave it be.

"What does she need to tell, about her and this Kaius person?" Mother's voice scratched out.

My parents had been so quiet, I'd forgotten they were here. I should be thrilled and aware of their presence, after I thought them dead for years. The fact that I could forget left my heart bleeding.

"Sorry. It doesn't matter. Tell me about you and Dad," I said.

"Not much to tell," Dad mumbled.

"You know better than to try and protect her." Mom sounded much clearer this time, probably after a nice long drink. "She's a grown woman now. Look at her. She can handle anything we tell her."

I sat up straighter, wanting to look like the woman they were speaking of, and not the scared youth I felt like. Somehow, finding my parents made me want to revert to when I lived with them, instead of my current age of twenty-nine.

"What I want to know," Mother said, using her *I-need-an-explanation-and-I-need-it-now* voice, "is how you knew where to find us. Why did you come looking for us? And your dad mentioned there was a neczar that specifically wanted *you*, which surprised me. What have you been doing all these years, to get in trouble with them?"

I tried not to curl in on myself, but her tone and scolding made my shoulders droop. A shift of sand, so soft it could only be Nikon, came toward our group. By the sound, he stopped a few feet away.

"And why does the Reding's brother have anything to do with my daughter, let alone help her?" Dad snapped. "Don't get me wrong—I think my daughter is a thousand times your worth—but I'm trying to understand how you two wound up working together."

On the journey here, they hadn't asked much, so it shouldn't have surprised me they wanted to know now. I didn't want to hash over a story that involved more than I knew how to process, so when Nikon told it, I was secretly relieved. He summarized the facts well enough, without adding too many unnecessary details, weaving it all together in a way much better than I would. Being so near him left a pang in my chest I didn't know if I would ever recover from.

When he finished, I turned toward where my parents sat. "I need to know—why did the Reding have you imprisoned?"

The ensuing silence, except for the distant chatter from the marauders, was telling. Whatever my parents had to say, it wasn't something they wanted to say to me. That was their problem, because I was done having people keep things from me.

"What is it? I have a right to know," I asked.

"The truth is," my mom said, "we don't understand, ourselves. At first, we believed it was something to do with our being a part of the rebellion in Kenti, but—"

"You were *what*?" Here I thought I'd heard everyone's secrets, yet more kept tumbling out.

Dad sighed. "Your mother and I didn't want you to know, because we didn't want to put you in any more danger than you already were."

"You were part of the rebellion." My words came out in a whisper as the impact of it shook through me. My parents had been against the leaders. It seemed I knew them little.

"I'm sorry we didn't tell you," Mom said.

But this couldn't be. It didn't make sense. Not with what I knew of them and what they'd done to me. "If you didn't like the way things were run, why did you put sand on my eyes, to make me an amant?"

"We didn't." Dad sounded exhausted.

Mom continued when he didn't. "We put sand on your eyes, to make it so you could fall in love as in times of old, how you wanted, and not only by first sight."

CHAPTER TWO

All this time, I thought my parents had tried to hurry along the amant process. To force me to be like them—a part of the class of people who had control. But no. They'd been trying to help me fall in love slowly, at will, like it was rumored to be done before the Govlin Wars. That belief was baseless, which was why their efforts hadn't worked on me.

I didn't know what to do or say, the swaying of my mind incomprehensible.

The world went on around me—a murmur of sounds, scratching sand, and the hot press of the day. But the revelation changed everything. A more shocking reveal than Nikon's had been. My mind swirled around, looking to hold on to something that would ground me back into my parents' actions. They didn't want me to be like them. They wanted me to have freedom to love. Instead, they blinded me. The agony that mistake must have caused them was great, yet I felt mine had been greater.

"We're so sorry," Dad said. "We never meant you any harm. There's nothing that's been able to let us forgive ourselves for doing so."

"We never should have tried it," Mom added.

Sorrow clogged my throat, but I understood.

When I finally found my voice, I said, "You were trying to do what was best for me, and it turned against us. I was angry for so long, and I had a right to be. Yet, somehow, it doesn't seem as important anymore. What you did was an act of love that went wrong. I don't understand why it had to turn out this way, but since it did, I learned to live like this. And I'm happy. Mom, Dad, if I can forgive you, then you can forgive yourselves."

And just like that, my Dad started crying again. I never knew a grown man to sob so much, but if it helped him work through his emotions, I was all for it.

Mother sniffed from close by.

"We don't deserve such a wonder as you for a daughter," my mom said, the noises telling me she was probably crying, letting the tears free her words.

I reached for them, and pulled them into a hug. Their frames were smaller than I remembered.

"We need to fatten you both up. I'm afraid you'll fall apart on us if we travel," I said.

They held on tight for a long minute, yet not long enough. I wanted to stay in the moment with them more than I was currently capable, but it slipped away despite my efforts.

When we pulled apart, the sobs had calmed on their end, but they felt threateningly close on mine. My parents. I never thought I'd feel their touch again.

"Are we traveling somewhere?" my mom asked.

"Somewhere out of the country would be best, if it were at all possible." Dad sounded uncertain.

Since the country was either surrounded by desert or encased by mountains, there were only two ways in or out. The waterfall by where I used to live—but I hadn't a clue how you'd be able to climb such a thing—or at the end of the Death River. We sent our dead down that river through the chasms that meant certain loss of life to any living who attempted it.

There was no escaping the Reding and Vading. We were stuck under their rule, with our only source of water being tainted, most likely by them.

It'd been quiet long enough. What was everyone thinking?

"I don't know where we can go," I said. "There's no place safe except here, but I'm certain Na'eehma is anxious to have us on our way, since we have the elite warriors and neczar after us."

"I'm afraid that's true," Nikon said. "She informed me that, while we've kept our word and helped them gather with the rebellion, it is a cause of stress, to have such dangers coming after them."

I tapped my finger on my leg that was almost dry by now. The marauders had done a better job helping us than they needed to. Plus, they didn't like the government telling them what to do, but he was right. We didn't want to cause more trouble for them. Should the Reding and Vading decide to send their warriors here, the people would not survive.

"He's right." Na'eehma's voice coming closer had me sitting straighter. "It appears you've captured the eye of the neczar and the high priest."

I shifted in my spot, wishing I had a grip on all those I cared about. Resisting the urge to pet Tewy in place of that, I said, "It is true."

"As much as I want to protect you, I can't. If we were to bring the wrath of the high priest and the rulers down on us more than we already have done, we could lose our camp. Our entire way of life, along with a safe place for those who would be harmed the most by them. I'm afraid I must ask you to leave."

Though her request wasn't surprising, it left a bitter taste on my tongue. "I understand," I said.

But what would we do?

"You can't send them back out there," Zoe said. "Not if the high priest and the neczar are after them. Cassandra and Nikon have enough of a problem with the warriors as it is. They've done so much. Please reconsider."

"I'm sorry. There's nothing left I can do but send them off with supplies." Na'eehma's tone was firm.

"There's one thing," Husani said.

I hadn't realized he'd joined us, but it was difficult to keep track of everyone with the noise of camp.

He went on. "I'll join you."

I widened my eyes. It was hard to believe he'd offer, yet he had warmed up to us after Na'eehma sent him to keep an eye on us. He'd been a large part of getting the marauders to help with the rebellion. But with the threat narrowing in on them, of course the marauders needed to get some space. I just wished it wasn't from us.

"But where will they go?" Zoe's voice was tight and shrill.

"Zo, let it go." Kaius's voice was soothing but held an edge of tension.

"It's fine," I said. "We'll figure this out." I didn't know how yet, but something had to turn up. Where could I take my parents, to keep them safe?

"Give them one night," Zoe said.

"That's not possible," Na'eehma replied. "They need to leave, so we will have the attention away from our camp."

We needed to go fast, show ourselves somewhere away from here, and not get caught. *Sands.* That was so not happening. Too bad there was no way to stop the neczar or prevent the high priest from hunting us. I knew of no way to counteract them.

While I wanted to think of a place to hide and struggled, I said to Zoe, "Will you and Kaius need any help? Is there anything we can do for the rebellion?"

"The Jackal is used to operating with just the two of us on an as-needed basis. We'll do what's needed and get the rebellion back on track. People might be scared, but by stealing prisoners, you've shown that the Reding and Vading can be challenged."

Maybe she had a point. I hadn't heard of anyone else escaping their dungeons. The thought didn't bring as much pleasure as it should, but before I could reply, my mother asked, "Who's the Jackal?"

There was much my parents didn't know, aside from what Nikon had already told them.

"It's me and my brother, Kaius," Zoe said, the lie of their relationship slipping easily off her tongue.

I was correct, then. It wasn't just Kaius that was the Jackal. They made a good pairing. What more was there to their story? There had to be pieces I'd missed because they were trying to keep their secret, but I would come back to it another time. Now, I had to figure out where to take my parents with Husani's help. Nikon would likely wish to come as well, but I needed to resolve my feelings about his deception.

There were some faint murmurs, and Zoe said, "Kaius and I will come with you."

"But what about the rebellion here?" I asked.

"I'll keep everyone in contact," Husani said. "It'll be less pressure anyway, if the Jackal is not in our camp either."

He had a point. "I'd be happy to have your company, Zoe and Kaius." I just hoped we didn't all get caught.

But where would we go? "We can't go to Sirya," I said. "Kenti was no good the last time we were there, and Itpy wasn't much better. Ruso, maybe?"

"It's close to the capital, but it'd be better than going to an outskirt city." Nikon made a good point. The cities farther away would seem more likely for people like us to escape to, so the soldiers would be searching for us there. I wished we could go back to my house by the waterfall, but Antonia was certain to have it guarded.

"What preparations do we need to make?" Mom asked.

Leave it to her to be on top of things despite the fact she just got out of the dungeons.

"We will provide what we can," Na'eehma said. "We may not be able to allow you to stay, but we won't let you go without. Do you know where you can stay in Ruso?"

This stopped me. I knew little of Ruso, other than its proximity to Sirya. "Nikon, do you have anyone there?"

"Some, but I'm not certain we should use them."

"I may have a connection," Dad said.

I jerked my head back. "How could you have one?"

"We were part of the rebellion before all this," Mom reminded me gently. "It might have been years, but we'll find a way with someone."

Dad added, "The person I'm thinking of may be gone, but there are other avenues we can tap. I'm sure we'll think of something on the way."

His words came out sounding so certain, I believed him despite it not making full sense. One niggling doubt continued to poke at me. "What if the warriors have already gotten to your connection?"

"Then we'll go from there," Mom said, a hint of warning in her tone. Many years ago, I asked where she'd been after getting home late one night and heard that tone. Looking back, it was probably due to working with the rebellion.

I hoped she was right that something would come up. My parents could be counted on despite being in poor condition. It was nice to leave the decisions up to someone else for a while, but it also left a familiar panic creeping up on me. They didn't realize I wasn't the blind girl they left behind, but a grown woman. "Is there anything else we need to know before we leave? Any information that could help?"

No one responded.

My dad said, "I wish I had more, but so little has happened to us over the years. We don't even know why they took us."

"Wasn't it because you were part of the rebellion?" Zoe asked.

"We thought so," Mom said, "but they didn't ask us anything about it. If Cassandra hadn't disappeared before we were taken, they would have imprisoned her as well."

"Thank the sands that didn't happen, but we were distraught when we couldn't find you," Dad added.

I scrunched my eyebrows. "I didn't disappear. Antonia told me you were dead and took me to live by the waterfall." Which reminded me of the somehow tainted river, with what or why, I didn't know. I hated the thought that my beloved river was no longer good enough for me to drink or play in.

"Antonia?" Mother asked. "The caretaker who came to us, offering to help you? She took you away?"

Something didn't make sense here. "She came to you? I thought you and Dad hired her."

"Of course she came to us. We thought hiring someone around your age to help was a good idea, but it wasn't ours."

I bit my lip. There was more to this than I was putting together, but should I uncover it? "You do know that Antonia is the Vading?"

"No." Dad snapped the word out.

"She was just a sweet youth who wanted to help you. She had nothing to do with the Reding," Mom added.

"That's because she didn't know him yet," I explained. "She must have come across him sometime after she moved us to the waterfall."

"And that was why she left?" my mother asked but kept going like it wasn't a question. "She became an amant. And not just any amant, but the Vading." The disgust in her tone was clear.

"I thought you knew. You understood about the Reding and his brother"—I couldn't bring myself to put the word together with *Nikon* just yet—"right away, so it made sense. Plus, you knew Antonia personally."

"I believed the Vading was a different Antonia, though the

name isn't common. Come to think of it, we never saw her while we were imprisoned." Mom's voice grew more hesitant.

"But you saw the Reding?" I asked.

"A few times," my dad confirmed.

Mom added, "His brother was in the background some of those times, in training to be an elite warrior. A weapon in the hands of the ruler. I hadn't seen him for a while—until our escape."

"Why did the Reding visit you personally?" I ignored the second half of her comment for now, but stored it away for later.

"That's the question, isn't it?" Dad sounded more thoughtful than upset, which surprised me. I would have thought he'd be more antagonistic toward the man who imprisoned him and whom he'd worked against with the rebellion.

"What did he ask about?" Nikon's question reminded me we weren't as alone as we probably should have been for this conversation.

"More than I can remember." Dad mumbled something that sounded an awful lot like *traitor*.

I couldn't figure out if he was glad Nikon had become a traitor to his brother, or upset that he'd betrayed the people by supporting the Reding for as long as he did. I wasn't about to ask for clarification. "This is important. Can either of you think of a few of the questions? It might give us a better idea of why they took you."

"Let me think," Dad said, as Tewy pranced around in my lap and finally settled down to curl up in a ball.

Mom quickly added, "They asked a lot about our family. We were often separated, so I tried to say nothing. They asked questions about our life and how we did things. Questions about you, Cassandra. I figured they were trying to get information about where you'd gone, so they could use you against us, to find out more about the rebellion. I never said anything, even after Nikon here left and they began torturing us." Her voice cracked on the last two words.

I wanted to reach out and comfort her but didn't know how. Her keeping silent had done a lot for me and the rebellion. "What about you, Dad?" I asked.

"I kept my silence as much as I could, as well. They tried a lot of different things when the brother wasn't around, but we held it together." His words were weary.

Did Nikon remember them? I'd like to think that, if he had, he would have helped me find them sooner. Maybe he didn't know them by name. It didn't seem like the best moment to ask Nikon about it.

I wanted to avoid thinking about what my parents had been through. The torture... It was near impossible to ignore. The Reding had ordered them hurt in more ways than I probably knew. I clenched my jaw against the pain of thinking about what may have happened. The things the warriors may have done. My heart ached more than my sore jaw.

If it wasn't because of their association with the rebellion, why were my parents specifically targeted?

"I'm sorry they did that to you both." Nikon's voice was soft.

"It is what it is." Mother's tone was strong, but someone sniffed like they were crying.

I rested my hand on Tewy's sleeping form. If only there was a way I could make it better... But nothing would fix this.

CHAPTER THREE

It didn't take long to gather supplies, say our goodbyes, and head out. We wanted the marauders safe as much as we wanted ourselves to be safe. I couldn't have the blood of an entire camp of people on my conscience, should we stay.

Tewy, the traitor, went to Nikon during the journey, while either of my parents, or Zoe, was with me. I was grateful for their help, but I missed Tewy. If I was being honest, I missed Nikon, too, despite being upset with him.

As we camped at night and walked during the day, I thought about how to approach him. There was much I could do. Just start speaking with him. Ask about him not telling me about his brother. Just be near him despite the awkward feelings bubbling up inside me.

I had to wonder if he felt the same toward me as at times, his silent presence seemed near, but I could never be sure. With so many people around, we wouldn't have a chance to talk. I wouldn't know what to say anyway.

"We're getting close to Ruso," Nikon said, farther off than I was accustomed to, despite the time we'd been more distant with each other.

"I should go ahead and see if our contact is here." Mom sounded stronger every time I heard her speak. We'd gone more slowly because of my parents. Thankfully, because of Na'eehma's provisions, we had enough supplies to get us through the desert without a problem.

"Not alone, you won't," Dad said. "I'm not having you captured again."

I wanted to volunteer, but I wasn't the best choice. Spending one-on-one time with my mother would have been nice. Making sure she stayed safe? Even better.

"I'll take her," Nikon said, surprising me. Since I captured him at my waterfall house, he usually opted to stay with me. It was a good thing to have him protect my mother.

Before I could say so, Dad said, "I may not like what your brother has done with this country, but you've taken good care of my daughter. I'd much appreciate you taking good care of my wife."

"I'll do my best," Nikon said.

"You can claim to be my son and say we're scouting out for our family." Mom's take-charge attitude was familiar. I took a step back, but she wrapped her arms around me. I hugged her back, as she whispered, "Stay safe."

"I'm more worried about you, but you're in good hands with Nikon."

Tewy squawked.

"No, boy. You can't take care of them." I pulled away from my mom. "You're too conspicuous. You need to stay with me."

He gave a whine, before little *thumps* sounded across the sand. I reached down to let him climb up my shoulder, and rubbed his chest. "That's a good monkey."

"Tewy is an oddly intelligent little thing, isn't he?" Dad said.

"I'm glad you have him." Mom's voice wafted farther away. "We should get going. I don't want to linger in the open longer than we have to."

Nikon's soft footsteps moved toward me, surprising me once again. "I'll watch out for her."

"Thank you."

He lowered his voice. "And perhaps when I return, we can talk."

I nodded. If I responded verbally, my throat was so tight it felt like it would crack and give away my emotions. Granted, my expression probably did that for me.

"Be on guard while I'm gone," Nikon said.

"I will, but Kaius and Zoe are here—you've trained them fairly well, plus my dad. And I've got my trusty staff." I patted the familiar stick in my grasp. "We'll be fine. Come back safe."

"We will."

As they left, we went silent. I didn't want to disturb the moment, the tension and fear in the air making me fear something bad might happen to my mother and Nikon if I did. I wanted them to return and find us on the very spot they'd left us, without a problem. But we couldn't count on that. I pressed my lips together, keeping in a call for them to come back.

"Let's make ourselves comfortable since we'll be here for a while," Zoe said, making me more grateful she and Kaius were with us. If they hadn't come, I doubted Nikon would have wanted to leave. As grateful as I was that he'd gone to protect my mother, without him here, something vital was missing. And maybe something was. He was my best friend, after all.

I took Tewy from my shoulder and popped him into my arms. The heat of the day waned into the shadowed coolness of the night, before my mother's shuffling was accompanied by Nikon's familiar steps. It took far longer than I would have liked for them to return.

I jumped to my feet. "Are you safe? News?"

"We're well." Mom sounded tired. Until I heard that note of weariness, it was easy to forget how much she'd been through lately, when she kept pushing on ahead like she did. "The first and second person I'd hoped to find weren't there, but I found a friend on our third try."

With her and Nikon here and well. That was all that mattered. But it was lucky she had a friend in Ruso. That person had better be trustworthy.

"You should rest before we get going," I said.

"We all should," Nikon said. "It wouldn't be wise to go back into town during the night. There weren't as many warriors as in Sirya, but there were enough to be concerning."

Mother took my hand in hers, which felt bony and chapped, and together we sat, me next to my dad.

"Will we be all right?" I asked.

"As well as anywhere now that so much is off limits," Nikon replied at my level. He probably sat when we did.

"How long are we going to stay?" I didn't like the thought of putting my life in another's hands for more than a couple of days.

"As long as it takes."

"Will we be able to help the rebellion from there?"

"I believe so," Nikon said.

Tewy climbed off my lap and scampered over to him. Lucky monkey had no qualms about getting Nikon's affection. Did I wish for the same?

"We should sleep," I said.

"I'll take first watch," Nikon said.

"I'll take second," Zoe offered.

"Third," Kaius added.

It didn't take long to get situated, but I lay awake for a long time, listening to the breathing of those I cared about. All those I loved—together in one place. I wanted to keep them close, but the fears of what could happen to them swirled around me, and I shivered.

CHAPTER FOUR

I woke to Tewy plugging my nose. I sputtered for air, then scolded him. The noise of the others moving about, getting their gear ready, perhaps, had me preparing myself for the journey.

We ate a quick meal, and headed into the city while it was early.

"Through here," Mom said as the ground changed from soft sand to a harder base with loose grains on it.

I tried not to grip Zoe's arm too tight. If only I had my staff... I'd given it to Dad for safekeeping, to make my blindness less obvious. The last thing we needed was for someone to turn me in to the warriors because of my lack of sight. Not only would I be swooped up and taken to be a slave, but I'd also be parted from my loved ones forever.

Tewy rode with someone else, so quiet I couldn't spot him. That was a nice change. If he didn't draw attention to us, maybe we'd have a chance.

We continued forward with a determined stride, like we had business around here. As much as I wanted to hurry to the safe place, a slower pace would be easier to keep up with, but I trusted Zoe to keep me from tripping over something.

Voices drifted over from somewhere to our left. People getting on with their day? That was both good and bad for us. More people going to work meant we'd look less out of place, but there were also more of those who might turn us in.

We went left, the sounds of talking growing louder but indistinguishable. Several house lengths forward, and then we turned to the right.

After a few steps, a female voice whispered, "Good. You made it. Hurry inside."

I was grateful Zoe didn't waste any time. We were steered into a space that felt enclosed, probably fairly small for this many of us, though we weren't pressed up against each other. A mid-sized room perhaps.

"Is everyone here?" I asked.

"We are." Nikon's words relaxed me.

"Were you followed?" asked the woman from before.

"No," Nikon replied.

"Pardon me—I don't know you, so I'm asking Edita," the woman said.

"This man can be trusted," Mom said. As she went on to explain, I feared she would say who he was. "He's a good friend of my daughter's, and watched out for her while Dorian and I were imprisoned."

"Is that so? All right. Follow me. We'll get you settled, and the space is going to be tight. We'll be safe enough in here. We only get raids once in a while, and we had one a few days ago. It should be a week or two before another. I'm Ramina, by the way."

"Thank you for your hospitality," I told her.

"I'm just grateful Edita and Dorian are alive. We all feared they were taken and killed by the warriors after you disappeared."

This woman knew me. Or of me. There had to be so much more I missed out on. "How did you know I disappeared?"

"Word spread fast throughout the rebellion."

"We're grateful as well that we survived," Mom commented as we continued down what I thought was a hall.

Everyone stopped, and Ramina said, "I have three extra rooms at the moment. Edita and Dorian, you can have one. The groups of women and the men can each take one of the other rooms. They're right down this hall. If you'll excuse me, I'll let you get settled while I make something for breakfast."

We'd have to find a way to pay her for the food, if she was going to feed us all, and we hadn't brought provisions for much longer. Zoe led me into a room on the left and let me explore, while Tewy jumped about. The little guy had better not cause any problems.

As I tapped my way around from the cane I'd gotten back, I found the room was on the small side—two beds scrunched in close together, and one dresser. A narrow walkway to the door was the only floor not taken up by furniture.

"Which bed would you like?" I asked.

"Whichever."

"I'll take this one." I sat on the one to my right. Tewy jumped on my lap, squawking away. "That's right—we're going to live here for a while. Stay out of everyone's way and maybe help the rebellion." Hopefully.

He continued to bounce around, chatting his monkey gibberish as he went, while Zoe and I settled in. I set my cane aside, knowing I could easily find it again since it always called out to me. It didn't take long to unpack, as we had few things, and then we went out to the breakfast Ramina had prepared for us. After eating, we stayed gathered around the table, as my mom and dad told Ramina what happened since they'd been captured.

I listened carefully, as Ramina responded, "We've heard news of other cities getting more raids and tightening restrictions.

The maveor has been fairly lenient here. So far. The rebellion has been flourishing, and with your return, we'll probably gain numbers. We have to get out from under the amant. The only thing that would help us more would be a boost from the Jackal."

Silence settled over the room like an uncomfortable cloak. The Jackal was already here, but I didn't know how comfortable Kaius and Zoe would be about sharing who they were. As the quiet stretched on, enclosing us, it was apparent they either weren't sure or didn't wish to say anything.

"That would be a boon," Mom eventually said.

"What would you have the Jackal do?" Kaius asked.

"Give words of advice to the people," Ramina said. "Let them know they're not alone, and that there are others out there, fighting against the injustices forced upon them."

A moment's pause. The nerves in me had me wanting to pace. I wished I knew what everyone was doing.

Zoe spoke up. "We could arrange to have the Jackal come."

"You?" Surprise colored Ramina's single word. "But you're so young."

I held in a laugh. I didn't know how old Ramina was, but Zoe was around my age, and I was no longer a youth. We were probably younger than Ramina, but why couldn't we take part in the rebellion?

"We are the next generation, and we are ready to do what's necessary." Zoe's response made me hold my head high.

"Forgive me. You're correct. It's hard to remember that sometimes, when all I deal with are people my age, and it gets to be difficult to find anyone older. We'd love any help you could give in getting the Jackal to cheer the people on. Despite our proximity to Sirya, we've had a lot of newcomers joining in Ruso lately, running from the oppression of other cities. Because of that, I believe the maveor will be forced to do something, or he'll get kicked out of his position. Warriors will soon follow. We need to prepare the people for that."

"When's the soonest we could meet with them?" I asked, eager to find something to do, to help.

"As soon as this afternoon, should you like," she replied. "I'll send word out right away, and we'll set up a time for people to start coming by. It'll be better if they come here on a visit, a few at a time, as I already get many of those in a week, than to have you congregate with a big group. Once you're familiar with many of them, we can figure out how to bring the Jackal in."

Knowing the Jackal was here gave me hope that Zoe and Kaius would reveal themselves as such if necessary.

"That sounds like a good plan," Zoe said. "If you don't mind, I think my brother and I are going to take time to talk through things privately."

"You can use our room," Nikon invited. "I needed to speak with Cassandra, anyway."

I didn't like the way he said my full name, instead of shortening it like he did when we were comfortable with each other. My anger and frustration didn't negate my missing the endearment. My back was stiff as I stood. Tewy gave a concerned hoot, and I told him, "You can come if you want, boy."

From the sound of things, he scrambled away, toward the room Zoe and I shared. I followed after, sweeping my staff ahead of me. Nikon's scent of metal and sand came to me before I reached him and made me pause.

He said, "Would you like to take my arm?"

"Thank you." My mind was numb. My emotions attempted to match it, but a light flutter went through my stomach. I hadn't touched him since the day my mother outed him and he admitted he was Reding Theodore's brother. A couple weeks, maybe. Doing so now felt as if he was saying something I didn't fully understand. I paused, my hand halfway up, but he didn't take hold of it and guide me to his arm, as he often did.

Slowly, I raised my hand, searching for him. When my fingers skimmed across the familiar slope of his cheek, peace settled in my chest and grew into something more as I firmly clasped his arm. His muscles were more known to me than anyone else's, and I couldn't help but notice how tense they were. The way they held taut with stress I didn't understand spoke to me of the burden he must have carried. Zoe was correct; I needed to forgive him, even if he didn't ask for it.

He led me down the hall and into my room, moving across from me and shifting down to sit on Zoe's bed. I'd half hoped, half dreaded he'd sit by me. At least it gave me an idea where we stood.

Tewy jumped between us like it was a sort of game, and I laughed. "All right, boy. Settle down. Nikon and I need to have a chat, and if you aren't good, I'll send you out of the room."

Shockingly enough, he popped onto my lap and stayed there, still and quiet. I set my staff to the side and petted him with both hands, needing the strength of my little monkey to get me through this.

Nikon didn't say anything, and I didn't know what to say either. I didn't want to keep wasting time like this until someone interrupted us. We needed to clear the air between us, no matter how difficult it was.

And I'd start. "So, you said we needed to talk?"

"Yes." Though a simple one-word reply, it held so much fear, it left me wondering what was going on in that mind of his.

The only way to know was to keep moving forward. "You're the Reding's brother."

"I am." There was a hesitant note in his tone.

"I wish you'd have told me." Tewy's fur was soft, but not enough to take the edge out of my words to a man I desperately cared about. I worked to soften them. "I know it must have been hard for you, but I thought we knew each other better than that."

"We did. We do. I wanted to tell you—so many times, I almost did—but I couldn't bring myself to. I was afraid you'd think of me differently." And probably fearfully, if I was reading his voice right.

I scooped up Tewy and went to sit directly next to Nikon, so our legs brushed against one another. It felt more real. Like I could read him better if I was closer. I wrapped my right arm around Tewy, and took a hold of Nikon's hand with my left.

The gesture was more intimate than we usually went for, but it was the right thing to do in that moment. Our hearts and bodies might never connect in a romantic way, but he could be my best friend, whom I cherished. If holding his hand let him know it, *by sands*, I would hold his hand. Besides, it felt really nice. Warm and comfortable. I wanted to lean in and rest my head against his shoulder, but I stopped myself before going that far.

"I understand." The words were easier to say than I thought they'd be, the next sentence spilling out easier. "I forgive you."

"You do?" His hand was tense in mine.

I gave it a squeeze. "Definitely. It was a shock, of course, but I understand. I do want to know one thing. Are there any other big surprises you have coming that I should be aware of?"

He chuckled softly. "Not that I know of."

"Good. I think I've had about enough of those." I sighed.

"I want you to know that you mean everything to me, Cass. Life hasn't always been kind, but you have. I don't know what I would have done if it wasn't for you."

I was grateful to hear my nickname from him again. "You're right. I am pretty great to you," I teased.

"You are. And I know you said you didn't want to hear this, but I have to say it one last time. I truly feel that, if things were different, we would have fallen in love."

I stiffened. *Different* as in, if I wasn't blind.

He put his hand over mine. "I know it's hard to hear. It's hard for me to say. It feels like there's a connection between us. Something so tangible, I can almost grasp on to it."

"But we'll never be anything more than friends." My voice was dull to my ears.

"The best of friends. I'll always be here for you."

When I sighed this time, I was letting go of things that could never be. I gave in and leaned my head against his shoulder, content to be so near him. "And I will always be here for you."

CHAPTER FIVE

We sat like this for shorter than I liked but longer than I expected. It was nice, being in Nikon's company. No, *nice* didn't have the right gravity. I needed a much, much stronger word, but I couldn't waste time trying to come up with it when there were other things I had to know.

"Now that I understand who you are, can you tell me a little about your family? What really happened to your parents? What made you decide to take the papyrus and run, if the Reding is your brother?"

"I don't know if we have enough time for my full story. Plus, it's boring."

"To you, maybe, but I'm interested." I tilted my head toward him. "Can you give me a brief overview?"

He went quiet. What was he thinking?

Tewy gave a soft *oooo*.

I patted his back, grateful I wasn't alone in my concern for Nikon and what he'd been through.

"My parents always favored Theodore. I came along as a mistake, and stayed that way throughout their lives," Nikon said.

I threaded my fingers through his, wishing there was a better way to comfort him through the memories.

"When I was nineteen, my family went for a visit to Peka Tower. We traveled often, so this was nothing new, but we didn't go to the high priest as much. I didn't like the man. Luckily, my parents made me wait in the river boat with the staff, so I didn't have to go in, but when they came out, both of them were upset. They wouldn't answer any of my questions about what had them out of sorts, and Theodore said he was frightened by the neczar. My parents had seen the beast before. It didn't seem to faze them. I never figured out what happened with the high priest, because on the way back to the pyramid, they got sick. Mother died first, and Father went the day after. Theodore became the Reding."

"And you became his right-hand man," I added when he didn't continue.

He shifted his weight away from me, then settled back beside me. "I was already an elite warrior by that point. I didn't think I had any other choice when he asked for me to accompany him places. It didn't bother me, until he fell in love. I never much cared for his wife, but the people seemed more content with their ruler being an amant."

I doubted the odiosom cared if they had been or not, but I wasn't about to bring it up. "She must have shown you more of her true colors than she showed me."

"When my brother was around, she was fine, but it didn't take long for her to become dismissive and rude when he wasn't. It wears at a person. That, mixed with my brother's growing disdain toward odiosom and me... When the chance arose to take the papyrus he'd been studying, it felt like the right thing to do. Problem is, I still don't know what it's about."

Not knowing what else to say, I rubbed my thumb in circles on the back of his hand.

"Sometimes, I wish I'd never left, but it was the right decision. Theodore makes bad choices. I couldn't stick around and watch him spiral from one poor decision to the next."

"It must be hard to see that coming from your own brother."

"Yes." His tone lightened. "But it led me to you."

"Ah, but you haven't done any chariot racing since I met you." I tried to lighten the moment, remembering how he'd previously said he'd love to do so.

"True. We'll have to remedy that as soon as things calm down."

If they ever did. My doubts grew by the day. More likely, when things evened out, it'd be because we were dead.

I shivered.

"Cold?"

"Anxious about the future."

"You and I both." He moved closer. "We'll figure it out. Together."

"True. We managed to find my parents. As long as we have each other, we can change things." And I believed it enough that I wanted to keep moving forward. "What can we do to assist the rebellion, while we're here? It sounds as if Zoe and Kaius have plans, but I don't know where that leaves us. I want to help them, as long as they don't try to kill Theodore and Antonia again without a trial. If they do..."

"We'll keep a close eye on things." His tone was deadly serious again. "At this point, I'm not certain I want to do more."

"Because of the warriors, searching for us?" I asked.

"And the neczar, wanting you."

I shivered. "You don't think he followed us to Ruso?"

"I want to say *no* and pretend it will all be fine, but I don't know."

Tewy gave a soft coo, putting his hand on mine and Nikon's.

"I agree, Tewy," I said. "We'll hope for the best. I don't know what I would do should anything happen to either of you, though."

"And I feel the same about you."

I bit my lip. Was there anything we could be doing while in hiding? If only there was somewhere safe we could go, but there was nowhere but the desert ruins, and those didn't seem any safer. Plus, supplies wouldn't be readily available there. That did raise the question— "What do you think is going on with the water?"

"I wish I knew more, but without asking Theodore outright, I don't know that we ever will."

"Is that something we should work toward?" I asked, half-wanting his answer to be a *yes* and half-hoping he said *no*. I mean, he would lie to us, but perhaps there was still information we could glean from however he chose to answer.

"For now, it's probably best that we don't. There's no way for us to get to him safely, and if we could enter the pyramid, we likely wouldn't be able to get out again. No, I think we'll have to accept the fact that something was changed about the river and we don't know what or how."

He was right. This needed fixing, but without knowing the specifics, it was impossible for us to move forward. "I wish we had more answers."

"So do I."

"We need to find them somehow." I stretched, reluctantly pulling away from him. "We should probably rejoin the others."

"Yes." But he didn't move.

It'd been so nice to be with him, I wasn't ready to let it go, but Zoe's voice murmured in the hall. I had to give him warning about her and Kaius. It was one thing not to tell Ramina, and another to keep it from Nikon. "There's something I should say, but I can't really. All I can say is that there's something Zoe and Kaius need to tell you."

"You mean that they're amant, pretending to be odiosom brother and sister?" He sounded so certain, I leaned back in surprise.

"You know?"

"Of course. You couldn't see them, but when we lived at the same house in Itpy, I often caught them giving each other long glances, or standing closer than a brother and sister should. It made me suspicious, but then I caught them kissing. They don't know it; I backed out of the room before they heard me. But it was clear they'd been hiding their relationship. Due to the rebellion, probably."

"Why, you sneaky man." I laughed. "Yes, they didn't think anyone would trust the Jackal if they knew the two of them were married. You should tell them you know."

"We'll see. I'd rather not have them more uncomfortable around me. But if you know it's only a matter of time before they share their secret with me..."

"She's been meaning to."

"I'm sure it's hard."

"Yes." It was hard to tell those you care about truths they wouldn't like hearing. I shifted, and Tewy jumped off my lap toward Nikon. Once I was on my feet, I turned toward the two. "Thank you for talking with me."

"Any time, Cass." The strength of his voice made my heart grow, despite the simplicity of his words.

We could do anything, as long as we had each other.

CHAPTER SIX

It was time for us to meet with the rebellion. I was to go arm in arm with Zoe, while Kaius, Tewy and Nikon went in their group. Nikon took my cane with him since he could handle it and still show he was sighted, so I wouldn't look suspicious to any warriors we might come across.

"We'll be together again soon," Nikon said, and they headed out.

After they'd been gone several minutes, I said goodbye to my parents and Ramina, who'd chosen to stay home. Zoe and I set out. I didn't know exactly where we were going, other than it was some distance away.

We'd gone down the street, turned left, and continued on a few paces, when a murmur of voices came to me. It sounded like a crowd.

"What's going on?" I whispered to Zoe.

"There are a lot of people ahead, but this is the quickest way to the meeting."

"We can maneuver through them, so you make it there on time."

"Only if you're certain."

"I am." If I was the reason she was late, guilt would eat at me. "Let's just hurry. It'll be fine."

She took a deep breath. "Here we go."

I followed, the noise of the crowd growing, the farther we went. People bumped into me, jostling me from side to side. Doing my best to stay upright and not be phased by the jumble, I listened to the shouts around me.

"Those odiosom, thinking they're better than us. Too many people having the nerve to come from other cities."

"We ought to do something about them."

"Put them to work."

"Or kick them out of our town altogether."

Frustrated with the remarks, I wanted to snap back at the speakers. Instead, I kept my hand on Zoe's elbow, making sure to keep a tight grip. If they were so against the odiosom, it was a sure thing they wouldn't want anything to do with the blind.

"Shut your mouths," a woman called out. "You amant are always lording over everyone else, with no good reason."

"Reason enough when amant are the ones favored by the sands."

A sickening smack of flesh hitting flesh sounded through the air, followed rapidly by more. Something jabbed me in the stomach. I doubled over, grasping for breath, as people pressed in all around me. I bit my lip, as I tried to catch my breath from the hit. *Zoe!* I lost her.

"Cassandra!" She called out for me, but her voice had already grown muffled from the crowd.

Should I call out to her? As much as I wanted to, calling more attention to myself in this group seemed like a bad idea. The fear skimming through me threatened to grow, but I tamped it down. No point in losing my wits now. I'd need every one of them to get out of this.

Why wasn't Zoe calling for me? Where were my friends? I needed help, but for whatever reason, they couldn't give it to me.

Likely they didn't want to bring more attention to me with so many already lashing out at the situation.

The crowd became louder, jostling me along as they shoved and pushed. No one lashed out at me purposefully as far as I could tell, but the elbows, hands, and knees connected with me all the same. I struggled to stay balanced. If only I had a sense of where to go.

That was it. I could find a sense of where to go. My cane. I could find the others by following the sensation to grab hold of it.

I tried to search for it, but the crowd tumbled me about so much, it was hard to focus on my cane—until two hands grabbed my upper arms and pulled me backward. I wanted to buck against them, but a woman's voice whispered in my ear, "I'm going to help you get out of here."

I froze for a moment, until I realized she was trying to drag me the same direction as my cane. It was better than nothing. "Thank you," I said.

She took my arm and linked it with hers, locking us together. We got pushed about, as some voices cried for justice for the odiosom and others demanded compassion from the amant. There were some voices of reason, but as the people grew more restless, I was grateful this woman was helping, though I didn't know why. I could only hope that Zoe was with the others I could sense us moving toward, the ones who had my cane.

The woman led me through the mass until it thinned out. The voices were quieter here, as if most were interested in what was going on, and not necessarily wanting to get into the fray.

Once we were clear of the group, I let her lead me a little farther. The noise grew distant before I finally dared speak. "Thank you for your help," I said, pulling away. Was that the right thing to do?

"Of course. I'm Lavti."

"Cassandra. Are you headed to—" I couldn't ask if she knew

anything about the rebellion meeting. For all I knew, she supported the rule of the amant.

"The rebellion meeting?" she asked.

She must know something about it, or she wouldn't have asked in the first place. My being blind probably encouraged her to trust me with the information.

"My friends are going," Lavti said. "I decided to join them last minute and see what it was all about. Are you going, as well?"

"Yes. I got separated from those I was going with." Feeling awkward, I added, "Would you mind helping me find the place? I have an idea as to where it may be, but with what we just went through, I don't want to wander the streets alone."

"I'm happy to help you make it."

"Thank you." My cheeks burned. I held out a hand for her, and was grateful when she gave me back her arm.

She walked at a quick pace, but keeping up was easy enough.

"Do you live in this part of town?" I asked.

"Close by, yes. I lived in Itpy for a while working at the market, making and selling clothes there, but I came here recently."

"Itpy? I used to live there. Do you know Hettie? She's a fantastic cook, who has a stall in the market."

"I know her. She moved to Ruso recently too. There are raids going on in Itpy that have forced people to find new places of refuge. We're almost there."

Hettie was in this city. It'd be good to see her and talk to her again. It was far too long since I'd tasted one of her delicious meals.

The soft murmur of voices reached me, and several steps later, Lavti said, "We're almost there."

As we neared the voices, a scampering caught my attention. *Tewy.* Elation jumped through me mixed with a strong dose of relief. I bent down for him. He raced up my arm, jabbering excitedly. I let go of Lavti, in order to hold him with both hands and allay his fears. "I'm fine."

"I'm so sorry. Where have you been? I've been looking everywhere for you" Zoe approached and wrapped me in a hug, Tewy squawking in protest at being squished between us. "I just arrived here to get help, but it looks like you didn't need it. We've been so worried," she said.

"I'm the one who insisted we continue on, but I'm fine now. Lavti here helped me."

Zoe pulled back. "Thank you for helping my friend. She's as dear to me as a sister, and I don't know what I would do if anything happened to her."

"It was nothing. I was on my way here, anyway," Lavti said.

"Where's Nikon?" I asked. Not that he needed to be here. Except, if I was honest—since Zoe got here first and told them I'd gotten lost—I'd expected him to be worried and come over first thing when I showed up.

"He's out looking for you," Zoe said. "I'll have someone fetch him."

Zoe asked someone to go find Nikon and let him know I was well, and I left Lavti with many *thanks*, so she could mingle with others.

Zoe said, "I'm grateful Lavti found you. I tried to, but there was no way in the crowd. Any number of things could have happened to you."

I bit my lip. True, I'd been shoved about, and would probably be bruised later, but there were far worse things that could have happened to me. I could have been turned in, made a slave, or killed outright.

"Something did happen, didn't it? Your parents will have all our heads, if Lavti hadn't come by with you," she said.

"I'm fine. There was a small... scuffle, but I'm well. Lavti got them to leave me be."

Zoe grasped me in another hug, and Tewy jumped out of the

way this time, to land on my shoulder before she could crush him against us. When she pulled away, she asked, "Do you need anything?"

"Truly, it was a little frightening, but nothing more. I would have had no problem, if I'd had my cane," I said.

Tewy made an affronted noise.

I laughed. "And you, Tewy, of course. I'm lost without you, but I suppose it's good for me to try things out by myself."

"I know you're right," Zoe said. "It's just hard not to worry, when the blind are treated so ill. But you weren't found by a warrior and taken. I'd never forgive myself if you had been."

"That's something neither of us want." I shivered at the thought, but quickly brought myself back to the present, where I was safe. "I can't hide forever. I need to learn to do more on my own."

"I understand, but I'm not certain Nikon will. He's so protective of you, it'll be difficult for him to come to terms with it, especially once he hears you had a run-in with an unruly crowd."

"True. But it's not like I plan on going out on my own. I just miss having more freedom."

She gave my shoulder a squeeze and whispered, "Nikon's coming toward us full steam. I'm surprised he hasn't knocked anyone over."

I wanted to laugh, but Nikon wouldn't appreciate it in such a moment as this. The thought of him bowling people over to get to me warmed my heart. There was a way for us to care about each other, no matter what the world might be like. It just never felt like enough.

The chatter around us fell silent, as people hurried away. I turned toward the direction their voices were going. It would be Nikon.

Without the warning of the usual sounds he made so I knew where he walked, Nikon crushed me into a bold and fierce hug, clinging on to me as if afraid I would disappear any moment. Tewy chatted animatedly, his little voice chipper.

After a few warming seconds, he moved slightly away but kept a grip on my upper arms. "Are you hurt?"

"No."

"When we realized you'd been separated from us and I couldn't find you, I—" He brought me into another hug, enfolding me in his arms. I settled my head against his shoulder, happy to have his arms around me. To feel important to him—though I would rather not have put him through the stress. Finally, he pulled back again, as voices drifted around us. "What happened?" he asked.

"Too many people, pushing this way and that. Who were they all?"

"Refugees and amant," he said. "I don't think they meant to separate you two."

"Nikon's wrath said otherwise," Zoe said.

I pressed my lips together, holding in the worry and giddiness bubbling inside me. "There are so many of them."

"Did any of them hurt you?" he asked.

I shook my head. "I'm a little startled is all. A woman helped me. I would like you to meet her. Zoe? Would you mind finding Lavti?"

"She's already heading this way," Zoe said.

Nikon threaded his fingers through my own, smooth and comforting. I basked in the feel of our hands pressed together—despite them being so only in friendship and worry. "You really don't have to worry. I got out before anything bad happened."

He squeezed my hand more tightly, as if afraid I'd disappear.

I whispered, "I'm well."

"I have to reassure myself of that."

"Cassandra," Lavti said. "I'm grateful to see you've found your friends."

"And we're gratefu—" Nikon gasped, mid-sentence.

My heart thudded in my chest. "What is it? Are the warriors here?"

Everyone continued to chatter around us, as if things were fine, but Nikon's grip went lax as I clutched him. "Nikon?"

"I think, maybe..." Zoe's voice drifted off.

Panic squeezed me, my pulse roaring so loud in my ears, it drowned out all other sound. "What is it? Please, tell me."

"Nikon should be the one to do that," she said.

When he didn't respond, stress pushed at my heart. I lifted our hands, sensing something different. A strangeness was there. Didn't matter. Nikon was more important.

"I..." His voice was tight but also held a strange note I'd never heard. A softness that grew as he spoke. "I've found her."

"Lavti?" Why such a fuss?

A thought niggled at me. The way Lavti had come over when Zoe went for her, when Nikon had never met her before... His gasp... His odd words...

But worst of all, the odd feeling on his hand.

I wiggled my fingers, feeling the tell-tale ridge that had formed.

Nikon had fallen in love, and it wasn't with me.

CHAPTER SEVEN

"That can't be." It couldn't. Not at all.

Panic ebbed through me, rapidly turning into a flow that made it difficult to breathe or do much of anything but clutch at my chest, as a *whoosh* sounded in my ears.

When Nikon spoke again, it was from in front of me and to the side, but not close, like I expected from when he'd seen me get upset before.

No, it was closer to where Lavti's voice had come from.

"It's you." His voice was barely audible above the din.

"I thought I would never find you." Lavti's words were clearly not meant for me.

An unexpected rush of anger pulsed through me, pummeling against my inaction. There had to be something I could do. Nikon couldn't fall in love with her. He couldn't. It felt wrong. It was so wrong.

I backed up, needing space and air. Lots of air. Why couldn't I breathe? What was my problem?

"I believed I was going to be an odiosom forever, doomed never to find love," Nikon said.

The shock in his voice shook me. More than that, the rage in me pounded on. Rage and something that felt oddly like fear. I took several steps back.

Tewy jabbered from somewhere close by, but not near enough to comfort me, which was all I wanted.

The rage was fading into something deeper. Darker. Despair.

When Lavti spoke again, her words were muffled, but I heard them clearly. "I've found you. I'm never letting you go."

I stumbled away, shaking my head. This couldn't be. It didn't make sense. I might be blind, but I'd almost believed Nikon and I—

But no. Of course nothing would be between Nikon and me. I was blind. Doomed to always be alone. I should be happy he'd found someone. But I couldn't stop the flow of emotions. The strange grip of *wrongness*, clenching around my heart.

Didn't matter what I told myself, as I turned and rushed away from them. Voices called back to me, my name on Zoe's tongue, frantic, but I raced on. I had to get back to Ramina's house. I had to get out of here. Had to find a place, where I could figure out what just happened and how I was supposed to feel about it.

Tewy scampered after me, and I paused only long enough to let him hop on my shoulder.

Part of me felt like a sphinx, wild and fierce, wanting to run back shrieking and take Lavti out. Which didn't make any sense. I barely knew the woman, and she'd helped me. She should be a good match for Nikon. Wasn't that what falling in love was? Finding the person that completed you and made you whole? I wanted that for Nikon.

Or I'd believed I did.

I clenched my jaw as I strode forward. At some point, I'd lost count of my steps—if I'd ever started counting them. My head was loud. Angry. My thinking was clouded and irrational.

And I was lost.

I stumbled to a stop. I had my cane. If someone tried to come after me, I could defend myself. "What do we do, Tewy? I don't know how to get back to the house."

He squawked and jumped off my shoulder.

"Where are you going?" If he left me now, I'd truly be alone. I headed toward where he made the noise. He hooted, this time from farther away, but not so far as to cause me more trouble.

We continued like that for a minute, when it dawned on me what he was doing. "Are you leading me to Ramina's?" I asked.

He gave a happy chirp. I took that as a *yes* and continued on, listening for his noises every so often, using my cane, and followed him.

My mind was so jumbled. If he hadn't helped, who knew where I would have ended up?

I focused on the sound of our steps, moving through the street. It was quiet besides us, but Ramina lived in an odiosom neighborhood and the residents worked during the day, so it made sense. I latched on to the normal thoughts, gripping at them tightly, but the ragged emotions wanted to boil up inside and leave me a mess of burning sand.

We turned left, and Tewy jumped up on my arm and scrambled up to my shoulder. I used my cane to find the step up into the house, and went in.

It was cooler here than it'd been out in the sun. Still, I wished I had somewhere else to go. A room that was all mine, and not one I shared with Zoe. I loved her like a sister, but it would have been better if she was with Kaius, and not pretending to be his sister instead of his wife.

Wife. Oh. Nikon would... With Lavti. They would—

Pain wrenched through me, howling like the desert winds through the worst storm, sand blasting every inch of me. I stumbled and fell, landing on my knee and tumbling to the ground.

"Cassandra?" Mother's voice came from far in the kitchen, before I heard her hurrying my way. "What's going on? Are you all right?" Her words were panicked now.

I scrambled to my feet, not wanting a scene. I wanted to tell her I was fine, but the brutal pounding inside said I was anything but. "I just need to sleep, I think."

"I'll take you to your room. Let me call for your father."

"No, no. Please don't worry him. I'm just tired. Please."

"If you insist."

The way to my room was muddled, barely registering voices or surroundings, until I made it to my bed. I lay on it, letting my cane drop from my hand and to the floor. Its familiar call came from below, where it must have rolled under the bed. The call that Nikon had helped me achieve.

He'd done so much for me. Taken me with him when I could have been captured. Insisted that he protect me. Taught me things I needed to know. Together, we'd faced a lot. I'd become a better, stronger person, because of his influence in my life. He had greater faith in me than I had in myself.

We'd been so close. I wanted to believe there was more between us than friendship. There was a stirring of something. A light in my chest that existed only when he was near. It hurt to think it, yet I wished for more.

And yet, he fell in love with another woman.

Someone who wasn't me.

It was stupid. I couldn't fall in love.

Didn't matter. The pain and mourning still reamed through me. I'd forever lost something I could never have anyway, but the spark of hope had been there, until his loving another snuffed it out.

I WOKE to Tewy jumping on my chest. I grunted. "I'm awake, Tewy. Go find someone else to torment."

He stopped but didn't get off my chest.

I groaned. Why did I feel so awful? My head pounded, my eyes heavy and swollen, but they were nothing compared to the pain stabbing my heart. The events of returning here in a haze of pain came back with a sickening clarity. I didn't want to think of what had happened. Not ever again.

Forcing *him* from my mind, I said, "Why are you waking me up? I just want to sleep after..." I gulped back the rest of my sentence.

"He's concerned about you, as we all are." Nikon's voice, usually so reassuring, left me feeling ripped to shreds.

Thinking of something nice to say was near impossible. I should have stayed quiet, but instead opted for, "Why aren't you out, enjoying your new amant status?"

The words came out harsh and cutting. I rolled over. He was probably sitting on Zoe's bed, by the sound of things, and it was far too near.

The bed shifted beside me. "Because you're my best friend. I'm worried about you."

Friend. That was all I ever was, and all I'd ever be. "Now isn't a good time to talk."

"What happened? Are you sick?" The concern in his voice made my eyes water.

I bunched in on myself, blinking heavily, not wanting him to see me cry. "I don't know. I just need time."

He put a hand on my shoulder, the touch at once comforting and torturous. Did I want to kick him away, or lean into him and curl myself around him?

I stayed as I was, rigid and tense, turned away from him.

I tried to ignore him, but he didn't leave or move. Just remained there, by my side. Tewy nudged my arms, until I wrapped them around him. At least Tewy wouldn't go and fall in love and leave me. That was one of the few things I could count on. Monkeys were not only rarer in this part of the world, but he'd never shown interest in girl monkeys. He never really cared much about their company, or he would have stayed behind when I left my home by the waterfall, where most others like him lived.

My heart ached for those simpler times. I might have been lonely, but there'd been less pain.

"Can you talk to me?" Nikon's voice was soft but worried. "Tell me what's wrong."

Tewy stirred, tail whipping against my left hand.

I wanted to speak, to tell them both how much it hurt to have Nikon fall in love and leave me. Despite how hard I tried, every time I opened my mouth, the words couldn't make it past the sand stuck in my throat.

"Cass? Please? I'm worried."

My heart tore a little more. It didn't make a difference. He'd know sooner or later, and I might as well tell him. I didn't want him concerned on my behalf. Besides, it wasn't his fault that people fell in love at first sight and he'd happened to finally meet the woman he was meant to be with.

Tears flowed harder, but my voice came out surprisingly clear. "You found Lavti."

A silent beat.

"I did. She's here, if you want to meet her." There was emotion in his tone, but I couldn't read it. Didn't want to, was more like it.

"I already did." My own voice was flat. Dead.

"Yes, but not as my future wife. I know there's much for us to handle, and I'll stick with you through it all, but she's anxious for that step."

She would be. Marriages usually took place within twenty-four hours of falling in love. And then the happy couple was accepted into amant society. They would likely struggle with concerns like money and where to live, but it would be easier for him. If he could keep people from knowing he was the Reding's brother, he could make it through. He might not be interested in the rebellion anymore.

I scooted away from him and knocked into Tewy. My monkey *ooooed* at me, nice and long, while putting a hand on my cheek. He probably understood what was going on less than I did, but he was here for me.

The entire thing was wrong. If only I could go back and have none of us ever meet Lavti.

No, I couldn't wish that. I wanted happiness for Nikon, even if it hurt me.

"Please, tell me why you're like this." Nikon's voice was soft but full of pain. He clearly worried about me, despite finding his perfect match.

I had to give him the truth. "You fell in love."

"How does that affect you being—? *That's* why you're upset. You're not ill; you don't want me to have fallen in love." It was as if the sands made it all clear to him.

"Yes. No. I don't know." My feelings were such a jumble, I didn't know how to explain them to myself, let alone him. "I'm glad you've found what you always wanted. I really am. It's just... I thought— I'd hoped..."

When I didn't finish, he said, "We'll always be friends. That's not going to change, Cass. You will always be my best friend."

He was right. We were friends. I needed to remember that. We'd always be friends.

Too bad I wanted more.

CHAPTER EIGHT

Everyone had eventually come home last night. Mom and Dad visited me, though I said little, and Zoe let me know she was there when I was ready to talk. Sleep had been a rough ride after that, but I stayed in bed anyway after everyone else got up. Tewy left at some point, probably to find food. I knew I needed to do the same, but moving was difficult.

No matter how I wished to stay in bed and mourn something that could never be, there were tasks to be done.

After forcing myself to roll out of bed, I grabbed my cane, made comforting noises at Tewy—more for me than him—and headed toward the main room, where voices drifted from.

"We have to move forward," Zoe said.

"We need to do so in a way that's kind to the amant," Lavti said. She was in a conversation about the rebellion? "Things are hard for the odiosom, yes, but the amant aren't that bad."

I opened my mouth to refute from the hall, but Nikon beat me to it. "Despite our becoming amant, we should think about what the odiosom are going through. They've lost much over the years, and it's only getting worse. Not to mention what the amant do to the blind."

"You mean like Cassandra?" Lavti's voice was soft.

I bit my lip, holding in a reply, so I could hear what was said in my absence. I probably shouldn't eavesdrop, but I couldn't help myself.

"Yes," Nikon said. "They would make her a slave—if they didn't outright kill her. It's horrifying that they would treat anyone that way."

Standing straighter, I thought more about his response. He was correct, and although we'd only ever be friends, it seemed his becoming an amant truly wouldn't harm anything I didn't want to change about our relationship.

"It's beyond wrong." Zoe's conviction strengthened her words.

"I would like to get to know Cassandra and the plight of the people whose lives you're trying to help improve," Lavti said.

It had been her plight before yesterday. But she was attempting to understand. As much as I wanted to find a reason to dislike her, to maintain my feelings of frustration for her, I didn't have anything to hold on to. She was a good person, as far as I could tell, and she would make Nikon a good match. He deserved such.

I needed to remember that.

Not wanting to dwell on it anymore, I entered the room, head held high. Tewy hooted and scampered over to me. I bent over, holding my arm out for him, and let him climb up to my shoulder, where he chattered animatedly into my ear.

"I know, boy," I told him, but that didn't do anything to ease his squawking. If anything, he got noisier. I talked over him. "What's the plan from the meeting? Any ideas about what to do next?"

"Cassandra, you're better." Zoe's relief was palpable, but the footsteps that came near were soft and familiar. When Nikon embraced me, I wasn't certain what to think—yet I had no problem embracing him in return.

He said, "We've been so worried about you."

The tone of his voice said they'd been more concerned than they were letting on. How could I say the problem was a broken heart over him? Instead, I said, "I'm fine enough." Or as well as could be expected, given the circumstances. "Nothing to fret over. Let's keep moving forward."

"Are you sure?" Nikon's question was a whisper of a balm against my tortured heart.

Nikon moved to the side, as Dad came barreling in and said, "We've been wondering if you were feeling well."

"Good enough." But I hugged him back tight, and Mom's arms closed around the both of us.

She added, "Perhaps not, but things could have happened to you."

"No more need to stress now. I'm up and feeling"—well, not like myself or much better, but—"well enough to get some things done."

"Let's get things done, then," Zoe said, a note of anxiety in her tone.

I would be concerned about her if she'd acted out of character, but I was grateful nonetheless.

Mom and Dad pulled away from me, but it was Nikon who led me to a seat next to him.

By this point, Tewy's chatter had almost calmed to a normal level of annoyance. I gave him a pat, to make sure he knew I hadn't forgotten him, as a question came to me. "Is Hettie here?"

"No," Lavti said. "She and my other friend went back to help the others from Itpy figure out where to go and what to do."

"How many of you from Itpy are there?" I asked.

"Twenty-three."

So enough that we couldn't take them in, but not so many that we couldn't help. As the others made plans for trying to find the refugees homes, I was very aware of Nikon, next to me. I tried to focus on what they said, but it was near impossible.

Nikon smelled of metal and soap, like he'd recently bathed. The fresh smell and his proximity had me wanting to grab hold of his hand, but I stopped myself. It wasn't something I would have done anyway, with so many people about, but never now that he was an amant.

"Cassandra," Zoe's tone implied it wasn't the first time she'd said my name. "Do you have any thoughts?"

About what? Sand blast me for not listening to the conversation. I needed to focus on what was important for the greater good. "Not at the moment."

"We'll move ahead, then," she said. "Keep recruiting in town, and see what we can do to help those from Itpy. We need to come up with a plan to deal with the Reding and Vading, as well, but that will take more time. The maveor may be sympathetic to our cause, but we should be cautious about how we proceed, here in town."

"We'll keep things quiet as we move forward," Mom said, "but we need to get going."

"People will be thrilled to know you two are alive, and that will help our cause," Ramina said. "That and Nikon's wishing to help despite becoming an amant will be high points in our favor."

"I'll help however I can, as well." Lavti's voice was smaller than when she was talking clothes, but still resolute.

And while everyone else was out helping, I'd have to figure out how to get through things without making a mess of their plans. There was little I could do from Ramina's house, but there had to be something that I could do, and I simply didn't know what it was yet.

I could think on the problem of the tainted water, or the neczar's chasing me for the high priest. Though I didn't know much about either at the moment, maybe I could come up with some ideas.

THE FOLLOWING WEEK went on slowly. While Lavti didn't move into Ramina's, she was here often. Most of her time she spent with Nikon, but she socialized with the rest of us as well. I was grateful to her for helping me, but I also had to hold in the twinges of jealousy I felt at her and Nikon's closeness. It wasn't like I was the only one allowed near him, especially since they were in love.

The thought left my stomach churning.

We were gathered together—Nikon, Lavti, Zoe, Kaius, and I —with Tewy running in and out of the room. While the others planned the next steps of the rebellion and pretend to be amant and warriors, I thought out how I could make a difference.

When the idea finally came to me, I said, "Lavti said she makes clothes, yes?"

"I do," she responded.

"Perfect. If we had more amant outfits and warriors' uniforms, we could have more of our people infiltrate those groups. We'd have better access to areas we were struggling with before. Disguises would also go a long way toward entering the pyramid in Sirya."

"It's a good idea," Nikon said. He used disguises a lot, so he was the best one to talk to about the subject. "Those of us who are more recognizable either need to stay in the background or further alter our appearance, but it would work."

"If you're willing to help, Lavti, I also believe it's a good idea." Zoe's confirmation mixed with Nikon's, to make me sit up a little straighter.

"It'd be good, to have a reason to sew and help others learn," she said. "The hard part may be getting the supplies we need. Both warriors' uniforms and amant outfits have difficult to get or expensive materials."

True, but I kept thinking on the beginning of her words. There was so much more than just learning to sew. We were working to topple an entire government.

"Leave that to me," Nikon said.
I didn't like the sound of that.

CHAPTER NINE

Two days later, I was learning to sew with Lavti at my side, on some cheap cloth Ramina had found for us, when Nikon burst in the back room. "I've got enough material to get you started."

"*Oh, Nikon.*" Lavti's chair screeched across the wooden floor, and her steps were soft and dainty as she went to him. "I can't believe you've found all this. Where did you get it?"

"I may be an outlaw, but I have connections."

I shook my head, freezing in place when I heard a smooch from their direction. They'd put off getting married until things were more secure, but she was affectionate. Which was good for him, but also hard to hear.

"Don't you see, Cassandra?" Lavti's voice caught. "My future husband is brilliant. He can make anything happen."

"Almost anything," I mumbled.

"What was that?" she asked.

I forced a smile. "Nothing. I'm happy he was able to get what we need. Was it dangerous, Nikon?"

"If only it had been. Things have been far too calm around here, lately." His words would have reassured me, had I trusted them. Nikon might like action, but there was a note in his tone that made me think he'd seen more fighting than he let on. Likely he'd had to go somewhere guarded to get the materials he needed and had broken in and out.

Lavti giggled. "It's nice to have things quiet. If they settle down enough, maybe you and I can return to Itpy, to live."

Tewy screeched from another room, the sound splitting through the air as he came roaring in. Apparently he liked the idea of Nikon living with someone else as much as I did.

"What is it, Tewy?" I asked, holding my arm out toward the sound.

He calmed and took the moment to hop up to my shoulder and pull my hair.

"Yes, yes. I know. I need to have it cut again. It's not worth howling over, though." My words did little to cease his tugging, but it did become a bit gentler.

"He's an interesting little thing, isn't he?" Lavti said. "I'll get started on these right away, for Kaius and Zoe. Cassandra seems ready to start making uniforms as well. She's surprisingly good at figuring things out."

I tried not to grit my teeth, and instead lightened the mood. "Just don't tell her about the time Tewy mixed up all my yarn."

Nikon laughed. "We'll be sure you have the right colors and Tewy doesn't get a hold of them."

The monkey in question stopped pulling on my hair to snort and slouch on my shoulder.

"There, there. I shouldn't have left you alone in that room so long. I would have gone stir crazy too," I said. Though perhaps not as much as he had.

He patted my cheek and went back to playing with my hair.

"What can I do, to help you get started?" Nikon asked.

It didn't take long before the material beneath my fingers was soft like the silk of water. Compared to the coarse cloth I'd been working with, it was divine—so much so, I worried my fingers would snag on it and leave marks.

Lavti told me I was doing fine, while Nikon sat nearby with Tewy. Zoe and Kaius had previously come in for measurements. My job was a matter of stitching where Lavti told me to. Simple enough, and leaving me far too much time to think.

"What do you think the Reding and Vading are planning next?" No one had yet told Lavti that Nikon was the Reding's brother, and I wasn't going to be the one to break it to her. Though she knew we were working with the rebellion, it was also clear she didn't know he used to be an elite warrior. Nikon would figure all that out. I couldn't imagine going from having friends in your life to suddenly having a person you loved more than anyone else, and in a romantic way, when you didn't know them.

It didn't sound much like love to me, but that was probably because I'd gotten lost in my odd ideals. Kaius and Zoe's relationship, like my parents' relationship, was one of trust, respect, and love. Sure, it'd started off like Nikon and Lavti's, but they'd grown it from there. Lavti and Nikon would do the same.

I shook myself, making my tiny stitches while I waited for Nikon to talk. There was a lot going on, without my always bringing things back to love. Lavti's presence might be an adjustment in our lives, but there were things more important than how I felt about them. The rebellion against Eppla's rulers, for one. Why the high priest wanted me and if he'd be able to get his hands on me, for another.

The thought sent a shiver down my spine.

I stretched my back, and continued with my sewing. "Well, Nikon? Any ideas?"

"I think they'll come around if we make an open line of communication with them," Lavti said.

It surprised me that she was the one to respond. What was Nikon thinking about? "Do you know much about the Reding and Vading?" I asked her.

"The bits and pieces everyone does. The rebellion is a great idea, and it will help get their attention, so we can change things around."

"Most people, I believe, are good. It's some who've gotten control of laws and power that have made it a struggle for everyone else who's trying their best." Nikon's words surprised me. I knew he didn't like the way things were run, but I didn't realize he was so hopeful about how they could be.

I needed to be more like him. We needed to be doing more. The time we tried to take down the Reding and Vading had been a good attempt, but with the plan going awry and people wanting to kill them, that wasn't the best option any more. Infiltrating the amant and the government seemed like a way to gain more information and help the rebellion overthrow the government, but would it be enough?

"Exactly," Lavti said. "And we can show them the way."

"I'm glad you joined the rebellion with us," he said.

"I am, as well."

All this mushy talk between them left me feeling like I was in the wrong place, at most definitely the wrong time. Sands knew I didn't want to interrupt them, but neither did I wish to draw attention to myself by leaving. I sunk further back into my hard, wooden chair.

"Cassandra here has done a lot to help. In fact, if it wasn't for her, I wouldn't be a part of it." Nikon's words buoyed me up.

"It was more those we know back in Itpy who got us started," I demurred. "I knew things were wrong, but I didn't believe something could be done about it. I'm rather hoping we're on the right track."

"We did have some luck there," he said.

"More luck than the time I had to spend in the sewer." I scrunched my nose at the memory.

He chuckled. "You smelled something awful."

"I wouldn't have, if you hadn't suggested it," I teased, but then let a serious note enter my voice. "And I would have been captured by the warriors and taken who knows where. To be a slave or..." To the high priest, maybe? I didn't want to think about that possibility.

"Sounds like you two have been through a lot," Lavti said.

I shrugged, focusing back on my sewing. "Hasn't everyone?"

"Interesting idea."

It didn't seem so novel to me. "Everyone goes through hard times, though they're different from another person's. Some hardships just happen to be more noticeable."

"Like your blindness."

"That's one way of putting it." I tied off my thread and held up the cloth. "How does this look?"

"You did a good job. It'll make Zoe look like the most fashionable amant." Lavti sounded enthused. She knew what she was doing, as far as I could tell, so I was grateful to have her think I'd done my project justice.

We spent the rest of the day sewing and putting together different outfits for people in the rebellion. Though we needed to create many more, we'd come a long enough way that people could start working with what we had. Now we needed to figure out how exactly we wanted to go forward.

CHAPTER TEN

I rubbed my temple to ease the forming headache. I'd been hunched over the material I'd been working on. Lavti and I had made many outfits over the past week, but with more material and people in the rebellion, there was always something to do. It was good work but exhausting.

"*Sand it*, I'm out of thread," Lavti said. "I'll have to go out and get some."

"Too bad we didn't realize before the others left. They could have picked some up on their way back from the meeting." Though I was secretly grateful for an excuse to get out of the house. I'd spent so much time cooped up with her, I was ready for some fresh air. Maybe the change could help me figure out how to accept her and Nikon's relationship. Spending time with her was a good chance to get to know her. "Would you like me to come with?"

"I would enjoy that."

"Let me get my cane, in case I need it, but you should hold it lest we attract suspicion."

"I can do that."

I finished tying off my thread, jumped up, and hurried to the room I shared with Zoe. I got my cane and enjoyed its familiar buzz in my hands. Lavti had been staying with her friends at night, but with the amount of time she spent at Ramina's, she should have moved in with us. I didn't want that, but I couldn't deny she was trying to be kind and helpful.

I returned to the room we'd turned into a workspace and held out my cane.

Lavti took it. "I've got it. Do you need anything else?"

"Nope, let's go."

I held out a hand, walking toward her, and she let me take hold of her arm. She led me out of the empty house, into the street. I wished Tewy or Nikon was with us, but they'd gone with the others to the meeting. It was good for us women to get to know each other better. Lavti would be in Nikon's life for the rest of it, which meant if I wanted to stay close to him, I needed to be comfortable with her.

We went out of the house, turned left down the street, and went along at a good pace. The midday air was hot but fresh with possibilities. My sandals slapped against the cobblestone. I should have left them off as they annoyed me. Too bad my feet weren't as tough as they used to be. Just as well. The people of Ruso thought it odd for someone to go without shoes, for some reason. Lavti's steps were far louder than mine, almost clomping.

Once we'd passed what must have been several houses, I asked, "How did you get started in clothing?"

"One thing led to another."

"Oh?" I prodded her on.

"You know—found one person who taught me, and I liked it so we went with it." She sounded excited despite offering no details.

"Have you been to the shop we're going to before? I know you went with Nikon, to get a few more materials"—I didn't want to come right out and say *stolen goods*—"he didn't find at first."

"I have been to that shop before, yes." Her footsteps quickened, and I hurried to follow suit.

"You're really excited about this, aren't you?"

"I'll admit to that."

A flutter tickled in my stomach. "Have you worked with many amant, then?"

"Yes. Almost there." She sounded as if she was distracted.

Were there many people around? I didn't want to ask and give myself away, but I suddenly wondered if it was such a good idea to come with her, after all. I'd never much learned my lesson on not going out.

It'd be fine. I went out—well—not often, but sometimes. I tried telling that to the flutter in my stomach that grew across my whole torso.

Lavti's breathing became louder, probably due to how fast we were walking. We turned a corner, and I didn't bother asking more questions. Her mind was clearly on something else, and I was too busy, listening for danger she might not recognize.

After a dozen more steps, she stopped and said, "Here you go."

"Are we there?" I asked, at the same time a man's voice asked, "Who's this?"

Did he run the shop? I kept my mouth shut, since we hadn't entered a building, the heat of the sun beating down on my skin.

"This is a blind woman I caught for you," Lavti said. "Thought she'd make a nice collection for Vading Antonia. I understand our ruler knows this one personally."

"*What?*" The word came out of my lips in almost a screech. The flutter morphed into a heavy pressure, so weighty it pulled my heart down. This couldn't be happening. We'd been trying to become friends, and she loved my best friend. That had to mean something.

Or maybe that was the problem. Perhaps she wanted me away from my best friend and her amant half.

The thought left me sick. She was betraying me for her own gain. "Lavti, no. Don't do this."

She ignored me, except to rip her arm away from my grasp and shove me forward. I stumbled, my brain struggling as much as my body to catch up on everything that just happened.

I lurched forward, heading for the one thing I could always locate that could help—my cane. It called out to me, screaming at me to grab it. I'd moved less than a step, when rough hands grabbed my upper arms and yanked me back away from her. I struggled against them, my mind stuttering against what happened.

"Thank you for doing your duty as a citizen of Eppla," the man said.

"Trust me," Lavti said from behind me, glee evident in her tone, "turning this one in is my pleasure."

"Lavti, please, don't. Nikon will never forgive you." I turned back toward her voice, panic making me want to run. But where to? Why hadn't I paid more attention to where we were going? I should have known Ruso better. Should have realized we weren't heading to the market district, like I believed.

"He'll never know," she replied.

I growled, letting out all my anger and fear. "We can be friends, if you get me out of this."

She laughed, the sound light and happy, with a twisted cruelness I hadn't suspected of her. "Oh, Cassandra, you really shouldn't be so trusting."

She continued, "Here's her cane. Make sure she doesn't get it, or she'll give you a good wallop with it. Despite her lack of sight, she's apparently quite something to behold with it. Glad I won't have to endure that comparison anymore." Lavti's tone somehow became more gleeful the longer she spoke. "I'd recommend taking it to the Vading with her. And be quick, if you don't want her rescued. She has friends in high places."

"Please, tell me you aren't having me sent to the pyramid,

Lavti." I pulled against my captor again, trying to free myself and reach my cane, which was now to the right side of me. The grip on me stayed firm and unmoving.

She laughed. "See you never again, blind freak."

I reared back as her noisy steps clipped away. The hurt and anger didn't stay long, as reality washed over me like the river of death, roaring into the southern chasm. I opened my mouth to scream for help, hoping I was somehow close to a rebellion member who would help me out. Before I could let out a sound, a hand clamped over my mouth.

"Let's get this scum where she belongs, so we can get our reward money and carry on with the day," my captor said.

Several people voiced their agreement—far more than I had suspected were near.

I had a sinking feeling we were near a warrior headquarters.

The man tugged at me, pulling me into the opposite direction Lavti and I had come from. I squirmed, trying to bite him or land a kick.

He was wily, not letting me get tooth or claw in him or his companions. There was nothing I could do against their strength and numbers. I was doomed to face Antonia and whatever came next. I'd been captured.

No. Lavti had turned me in.

CHAPTER ELEVEN

After screaming and yelling to pound out my feelings by angrily pacing my cell, I'd only been ignored. My voice sounded hoarse, but it was nothing to the agony inside at what Lavti had done. And Nikon would likely never know.

I'd been by myself in the Ruso jail and dealt with being imprisoned. I'd lived alone for years, so it hadn't been anything new. Yet it was different without freedom or Tewy. Everything was different. The love Nikon had wanted—and finally gained—led to my own capture.

It felt as though years passed, as I tried to figure out a way to escape. There was nothing but bars spaced evenly apart where one wall should have been and brick on the other three. I knew, because I'd checked while the other prisoners in different cells ignored me. The guards couldn't keep me in here forever. When I got out, Lavti would pay.

Except, there would only be slavery in my future, unless I escaped.

I plopped down to the cold, hard floor, half-grateful to find a different texture and half-angry to be feeling at all. I curled my legs up and wrapped my arms around them. Without my cane, Tewy, Nikon, and my other loved ones, I was useless.

And Lavti knew it.

She'd exploited the one weakness I'd worried about. The thought gave me a rush of energy again. I jumped to my feet and resumed pacing the cell, careful to measure my steps so I didn't run into the bars in the front or walls on the sides. It was hard to tell why I bothered, though. Running into jail bars was the least of my problems.

Several hours later, footsteps approached my cell and the lock clicked.

They pitied me and were letting me go. My hope quickly deflated when I remembered how criminal it was to be blind. They would only take me out to a new life of slavery. They wouldn't release me unless it was by way of death.

Holding my head high, though I wanted to curl up in a ball and cry, I crossed my arms in front of my chest and asked, "Decided you made a mistake?"

"We're taking you where you belong," a man replied, his voice harsh.

"And where might that be?"

"With the other slaves."

The unknown waited for me, as Nikon's mind was poisoned by his future bride. I gulped back my fear, doing my best not to let it show, as they took me from the jail. They marched me out of the city, onto a path I'd ever used.

A week later, we reached what my guards said was Sirya. Back to where I didn't want to be, to become the rulers' slave.

Sand it all.

As we walked through the streets of the capital, the voices around us were mostly murmurs, with the occasional stupid person calling out something along the lines of, "Odiosom trash."

They didn't know I had unwillingly committed the worse

crime of being blind. The thought of something so uncontrollable being punishable by law made my anger fiery hot.

I was more than ready to take out these guards with the staff they'd brought along. Unfortunately, they listened to Lavti and kept it out of my reach.

We came to a stop, and a woman's voice called out, "Who have you here?"

"We sent a note ahead, about this prisoner. She's to become a slave, but the woman who turned her in said the Vading would have a personal interest in her." He shoved me around, as if used to speaking with his hands, but didn't let go of me while doing so. Smart of him. I might not have been able to get away, but I would have tried and done what I could to hurt them in the process.

"Ah, yes. I know this one," said the woman. "I'll take her from here."

The man jerked me back. "No offense, but we'll deliver the goods ourselves. The blind thing's name is *Cassandra.* Got to make sure we get the reward you see, and if the Vading does have an interest in her, we expect the reward may be higher than for a simple slave."

The woman sighed. "Fine. Come along. But make sure she doesn't cause a fuss. I won't have any more of that around here."

I pursed my lips together in anger. Being handled by these people made me want to writhe and scream. Nothing I'd said on the way over made a difference, and I doubted anything I said to this woman would do any better.

Trying not to show my frustration at the situation and my growing apprehension of being brought before Antonia again, I was forced along as they marched forward.

Had Nikon found me gone by now? Did he realize Lavti was the one who'd turned me in? Fury at her for doing this to me ate at me. Yes, I'd been possessive of Nikon, and he wasn't my amant half. I sure had a lot of feelings for him that might have caused the jealousy, but I wasn't about to give her any slack. She'd done all of us wrong.

The slant of the floor beneath me was familiar, taking me back to when I'd walked this way before. Both times, I'd been with Nikon. The first, we were brought before the Reding and Vading after Tewy called out to Antonia in a crowd. The second, when the rebellion thought they could kill the Reding and Vading to solve all the country's problems, and Nikon and I thought saving them for a punishment less harsh than death would be the best option. Maybe we were wrong.

Without Nikon's near-silent presence comforting me through what was to come, I was left alone to deal with this. My shoulders wanted to slump, but I pushed my back straight and held my head high, as we made a tight turn to the right and came to a stop.

"Wait here," the woman said.

She left, the warriors with me rumbling into talk as soon as her footsteps faded.

"You think we're going to get a good reward?"

"Better be, with all the extra work we did, to bring her ourselves. If that woman lied to us about how important this one was, I'll hunt her down myself."

"We'll find out soon enough. The name seemed to make an impact."

"My pockets need to feel that impact."

"Your pockets are lined with blood money," I snapped.

"Oooh, little blind girl finally has something to say," the man Lavti delivered me to said. "What I wouldn't give, to teach you a lesson. If you weren't so valuable, I'd make certain you felt my fist. Might still do it if the Vading doesn't want you like we were told."

I had the strongest urge to spit on him, but held it in. No sense making him angrier toward me, to the point where he lost his temper. From the sound of things, I was lucky I got this far without feeling his wrath.

Though I did wonder what experience he'd had with the blind, to feel this way. Did he simply hate us because he was told to, or had something happened that made him believe the Reding and Vading's awful rhetoric?

The woman's footsteps echoed back into the room.

"Seems you warriors have found yourselves a prize," the woman said. "Let's go see if she's who you say she is, and if you'll be rewarded or feel the wrath of the Vading for wasting her time."

"*Wasting her time?*" the man asked. "We wouldn't do that."

"There's a distinct possibility you are." I didn't care about the fate of those who brought me here. They'd made their choice, when I had none.

"But you are this Cassandra the woman who turned you in spoke of. Aren't you?" the man asked.

I shrugged.

He grumbled, took a hold of my arm hard enough to leave bruises, and pulled me forward with him.

Sure, he was about to be rewarded, but he could quiver in fear a little bit before Antonia paid for me. How much was I worth to her? Not much—she'd made that very evident.

And yet, it did sound like there was a reward for me. Odd.

We walked around the pyramid, the way getting steeper with each turn. It wasn't long before the ground leveled out and we entered a flat room that the air moved around in. If I had to guess, we were at the throne room at the top of the pyramid—but then, the last two times I'd been here, there'd been some chatter. Today, it was silent. Heavily so.

I was pulled forward, before being shoved to the ground, my knees screaming in protest at the hard rock floor beneath them that I was now bleeding on. It wasn't bad, but there was definitely liquid coming out of my stinging knees.

Someone grabbed me by the hair and yanked my head up.

Then nothing. I hated the waiting. I'd rather get on with whatever was to come. When I heard Antonia's familiar laugh—one that used to fill me with comfort but now filled me with dread—I knew there was no way to escape her this time.

CHAPTER TWELVE

"What do we have here?" Antonia asked. "Is this Cassandra?"

A soft clicking of a person walked toward me, and slim fingers gripped my chin. I tried to jerk away from the cruel grasp, not willing to make this easy for her, but the hand gripping me from behind held my head firm.

I growled. I may have been brought to the pyramid under someone else's control, and soon to be a slave—or worse—but I wouldn't allow Antonia the satisfaction of seeing me down and succumbing to my situation.

"You have no idea how much I regretted letting you get away twice now. There won't be a third time." Her voice was cold.

She had me under her power. There was nothing I could do except hide how much it got to me. How much it dragged me down.

Someone snapped their fingers. Her.

"Yes, my Vading?" the woman who'd accompanied us inside the pyramid asked.

"How did you find her?" Antonia asked.

"These warriors brought her in."

"Well?" Antonia's tone was demanding.

"She was handed to us by a woman," said the male warrior who'd threatened me with physical violence.

"Do you know who it was?" she asked.

"No. She had a scarf around her face and didn't look familiar. Though it was in Ruso, not here."

I wanted to open my mouth and give Lavti away, but stopped myself before I said her name. Giving her away would mean putting Nikon and the others in danger—something I'd never allow. Antonia would do things far worse to me if she had access to my loved ones to torment.

Sandblasted traitor. If I ever got out of here and was around Lavti again, there'd be sand to pay.

"Hmmm." Antonia was close enough I could have lashed out at her if the grip on my hair wasn't tight enough to make my eyes water. "Very well, then. I don't care, as long as she's here. Though my husband will want you to keep an eye out in Ruso for the former elite warrior, Nikon. He was likely with her, so keep watch for him."

"And our reward?" the man asked.

Antonia's voice softened. "Yes. You'll be handsomely rewarded for bringing her in. Remember there's more to come, should you capture the man as well."

"Thank you, Vading," he replied. "This was brought with her. We were told to be careful not to let her get it. Apparently, her fighting skills with it are better than one would believe."

"Ah. Is that how you managed to defeat so many warriors, Cassandra?" she said. "That will certainly have to be studied."

I held in a cringe, not wanting her to know how much the loss of my cane meant to me. Finding my way around without it was harder, but more than that, I wasn't able to hit all these nitwits in the head with it.

"You, there," Antonia said, pulling me from my thoughts. "Yes, you. Take these men to receive the reward for Cassandra's capture, and then I want you to send word to the high priest that I have what he's been looking for."

I gulped down the fear pushing up my throat. What did he want me for, and how was she involved? The thought sent bile to my mouth. Maybe I was reading too much into this. Maybe she sent all the blind to the high priest, and she didn't know that he was looking for me personally. Why wouldn't she, though?

"While we wait for his arrival," Antonia continued, "you should learn exactly what I want to do to you, Cassandra."

From the tone of her voice, I had a feeling it wouldn't be something I wished to hear.

Though the feelings of despair pulsed through me, I did what I could against them. They ached in my chest, no matter how hard I wanted to move them aside. I couldn't give in yet. My friends would find me.

Yet, now that I thought about it, they would have no idea where I went. Lavti would have told them I up and left. Or that she went out to get thread, and I was gone when she returned.

No. I was my only hope and with what I had right now, that meant no hope at all.

CHAPTER THIRTEEN

With my head aching from where my hair had been pulled for far too long, and my knees sticky with dried blood, I was taken to the slave quarters and shoved inside.

My surroundings were an empty map. Nikon would know where we were if he was here, but then, he wasn't blind and might have never been in this part of the pyramid. He'd have more of a clue than I did, but I was grateful he hadn't been captured as well. My stress was higher than before because I'd gone into a dark world, with nothing familiar or helpful except for the far too distant call of my cane. So useless.

I slouched as the door slammed closed behind me. What should I do? The room was silent. I bit my cheek to keep from crying out as the sounds from the other side of the door receded. The stale dust settled in my nose, making me sneeze.

"New slave?" a woman called out, her tone soft and trembling with age.

I swallowed down what I could of my fear, frustrated when far too much of it stayed, making my voice crack. "Afraid so."

"It's all right. We're slaves also. These are the slaves' quarters, such as they are. I'm Elata."

"Cassandra."

"I'd say it was a pleasure to meet you, but it never is where no one wants to meet. Come along, then. You've arrived just as I was about to start my chores for the second part of the day."

I nodded, realized she couldn't see me—unlike the others I was usually with—and croaked out, "Thank you."

"Don't thank me yet. I'll do what I can to teach you how to stay safe in this place, but it's a nest of scorpions. Worse, I found a scarab yesterday while cleaning, so I don't expect to stay long."

I hissed out a breath. A scarab was never a good omen.

"We stick to the slave quarters as much as possible, where we are out of everyone's way, but I'm afraid the space isn't all that much. They work us until we drop, but we can only do so here. You'll stick with one of us at all times. We never go anywhere alone, which was why I was in here, waiting for a partner. You see, we've been uneven since the last slave was... Well, never mind that. Keep in mind we stick together in pairs."

I gulped down another bout of fear and hopelessness, and asked a question I probably shouldn't. "Was the last slave taken by the high priest?"

"Dear woman, don't mention him. The scarabs won't be a strong enough sign of the horrors you'd have to endure should that come to pass. Why would you say such things?"

I pressed my lips together. How much should I say to her? I didn't know where I stood. "Just wondering."

"Well, don't. When he was here last, several of the slaves were taken as experiments, only to be discarded back among our ranks after he left. They're trying to get over their shock and horror, most unwilling to say much about it."

"I understand." Though I didn't. What experiments? And why would he want me? I assumed he kept in touch with the Reding and Vading, but that didn't mean they'd talk about me with him. There was nothing important enough about me to draw such powerful people's attention.

Except perhaps the annoyance I'd caused Antonia.

Elata bustled over to me. "I hope you do. Grab hold of this bucket I've got. It's full of soapy water and a rag."

I reached out and found a handle right in the perfect place. Keeping a steady grip on it, I prepared myself to do whatever the day would bring.

She instructed me to take hold of her hand and do my best to keep up.

We hurried through the halls at such a fast pace, I lost count of steps and directions in my head.

"I know it's a lot," she said at one point, "but you'll get used to it. I'm only mostly blind. Can see a bit, so I've got a little advantage. How well do you see?"

"Everything's completely black for me. Has been, since I was a teenager."

She clucked her tongue and spoke low. "Unfortunate for you to lose your sight, but we have to make of it what we can. I'm the most sighted one here, but see little enough that they had no problem turning me into a slave." In a quieter whisper, she added, "Makes me want to kick someone in the teeth, but there's little I can do. I'm getting old enough that one misstep on my end, and I'll go down the river of death, if they are gracious enough not to throw me in a pit instead. Have to be careful, around these parts."

There was barely any time to process all that, when she continued in soft tones. "This is the hall to the Vading's rooms. How much do you know about her?"

"Erm... Far more than I want to. We—uh—know each other. I'm afraid she's a big part of the reason I've been captured."

"Oh dear. That does pose a challenge. I work a lot under the Vading, but if she knows you personally, it may get tricky. We'll do what we can, though. Try to follow my lead while you're learning, and if she's ever around, be absolutely silent."

"Understood." All too well. Though nothing would be enough to escape under her heavy gaze.

She turned into a room and said, "Let's clean. This is a sitting room they use once every week or so, and it was used this week, so we don't need to worry about anyone interrupting us while you're learning."

She helped me in and started teaching me what to do. It wasn't hard work, but it was a bit mind-numbing, leaving me far too free to think of all the could-have-beens.

Too many of those. I wanted to not think about them, but there was no way around the thoughts blaring through my mind as we made our way through the stone rooms. Occasionally, there'd be a rug underfoot, but my sandals mostly smacked against stone.

When we were on our fourth room, I couldn't take my questions anymore and finally had the courage to ask, "Do you know why they want us as slaves?"

Elata grunted from across the room. "Don't know, exactly. They've been gathering us for years—ever since the Vading came into power."

I was mindful of the fact that, if someone was as silent as Nikon could be, they could sneak up on us and listen in on our conversation without us being any the wiser. Still, I had to have answers. "What about the Reding? Doesn't he want slaves as well?"

Her footsteps came closer, as I wiped down the desk she'd assigned me to. When she stopped next to me, I continued to scrub the same spot, leaning in to hear her speak. "It's said the Reding doesn't care for having the blind for slaves. It's all the Vading."

"That doesn't make any sense." But then again, maybe it did, and I simply didn't have all the pieces I needed. He seemed as awful as Antonia, but if he didn't want slaves, was that really the truth?

"Perhaps, but that is the way of things. The Reding is said to have fought her on it after they were first married, but the high priest stepped in and sanctioned it. Took many of the blind back for his own use."

I shivered at the memory of what she'd said earlier about the high priest. "They probably attend to tasks like what we do here," I said, though I feared they were actually being experimented on. "Keep things clean and tidy."

Her voice grew quieter than before. "The rumors are worse. They speak of tortures and experiments, though no one really knows what they entail, other than that they're upon the blind. But I shouldn't be telling you all that. You'll be safe from him here, with me. Let's go to the next room."

The high priest did want me, and Antonia had sent word to him about me. It seemed I was to become one of his experiments.

My muscles froze, screaming at me to run and hide. I didn't know what to think or do.

"Cassandra? Are you well?" Elata asked.

Not at all. "I don't rightly know."

"Well, you have to keep going. Unless we're on our death bed, there's no break for us."

Instead of shying away from the call of death, for the first time in my life, I wondered if it was a better option than the alternate future that awaited me.

If the high priest took and tortured me, what would it mean for my family? My friends? Nikon? Tewy? And what did it mean for me? I wasn't certain I wanted to know.

Getting back to work, I followed Elata through to another room. I worked the rest of the day, and fell into a hammock of a bed at night, exhausted. The next morning came far too soon, with Elata calling me out of bed after it felt like I'd just fell asleep.

The days came together in a blur of housekeeping. If I focused on my chores instead of my loved ones and impending slavery to the high priest, it wasn't as bad as I expected. It didn't take as long as I thought it would, to find my way around the area of the pyramid where Elata and I were. Especially with moving through it so much to keep the place as tidy as the amant wanted it to be, which was far more than I ever thought someone would want.

As I scrubbed down the stone floor in a sitting room on the third day, I had to wonder if they kept us busy because they wanted us to keep working, rather than because they needed the chores done so often. It was tempting to ask Elata what she thought, but I didn't know how my words would be received. Between not knowing if anyone was around and her thoughts on our situation, I found it difficult to ask.

I crawled backward over the stones, my knees aching from their previous injury and the repetitive movements I'd been doing on the hard surface for so long. Though I was almost to the end of the room, where I should meet Elata, it felt far away. How much more strain on my body would I be able to handle?

Though the strain on my emotions was worse.

I paused, stretched, and sat back on my feet, to ease some of the burden on my knees. Footsteps sounded coming down the hall, which was a common occurrence. It didn't bother me, until the sound came toward the room we currently worked in. Not wanting to get caught slacking on the job and get a smack on the face—like I got yesterday—I hurried back to scrubbing, doing my best to ignore the tension on my knees and back.

The footsteps stopped near the doorway. A man said, "Cassandra, you're wanted. This other slave must come too."

"We're not finished with the room," Elata said in a humble tone.

"Not my problem." The man's words came out impatiently.

I gathered my things together; I didn't think our lack of finishing would matter because we'd already spent so much time cleaning. I grunted as I stood, grabbing my bucket and throwing my rag in it. My body protested the movement, yelling out in pain, but Elata's soft steps were already on the move toward the door. I hurried to follow. There was little tolerance for those left behind—especially if I was the one they wanted.

But what for?

I choked down the fear, as the man said, "Let's go."

I rushed to follow the pounding of his steps down the hall. Where were we, in relation to Nikon's old room and the secret halls we'd gone through the first time I was here? It was easier to figure that out than worry over what I was summoned for.

Despite my time here, I hadn't been called on since my arrival, and the only reason I could think of for why I was wanted now was the high priest. It was doubtful he'd be here that fast, though, unless he used magic to speed his way here, but that didn't explain why he would.

I focused on the turns we made and the number of steps I took, as it was likely we'd be on our own to get back to our job. I didn't want to think that I might not return. My friends and family didn't know where I was, but if I was transferred to Peka Tower, it'd be more difficult for them to find me. Not only that, but my life—what little of it was left—would also be more miserable than it currently was. The idea of things getting worse made me stumble, but I caught myself and continued on, grateful when I didn't hear any water from my bucket splashing on the hall floor.

I had to believe my loved ones were searching for me. They might not be able to get me out, but there was a chance one of the rebels would stumble upon me here.

Shaking the thoughts away as more voices came into hearing range, I strove to focus back on the sounds of the man leading us. It was a good thing too, because moments later, he stopped.

I came to a halt but had to be close to him, judging from where I last heard his thundering about.

Next to me, Elata brushed my arm. I placed my hand on her

elbow, linking us together. Hopefully, we could find our way back once the time came. If the time came.

I growled internally. No *ifs* allowed.

The voices of those ahead droned on about odiosom and the troubles they caused. I wanted to disagree with them. To fight against their words. We'd done nothing to cause trouble unless we needed to get our voices heard. Of course, their perspective was different, and to them I was nothing more than a slave.

"I've heard enough." Antonia's voice sent an odd mix of longing to be with my former friend and a shiver of fear running through me.

Part of me wished we could remain friends, even if that was never what we were. I thought we had, and I wanted those more peaceful days.

She continued. "Get out. All of you. And don't come back until you have answers to the problem. I don't want any more odiosom causing trouble in Eppla's cities."

The rush of footsteps came toward us. I squeezed closer to Elata, as they passed by in a wind of hurry. I didn't blame them, only wished I could go out with them.

"You have her?" Antonia demanded.

I had an awful feeling she spoke about me.

"Right here, Vading," the man who brought us said.

"Bring her in but leave the other slave behind. I'm not dealing with more of them than I have to."

Why did she harbor so much hatred for the blind, enough to turn us into slaves against the wishes of the Reding?

"Yes, Vading." The man grabbed my upper arm and yanked me away from Elata. Though I wanted to hold on to her, I didn't want to cause her any pain or problems. I let go, a twist stabbing my heart as my pulse sped up. I hadn't left her since I arrived, though I was no longer certain when that was. The woman had been kind to take me under her wing. I'd much rather stay with her, than go in front of what might be my doom.

I stumbled forward, ignoring the ache in my knees, and allowed the man to lead me. We went fairly deep into the room, which was larger than I expected. The throne room again, perhaps?

He came to a halt and shoved me to the ground.

My hands took the brunt of the fall, stinging ran up through my elbows, but pain also rushed my knees, as the wounds on them opened again.

I never thought I would have to kneel to Antonia.

"She looks a mess." Antonia sounded disgusted.

"It's the way I found her," the man said.

"Very well," she replied. "Take the other slave and go far from hearing. I need to have words with this... thing." She lingered on the last word, as if she'd rather call me something much worse.

There couldn't be anything Antonia wanted with me alone, so why the bother?

The guard's footsteps receded, until I could no longer hear his thundering. As far as I knew, I was alone with Antonia, but she had the advantage. Despite wanting to know what was going on, I held my head high and said nothing. As I tried to take in my surroundings, the call of my cane that'd been so faint was now nearby—closer than it'd been since I was parted from it on my arrival. In this room, perhaps?

Trying not to give away that I knew it was here, I honed in on it with that extra sense I'd gained. Would I be able to take Antonia out with it?

The thought struck me. I was ready to maim or kill the woman I once considered a friend. I wasn't the girl I was when we were last together. Now that I was willing to do such damage, I would never be that person ever again.

CHAPTER FOURTEEN

The *clack-clack* of fingernails drumming against stone sounded ahead of me, not too far from where my cane was stashed. Antonia must have been close to it. If I could just reach it...

Could I really hurt her?

"It seems a lot has changed between us," she said, pulling me from my thoughts. "I wonder what it is you're thinking. You are highly focused on something."

Deciding if I should hurt you, was what I wanted to spit out, but I kept the words buried deep inside. No sense in antagonizing her further. Since I had nothing else to say, I kept silent.

She sighed. "Grandfather seems to think you're the key to what he wants and to my freedom, but I'm not. I'm less sure than when I was forced to spend all that time with you. What makes you so special?" More clacking.

What was she was talking about? This grandfather of hers... She'd never mentioned him before. And if he thought I was the key to something, it wouldn't be a good sort of key.

Another thought tugged at me. What did Antonia need

freedom from? She was the female ruler of all of Eppla. There was nothing freer than that.

"Ah, I see I've piqued your curiosity. No matter. We'll deal with it soon enough. Or who knows? Perhaps you'll have to be dead, for the answer to come. Your death might lead to it, but then if it didn't, we wouldn't have you around anymore. Hmm... It bears thinking on. In the meantime, I'm to experiment with you until he gets here."

I swallowed the sludge of wet sand lodged in my throat. If *he* was who I thought, I was in trouble. The high priest. He was the only person I knew of that she'd told about my presence; he was also the only one I knew who conducted experiments on people. I shivered uncontrollably at the thought of being experimented upon.

"Yes, I see your fear. Don't worry, little Cassandra. It won't hurt. Much."

Instead of giving in to my worries, I forced my expression to ease. "As if you could do anything that would bother me."

"Ah, so you do speak. I was afraid you'd gone mute." Cloth shifted and rustled, before heavy steps came toward me. For being so certain of herself, she sure was loud. Though I'd been there before, it was satisfying to know I wasn't as bad giving in as I used to be. And as for me being *little Cassandra...* I might be smaller than her, but it was easy to tell which of us was the bigger person.

"What's that smirk for?" She was close now, but I doubted I could reach out and touch her. What was more, my cane hadn't come with her. It was behind her, by where she'd been when I first entered the room. I cursed my bad luck. Could I sprint to it before I ran into any problems?

A slap shocked me to the present, making me sway painfully back on my knees. I hoped my blood stained her floor.

She laughed—a mirthless sound. "I should have had you be a

slave from the start, but Grandfather thought we'd get more use out of you if you were happy and pliable." She scoffed. "Didn't do us any good. Until now. Look as us—me, the Vading, and you, a servant. Oh wait. You can't, because you're blind."

Anger built in my chest, burning hot enough I wanted to rage at her. Why was she so cruel to me? And what did her grandfather have to do with anything? There had to be a reason she turned so wrathful.

The heat continued to build in me. Despite the aches and bruises in my body and the liquid oozing from my knees, I shot to my feet. Before I could move any farther, metal kissed my neck.

"Ah-ah," she said. "I have loyal elite warriors who won't let a thing happen to me. You didn't think we'd be all alone, did you, little Cassandra? If so, you're far stupider than I thought."

I gritted my teeth. If we were alone, I'd show her what coursed through me.

The disgust building was probably evident on my expression, but I didn't care. Let her sense how I really felt toward her.

The metal left my neck, and a swift kick landed on my back. I hurtled down to the floor, smacking my hands against the stone, then my knees, then my face. Pain screamed up at me, making me call out against my will. There wasn't anything I could do about it. Didn't mean I couldn't land blows in other ways, though.

I hissed through the pain, catching my breath. When it felt as though I could handle myself and knew there weren't any broken bones, just bruised ones, I sat back on my feet and tilted my head toward where her face should be. "You've never been a fraction of the person I once thought you were."

"Oh no. The blind girl hurt my feelings," she said in a mocking tone, and laughed. "You didn't really think I'd care, did you? I'm the Vading. Whatever I say is law."

"You could have used your power for good. Instead, you let awful things happen to good people. Odiosom are being treated like garbage. Blind people become slaves. And you're a part of it all, when you could have stood up to the injustices. I pity you."

"If anyone needs pitying, it's you. I'm the one who convinced the Reding that the odiosom were so worthless and the blind needed to be enslaved."

I'd heard that from Elata, but Antonia's confirming it so blatantly jolted my system. "*You didn't*," I said. "Why would you do such a thing?"

"I have my reasons. Now, I need to know—how do you find the water?" Though her tone was amicable, there was a hint of something to it. Something almost sinister.

"The water?" Oh no. This couldn't be. She was somehow involved in whatever was happening to the water supply. The truth of it was beyond me, but there had to be something. "Is that why you had us live by the waterfall?"

"She finally uses that small brain of hers. But we're not talking about the house or what could have been there. What I want to know is if you've been drinking the water from the river, like you did when we lived together."

"What else is there to drink?" I was truly baffled. This conversation wasn't going where I thought it would. Was this what she meant by *experimenting*? If so, it was something I could handle.

"Good answer. Yet something is off, if you're the key. My sources say you've been awfully close to that horrid brother of Theodore's, and that might have something to do with it."

What in all of Eppla and sands was she talking about? "What brother?" I knew she was speaking of Nikon, but I hoped to get more information out of her as to what was going on. No, I was more confused about the water and Nikon—how they went together. Maybe it was because he stole the papyrus?

"Nikon hasn't told you who he is, then? That's so like him. He always kept secrets, ever since I've known him. Never seemed to trust me."

"He has sense," I spat at her.

"More than you do, it appears."

Nothing about my words seemed to bother her in the least. Didn't mean I'd stop trying. "And far more than you, may scarabs find you."

"You're not worth my time, to continue this."

Someone snapped, and a hand gripped the back of my head, once again yanking my hair back so my face was forced upward. I grunted. Once the shock wore off, I kept my jaw clenched and worked to hide the pain, though my eyes watered anyway. Between the screaming in my knees and now in my neck and head, I wanted to restart this conversation and go straight for my cane.

"What happened, to make you blind?" Antonia demanded.

I blinked, tears streaming down my temples as I tried to process my shock. The person holding my head pulled on my hair, and a man grumbled, "Answer the Vading."

I eked out, "I thought you knew." I needed to buy time, to figure out what she didn't have and was trying to get. There had to be a reason she wanted to know.

"Tell me," she said.

If she didn't know, I should probably keep it a secret despite not understanding why. I hoped I could last through whatever was to come. "Didn't you hear? I was in the desert too long, looking at the sun."

"That's not it. You may want me to believe it is, but it can't possibly be. Not with the shift Grandfather noticed in his experiments around the same time as we heard rumors of your parents losing their senses when you became blind. Tell me the truth." The rage in her voice might have been subtle, but it meant she was at her tipping point.

I clamped my mouth shut, not wanting to get myself in more trouble. *The rumors?* And what shift? I hated that she was so vague.

"Fine."

Another snap, and my head was released. I crumpled to the ground in an awkward heap. Despite my gratitude for being let go, I couldn't help but worry over what would come next. Though maybe she'd leave me alone.

I wanted to believe that but couldn't.

Sharp metal pierced my left upper arm. I hissed in a breath at the jolting pain, wishing I could do something to make it leave. The tip of what must have been a knife or dagger dug deeper before halting. The misery stood sharp. Agonizing.

I let myself stay a lump on the floor, as I worked through the fog of pain and despair. I hurt too much to think or do much of anything, but I would get this figured out. I had to.

"How did you become blind?" Antonia demanded again.

"Already... told you." I barely managed to get the words out between gritted teeth.

"How would you like a lovely scar, going down your arm? That should loosen your tongue if nothing else will."

"Why do you care so much?" I asked to distract her from giving the order. Though the pain was unbearable, as the tip of the metal stayed in my arm, making me want to smack the person holding it with my cane. I didn't care about a scar, but I did hate being in pain, bleeding too much, and possibly being injured so badly that I'd never manage to fight again. I doubted Antonia would allow anyone to treat me with magic to prevent such things. She only needed me alive, nothing more.

Antonia sniffed—a short, upset sound.

I waited for her to speak, wishing there was some way to get this weapon off of me. Aching to get it out. It burned my muscle.

"You should have figured that out by now," she said finally. "If you haven't, you never will."

I hadn't a clue what she was talking about. The sharpness grew so intense, everything slurred together. The room was heavy. Oppressive. Torturous.

She said something else, but it was a jumble. Another snap. The metal pulled out of me. I gasped in pain, as blood soaked my skin.

"Bandage her up." Antonia's sharp words surprised me. I hadn't expected her to want me healed. It had to be so she could torture me again later, before giving me over to the high priest.

Rough hands grabbed me and tied a scratchy piece of cloth around my upper arm. It was better than nothing, and must have had some pain-numbing ointment on it, because the throbbing lessened and my mind felt clearer.

"I promise it will be so much easier if you tell me, instead of letting my grandfather get the answer out of you."

I didn't respond. *Her grandfather.* The words echoed in my head. I was going to him. No, I was going to the high priest. Or wait, maybe they were the same person. I gasped at the thought. It didn't make sense that the Vading and high priest were related. None of this made sense.

She smacked me hard across the face.

I didn't move. Didn't want to fight. Pain was enough to scatter my concentration.

"Did your parents tell you what they went through, every time the high priest came into town?" Her voice grew sweet, cloying. I hoped she suffocated on it.

"I know... he tortured them." The words spat out of me in stuttering gasps as I struggled to come to grips with myself again.

"That's right, Cassandra. My grandfather tortured your parents for information about you, but they never gave in. No matter how much pressure he or I applied, there was nothing we could do against their willpower. But I know you. Far better than I would like. You're so much weaker than your parents. Ungrateful little brat. You're going to make all their hard work for naught."

Whatever she thought her words would do to make me feel like I would fail, they had the opposite effect, making me want to uphold their effort. I would get through this, no matter what it took. She would attack me, and so would her grandfather—all of the amant could—but I would not give in.

"I'm sorry," I said, "that you had such a sad life to make you turn out like this." My voice came out stronger than I thought it was going to, but I was grateful. I sat up straight. The jostling made my arm hurt, but I didn't care. I held my head high.

Until she smacked it back.

"You don't know what you're talking about." It was more hiss than words.

I teetered backward a moment, before righting myself. "I know you wouldn't be so bitter and mean if things had been different for you."

I braced myself for another hit, but instead of hurting me, she laughed. "You don't understand the wondrous life I've had. Grandfather took me in when my parents died, and treated me better than anyone else ever has. He's taken care of me and taught me everything I need to know."

"And what's that?" I asked. "How to torture people? Seems a depressing life."

She scoffed. "Tell me how you became blind."

I'd been hoping my conversation would have diverted her from that question, but she wouldn't be deterred. No answer I was willing to give would make her happy, so I locked my jaws together, determined to stay quiet.

"*Tell me*," she yelled so close, it hurt my ears.

Despite the anger and fear of what she'd do to me if I didn't comply, I held my silence. It stretched across the room like a living thing, the quiet an echo of my fear.

When she spoke, her voice was directed away from me. "Find Nikon. That'll loosen her tongue."

"We're trying, but—" a woman's voice said. It sounded familiar, but I couldn't place it.

"No more excuses. I'm through with them. She'll talk if we threaten him. I know it. I want him within the week."

"Yes, Vading."

I tried not to shrink and shiver in fear, but I failed. She was right. If they found Nikon and tortured him, I would tell them anything they wanted to know.

CHAPTER FIFTEEN

Elata gently patted my arm with a rag, but I sucked in a breath at the pain.

"What did you do, to bring the Vading's ire on you?" she asked.

"Honestly, I'm not certain." Would telling her make a difference? At this point, I didn't see the harm. Antonia might try to use Elata against me, but I wouldn't say anything they could give her grief for. What I'd share wasn't common knowledge, but close to. "We used to be friends. Or—well—I thought we were. When I first became blind, my parents hired her to help take care of me. We are about the same age, and they thought we had similar interests. She was kind, though sometimes sharp. I used to think the world of her."

"What happened?" Elata prompted, as she wrapped a new piece of cloth around my wound.

I focused on my story, and not the throbbing. "One day, she disappeared. I was left alone, with no one but my monkey for company." Thank the sands for Tewy. If he was here now, I'd no doubt hug him so tight he protested and pulled my hair.

For once, I missed his tugging on my hair.

"How did the Vading come to be hired as a caretaker? Not much is known about her before she became amant to the Reding."

Good question. I told her the little I knew of my life with Antonia, but the more I spoke, the more I realized how little that was. What she'd said in the throne room had revealed more about her true self than any of our time together had.

When I finished, Elata asked, "How did your parents come to find her?"

"At first, I thought they sought her out, but I found out recently that it was the other way around. She came to them. She was sort of just there one day, after I went blind, offering me the comfort I needed to get through life. My parents were so devastated they kept their distance." Causing my blindness couldn't have been easy for them.

And what did Antonia want with that information?

She wasn't a friend when she helped me, or any time after, as much as I wished things were different. There was more to all this than I'd ever imagined. The thought left me sick.

There was clearly something she wanted from me. She and her grandfather, the high priest. I had to figure out what so I could stop it. Perhaps then, they wouldn't want me anymore.

But why would it matter to them how I became blind?

"What would the Vading have wanted with you back then?" Elata asked. "There had to be something."

"I don't know," I said. "How did she find out about my blindness? I didn't think my parents had told anyo— Except, maybe they did." They were a part of the rebellion. They could have said something there, to keep from being part of the group trying to take down the amant's rule. It was too difficult emotionally with the grief they were trying to deal with. "What if they did tell someone? What if word got out to the wrong people?" What if someone they trusted really was a spy? We'd been betrayed so many times, I wasn't surprised they had been as well. I sneered.

"And why would those people want a newly blinded youth? We were hated back then, but not yet criminal."

She was right. What would Antonia and the high priest have wanted with someone like me? The only thing that came to mind was what Antonia was asking for—*how* I became blind. That was all I could think of that would have drawn their attention to me, rather than someone else. From whatever source, Antonia knew I'd become blind in a unique way, but not exactly what that was. For whatever reason, that mattered to her and the high priest.

Magic was the difference. It had to be. I'd never heard of anyone else losing their sight because of it. The tainted water and my blindness—they had to be related. But how? And why?

"I wish I knew—"

Footsteps coming toward the slave quarters cut off Elata. I grumbled, as she finished tying my bandage. I wished we could continue the conversation. It felt as if I was on the edge of falling off a cliff—one with a very dangerous bottom, possibly deadly. At the same time, though, it might lead me to a place I wanted to go, in order to understand.

The footsteps came and left. A guard, most likely, which made it all the more imperative that we kept our voices down and not let anyone onto what we were thinking or the information I had gleaned from Antonia.

Despite trusting Elata—whether that was good or bad judgment on my part—I couldn't tell her about the magic. If the information got back to Antonia, I would never forgive myself.

After several minutes of silence, Elata pulled away from me, my bandages arranged. She was close enough I could hear when she whispered, "I wish I knew more. What do we have to do?"

I tapped a finger on my knee. "We've got to figure out what's going on. I wish there was a way to get out of here."

"It would be next to impossible to escape."

I wanted—needed—out, but she was correct. "We'd have to

know the pyramid better. The areas we don't usually go in. And the warriors' schedules."

"You're thinking of trying, aren't you?"

"I can't live my life here. There are too many people who need me out there." And too much dangerous information I apparently carried, to stay here. Besides, the thought of what Lavti had done, and Nikon never knowing it, made me want to slam my fist into something. Preferably her face. Though I didn't consider myself a violent person, I was willing to make an exception. Nothing would feel as good as my fist making a resounding *crunch* against Lavti's face. I'd settle for her stomach, though. It might be easier to aim for.

"I don't know of any ways out. If I did, I would have tried them already." Elata's words brought me back to the present problem.

If only I had my cane, Tewy, and Nikon, I could make it out of here. Without them, what could I do? "Do you know of a way to get my cane from Antonia?"

"You refer to the Vading with such familiarity, but I suppose that makes sense." She sighed. "None of us are allowed anything that would help us get around, so if you did get it, someone would take it away. You've been figuring your way around fairly well, though. What do you need it for? After you escape? If you can ever manage."

"No." Should I tell her? I didn't see the harm in it, since Antonia would figure it out if she put a little effort into it. The Vading already knew something was going on with the object. "My cane has been treated with magic. I can use it to find my way around, yes, but it also comes apart into fighting sticks I can use to sense those attacking me."

"Oooh. That would not only be useful, but also an interesting new sensation. I'd like to try something like that."

"If we ever make it out of here, I'll have Nikon make you one that we can treat with magic." I slowly lay back on a bed, trying to pretend I had no aches and pains, and failing.

"Nikon? As in *the* Nikon? The elite warrior who was the Reding's closest guard?"

And brother, I added silently. "Yes. Why? What do you know of him?"

"I used to clean his room before he disappeared. He always was kind to us blind."

"I didn't know we'd been in that part of the pyramid."

"We haven't. I was there a while back, and since he left, no one of note really lives in that area. It gets cleaned, but less regularly."

An idea sprung to mind. "Do you think you could get me back there?"

"I don't know. We'd have to time it right, so no one gets suspicious of our being there. Why do you ask? They cleaned out his room after he escaped from the Reding and Vading a second time. Didn't want him getting any more things from there."

"That shouldn't be a problem." Did I dare tell her about how I got in there before? I bit my lip. I liked her well enough, and trusted her, but how well did I know her, really? It'd only been a matter of days. Besides, people I thought I'd known well turned out to be deceitful.

Could I trust Elata or not?

While my heart wanted to say *yes*, my mind didn't dare, for fear of all the problems I'd had in the past. Besides, if she was captured, she'd spill everything she knew, whether she wanted to or not. I did want to help her—and all who were enslaved—get out of here, but until I had the opportunity, I'd have to think of an excuse for wanting to visit Nikon's room. "I've been there before."

"Truly? What's there to help us escape?"

Her forthright question left me muddled. Might as well help her get where I was coming from. "Though I'd love to tell you,

I've been betrayed enough in my life. I don't know if I should." Saying what I had was dangerous without any more. I hoped she didn't hate me for what I said.

"I understand."

I perked up. "You do?"

"Yes. From the little you've said of your story, and what I know of people, it makes sense you'd want to keep information close to you. Not that I like it, mind you, but I understand. I don't know if I can get us there, but we'll do our best," she said.

"Good. The sooner the better. I have a feeling that once the high priest gets here, I might as well give up." The thought of giving up after all I'd been through put a rod of metal in my back. I wouldn't quit if I could help it. My parents were probably tortured in front of each other for my sake, and remained silent on matters concerning me. If they could do it, I would do the same, but in the meantime, I would do everything to escape this place.

CHAPTER SIXTEEN

Days passed, yet there was never an opportunity for me and Elata to get to Nikon's room. We were confined to the slave room when not working, and a guard had taken to following us around. Did Antonia suspect I'd try something, or was she just being cautious? I wasn't keen to find out, as that would mean I'd have to speak with her again.

With time moving on, the urge to do something to aid an escape grew. The longer I stayed, the more likely the high priest would have me in his clutches. I'd faced down a neczar, but when I was being honest with myself, the high priest scared me more.

As we finished cleaning our last room, I expected Elata and I would go back to the slave quarters. As we turned and headed in that direction, our guard for the day said in her high voice, "Not yet. You're to see the Vading."

I tried not to cringe. I wanted to go anywhere else in the pyramid except to her. The Reding would be preferable. Did he know about her plans with the water? Nikon had stolen them from him, but had the Reding read them first or written them? And if so, did he understand better than us what the tainted water meant?

My focus should shift to what was coming. I needed to prepare myself for them catching Nikon. If Antonia had him, I needed to do my best to hold it together, but could I? He was tough, I knew that, but could I let them hurt him for information I possessed?

I missed Nikon. Missed his solid presence in my life. Would his brother care, if he knew Nikon's wife was torturing him? I didn't think he would. In fact, he likely sanctioned the whole thing, from the little I knew of him.

Then again, it wouldn't hurt to mention it, should I happen to run across him. I doubted I would, though. For being amant, the Reding and Vading didn't seem to spend a lot of time together—not while I was around.

The way Elata led me was familiar, but different enough that it took my concentration for the rest of the turns. I wanted to learn my way around. The distraction was welcome. If thinking was hard, I might not worry about what was to come.

Sands. I didn't want to think that. My chest felt as if it dropped with a *splat* to the stone floor we walked on, and stayed behind as we went. I didn't want to abandon my bravery, but it was failing me anyway.

This time, there were no warning voices—only the faint tips of my memory told me we'd reached the Vading's throne room, where she *hosted* me the last time I met with her.

I knew I was unfortunately not wrong when her voice lashed out. "Finally. Take the other slave back to the quarters. I'll send someone with this one when I'm finished with her. If there's anything left."

I wanted to dry heave, but did what I could to breathe through it.

I gave Elata's arm a quick squeeze, before turning my attention to where Antonia's voice had come from. Elata's and the guard's footsteps retreated behind me, completely out of hearing before Antonia said anything further.

I didn't hear Nikon. Though he could be absolutely quiet, he'd likely make a sound to let me know he was here if he could. The fact there was no noise depressed me, but the call of my cane lifted my spirits a little. I might not have everything I needed, but that would help, should I ever get my hands on it. Sadly, that wasn't likely.

"Are you ready to speak to me about how you became blind?" Her voice held a bit of menace that made my recovering upper left arm ache.

She didn't say anything about Nikon. Was she going to hover that over me, or had they not found him yet?

Instead of answering her, I focused in on my only hope. The cane. Right where I expected it to be—next to her, only I was farther back from it than I'd been before. Close to the entryway. I couldn't reach it, and if there were warriors about again, there was no way I could sprint for it before they trampled me to the ground.

"Bring her here," Antonia commanded.

This was it. This was when they were going to tell me Nikon was captured.

Rough hands grabbed me on both sides. The pain in my left arm made me grunt, but I sucked in the hurt, so I wouldn't give away what I felt to Antonia. She likely already knew, but I wouldn't make it easier for her than I had to.

They dragged me forward more than letting me walk, though I tried to keep up. I stumbled, and they threw me to the ground, leaving me there for nothing but Antonia to command me to be tortured. Or worse—to torture Nikon.

The only highlight was that my cane was almost within reach. Just a little farther, and I'd be able to grab it. To what end, though? If I took out a few people, I'd still be a slave, surrounded by warriors.

"Tell me how you became blind." Antonia sounded less patient than before.

The problem with the theory Elata and I had come up with hit me. If Antonia knew my blindness came from magic my parents used, why would she be asking?

"You know already," I said.

She scoffed, angry and curt. "All those years, I tried every way but torture to get you to tell me, and you never mentioned more than your parents and magic. No specifics. What exactly happened, you never divulged. Well, that changes today."

Nikon. She had him. She wouldn't be this confident without him, would she? She sounded frustrated more than anything.

She didn't have Nikon.

Despite my position, a burst of calm came over me. She didn't have Nikon. What was more, she didn't know what my parents had done—what they'd been thinking—when they'd used magic on me. Didn't know they'd wanted me to be free of falling in love at first sight so I could fall in love slowly, at will.

Nikon was safe. My loved ones were safe. Better—Antonia knew less than I thought, and I held more power than I expected.

A hard *smack* across the face sent me tumbling the rest of the way down. Though my face hit the stone, I was more surprised than anything. The pain would hit later, but for now, I was in shock.

"Don't you smirk at me. You have no right. Tell me what happened."

Doing my best to lift my face despite the throbbing, I turned toward her and smiled again. "Never."

A punch this time, one that knocked me to the ground so fast, I thought my head would erupt like one of Nikon's exploding sand-magic bombs.

"Don't you dare speak to me that way. I've had enough. Give me answers. Now." Antonia's voice was low, but it might as well have been a scream, for how it made my head pound.

The throbbing pulled my thoughts toward her words. This

time, I rolled over. If she wanted to hit me again, it wouldn't send me flying. "Never."

"I won't fail again. You must tell me." Her tone held so much fury, I expected her to start beating on me, but it never came. Maybe she really would wait for a reply.

There had to be a reason she was so intent on getting answers from me at this moment. She must have heard back from the high priest, and he demanded them.

I choked out a reply, my words growing stronger the longer I spoke. "Why are you so insistent that you find out for him? It doesn't make sense. We were together so long. Why would you give me up like you did? Why would you leave me alone? I just want to understand what happened to the relationship I thought we had."

"And give you the satisfaction of answers, when you're giving me none? I don't think so."

"You know, you don't sound like a Vading," I said.

She snarled. "And you don't sound like the woman who'd break the work my grandfather did to ruin love."

I held very, very still. Did I hear correctly? She'd said her grandfather worked to ruin love, or was my head throbbing too much for me to really understand what was going on? They said in previous times that people fell in love however they wanted. If the high priest manipulated the water somehow, to make people only fall in love at first sight...

No. It was a monstrous idea.

Yet, the longer I thought about it, the more certain I was I'd heard her correctly.

The room remained silent, nothing but my struggling breaths to tell me someone was here. That *someone* was me, and I might be in pain physically, but I'd just been given more than I knew before.

I tried to put the facts together, through the haze of pain and silence. Her grandfather was the high priest, and he had done something to ruin love. Her husband was the Reding, who was looking into something that happened to the water. Could those two *somethings* be related to each other and have to do with the high priest ruining love? I wanted to know how it was done so I could fix it. Not that I could fix myself at this point.

Most of all, I was curious to know my part in all this. There had to be a reason they wanted me.

"Thank you," I finally said. "I always wanted to know what was going on. I've felt so lost, in a world bigger than me, but I've found great pleasure in—"

Fingers snapped, and someone kicked me from the left side—straight in the stomach. Again, they kicked, and I flinched, gasping for breath and struggling against the agony in both my head and torso.

My thoughts fogged. I couldn't move. Trembling, I lay there.

The floor was cold against my skin. The air was warmer, but only just. It was a good day to be beaten. The swelling could be managed somewhat by the coolness.

I thought of my river—the joy I used to find, swimming in its rush. The time I'd been with it, and how much it'd given me.

What I would give, for just a small portion of sand from its bottom...

But Antonia would never allow it.

Someone shifted closer, until hot breath smudged against my cheek. The breath came with Antonia's voice, saying, "You don't know what you're talking about or whom you're dealing with."

"Apparently... you don't... either." I gasped out the words, surprised I could manage them.

Another snap, and she rustled away from me, the slap of sandals fading as the beating began. I curled into myself, doing my best to protect my head with my arms.

I could take it.

I would make it.

I had to.

Zoe.

Mom. Dad.

Tewy.

Nikon.

Kicks kept coming. Pain—awful, *terrible*—the only thing I felt.

My limbs didn't respond. Didn't move to protect me.

Something slammed into my head.

The world went dark.

CHAPTER SEVENTEEN

Agony ratcheted through me.

Sharp and dull aches everywhere.

I blinked but didn't move. The pain was all-consuming.

As I lay there and struggled not to feel, I heard a tapping sound. It must have woken me and was coming toward me.

Footsteps. Sandals. A woman—someone familiar. Antonia? No. She had me beaten past what I thought I could endure, but this woman's sound comforted me.

But she wouldn't have the magic needed to heal me from this torment.

Elata's steps—I thought it was her—were almost to me. My guess was confirmed when I heard her voice.

"Cassandra? Are you here?"

"Sort of." I was grateful my mouth responded to my thoughts.

"Thank the sands in the river below. I never thought I would hear your voice again, after the guards talked about how you'd been left in a bloody mess." Moments later, her soft hand touched my cheek.

"Ow."

She jerked away. "Sorry. How bad is it?"

"Bad." So very bad.

"I brought some healing ointment. It won't fix everything, but it'll help numb your pain."

Was I going to die from my injuries? Maybe, if I'd lost enough blood or my insides were damaged too much. I didn't think they were, but I almost felt like I wanted to pass away. I'd been through so much horror in the last... "How long was I gone?" I managed to get out.

"It's early, early morning, before the warmth of the sun comes. I managed to wait until the guards left, before sneaking out."

I groaned. "Shouldn't have. You're going to be in trouble."

"Hush now. It's fine. They need you alive."

But did they, really? If so, why would they leave me like this? They might know I wasn't going to die, but that I would feel like it. Probably seemed a just punishment, for speaking to the Vading in such a tone.

Antonia. Egh. I didn't want to think about her ever again.

"You're going to be just fine." Elata kept murmuring soft reassurances the entire time, offering as much comfort as the numbing cream she smeared over me. That wasn't all she did, though. She spent time, cleaning off the dried blood around my mouth—my lip did feel split—and caring for me in a way that reminded me of my mother.

Bad move to remind myself of her. "I've got to get out of here."

"Soon, I fear," Elata agreed.

"How much more I can live through?" And not give answers. When the high priest came, there would be nothing left of my life but more of this torture. Probably worse, but that was difficult to imagine right now. There was a tug of a thought.

"I don't know if you can move. Unless there's a spring linked to magic and sand in Nikon's old room, there's no way to get you out."

"There is something. I don't know what yet." It was close. It called to me, pulling at my thoughts and my hands.

What was it?

"Never mind that for now. We should get you out of here. If you're here when she comes back..."

I didn't want to think of the consequences either, but I also didn't want to stand, despite the numbing concoction doing a wondrous job. I didn't want to do anything that painful.

Despite my reluctance, I forced myself to a sitting position. Elata was correct. And when Antonia's grandfather came...

I shivered. "I've got it. I can do this." My voice cracked, but I moved toward the feeling, as I crawled to my feet.

"Where are you going? That's the wrong direction."

As soon as she said the words, I realized what was calling me. My cane. I sucked in a breath, quick and excited. I stepped forward, reached out, and wrapped my hand around the familiar wood that had helped me through so much. Grasping it made me feel stronger.

Or maybe that was Elata's concoction. Still, I felt more in control.

"Cassandra?" Elata sounded worried.

"I'm here. I've got my cane."

Her voice hushed. "The one you told me about?"

"Yes. They must have forgotten it was here after they beat me and left." I was grateful. I knew my way around enough that I didn't have to have it, but it would help me move around in my condition, and more if we came upon any guards—and I remembered exactly what we had to do, no matter how hard it was. "You've got to take me to Nikon's room. Now."

"Are you certain? If we get caught, it'll mean more trouble."

"Now that I have my fighting sticks, it'll mean trouble for them." I strode forward, wishing I could put the confidence I felt into my steps, but even with the care Elata had shown, I hurt. "Let's go."

"But what if the guards come after us and you can't fight?" she asked.

Despite her hesitation, when I found her hand, she rested it on my arm and started to follow my lead.

"I'll take care of anyone we come across. I promise you that. You just get us to Nikon's old room as quietly as you can."

"I hope I don't turn in the wrong direction," she muttered.

We fell silent, save our footsteps, hurrying as quickly as possible across the hall. Though I didn't hear anyone approaching, I was overly aware that the warriors could find us at any moment. I picked up the pace and hoped I was in good enough condition to actually take out anyone who came our way.

I pressed myself on, and Elata must have caught on to my urgency, for she sped up. Though I didn't know how I'd make it through our escape path, I was determined to do it. I only hoped she and I would both make it. Between the two of us being blind and me injured, it would be near impossible.

No. I shouldn't think like that.

Pulling away from the negative side of things, I went forward until footsteps caught my ear. I hesitated, but Elata pulled me on faster. As we made another turn, I wanted to stop and figure out if the steps were coming our way, but she pushed us on. She was right to do so. Though I could fight, it probably wasn't smart. A fight could go either way, no matter the magic I had on my side.

Despair tried to fill me. Tried to drag me down to the stone floor that sloped further downward beneath our feet. I wanted to give in, but I wouldn't. Not now. I had more than myself to worry about. Not only Elata either, though getting us both out was a primary concern. No, I needed to get the information I had to the rebels. If Lavti was there...

Didn't matter. I had to share what I knew.

The water. The high priest. Antonia. That amant and the

odiosom. The change that been said to happen back in the Govlin Wars, when people stopped falling in love slowly. The high priest was old enough to have seen it. In fact, if he was anyone other than the high priest, he likely would have been killed for his age if he wasn't useful.

If I could glean a little more information, I could figure out not only how to stop the high priest and Antonia, but perhaps also how to restore the world to what it once was, with people coming to love naturally, and not only at first sight. The latter felt wrong, especially now that I knew it'd been forced upon us.

The thoughts gave me hope and joy, despite not having any where Nikon was concerned. He and thousands of others had already fallen in love. What I wanted to change was the future, so nobody was destined to be one with a person they happened to lock gazes with. No. I wanted more.

Steps echoed down the hall again. Elata and I sped up. I couldn't tell where the sounds came from, as they seemed to be everywhere.. Someone was hunting us. I swept my cane closer, ready to let go of Elata, pull it apart, and smack someone with it.

It'd feel far too satisfying, after all I'd been through.

The people moved faster, giving me the opportunity far sooner than I expected. I dropped Elata's arm, twisted my cane, and brought my sticks up in front of me in a solid motion.

The steps closed in from behind.

I turned as I called out to Elata, "Move to the side."

Her familiar sounds moved away, far lighter than the ones approaching. Three sets of feet, if I wasn't mistaken now.

I loosened my stand, ready to take on whoever came my way.

"Who are you and what are you doing?" a woman called out. To me, I assumed.

"Just going on our way." I slowly lowered my sticks, pretending to listen as I continued. "Sorry. You startled us."

The people slowed but didn't stop. I could make out their

sound better now that they'd turned down our hall. Definitely three pairs, and they hadn't come close enough for me to hit—yet.

The woman said, "Which slaves are you and why are you out this early?"

"I could be asking you the same question." Stalling was the best I could do, to get them to come within cane-reach. If one of them got away, they'd warn others.

I asked much of myself. I hoped I could deliver.

"We are elite warriors, in case you slaves couldn't tell," she spat. "We belong here. I don't think you do."

She had a general idea of who we were, if not specifically. That would change when the warriors heard of my escape. Once they knew for certain who I was, they wouldn't stop for a chat. Or maybe that was why they were stopping for a chat—get me to loosen up while one of them sneaked back for help.

Too bad Nikon had trained me to know better.

I ran forward, swiping my sticks out as I went. It didn't matter if I knew their exact positions. If I could provoke them into a fight, the magic would do the rest.

I banged into something that had give, like a stomach, my other stick catching air.

"*Ugh*," someone shouted, sounding out of breath.

The real test began.

They rushed me, my senses flowing to life. I caught two of them, banging my sticks against their swords, grateful the wood wouldn't break. As soon as an opening presented itself, I tried to bash against them. Instead of connecting with skin, some other weapon flew into the fray.

They must have had two weapons each.

Cursing the fact that they were elite warriors, I continued fighting. I didn't have enough sticks to counter all their weapons, but what I lacked in defenses, I made up for in speed. Practice had been good for me, toning me into a better fighter when I needed it the most, though not as much as I wanted since it had been days since I'd practiced. The constant scrubbing had left me with muscle, though. The magic from my sticks flowed through my limbs, bringing them to life against the people coming at me.

Despite the beating I endured yesterday, I flung myself into the fight, the stone ground smooth beneath my bare feet. While their sandals smacked against the hard rock, I breathed heavy and grunted as we fought. I attempted to figure out where the third elite warrior was.

I couldn't make out a third person, and the two attacking me didn't leave much time for searching. I worked up a sweat, keeping them from getting past my weapons. I attempted to move forward, but instead, I had to back up as their attack on me pressed in.

There had to be a way to stop them.

The pressure of having Elata somewhere at my back sent a rush of worry flinging through me. I didn't want to bring the fight to her. She'd be injured for certain.

I hit high, and followed it with a burst of action toward the warrior on my right, bashing against someone. With no time to celebrate, I whacked at my other opponent, but I was blocked.

I gritted my teeth as pain lanced through the side of my torso where I'd been kicked, but I managed to push my attacker back. Despite the growing wetness to my clothes from sweat—and I didn't want to think what else—I pressed on, trying to find a weakness.

The way they worked together was reminiscent of me and Nikon.

The thought of him yanked me from the fight. I shoved myself back in with a fury, not willing to let any emotion cloud my mind. Elata and I—and all others wishing to change how things were—couldn't afford it.

I held my ground, instead of falling toward Elata like I had been. There wasn't much room to work, which was to my advantage, since I had more space than the warriors. I used the space to widen my swing and bring my full force on my right stick, to knock a weapon out of the way before slamming my left one against my opponent.

I hit as hard as I could, when the *clack* of someone running away from the fight made it through the noise. The third warrior was getting away down the hall.

Sand it all.

I couldn't break into a run after them. Instead, I was forced to continue moving as the other two pressed on. I struggled to know what to do. The feeling of failure ripped at me, sinking its claws into my wounds and Elata's freedom.

With a growl, I swung harder than ever. My body ached less than I anticipated, as I added a burst of speed into my actions. I didn't want to hurt anyone, but our freedom was more important.

Sweat dripped down my face, as my pulse rushed in my ears. I needed to be better and faster, but all I was was me.

I needed an opening— *There.* I took the area between the weapons I sensed coming at me, and bashed into the warrior on my right again. The attacker fell back, as I blocked the weapon on my left. One opponent remained. Though I couldn't tell if the person leaving the fight left the hall, it didn't matter at this point. I just needed to get Elata away from here as quick as possible.

I concentrated on the person before me. With little to stop me, now that I wasn't being attacked on all sides, I quickly knocked through the defenses of the remaining warrior, forcing them to back off. Though everything in me screamed to continue after them, I held back, my body weak.

Elata needed me, and now that the fight didn't rage around me, my limbs were drooping. The wetness of my dress reminded me of why. I waited a few moments, to make certain all signs of the warriors retreated. All three were gone from hearing range. It was bad, but better than having them kill or capture us.

I softly called out, "Elata?"

"You survived?" She sounded astonished.

"Barely." To my ears, I sounded winded. "We need to go. They'll be back with help."

A sudden pressure to my side had me thrusting my stick up and blocking a sneak attack. I growled and threw myself back into the fight.

One of the attackers had somehow remained behind, to finish us off or recapture us. I wouldn't let that happen.

I put my fury into the attack, though not with reckless abandon. Just enough to keep my movements going, until I managed to get past their weapons and bash what had to be their head several times. I moved my arms again, slamming my cane forward at the same time a *thump* sounded. I hit nothing but air, which left me off balance. The attacker must have fallen to the ground.

I caught myself. Hissing in pain, I turned back to Elata. "We go now."

"I'm here."

We found each other in moments, and I let her lead me as I continued to bleed, not hooking my cane back together. She pulled me forward by the arm, and we made quick progress away from the scene of the fight.

If I never met an elite warrior again, it would be too soon.

CHAPTER EIGHTEEN

My breathing came in labored, as Elata said, "We're almost there."

I hadn't told her I was injured, but with the way her voice echoed with concern, she seemed to sense it. That, or she realized that, with some of the warriors having found us, it wouldn't be long until others did as well.

My head swam from the fight, but enough thoughts of danger broke through that I forced her to stop. "I need to bind my wound."

"I should have stopped us sooner." She quickly went about her task, tearing something—probably her dress. "Where is it?"

We worked together to tie the fabric around my waist.

"Don't ever do that to me again. I swear, Cassandra, listening to you fight was rough, but knowing you got hurt and didn't tell me was worse." She clacked her tongue.

I panted, as I rested against the wall. "Wasn't any time. We needed to get away."

"That may be, but you probably left a trail of blood right to us."

I grimaced. "Do you think they'll know where we're going?"

"We're in the main section, but the turn to the area we want is up ahead. We have some leeway."

"So they'll possibly know."

"Yes." Her tone was resigned.

"We need to get moving, then."

Since I hadn't put my cane back together, she grabbed me by the arm again and continued on. Though I wanted to run, we walked at a slower pace than before. My injuries weren't a reality I wanted to handle. Without magic, there was little we could do with all the wounds I received, and each and every one of them threatened our escape.

I gritted my teeth and forced myself on, only the thought of Nikon in love with that scarab, Lavti, keeping me going.

We took several turns, the area around us sounding empty—thankfully. We needed something to go our way.

"Almost there. It's not far into this area," Elata whispered. "Though I don't know what we're going to find here, to help us get out of this place, and after what you just did, I'm afraid of what they'll do to us when we get back. You, they'll keep around for the high priest, if nothing else. Me? I don't know."

"Don't say things like that." I pushed forward. "We'll escape."

"We will? How? Someone you know?" Elata asked. "Where will we meet them? How are they going to get us out? Did you arrange something? How?"

"No. We're getting out on our own." Though at the moment, that felt far away. How would I not only climb up to the hidden spot, but also down the rest of the pyramid? It'd seemed huge the first time Nikon and I climbed down, and I'd had his help along the way. Plus, we'd only gone partway.

I might have set an impossible task before Elata and me, but I wouldn't stop now. There wasn't any turning back.

"How?" Elata sounded more confused than upset. That would soon change. "Just a moment. We're here."

She stopped and fiddled with the door before it opened.

Together, we hurried in and closed it behind us. I was grateful to find a lock on it, and turned the key. It wouldn't be a fix-all, and might give us away if someone came looking for us and knew it was supposed to be open. Then again, it could also give us needed time. The latter felt better, so I went with it.

"Search the room. There should be a desk or something. We need to find it and push it over, in front of a tapestry that hides a hidden entrance. That's our way out."

"And then what? We're high up." As was her voice. "Does it have a passage down?"

"We'll have to climb down. We can do it. I know we can."

"But—"

"No. We'll do it." We had to. "I've done part of it before."

She huffed but shuffled away. I twisted the two parts of my cane back together, trusting that if I needed them again, I'd have warning this time. Cane in hand, I searched the room. As I found the closet, memories of Tewy and Nikon flooded me. I missed them both terribly. The three of us being shoved together in there hadn't been ideal, but I'd give anything for it to happen again. If Lavti did something to them... But no, she saved her scheming for me.

Not *if*. *When*. I needed my loved ones back in my life. I hoped they were alive and well. Just thinking about something different made me sway with faintness.

No. I had to be strong, to get out of here. I moved on from the closet and continued around the room. Something was odd. There wasn't anything in here. It was barer than I thought it'd be from Elata's description. They really didn't want Nikon coming back and using more things from his room.

That was bad news for Elata and me. "We're going to have to climb up to the opening."

"Climb what?" Her voice went higher.

"The wall. More like, I'll boost you up, and then I'll have to jump and you'll have to pull me through." That had to be the best way to do it. Nikon was far stronger than she, so I wasn't certain if the plan would work. Though doubts pummeled me, I didn't say them. I was light, and she was strong for an older woman. It had to work.

"I don't know about this," Elata said.

"What's the worst that can happen?" I asked with a confidence I didn't feel. Before she could respond, I hurried to add, "Never mind. Don't answer that. Let's try."

By now, she'd found me, and stood near me as I estimated where the hidden entrance should be. "If I can get you up here, round about, we should be able to find it."

A worse thought hit me. If everything was taken from this room, what if the tapestry was gone? What if they'd found the hideout and kept it guarded? Worse, what if they sealed it off?

Gulping down my fears, I said, "You can do this. Just climb up me, and then stretch as much as possible. I'll keep as steady as I can, while you search for the hidden tunnel."

"I don't know about this," she said again.

"You can do it. I know you can." I put the last remaining hope I had into those words. If she protested more, I'd have nothing left to give.

She sighed. "I'm afraid of falling, but I'll try."

"That's it. You're strong, from all the cleaning and moving furniture you do. Let's go for it."

I reached out to her, and she attempted to use me as a ladder. Her foot slipped against my shin, but she grabbed my shoulders, to pull herself up at the same time she tried to climb with her feet. That didn't last much longer, as she didn't gain any headway.

"Let me help." I tried lifting her by the waist, as she pulled and pushed against me. Though she got higher, she didn't make it all the way.

Every moment we stayed down here was another moment the elite warriors would be gaining on us. I hoped the blood trail I left wasn't as bad as I thought it was. It couldn't be, if the sands were with us.

With a sudden lurch, she tried one more time. I hoisted as she climbed, and we somehow wound up with her on my shoulders.

"It's a good thing you're light," I said. Until she had to lift me.

I shook away the thought. We'd deal with that when it was time. If nothing else, she might escape and send word for help. If Lavti hadn't completely gotten her pincers in Nikon yet.

I shivered. If she had, he might leave me to be experimented on.

I stepped closer to the wall, careful to keep my hands around her calves. "Feel along and see if you can find a tapestry or anything like that. It should be hanging in front of the hidden entrance."

"There's one to my right."

Surprised she found it so quickly, I carefully took some steps to the side. "Reach behind it."

The whip of the tapestry moving reached me, followed by the smacking of skin against stone. She leaned forward, which made me wobble. I caught myself on the wall before putting my hands back on her shins. "Did you find it?"

"There's nothing here," she said.

"What?" I kept my voice calm, but my insides raged like an out-of-control sandstorm.

"Nothing." The slap of hands came again.

I wanted to scream. How had they found it? Why had they left it covered, if they'd blocked it off anyway?

Didn't matter. We were lost to the warriors. That, or we'd hide here until we starved to death.

"Maybe it's on another wall?" she asked.

Not wanting to admit we were doomed, I humored her. "We can check."

Slowly, I walked around the room, as she swayed and the sound of her slapping the walls continued. It was little use, other than to give me time to think of a plan. Only problem was this was *the* plan. There was nothing else. I didn't know how to get us out of here without that escape route. It'd been a slim chance anyway, but now it felt hopeless. Entirely worthless.

We passed by the hangings over the closet and continued to the other side. How did I tell her? She would be heartbroken and know death was coming. It was my fault, for leading her hopes up to begin with.

And Nikon? Tewy? What would happen, without me there to help them? My parents, Zoe and Kaius... So many others.

I needed them. We were friends, and they'd be as hurt as I was at the thought of not seeing each other again. But they'd get along without me. Eventually.

I stepped to the side, ruminating what to do. With our circumstances, it was near impossible to think this would end well. I had to figure out how to save Elata, because she was correct. Antonia and the high priest would keep me to gain information until they were done with me, but her? I didn't know that they found her to be of value—though I found her to be greatly so.

As I stepped to the side again, there was a rustle above me.

"Found it," Elata said.

"I know. I'm sorr— What?"

"It was hidden behind this tapestry, like you said."

I wanted to sink with relief but couldn't let her fall. I'd picked the wrong direction, and there were more than one tapestry. The comfort filling my chest overwhelmed me. I leaned against the wall for support, doing my best to maintain strong and upright legs.

"Cassandra?" Elata called down to me.

"Sorry. Just want to get out of here." Which was true. I didn't want to admit to how close I'd thought we'd come to not having a way out, though I might tell her in the future—if we had one.

There were lots of ways we could wind up back in Antonia's hands, but now we had a chance.

"I'm going to try climbing through the hole, then."

I braced myself, to give her the steadiest base to pull herself up from. She jostled around on my shoulders, shifting her weight around until she pulled up and got her feet off my shoulders.

I backed up a step, getting ready to catch her if she should fall.

All that happened was that she said softly, "Made it." Her voice was distant and muffled. "I don't know if I'm going to be able to turn around."

I smacked my forehead. Blast the scorpions to the death river. I'd forgotten the space was so narrow. She couldn't help me up unless she went all the way out, turned around, and came back down. It'd cost precious time.

I bit my lip. What should I do? There was nothing else I could think of. "You're going to have to crawl the whole way down, and come back through the tunnel to help me up. Be careful of the edge on the outside."

Silence.

"I'll pretend I'm not afraid of heights." The fear in her voice said it'd be difficult, but I was grateful she was willing to try.

"You go on," I said. "I'll see if I can get up on my own." As slim a chance as that was.

"I'll come back for you." Though her voice was muffled, her determination shone through.

The soft scraping of her leaving sounded above me. I wanted to lie on the floor and nap until she got back, but it'd be better to see if there was something I could do.

I rolled my shoulders, and the cut in my arm ached. Wrong move. I picked up my cane. There was no way I would leave it behind. It wasn't only that I wanted to keep it, but I also didn't want to leave behind evidence that we'd been here. Plus, I had a feeling we might need it, once we climbed down from the pyramid and headed out of here. Wherever we ended up.

Cane in my left hand, I jumped, reaching with my free, right hand. My fingers brushed against thin cloth that must have been the tapestry. I slammed back to the floor, the stones surprising me as I'd been concentrating too hard on what was above me.

Jumping again, I pushed my hand forward. The tapestry gave more than I expected, but I didn't make it to where I could grasp a hold of the ledge. Though I jumped a handful more times, it was clear I wouldn't be able to get up there by that alone. I needed help.

I gritted my teeth and ran my hand along the wall.

A few stones jutted out, but not as much as I hoped. I might be able to get a small grip on some, but would it be enough?

I found one just above my shoulder and attempted to grip on to it as tightly as I could. I needed more room for my fingers to really stay on the wall, but it was better than nothing. Since the stones weren't smooth, it might just work.

Moving my toes around, I found a slim foothold. I braced my foot on it sideways and pulled myself up. With my other hand, I searched for more stones that jutted out. Finding another, I pulled myself up, but with the thin ledge and the cane in my hand, I slipped and fell back to the ground.

I growled, and tried again and again, only to face the same results. Without someone to help, I was bound to land on the floor every time. Perhaps, if I could give my cane to Elata when she returned, I could climb up without help. Or with help she'd be able to provide.

I prowled across the room, pacing between walls that felt as if they grew closer together at every turn. Though I wanted more space, I didn't dare go into the hall. If someone found me, I was done for. My chest clenched at the thought, tightening uncomfortably. I'd have to wait it out in here. Elata would come back for me.

My thoughts kept oscillating between my need to escape and my family and friends. I didn't know where Nikon fit in exactly—friends or family—especially now. I wanted to believe he was like family, but who knew. Tewy, though... He was as close as any family member, and teased me like a sibling I never had. So what if he was tiny and furry all over?

I couldn't believe they were all with Lavti now. I smacked my cane on my other hand. How could I have trusted her?

Didn't matter. I only hoped I made it out of here. Someone would believe me when I told them. They had to. If we made it back to Ruso. I hissed out a breath, thinking of the task before us. If I focused on one step at a time, we'd make a plan.

And Nikon? Before, I would have said he'd believe me, but with him in love with her? It was much less certain.

Voices sounded outside the room, in the hall somewhere. Fear had me jumping to the side. I found the closet and hid behind the cloth hanging there.

The people grew closer, sounds rumbling through the door. Elata had said this area was barely used anymore. Unless she was wrong—which I doubted—they were likely searching for us.

A man outside the door said, "I'll check here. You go on down to the next room."

I pressed against the far wall of the closet as hard as I could, willing myself to be invisible and wishing it would work. I held my cane steady, slowly twisting it apart. I hoped it didn't come to a fight.

A jiggling sounded, like someone trying to turn a doorknob. Thank the sands I'd locked the door. I swallowed the bile building inside me. This was the wrong time to lose it. I had to make it until Elata came for me, but if they found me, I was doomed.

Silently, I cursed myself for not telling Elata how to find those I knew and trusted.

The knob was jostled again, and the man called out, "It's locked."

The response was too far away for me to make out behind the wall and in the closet, but the man sounded annoyed. "I'm not bothering with that. They couldn't have made it past a locked door."

I held in a snort, hoping his stupidity extended to his companion.

"No, I don't think so. Let's keep going."

This time, I heard a second man's muffled reply. "They could be in there. We have to check. If the Vading finds out we let them get away, she'll have our heads."

Sands.

They weren't going to leave it be. There were only two of them, but if they found me and one got away to tell others, it wouldn't end well.

"Go get the key," the second man said. "And hurry up."

"I'm going. I don't want to lose my head over a couple of blind slaves either."

They stopped talking, and I made out the faint sound of footsteps leaving. As much as I wanted to be grateful there was only one warrior out there, the thought didn't bring any comfort. I could take one out, but if I did, the other would know something was going on down here, for certain. Elata had better hurry, and if there was an extra key it had better have been far off.

As silently as possible, I went back to the secret entrance area and climbed the wall again. Despite my best efforts, I fell back as time slipped away. There wasn't any way I would come up this wall.

Unless... What if I found a way to tie the cane to me? It was worth an attempt.

Carefully, I went back into the closet, to muffle the sound I was about to make, and worked to rip the skirt of my dress. The fabric strained against my pulling it from two sides, but didn't give. I yanked harder, till the sound of tearing filled the small space. I sent silent wishes to the far-off sand that the warrior wouldn't hear it as well.

I chose a spot on the other side that would yield a thick strip of cloth, yanked again and it gave beneath my tug. I tied the strip around my cane, making certain it was high enough to not get in my way but also tight enough against my body that it wouldn't fall.

I went back to the wall and found the stones I'd used previously. The first steps went the same, but without the cane in hand, I was able to grip onto the slim ledge and heft myself upwards.

I ran my hand across the wall, until I found another jut to hang on to. I went up three more stones before I reached the tapestry and the emptiness of the hidden entrance behind it. I gritted my teeth and hoisted myself up, as I gave praises to the sands. I needed this, and somehow, I was making it happen.

I was over halfway up, when my cane caught against the entrance. Having been laid horizontally across my body, it wouldn't turn. With a curse, I reached back, attempting to half hold myself partway in the entrance, and with my legs and my free hand, readjust my cane. The wood wobbled beneath my touch but didn't move as far as I needed it to.

"Got it," a faint voice called out.

Sand blast it all. I was going to be caught after coming so close to freedom. No. I wouldn't let that happen. I shoved the cane aside, got the tip to swing across the wall until it came into the tunnel with me, sliding up against my left leg.

As there was the familiar jostling of the door, I yanked myself forward, kicking my legs and pulling with my arms, to get as far as I could. My bottom half was a ways in, from the feel of things. I kicked the tapestry, to make sure it wasn't folded up in the tunnel with me.

I was in all the way, just barely, when the voices came back, this time clear.

"See? Nothing," the first man said. "I brought all these extra warriors and the key for nothing."

I clenched my teeth and took shallow breaths, pleading with the sands they wouldn't think to look behind the tapestries or didn't hear my struggles. So many warriors for just little old me and Elata.

"There was a noise while you were gone."

Maybe they found me, after all.

CHAPTER NINETEEN

"There's nothing here," the first man insisted.

"I could have sworn I heard something," the second replied.

"Both of you, stop standing around, get out of the doorway, and get in there to look around," a woman snapped. Her voice was familiar. Hauntingly so.

Valeriana. The woman I'd heard before, in the throne room, whom I couldn't place. Recalling the sound of her brought memories of her at my waterfall home, searching for Nikon. She knew him all too well, and he didn't care for her.

I didn't either.

What was she doing here? I shook off the fear. It was more for Nikon than myself, but hearing her sent me to a place I didn't want to go. Instead, I wanted to rush forward and get out of here. Too bad that'd make too much noise. I was stuck here, far too close to them.

Many footsteps entered the room and moved around. When Valeriana spoke again, I hated that I could hear her and knew I was so close to being caught.

"It is suspicious that this specific room was locked."

"Why is that?" the second, more sensible man asked.

"Don't you know?" the first interjected. "This is the infamous Nikon's old room."

The silence that followed was more worrisome than if they'd continued to jabber.

Someone shuffled their feet around, but nobody spoke, until the sensible one said, "There's no one in the closet. No one here at all."

"We're missing something." Valeriana sounded so certain, I was shocked she hadn't pinpointed my location yet.

I shifted to put a hand over my mouth to keep myself from doing something stupid. Or maybe I was trying to keep my fear from escaping because she seemed to be able to smell it.

Though I could make out faint breathing from below, they no longer moved about.

Valeriana said, "I want a guard posted in this room day and night, until they're found."

"Yes ma'am," a group of men and women called out.

It was quiet for another moment, before the footsteps headed out. I rested my forehead against the cool stone beneath me, not caring that it was rough. I might have escaped Valeriana's notice, but how was I ever going to get out of here if a warrior was constantly posted in here? They'd hear my movements. I shook my head, not wanting to believe it was so. There had to be a way out. I was so close to escaping.

"Good job, scarab lover," a new woman's voice said. "Now we're stuck with another two of us guarding, instead of being out there, looking for real evidence of where those slaves went."

"It's his fault," the man who'd gone for the key said.

"I could have sworn I heard something..." The man who'd sent him for it sounded thoughtful.

Though I couldn't move, I also couldn't stick around here, waiting for them to figure out where Elata and I had gone. And if Elata managed to come back without realizing there were warriors in the room, she could give us away. I had to get out of here.

As they continued their discussion of who would get the first round of guard duty, I inched forward. I was annoyed I had to move so slowly. At this point, I'd never make it out of here before I died of thirst.

The guards sounded just as close as before. I pressed on, continuing my arduous journey. My forearms soon ached with the added strain of moving silently. The remaining warriors made barely any noise, just the occasional scuff against the stone floor or wall.

After going some distance and not hearing them for a moment, I started moving faster. Not a lot, but enough to actually make progress.

My cane tapped against the wall of the tunnel as it shifted next to me.

I froze at the sound, listening to the warriors.

The man asked, "Did you hear that?"

"Hear what?" the woman asked.

"I don't know. I thought I heard something again." He sounded far too thoughtful for my liking.

They didn't speak, but I waited a while before continuing. When I finally did, I went back to my ridiculously slow speed. I internally grunted at the agonizing pace, but I couldn't risk more. At some point, I reached back, grabbed my cane, and slowly brought it up beside me, so I had better control over what it was doing. Plus, it felt good to have it in my grasp and not just bouncing at my side.

My dress tugged up some with the motion, but I didn't care that it left my legs more exposed, to get roughed up by the stones. If it meant getting to safety, I'd do whatever it took.

Grateful for the numbing concoction Elata had slathered on me, I took my forever-forward journey, going on and on. I didn't know how far I'd gone, when I heard breathing coming ahead of me. My heart jumped out of my chest, before I realized it was probably Elata.

What to do? I didn't want to scare her and risk a shriek of fear, but talking was dangerous. I weighted my options, and finally settled on saying in the softest whisper, "Elata, warriors in the room."

The breathing hitched, and then came across more rapidly. I strained to hear any sign of life behind me—a word or shifting or a sword being drawn... anything—but none came.

Braving another whisper, I said, "Go back."

At first, her breathing was some distance off. It was a comfort to have her so close. Knowing nothing bad had happened to her when I sent her off alone slightly relaxed my worry over her.

I continued on my journey, letting myself go a little faster than previously. Shortly thereafter, Elata shifted. She was doing as I asked and moving away from the area.

I sent a silent *thanks* to the sands, for once again saving us.

We scooted through, and the farther we went, the more at ease I became. We might make it out of this mess. Or out of the pyramid. As distant as that seemed only a short while ago.

We'd gone some distance. Salty drops ran down my cheek. Not tears. Sweat. The temperature had increased. "We're near the end."

"I think so." Elata kept her voice soft, as we both came to a stop.

"We should stay until night," I said.

"Is it safe?" Her voice trembled.

I didn't want to admit how much danger we were in, but neither did I wish to lie to her. "Honestly, I'm not certain. If they find where the hidden tunnel is, we'll be in trouble. But if we try to climb down the pyramid during the day, we'll be seen. We'll have to wait until it's dark for them, and hope to the sands they don't figure out where we went."

She sighed, and I agreed with the sound. There was small

chance of success for all we needed to do, but we had to keep going. "Let's wait until the temperature cools. I'm going to try and sleep until then."

I didn't want to admit it, but the numbing medicine she'd used on me no longer felt like enough. I wanted to lie somewhere soft and not move for a long, long time. Still, my desire to save my loved ones from Lavti's claws grew stronger, the closer to freedom we got. I doubted she would hurt them or turn others in like she had me, but she had to be manipulating their thoughts about what happened to me. There was a possibility that, if someone else got in her way, she'd turn them in as well. I needed to make certain my loved ones were well, but I'd never make it down the rest of the pyramid like this.

"Elata, do you have any more of your concoction?" I asked.

"Not much."

"Can I use it?"

"Yes, but perhaps right before we get going again. We don't want to have it wear off before we get to the ground."

"Right."

She went quiet, and I rested as much as I could. The heat was strong, but not any more intense than I'd dealt with before. It added to my sleepiness. I slipped in and out, until something brushed against my hand. I jolted back.

Elata said, "Sorry. I didn't mean to scare you. I think it's been night for some time."

It hadn't dawned on me until she spoke, but it was cooler.

The thought of climbing down the pyramid left me wanting to hole up in the tunnel until someone came to save me. Holding in a groan, I said, "Let's get out of here."

"I'm scared."

That reinforced my fears. "It's going to be all right. It's high, but we'll make it to safety, even if it takes all night."

"No, it's not that. Well, some of it is. But mostly, it's that I haven't been outside the pyramid in many years. I'm not sure I'm ready to face whatever is out there."

A pang of sadness ran through me. "I'm sorry you've had such a life. It's not the way it should be, for anyone. We'll find somewhere safe for you to go, with people who care for each other and won't make you a slave just because you're blind. I promise."

"Such a place seems unreal after these last years."

I reached out, searching for her hand until I found it. "It's there, waiting for us. Let's go find it."

CHAPTER TWENTY

When we got out of the tunnel, wind buffeted me from our spot that must have been a decent height up. I applied the last of the numbing concoction. The climb down was more straining and stressful than I remembered. We'd been heading toward the ground, helping one another get from a pyramid step to the next, for what felt like days.

My arm burned with pain where I'd been stabbed. The rest of me wasn't much better, but the salve seemed to take the brunt of the agony away, so I could keep going. Keep moving.

How much longer could I continue on, though?

We'd been silent for the most part, since leaving the relative safety of the tunnel, only communicating when absolutely necessary. It was dangerous to do anything more. As I helped Elata down the next step, it felt like forever. I stretched out, lowering her until I could go no more. She dropped like we'd been doing so far.

I handed her my cane, as we'd practiced the last hundreds of levels. Not that there were really that many. I'd lost count after *thirty-something*. How many remained was impossible to say, and

I didn't want to keep count when I had no idea where the end was.

I turned around and slowly lowered myself, clinging on to the ledge as long as possible, until my burning arms stretched all the way above me. My wound pulsed. I dropped the rest of the way and landed on my feet with a soft *thump*.

Despite the beating I'd taken, I'd made it this far. Though my muscles were more tender than I'd have ever guessed they could be, I had to push on. If I hadn't trained so hard before this, I wouldn't have managed.

Elata wasn't faring much better, from the sound of her heavy breathing, but she never complained.

Once I had my bearings, she handed me my cane, and together, we crept forward. As I stretched out my cane, dreading finding the ledge because it meant more moving downward, a sensation broke through the monotony of the climbing. The ground beneath my feet was different.

Instead of hard rock peppered with loose sand that had blown onto the pyramid steps, the path was softer. Looser. I continued searching for the ledge, but it wasn't there. We'd made it down the pyramid.

"We made it," I whispered to Elata.

For one brief moment, I wanted to fall to my knees and cry praises to the sands of magic that we'd made it down, but a more serious thought hit me. The real danger began now.

I had no idea where we were relative to the entrance. We'd exhausted ourselves, but now it was time to deal with any warriors on the pyramid grounds. No to mention the fact that we needed to find our way back to Ruso. I wilted, ready to sit down and sob, but instead pulled myself together the best I could and pushed forward.

Moving closer to Elata, I said, "We've got to be super careful now. I'll get us out, though."

She squeezed my arm in agreement, and we went forward,

me leading the way with my sticks out to fight. I made my way careful, each step measured and sure before I went on to the next.

Wishing I knew my way around, I went straight, away from the great building, feeling vulnerable. Without a map in my head of where to go—or indeed, a direction of any kind—I was almost as lost as Elata, who hadn't been out for years.

Each step felt more dangerous than the last. Memories of leaving my waterfall home with Nikon flooded me. I'd had him, despite not fully trusting him yet. I had been learning to, and he'd been my eyes. Now, a warrior could sneak upon Elata and me, and the only warning we'd have would be my cane, unless they made a mistake and let out a noise.

I shoved the thoughts away, as we continued into the abyss of a world, walking slower than I wanted. It was more likely we'd be seen this way, but then, we'd be found if we hurried along and ran into something. To come all this way only to be caught wasn't an option.

I stepped forward, but paused when my cane whacked into something.

Elata stopped beside me and whispered, "What is it?"

Laughter filled the air in front of us from many people, at least five or six. A woman said, "Did you really think we wouldn't notice a couple of blind women, stumbling around our grounds?" She laughed harder. "Take them."

I didn't wait for a sensation coming through my cane. I pushed Elata out of striking range, untwisted my cane, and struck out toward the laughing woman. I connected with a *thwamp*.

Someone called out in anger, kindling my own rage. I did not come this far only to go right back to Antonia. I would fight to the death, rather than be retaken.

I swung again and smacked into a solid object in front of me. The vibration through my sticks and up my arms let me know someone swung at me. I blocked with a growl.

No. They would not take me again.

Despite my aches and pains, I put my all into the fight, pushing myself on, determined to find a way to die, before I let them take me back to Antonia. I could float down the river of death and go to the afterlife until my loved ones joined me. It would be a relief to have a break, after everything I'd been through.

I slammed my right stick into someone, before blocking a strike with my left, slipping around their defenses, and bashing into skin.

Despite the number of people I'd heard laughing, it didn't feel as if I fought many opponents. And was that the sound of a separate fight over the one I was involved in?

There wasn't time to stop and figure out what was going on. I pressed on, fighting for my freedom and Elata's life. Maybe death wasn't coming for me after all. A wave of hope tried to spring through me—were others fighting the same warriors I was?—but it couldn't be. It didn't make sense. I smashed the hope down, as I smashed someone in the torso.

My weapons flew around me, though my arms were quickly weakened. I'd simply done far too much to put in the fight I wanted. My hits weren't as strong as before, despite magic powering my movements.

The sounds of fighting nearby continued, though no new attacks pressed in on me. I took several steps back, keeping my sticks up and ready to hit the next person who came at me. Grunts and gasps filled the air in front of me, as many as laughed before.

I took another step back and whispered over my shoulder, "Elata?"

"Here." She latched on to my arm.

I didn't waste time, as the fighting continued to ring through the air. It wasn't a full-blown cacophony, but before long, it would draw more attention this way. I scooted far to the side, hoping to make it around.

We'd only gone a short ways, when the clang of swords died off in exchange for people gasping for air. I quickened my pace, not wanting to meet with the winners. Without my cane put together, to guide me and let me know if it was clear, I hoped I'd know if I was in danger before tripping over something.

We'd gone a handful of steps, when a man called out from the area of the fight. "Ho, there. Wait. We're on your side."

I pretended not to hear him. Were they really on our side, or did they want us to come to them without a fight?

Several sets of footsteps neared and I stopped, knowing it was useless, and the man spoke again. "Are you Cassandra?

Elata and I couldn't outrun them. Hoping they were truly on our side, I asked, "Who wants to know?"

"Nikon and the Jackal are searching for you. I'm an old acquaintance of Nikon's from the pyramid, turned rebel. I'm on your side, despite being a warrior, as are we all here. I'm Kilno. We've been keeping an eye out for you. Just fought the warriors trying to attack you. We're with the rebellion." The last part was said in a whisper.

The wave of hope crescendoed, but what he said didn't mean anything. Anyone could claim to be with the rebellion. But Nikon's name mixed with the Jackal...

"They're searching for me?" They were the words I'd latched on to, as soon as I'd heard them. Was it true? Nikon hadn't given up on me, even with whatever hold Lavti had on him? Not to mention the lies she'd probably spun?

"He is. We have to get you two out of here, before more warriors loyal to the rulers show up. I'm afraid we've broken our cover with fighting the warriors. We can take you to him."

"He's here in the city?" I'd thought he'd be in Ruso.

"Yes. Please. We need to hurry."

"Can I hold your arm? It would help us get around." It could be a trap, but I was inclined to believe him. I reached out a hand, cane put together in my other hand. As soon as someone gave me their arm, I walked along with them, Elata close to my side.

How had Nikon gotten here, in the city? Did he know I was in the capital? I could send positive vibes to the sands that this would all work out. I thought Lavti would have talked him into going somewhere far away from me. A place where the two of them could make a home, away from the rebellion.

The thought made me sick. I wanted to snarl.

As we hurried through the streets, cobblestones bumpy beneath my sore feet, no one bothered us. If I had to guess, it was because those taking us to Nikon wore warrior garb. Without asking or touching, though, I didn't know for certain.

We twisted and turned, getting farther and farther from the pyramid, each step exhausting but filled with the belief that this would turn out well. I let that belief grow, until I heard a loud hoot rent the air, and a scampering monkey come bounding toward us.

I didn't wait for direction. I stopped where I was, bent down, and reached an arm out. Tewy climbed up and chatted animatedly, as he moved from shoulder to shoulder, patting my face, hair, shoulders—any part of me he could touch.

"Tewy." My eyes stung with tears, as he continued his insistent noises back at me. As soon as he paused, I said, "I thought I'd never find you again."

"And we thought the same about you," Nikon said from somewhere ahead. "From the looks of you, you were lucky to survive."

CHAPTER TWENTY-ONE

There was so much I wanted to say upon hearing his voice, but it was as if a vice tightened around my throat. I needed to do something, but nothing I tried helped.

Before I could clear my thoughts, his faint steps came rushing toward me, and the next thing I knew, I was wrapped in his arms. Warmth stirred deep within my chest, bringing my heart back to life with a heat that grew happier and more intense by the moment.

I needed him as much as I needed to do things for myself.

Tewy patted my wet cheek. I was crying? I pressed my other cheek to Nikon's chest and slumped against him.

I was tired. So tired. I didn't have to stay strong any more—but I did have to tell him about Lavti.

"We need to move inside," Kilno said.

Nikon shifted, but before he could go, I grabbed his shoulder and pulled him back to me. "Wait. Lavti."

"What about her?" His voice took on a new note, a hint of gruff emotion. Was it love, frustration, or both, combined in a new feeling?

Didn't matter. I had to tell him. "She handed me to the warriors."

He stiffened. "*Sand it all.*"

"I'm so—"

"I've got to take care of this. Now." Nikon shifted away. "Please believe that I'll be back for you as soon as I can. Kilno, make sure she gets somewhere safe, have a healer see her, and don't leave her until I get back."

"Understood, sir."

That familiar *sir* came out like he'd said it to Nikon thousands of times before, though I knew Nikon didn't care for it.

As Nikon left without a sound, I was grateful Tewy stayed. I had him for comfort and Elata was with me.

"This way, Cassandra," Kilno said from my left.

I found his arm, and he led me away, as I called back, "Elata, are you with me?"

"Here. Tired."

"You've more than earned some sleep." I rather felt like falling apart myself, but I didn't know what waited for us at our destination. I hoped my friends and family were here.

We soon entered a house without stopping to knock.

I'd only stepped in, when Zoe's voice came from my right. "Cassandra, you're back." It sounded as if she was crying.

"I'm here. Sorry I didn't get out sooner." I let go of Kilno, only to be embraced by her.

People shifted around us, moving and talking, but I focused on keeping a close hold on Zoe and making certain Tewy didn't leave me.

"Out of where sooner?" she asked—more like demanded. "Where have you been? We heard rumors, but we didn't know. We came home one day to find an empty house, you missing. Tewy and Nikon have been beside themselves. I don't know which of them is more lost without you."

"What about Lavti?" The question couldn't be helped. I was

anxious to know how he'd acted toward her while I'd been gone. Had he married her? I sunk down onto a couch, resting my sore body back on it.

"Nikon refused to marry her until you got back, saying it wasn't right to celebrate while his best friend was missing. She's upset that they pushed off the wedding again. Keeps harping at him, to get it back on. Instead of doing something useful, she's stuck close to him—which makes sense—but mostly to insist you probably ran off, or something similar. Nikon and the rest of us refused to believe it. Even if you were upset about his falling in love, you wouldn't do something like that. But where were you? Were you caught and taken to the pyramid?"

Peace warred in my heart with the conflict over Lavti's betrayal, and knowing I'd remained dear to Nikon even when he'd fallen in love with another. My body ached with the need for sleep, but the need to protect the others was stronger. "I was. Lavti betrayed me to them."

Zoe gasped, tightening her grip on my hand.

I shifted into a more comfortable position. Everything hurt.

"Lavti did what?" Zoe shrieked.

The room went silent.

I didn't bother moving from my spot, lying back with my eyes closed.

The chatter started back up again, quieter this time, as if people were listening in on our conversation.

I didn't care; I wanted to feel like myself again. "Where are my parents?" I asked.

"They stayed behind in Ruso, in case the rumors we heard that you'd been seen with warriors coming this way were wrong and you were there. You were with the Vading and Reding, weren't you?"

I yawned. Exhaustion was going to take over soon, no matter what I did. "I just escaped with Elata. Where is she?"

"The woman you came with?"

"Yes."

"Kaius took her to get settled. She looked about to fall over. You do too, though you're practically lying down. Can I get you anything? Do you feel like telling me what happened?"

"I've sent for a healer," Kilno said from nearby.

I nodded. "I only need to heal, which can't be done quickly, except by the sands, but I don't feel good enough to walk there." I yawned again and rubbed my eyes. My face—no, my entire body—was grimy. I should have cared I was making a mess, but I was grateful to have a place to rest. With Zoe's presence and Tewy, gently resting in my lap, I felt more at peace and like I could hold on a little longer.

Tewy clung to my torso, soft and comforting, as if afraid I would disappear at any moment.

I ran my hand over his coat. "I know, little guy. I missed you too. I don't ever want to go anywhere without you again."

Oooooo oo ooooo oooooo oo.

"Sounds like you have stories to tell," I said.

"Probably not as many as you do," Zoe interrupted. "He's mostly been moping around the place. Tell us—what happened to you?"

I sighed, holding Tewy close. "When Nikon returns. I'd prefer to tell the entire story only once."

"I understand. I'm anxious for the healer to arrive. Would you like something to eat? You're skinnier than when I last saw you."

"I haven't been gone that long, but yes, I'm famished."

"Long enough to be nothing but bones. I'll be right back."

The cushion shifted beside me, and her familiar steps hurried away. I didn't move a muscle, just let Tewy stay attached to me.

I must have drifted off at some point, because I woke to voices.

Zoe whispered, "Where's Lavti?"

"Locked up for now." Nikon's voice sounded tortured and angry.

"Good." I slurred the word more than I meant to.

"Sorry," Zoe said, coming over. "I didn't mean to wake you." A hand brushed hair off my face and felt my forehead, as if for a fever. "Would you like me to bring that food I promised you before you fell asleep?"

The more I came to, the more everything in me ached and burned with pain. I didn't want to move, but I needed to tell them all that had happened, before I fell back asleep.

And I really was famished.

I stretched, a sharp gnawing in my side making me call out.

"What is it?" Nikon was by me in an instant.

I placed a hand on the side of my stomach, as Tewy scurried out of the way. "I got stabbed."

"Where's the healer I told you to get?" Nikon shouted.

"I sent men for one as soon as we got back," Kilno said. "They should be here any moment."

Nikon growled under his breath. "I'm sorry I didn't realize sooner, Cass. There's just so much—"

"*So much* what?" I asked, breathing through my teeth.

"Erm... blood, bruises, and dirt. I didn't know if they were past injuries, but I knew you needed help, and I should have gotten it to you sooner. We'll get you fixed up. Everything is going to be fine now."

"Bet I'll have a scar to show for it." Better to focus on the humor, than the blinding pain.

He gave a short, mirthless laugh. "Maybe. If they bring sand, you might end up without a mark."

"You never know."

"Let's see it, or the worst of your wounds. I'll start treating it with what I know before the healer gets here."

I shifted upward with a groan, Tewy coming back to cling to me. "I may have some internal injuries; I was beaten before we escaped. But you should be able to do something about the side wound."

He cursed, as I fumbled for the knot Elata had made with the cloth she'd torn from her skirt.

"That's binding your wound? It's filthy."

"It's all we had." I grunted as his fingers brushed mine, taking over the job of untying it.

Within moments, he stopped and used a knife to cut through the makeshift bandage. He said, "We won't want to use that for anything again, anyway. Lie down."

I groaned, Tewy frantically moving around my body except the side that Nikon protected. My monkey would only stop on occasion to pat my cheek.

Nikon cursed again. "This should have been treated already. They'd better hurry with that healer. These bruises are from the beating? Who ordered that?"

The pain was making my head too fuzzy. "Tell you later." My voice came out sleepy. How much longer could I fight the pain and tiredness pulling down on me?

"*Sand it*, Cass. Don't you give up on me now."

"Not. Just been... through... a lot."

He took my hand, more gently than I expected, given his stern tone. "I'm so sorry. I promise I'll fix this."

"Sounds like she's already. Locked up," I managed between panted breaths.

"She is." He sounded more tired than I felt.

A door burst open, and footsteps hurried my way. I didn't want to let go of Nikon, and apparently he felt the same, as he switched from being by my waist to sitting beside my shoulder, keeping hold of my hand, so my arm was bent at the elbow.

"What happened?" a woman asked. The healer, if I had to guess, as fingers swiftly got to work, probing me.

"Where?" I asked back.

"A sense of humor—that's good. Is this wound on your stomach the worst of it?"

"It is. I think. Hard to know. More damage could be inside, or infection started somewhere else."

"I'll start there, and we'll work through... everything."

My eyelids fluttered, as I fought off sleep. "Don't leave. Tewy. Nikon."

"We aren't going anywhere," Nikon said.

Tewy replied in a soft *ooo*. I didn't know he could use such a quiet voice.

Hearing both of them made me relax in a way I hadn't since Lavti turned me in.

CHAPTER TWENTY-TWO

The healer took some time with me, before attending to Elata. She had magic sand with her, but not enough to completely heal me. She didn't think I had any internal injuries, and the worst of my wounds were better. Except, my arm would likely scar. It was a silly thing to worry about, but easier focusing on that, than thinking of all that had happened.

Elata was in better condition than I was, but still required healing.

I remained sore, but after dozing off and on for some time—finding Tewy and Nikon always there when I reached out for them, Zoe often with them—I finally felt awake enough to tell them what happened.

As I told my story and what I'd found out to Nikon, Tewy, Zoe, and Kaius, they were silent, though Nikon's grip on my hand gradually tightened.

Tewy interrupted with the occasional jabbering, his monkey chatter sounding thoroughly disgusted.

I felt the same.

Once I finished, the room was silent. Someone gave me a cup

of water, and I drank the entire thing, letting it soothe my throat after all that talking.

"I can't believe the Vading is related to the high priest," Zoe said.

Nikon stirred, though he didn't let go of my hand. "It makes sense. The two of them always seemed closer than was reasonable. I always dismissed it as them having the same idea."

"What do we do now?" I asked.

"You rest," Zoe said. "We've sent word to your parents, so there's nothing else for you to stress over, for the moment."

"I've done enough of that. I'm ready to do whatever needs to be done, to rid the world of Antonia and the high priest's influence. Especially if they've affected love through tainting the water. We've got to stop them." I wished to know why they'd done all of this, but that was minor, compared to stopping them.

"How do we do that?" Kaius asked.

I let Tewy grab my finger and wrap his hand around it. I was going to sound crazy, but I sucked in a sustaining breath and went ahead anyway. "We tell the Reding."

"What?" Nikon sounded a strange mix of hopeful and doubtful.

"Are you certain that's a good idea?" Zoe asked. "We've not had great results with any conversation in the past."

"Not entirely true," I replied. "I mean, we tried, but Antonia has always been there. I think—or hope—that if we can get him on his own, he'll listen to us. If not us, perhaps Nikon."

"I'm not sure I hold that kind of sway with him, anymore." Yet Nikon sounded more thoughtful than dismissive.

"And how do we find a way to speak with him?" Zoe asked.

I worked to refrain from biting my lip. I didn't want to bring Nikon any pain, but I had to do this. "Logistically, it would be tricky, but we can make it happen. I'm more concerned with what Nikon thinks of the idea." Especially since his grip had become loose.

He didn't answer right away, but when he did, his words were careful. "My brother and I haven't gotten along for some time, but we used to be fairly close. I don't know if he'd listen to me, but if his relationship with the Vading is anything like my relationship with Lavti, there might be reason to hope."

"What do you mean?" Zoe asked, though I thought I knew.

His grip around my hand turned firmer. "I feel this pull toward Lavti—love her—but I also hate her. There's this connection to her, a strange feeling that makes me want to be with her, but I don't trust her and would actively work against her. From what I know of Theodore and his wife, their relationship may be similar. They try to present a united front for the people, but behind closed doors, they often seemed annoyed with one another. When I left the pyramid, they no longer shared a room."

The thought was sad for other couples who might be in the same situation, but I didn't care about Antonia at this point. It also gave me hope. "We have to try to talk to him."

"I could be wrong. He could be as involved as the Vading is. He has been pushing lowering the odiosom, all these years."

"Isn't it worth a try?"

"Theodore was a different person before *she* came along." Nikon sounded tired. "If we can find a way to approach him safely, I say we try for it."

I perked up. This might make a difference. He was the Reding. He must have power over Antonia but hadn't known how desperately she needed to be stopped.

"No matter how safe we attempt to make it, trying to talk to him will be dangerous," Kaius said.

"But with the Jackal on our side and Nikon's resources and relationship to the Reding, we can make it work."

Nikon said, "Don't forget the hope you inspire in people, Cass. They look up to you, far more than you realize."

My cheeks heated at the thought. It didn't feel true, but maybe it was. "Let's not waste time. How can we move forward?'

"I'll talk to Kilno," Nikon said. "From the little I've discussed with him since he joined us at the house, there are many other warriors tired of the way things are. So many of them are odiosom and being treated like lesser people. The amant who are friends with them want to make a change. Being amant doesn't mean they're against us. I think having amant help us will give us more sway with the population as a whole."

"Kaius and I should tell you something," Zoe said, sounding hesitant. "We're not brother and sister. We're married. We've been hiding our marks with magic."

"I know," Nikon said.

"You do?" Kaius sounded surprised.

"It was easy to figure out, after living with you. And I understand why the two of you wanted to keep it quiet, but it might do more for the rebellion, to know the Jackal is a married couple, willing to fight for everyone's rights."

Nikon's words had me nodding my head. "I agree." Wholeheartedly.

"I always thought people would despise us, because we have something they don't," Zoe said.

Kaius added, "And definitely not want us to lead the rebellion."

"It's the other way around. They'd want to follow you, because you see what others like you don't," I said. "You can help unite people."

Silence, during which Nikon increased the pressure against my hand. It felt good to have his fingers wrapped around mine. I'd missed it. Only, I wanted so much more.

Silly thoughts, making me crave what I couldn't have.

Zoe said, "Maybe you're correct. We'll consider it."

"And while you do so," Nikon said, "we'll see what Kilno has to say about talking to the Reding."

"That's the best place to start," Kaius added.

"Elata might have some insights, as to the Reding's and

Vading's current schedules." She'd been there far longer than I had and would know their comings and goings better than I did.

Zoe said, "I'll go speak with her. She's been resting. When we can make her, anyway. She's determined to work, which makes sense because that's all she's known for so long, but I wish I could get her to relax a little."

Grateful I'd gotten Elata out of there, I worried over the rest of the slaves left behind. I'd never gotten to know them, but they'd been there, struggling under the Vading's rule, just as much as we had. If only there was something I could do for them.

If I knew why Antonia enslaved the blind in the first place, it might make a difference. I could discover how to invalidate that reason and rescue them that way. A far-off hope at the moment.

Zoe's light steps left the room, starting a chain of people coming and going. I was far stronger than I had been. I dozed throughout their meetings and attempts to figure something out. I'd contributed what I could. I didn't see them letting me come on the journey to where they'd meet the Reding, and had no new thoughts of how to help. I did enjoy having Tewy and Nikon with me, while the voices of Zoe and Kaius drifted close by. It'd be nice if my parents were here as well, but word had been sent to them, so they could relax somewhat.

The discussions lasted well into the night. I wasn't certain how late exactly, when I woke to the murmur of people speaking, but by the coolness of the room, I suspected it was more early morning than late night.

"What's going on?" I asked, stroking Tewy's fur.

I heard Nikon's faint movements coming toward me, and made room for him to sit next to me.

He did so and said, "It seems Kilno is right about his contacts in the pyramid. Those not under Valeriana's influence are far more likely to join our cause than the rulers' side. Given that many of them are odiosom or lower-class amant, it only makes sense. They're as tired of being oppressed as we are."

"So you have warriors in the pyramid. What good does that do?" Hupsheta's voice came from across the room.

I turned on her, not wanting to accuse her of anything, but also wanting to kick her out of the house. She held something over Nikon, for housing us in the capital before we'd found my parents. I didn't know what, but the fact that she did made me want to throw sand in her eyes.

That woman would hold your life over your head, if it meant she got something out of it.

Leaning toward Nikon, I whispered, "When did she get here?"

He hesitated, and I knew I wasn't going to like his answer. "We're at her house."

I stiffened. "We're not in the hideout, though."

"No. Too many of us for that, and I didn't want to drag you down there, when you need time to heal."

"And she's working with us?"

"Sort of." From the tone of his voice, I didn't think he was much happier about this arrangement than I was.

"Whatever you two are whispering about," Hupsheta said, "we need to move on. I've got to get my beauty rest, after all."

More like, find out our plans and turn them to her advantage.

"We can have those warriors help us," Nikon said to her. "Perhaps you can get your beauty rest while we figure out the rest of the details."

Cloth shifted in her direction. "Fine. I can tell when I'm not wanted. But remember our agreement, Nikon. I want to be kept in the loop with this."

"Understood." Though his word came out calm enough, he was as tense as a snake about to spring.

Several moments after the sound of her leaving faded, Nikon continued as if she'd never interrupted. I wished she hadn't. Wished we didn't have to be staying at her place once again.

"We're going to have some of the warriors kidnap Theodore."

Instead of sounding sorry about the prospect of arranging for his brother to be taken against his will, Nikon sounded overly happy about it. We should arrange kidnappings more often, if that was the case.

"Where will they take him?" I asked.

"Outside the city, where you and I can speak with him about what we've learned. The papyrus I stole from him that Kaius read had information about some of what is happening, but not near close to what we've learned. If he doesn't know more about it, we should tell him what we do know."

"You want me to help?" A rush of energy tingled through my skin.

"If you're up for it, you're one of the best resources we have, to convince him."

My face burned with his words. "I do have a firsthand account of what Antonia has said and done over the years, as well as what she did recently." But the Reding, the ruler of all Eppla... Would he want to hear from me? "Do you think your brother will listen? I mean, yes, the order to enslave the blind didn't come until after he married Antonia, but he must have agreed to it, or the law wouldn't have come to pass."

"I don't think he knew enough about the blind to be overly upset." In a quieter voice, Nikon added, "I know I didn't."

"That makes sense. You didn't interact with anyone who couldn't see."

"It doesn't excuse my behavior. I did many wrong things, over my time as part of the royal family and as an elite warrior. It pains me, to realize how much damage I've done."

"We all make mistakes. And you're working on correcting yours now."

"That's true."

Tewy jabbered something, climbing from my lap for the first time since I'd returned, to head toward Nikon.

"See?" I said. "If Tewy believes in you, everyone else should as well. Now you just have to believe in yourself."

I let the information sink in, hoping it would do some good. But I couldn't wait too much longer; there was much to be done. "Where will we meet with the Reding?" I asked.

Tewy hopped back onto my lap, hooting.

"In the desert, away from the city. I know a spot that has some trees but isn't visited often. It should afford us the privacy and access to both the river and desert, should we need it." Nikon's confident answer reassured me.

"When do we leave?" I asked.

He chuckled. "So anxious to talk to my brother, are you?"

"I want to hear all the embarrassing stories from when you were a child." If only we could get it to go that well.

"Oh no, you don't." Despite his words, he laughed harder.

Whatever it took, to keep him happy. It was good to hear a sound I'd so desperately missed. "When is it, then?"

"We're going to wrap up a few loose ends, and then we will go out to wait at the appointed meeting spot. We're going to have enough former warriors with us to keep everyone safe, though if all goes to plan, we shouldn't need them."

"That would be for the best." My mind drifted away from the next task at hand. Though I should focus on tonight, I couldn't help but ask, "What's happening with Lavti?"

His sigh was so heavy, I expected it to weigh the couch down further. "There doesn't seem to be an easy answer. I'm furious at her, but there's that strange pull toward her. I don't know what to do."

Neither did I.

CHAPTER TWENTY-THREE

The wait at the rendezvous point grew unbearable. I hoped my suggestion worked and didn't make things worse. However long it'd been, the cold night air brushing across my skin spoke of many hours spent waiting for those appointed to bring the Reding to us.

It was a dangerous job.

Though I hated to ask, I couldn't put it off anymore. I turned toward Nikon, who stood near me, while Tewy darted between us, playing. "What if something happened to them?" I asked.

"We knew it could take a while. Everything is going to go well. You'll see."

"No, I won't." I added a hint of a laugh to my words but quickly sobered. "I wish my parents were here. They could add valuable insight with their experiences. He tortured them, yes? Maybe we're making a mistake."

"Did he torture them? That doesn't sound like my brother. I thought it was just orders from Antonia, but maybe he changed."

"I just know they were tortured while in the pyramid. I assumed it was her that ordered it so, but now I'm doubting."

"We'll be careful," Nikon said.

But the worry nagged at me. If the Reding was the type to torture people, he was going to be more on the Vading's side than we assumed. What had made me think we could talk to him? Bringing him into this didn't seem like such a good idea anymore. I wished I'd thought of it sooner. If the warriors helping us had ended up captured, and he did something to them, I would be furious at myself.

Time continued to drag on, leaving me as restless as Tewy was. When the sands scratched in the distance, I strained to hear if the noise would continue. It did, growing and heading our way.

"Do you hear that?" I whispered to Nikon.

"I do."

Tewy held steady on my shoulder, as I gripped my cane. It was good to have the weapon, giving me some peace of mind. These could be our people, but they could also be warriors on the Reding's side, who'd found out the plan.

The steps came closer, slapping the sand.

I twisted my hand around my cane, ready to take it apart, but Nikon whispered, "It's them."

Though I eased somewhat, I didn't let go of my cane.

Tewy gave a soft *ooo* and climbed up my arm, to sit on my shoulder.

Nikon said, "Any problems?"

"Nothing we couldn't handle," a woman replied.

"Good."

"I should have known you were behind this," the Reding said. Though his voice wasn't as angry as I expected, something else dawned on me. It was amazing I hadn't realized they were related sooner. Hearing Theodore's voice now, the inflections and tones were similar to Nikon's.

I stood straighter, willing myself to be ready for this, and hoping to the sands the Reding would listen to what we had to say.

"We only want what's best for everyone," Nikon replied.

The footsteps stopped within striking distance if I didn't take my cane apart to swing it.

"My elite warriors will find you," the Reding spat out. "You won't be able to keep me for long. Valeriana has had it out for you ever since you left. She'll be more than happy when I give her the order to have you executed."

"That's not the way I'd like our reunion to go."

Though surprised Nikon was going that route, I held my tongue and waited for my turn to talk, eager for his brother to hear us.

The Reding scoffed, but Nikon continued. "We have news we wanted to share with you. We mean you no harm."

"Then why send these warriors after me, who should be loyal to me? I should have known you'd steal my men away from me."

Despite the ill will in the Reding's words, Nikon remained calm and steady—much better than I would have done. "The warriors come to us because they want to. Because they're tired of the way things are and know the rules should be better for all people, and not just good for the amant."

"You manipulate them. Get them to think things are worse than they really are."

"I'm here to tell you the truth of what's been going on with the amant and the odiosom. Mostly, though, Cassandra is here to tell you what she's heard straight from your wife's lips about her and the high priest."

I shifted my feet at the sound of my name, but continued to hold myself tall.

The Reding's tone changed from accusatory to suspicious. "What information could either of you possibly have that I would want to hear?"

"Cassandra, tell him what happened."

I wanted to ask if I should start before or after Antonia had beaten me to make a point, but I refrained from being so petty. "I will. But first, Reding, I would like you to know what I say is true.

I promise I'm not trying to hurt you—only give you the information you need, to act. The only proof we have is the words I've heard, but they are the truth."

"As if the word of a blind person is of any worth."

I held my chin higher, and before anyone could come to my defense, said, "Take my words as you will, but know that, if you don't believe me, it'll be because of your own hard head and to the country's detriment." I asked, "Did you know Antonia is the high priest's granddaughter?"

Silence followed.

"I'll take that as a *no*, but also that it makes sense, since you're not contradicting me." I relaxed my stance. If only I could grab hold of something that would give me more bravery... But since there was no such thing, I continued of my own will, grateful to have Tewy on my shoulder and Nikon at my side. "She told me herself, after she made me one of her slaves. She wanted to give me to him, to torture and get answers for something. Though I'm not certain on the specifics, I believe it has something to do with how I became blind, and includes the river.

"The people's very liquid of life has been toyed with, to make it so people fall in love at first sight or not at all. The two of them have changed the very nature of love, and with that, created a class of people who consider themselves better just because they can fall in love. Your wife seemed to think how I became blind is important to the whole process. I just haven't figured out why yet." I steadied my grip on my cane.

That was enough information for now. I didn't want to overload him, and we needed to gauge how he'd respond to what I already said. I hoped it was on the positive side of things.

The longer the silence stretched, the more I thought he might not believe me. I wanted to ask Nikon what was going on—how the Reding looked and what he was doing—but didn't want to undermine my credibility by worrying.

"I want to say I don't believe you, but some of what you say rings true with what I know of my wife." The last words sounded bitter.

"I'm sorry." And I was. No one should have to find things out like that about their spouse.

"Are you, really?" The Reding sounded genuinely curious.

Though it might not help, I wanted to be as genuine as possible. "Antonia was my friend for a long time. Or I thought she was, but she must have seen herself as only my sole caretaker. Going from that, to her leaving me all alone at a house by the waterfall, was difficult for me. Later, I learned that she had to leave because she fell in love with you, but she didn't tell me. She was just gone one day, with all her things," I said. "You saw what happened when you both captured Nikon and me. Worse, though, was when I was delivered to the warriors and became her slave. She... wasn't kind."

"Is that where all your bruises and cuts are from?" His tone was harder to read now.

I was determined to keep going. "Yes. She was trying to get information from me, about how exactly I became blind, and I wasn't willing to divulge it. She lost her temper."

"And this is after the healer has seen to her, Theodore," Nikon said.

A heavy sigh was followed by the Reding's saying, "I've seen her cruelty more frequently a couple of years into our marriage, but she knows I don't like it, so she's reined it in. I only agreed to it to keep her and the high priest happy. I didn't think her behavior continued, but it could be happening out of sight instead. I've heard rumors, but... The odiosom are a different story. You know how we were raised, Nikon. Mother and Father believed those who couldn't fall in love were worthless. I think the same. Them and the blind. Anyone who can't fall in love isn't chosen. Doesn't have a place anywhere, except as a worker to keep society running."

"They did teach us that, but you were odiosom for so long.

Did you feel you were worthless then? I only recently became an amant, and I don't think my worth was less to yours when I was your top elite warrior without a wife. Just because people don't have that in their lives doesn't make them inferior to those who do."

"Do you understand that, if I believe all that you're saying, it will change everything about our society?"

"I do. Far better than you realize." Nikon's words were soft but carried conviction.

"It's why we're part of the rebellion," I said. "I don't necessarily want to overthrow you as a person, but I do want to change the current ideals toward the blind, odiosom and elderly."

"Your rebellion wanted me and Antonia dead." The Reding's voice went flat.

"That was my fault," Kaius said from behind and to the left of us.

"Our fault," Zoe corrected him. "We thought that, if we got rid of you both, we could take better strides with the people who were being neglected. Nikon and Cassandra tried to talk us out of it."

"And in fact," I said, hoping Zoe and Kaius weren't angry with us when the truth came out, "Nikon and I made arrangements to kidnap you and Antonia and bring things down a different way, rather than kill you. We don't want to hurt you. We just want what's best for the people of Eppla. All people."

"Who are you, to decide what's best for the people?" the Reding asked.

"Someone who's seen the way of life that's not fair to all. And not just from my experience." Though it had been a rough go of things, especially lately. "I don't want to make the decisions, but something needs to be done. When no one else was stepping up, I had to make a difficult choice and hope it would help bring about better things. That's why we're here, talking to you. Antonia and the high priest are taking the country somewhere it shouldn't go.

The magic sands of Eppla are being mistreated, and I can't be idle while that affects the people."

"You make an impassioned plea. You have to understand, though, I can't simply switch things up because you want me to," the Reding said, making my heart sink. "But I've had my own concerns. The reason I was so angry when Nikon stole the papyrus was because I was looking into the high priest and his association with the water. It appears you know more about it than I do after pooling my resources together. I want to do what's best, but I'm not certain I know what that is anymore."

"Wanting to fix things is the first step." I kept my voice soft, like I would with a frightened animal.

Tewy wasn't so hesitant. He gibbered something fierce, before calming into his chatter. Whatever he thought about the Reding, he wasn't afraid to speak his monkey mind about it. But the Reding said nothing.

"Someone give the man a sword," I said.

"What? No." Nikon's words were firm.

"Why?" The Reding asked.

"Because if you are going to hurt the blind, if you won't listen to me, you might as well stab me now." I turned toward Nikon. "I'm serious. Give him a weapon. Let him prove himself. Let him look me in the blind eyes and if he still feels like he should hurt me, he can." I turned back toward the Reding. "But instead, if you find that my humanity holds you back, you should seriously consider what we've said."

Silence. As much as I wanted to say something, I let the quiet seep into the moment, giving time for the Reding to think on what I'd said. I doubted Nikon would give him a sword and let him stab me, but I hoped the point came across.

There was a cling of metal, a sword leaving its sheath. Nikon said, "Can you kill an innocent woman? Take my weapon. Do it if you can. Know before you do so that she's a full, complex woman. She knits the most wonderful things. She cares deeply.

She has parents who love her. She's a fantastic warrior. She has depth and life. Yes, she's blind, but she's so much more."

People shifted. Nikon's words warmed me, giving me strength. I kept my head steady. Let Theodore see me as I was.

The Reding said, "I want change. Where do we go from here?"

CHAPTER TWENTY-FOUR

Change was a good first step. We all formed a circle, sitting on the sand amongst the trees. The Reding spoke as if he wanted to help us, but part of me worried it was a ploy to get us to ease up around him. I kept a hold of my cane, just in case, but I hoped he was as sincere as he said.

"If I go forward with you," the Reding said, "what do you need of me?"

"We need to first discover what exactly the high priest is doing to the water. If there's something we can do to fix it." Nikon sat on my left, close to me.

Tewy curled up in my lap, likely wanting to sleep. I couldn't blame him; I was ready for bed myself. But there was much to be done before we went back to Hupsheta's. *Ugh.* I wished we didn't have to go there at all. I trusted that woman as far as I could see.

"He's coming to Sirya as we speak," the Reding said. "It was an odd decision, because he was just here and doesn't typically visit that often, preferring to stay in Peka Tower."

"He was coming to glean knowledge from me." Which was a nice way of putting it. "Do you think it'd be better to try and get information from him in Peka Tower?"

"I'd been thinking of seeking it from him directly, but now I'm thinking his tower might be a better way to go. There's a lot of information stored there, and if he's here, there'll be less warriors and neczar to stop you," the Reding said.

"Don't you have power to command the tower to be searched?" I asked.

"If I want a fight on my hands. Having someone sneak in would be more likely to produce answers."

"Going there will be dangerous," Zoe said.

"But less dangerous than staying here, where he'll be surrounded by the neczar and be on the lookout for me," I said.

"Though she has a point, I don't like it," Nikon said. "Theodore, do you think you could distract the high priest while he's here? Get him to stay longer, so we'd have more time?"

"It's difficult to say. The man is mercurial. You never know what he's going to do or say. I may be able to keep him here, but if I do, it will be a tight spot to be in. One I probably deserve, for listening to Antonia for so long." The begrudging tone in his voice made me wish I'd tried to communicate with him sooner, not just arranged to circumvent and kidnap him.

"Is it something you're willing to do, though?" Nikon asked.

The Reding sighed. "Yes, but only because I'm one of the few people he can't kill without getting in trouble."

"Thank you," I said. "What can we do, to help?"

"I need a reason why I was out. And any warriors who are willing to come back with me and report to me instead of Antonia would assist. I don't know whom to trust in the pyramid. Everyone seems to be scared of her, for good reason. Valeriana has tried to take your place as my top elite warrior, Nikon, but I've deferred her enough that she's mostly been working for Antonia. I have two strong women teaming up against me in my own home. I need some reassurance of safety and a way to communicate with you all that won't draw attention."

"Maybe you could say you wanted to see Sirya during the night? Or that you needed some fresh air?" Nikon asked.

"Something like that would probably work. Antonia rarely pays me much attention anyway, unless she has something she wants me to do." Theodore sounded sad.

Poor guy might be the ruler of the country, but he clearly had issues like the rest of us.

"That will work, then," Nikon replied. "We'll choose some warriors for you and come up with a message system. We're going to get out of Sirya for now."

"Where will you go after Peka Tower? How can I find you?" Theodore asked.

"I don't want you to know where Cassandra is. If I believe you're on our side, if you get captured, the high priest won't be easy on you, to figure out what you know." Nikon's words were delivered solemnly, leaving me shivering. "We'll make certain the line of communication remains open."

"Just try not to kidnap me again, will you?" Theodore's voice came out dry.

"I'll do my best, but no promises." And Nikon sounded teasing.

I didn't know what to expect from their relationship, but I'd guessed more like when we first met and things were tense than the teasing they were doing now. It also left me wondering what Nikon was feeling. It was the first time I'd heard a hint of happiness from him since Lavti's imprisonment.

They made arrangements for Theodore, including ways to keep in contact, but before he left, he stopped in front of me. "You seem good for my brother. Keep him on his toes, will you?"

I laughed softly. "I'll do my best."

"Don't give her any ideas," Nikon said. "She has enough of those on her own, as it is."

Theodore chuckled. "I'd best get back before morning. I can't believe I'm saying this, but thank you for kidnapping me. We'll meet again soon."

"Probably not soon enough for our taste, but too soon for the high priest's. Let's hope this goes well." From nearby Nikon, there was a thick slapping sound, like men hitting each other's backs during a hug. Things were turning around for us. We had Reding Theodore on our side.

Would it be enough against his wife and the high priest, though? The two had been playing the political game far longer than we had. Probably longer than we suspected, as well. I didn't know if it would be helpful, but I pleaded with the sands that we'd figure out what was going on and how to stop it.

Once the Reding was gone, accompanied by the warriors that brought him, the rest of us moved to a new location. We stayed outside, but at another area, where we could be more confident we wouldn't be traced back to our last meeting point, if the Reding had lied to us.

After snatching a few hours of rest and a simple meal of dates and flatbread, we gathered together, to decide how to move forward. Before anyone could speak—or make it so I couldn't—I said, "I should go to Peka Tower."

Zoe and Kaius protested vehemently.

I held up my hand to stop them. "Hear me out. I know I'm a liability at times, but I can't be around the marauders, because the warriors are looking for me. For that same reason, I can't be in most cities. It makes sense for me to go, and do what I can to help where I can. I don't want to put anyone in danger, but this will be the best way to keep everyone as safe as possible."

Quiet followed my words.

"I don't want anything bad to happen to you," Zoe said in a small voice.

"That makes two of us," I countered.

"Nope. Three." Kaius's response surprised me. I knew he was

a good man, but I didn't know he thought of me as a friend like that.

Nikon grabbed my hand. "Four."

Tewy jumped up from my lap, making hoots loud enough that the warriors could probably hear us from Sirya.

I grabbed the little monkey and pulled him close. "All right. I get it. You all want me to stay safe. And that's good, but the safest place for me might be what's most useful for all of us."

Tewy settled, but squeaked a couple more times before quieting all the way.

"We're concerned about taking you to where the high priest wants you," Nikon said.

"And when you're still recovering from the Vading," Zoe added.

It was nice to know they cared, but I couldn't let it stop me. "I'll be fine. We can go on the river. They won't expect us there. We'll have access to magic, which has been more favorable to me as of late. Besides, the high priest is going to be in the capital. This will be the best time to search his tower."

"I don't know," Zoe said.

Nikon drummed his thumb on the back of my hand. "Cass is right. I hate to take her closer to danger, but it might be worse to stay near where they expect us. They won't expect us to go to Peka Tower."

Unless the Reding betrayed us and told them we were headed there. He didn't know I was planning on going, and I doubted they'd expect it. "He's right. We should go. The sooner, the better."

"I don't have to like it, but I can understand where you're coming from, and respect that decision," Zoe said. "Unfortunately, this is a critical time for the rebellion. I want to go with you, but I don't think the Jackal can afford to leave."

"The Jackal is greatly needed," Kaius agreed.

"I understand." But that didn't mean I wouldn't miss them.

"It will be easier to sneak into Peka Tower in smaller numbers, anyway," Nikon said.

I didn't want to think how we were going to manage this impossible task. "We should get going. The sooner we go, the more likely we'll miss the high priest and discover what he's been up to."

"That makes sense, but there's one more thing I wanted to clarify," Zoe said. "Did you and Nikon really plan on apprehending the Reding and Vading, instead of letting us execute them like we planned?"

I hesitated, but only briefly. "Yes. We both thought it would be for the best. We tried talking to you about it, but it didn't go over as well as we would have liked. We made alternate plans instead, though it turns out no one's plans worked out."

"I'm sorry I didn't listen. I know now you were making a better choice."

"Maybe. We think they should be held accountable for what they've done, but I'm starting to think the Reding's biggest crime is ignorance."

"I would have to agree."

"You won't hear me complain about that assessment," Nikon said. "Older brothers can be a pain, though, so I may not be the best judge."

I snickered. "It's good we were able to speak with him. I hope it helps get us where we need to be."

"One can hope," Nikon said. And there was that note of optimism in his words that made me think he was rooting for his brother now, more than ever.

"We'd best get you both on the road," Zoe said.

I wished my parents were here to say goodbye to, in case I ended up down the river for good. "When my parents arrive, will you let them know what's going on?"

"Of course," Zoe replied.

We quickly gathered together what supplies we had, and Zoe

asked, "Are you sure you don't want to come back to Hupsheta's? We could make certain you were more prepared."

"No," I said, at the same time as Nikon said, "Absolutely not."

That we could definitely agree on, though I wished I knew more of what was going on with him.

I reached out for Zoe, and she gave me a hug. "I'll miss you, dear friend. Please, be safe," I said.

"I'm more worried about the two of you." She shivered. "I hope the Reding can keep the high priest away long enough for you to do what's needed."

That made two of us.

CHAPTER TWENTY-FIVE

I missed Zoe and Kaius already, but Nikon and I had Tewy with us. If he brought trouble along the way, though, I'd come to regret it.

It was going to be a long journey, but we'd had long journeys before. Pesky grains of sand slipped into my sandals as we walked. I did my best to ignore them. We'd decided to go through the desert until we got past Sirya. There, Nikon planned on buying or stealing a boat, to take us down to Peka Tower. Not many traveled that way, so we wouldn't run into others we needed to worry about—most likely. Plus, everyone should be focused on Sirya, as preparations for the high priest's arrival should begin at any hour.

"We should talk about our plans, going forward."

"Because it won't take long to be on the other side of Sirya?"

"Correct. We should be there a little after dark. It might be better to steal a boat when no one is around. Though it will draw attention, it will be less than if we purchase one and are seen going down the river."

True. The pang in my chest told me I wouldn't feel good

about it, though. "It's stealing. What if the owner needs the boat for their livelihood?"

"I know it's wrong but it keeps us from being more exposed."

"Can't we leave some money where the boat will be tied up?"

Tewy *ooooo*ed.

I wished he was on my shoulder instead of Nikon's, so I could pet him.

Nikon sighed. "I'd like to, but that would be more talk-worthy than a boat getting stolen."

I scowled. It was a terrible position to be in. Still, the country needed answers. *I* needed answers. Nikon and I would have to do what we could, to make that happen. Tewy would just be along for the ride.

"Fine, but know that I'm not happy," I said.

"That makes two of us. I'll find a spot safely downstream, where you can wait until I bring the boat over."

"Or I could save time and come with you."

He didn't respond.

I huffed. "It's going to be a dangerous journey, and a more dangerous destination. I might as well go with now, so we stay together."

"If I'm honest, I wouldn't mind. You're more than capable. I was thinking about Tewy. He's a good monkey when he wants to be, but I don't know if we can trust him to keep quiet."

Tewy gave an angry hoot and jumped onto my shoulder. There was one way to get him near when he wandered.

"Sorry, guy, but it's true," Nikon replied. "Cass, keeping you downstream with him will ensure he stays there and isn't within hearing distance of the shore. Or far enough away that his noises will be perceived as normal sounds of wildlife by the river."

I wanted to pout but was far too old for that. "I understand."

"I've upset you."

"Perhaps, but it's the way these things must be."

"Unfortunately."

Which meant I also likely wouldn't go in Peka Tower with him, to search. Just as well. If I was honest, it wasn't a place I was eager to go. I could wait outside with the best of them. And, I would still be out of the reach of the high priest.

We trudged through the sand, going around the city as the heat rose and fell for the day. I was tired—bone-achingly so—but the magic of the river should help with that.

When the faint sound of rushing water came to me, I relaxed some. Being on this side of Sirya was a step closer to where we needed to be. Antonia's warriors hadn't found us, and Theodore's people didn't seem to be coming after us. It was possible he did believe us, and was actually going to do what he could to help us.

I kept my voice low. "I have to admit, I'm anxious. What if this doesn't work out? What if there's no sign of why or how the water is tainted at Peka Tower? The high priest could keep all the information he has in his mind. This entire trip could be for naught."

"He's the type to keep copious notes. The real trick will be knowing what will be useful to take with us."

"Do you think he'll notice if we take anything?"

"Definitely, but by then, we should be long gone and on the way to Theodore. We'll figure this out, Cass."

I hoped so. "How close are we? The river sounds near."

"We're almost there. I think I see a spot for you and Tewy to wait."

Silly monkey, forcing me to stay behind. It might be for the best, but that didn't mean I had to like it. We went a dozen steps forward, turned, and took a couple more steps, vegetation brushing up against me.

Nikon said, "Need anything?"

"Just for you to be safe."

"I will be." He squeezed my hand. "I'll be back as soon as I can."

I didn't hear him go, but the warmth of him no longer clung to me. It was Tewy and me, until Nikon found a boat to steal.

I should have sat, but the nerves jangling through me kept me shifting from foot to foot. Tewy *oooo oooo*ed occasionally, but otherwise there was nothing but the soft sound of the river. It was so quiet, a crocodile creeping up on me from the river popped into my thoughts. I gripped my cane so I could smack the beast in the head if it came to it. I didn't come this far, through so much, only to be taken out by a hungry animal.

Trying to figure out what to do, I bit my lip. Nikon wouldn't have left me anywhere unsafe, but that didn't mean something couldn't meander along and find me. Though I wanted to know about the area and whether a creature like a crocodile would come upon me, I stayed still. I strained to listen for any sign of a wild animal approaching. Or worse, a person. Only the rush of the river met my ears.

All the trauma I'd gone through had me overreacting. Tewy or my cane would warn me. That didn't mean I was any less scared. I wanted to do something to calm my fears, but had nothing except Tewy. I ran my free hand through his fur, grateful he'd come with us.

Time kept dragging by, leaving me tenser and tenser.. It didn't help that he grew quiet, his little body becoming heavier. I pulled him into my left arm, cradling him while at the same time holding my staff so I could *thunk* anything that came by.

As Tewy fell asleep on me, I was jealous of his ability to sleep. Certainly, I could try to do the same, and Nikon would wake me when he returned, but the tension pouring through me wouldn't allow me to relax enough.

The night deepened, bringing a soft breeze of cool air, but no Nikon. It could be he was having a difficult time stealing a boat. Or worse, he might be captured.

I bit my cheek. It could be a long time while I was here alone, before I figured out if he would make it back. But no. Nikon would manage to get in and out of Sirya without anyone the wiser. He was smart and had lots of practice sneaking around. He'd be fine.

But if that was the case, where was he?

Time to think of something else. I couldn't keep pondering his well-being, when it left me fretting over things I couldn't control. Easier thought than done. The only other thing on my mind was what Peka Tower would be like. With the high priest and his neczar away, we wouldn't have much trouble.

I hoped.

"It's me." Though Nikon's soft voice eased a stretch of worry in me, there was a slight edge to it. "Can you hurry toward my voice? I'm being followed," he said.

Just what we needed—someone following and capturing us. I couldn't let that happen.

CHAPTER TWENTY-SIX

I rushed toward Nikon, Tewy stirring in my arms before settling back to sleep. He wasn't hooting and giving us away.

"Almost to me," Nikon said, as I swiped my staff in front of me.

Moments later, his calloused hand gripped my elbow and guided me into a boat which rocked beneath us as I climbed in.

I sat, and soon heard the soft dip of a paddle in the water, the vessel shifting more as we pulled away from land.

I wanted to ask about how he'd stolen the boat, but didn't know if it was safe to talk. Since he didn't say anything, I kept my questions to myself. Tewy curled up in my lap, blissfully unaware of the danger we were in. I almost wished I could be that ignorant, but I had some idea of what trouble we were facing.

As we went, I ran my hands around the boat. Though I couldn't reach far without getting up, there wasn't much to touch anyway. The wood curved out behind me, the sides not far from where I sat. If it was similar on Nikon's side, it was a small, two-person boat. We didn't need anything bigger. I hoped whoever he'd taken it from wouldn't be too put out.

More than that, I hoped whoever was following us didn't catch up.

As time wore on, my eyes grew heavy with sleep, the rush of the river and the rocking of the boat lulling me into a false sense of peace.

"We should be clear now." Nikon sounded rather breathless.

Maybe not so false after all. "We're no longer being followed?"

"We might be, but I've gotten us far enough ahead of them that we'll be fine. They may not have given chase very far. I left enough coin to pay for the boat."

"We're the strangest thieves ever."

He gave a soft chuckle.

"You're a good man."

He scoffed. "More like I have much to make up for."

I let the quiet shower down around us for a moment. It was easy to be thankful he was safe and we had a boat, but the fact that he was so hard on himself made me worry. There were some things I couldn't get around—things he'd have to overcome himself—but I wanted to do what I could to assist.

"Do you want to talk about it? I know it's hard for you to discuss your past life, but it could help."

He grunted. "I'm going to keep going for a while, as long as I feel awake enough and until I find a safe place to put the boat."

"I understand." And I did. He didn't want to talk to me about such hard things.

I let my fingers trail against the smoothed wood of the boat. How many people had Nikon hurt along the way? I had my doubts they were as many as he thought.

"Back when I lived at the pyramid, after my parents died and Theodore took over as the Reding, neither of us really knew what we were doing."

Nikon's words surprised me. I didn't expect him to get into how he felt, but since he was doing so, I sat back to listen.

"We let the high priest influence us the way he wanted us to go, mostly via messengers. And then came the time that Theodore fell in love. Antonia was... different. Angry. We followed her and the high priest's guidance more often than we should. It wasn't what I wanted, and deep down, I felt bad about it. Didn't matter, though. I hurt people who didn't deserve it."

It was hard to hear him being so down on himself, but I let his words wash over me anyway. He clearly needed to let them out. I leaned forward, to show him I wanted to hear more, without interrupting.

"I didn't torture people—not like the high priest did—but I didn't stop him, either. I should have put my foot down more. Should have let him know what I thought. Instead, I let him and Antonia put more ideas into my brother's head I didn't agree with. About the blind and the elderly. Things that he hadn't agreed with either before they came along. My parents weren't perfect by any stretch of the imagination, but Theodore always wanted to be better. Strived to be more. I thought I could help, and instead, I went down the dark path with him."

I let his words fade into the night, the silence between us filled with something else. Something more. I reached across the boat and rested a hand on his knee. For a brief moment, the oars stopped their dipping, before continuing on.

I hoped he felt what I wanted to convey, but words might help, in case he didn't. "It's hard when you go through a change, especially when you're younger and look to someone older than you, like the high priest. From what I gather, he's a force to be reckoned with. Believing in him—what he stood for and said—doesn't make you a bad person. If anything, you're stronger, for not only having left your brother, but also going back to teach him what you've learned."

"I wouldn't have done that if it wasn't for you," he said.

"There's no reason to say you wouldn't have come to the conclusion on your own."

"It was easy with you around, though."

"Sweet of you to say, but you need to give yourself more credit," I said.

The dip of the oars shifted. Nikon said, "The same could be said about you."

I softly laughed. "We'll have to work on it together, then."

"It's a deal."

I pressed my lips together. It'd been a whirlwind since I found my parents, but it didn't change a thing about how I felt toward him. If anything, despite his being the Reding's brother and not telling me about it, my feelings for him were deeper than ever. But there was a big obstacle in the way.

"Will Lavti stay locked up where you left her, while we're away?"

"She won't be going anywhere. Kilno and some of the other former warriors are making certain of that. We don't want her doing any more damage than she's already done to you. I fear she'd continue on that path, and she might tell what she knows about the rebellion. If Antonia or Valeriana got a hold of her, things would be very bad for all of us."

"It's good to know you have people you can trust."

The rowing stopped, and he grabbed my hand that rested on his knee. "You're the only one I trust."

Though he let go of my hand and I slid it back onto my side of the boat, warmth rushed up my fingers, to my arm and shoulder, filling all of me.

What was it about Nikon? If I didn't know it was impossible to fall in love with him, I'd think that was what I was doing. Or had already done.

The depth of my emotions—the strength behind them—surprised me. I wanted to love him and protect him and curl up against him. I licked my lips. Maybe there was more going on here than either of us thought.

"Nikon?" I asked.

"Hmm?"

"Do you think... That is to say, I..."

"What is it?" His rowing slowed but didn't stop.

I swallowed past the tightness in my throat. There had to be a way to explain what I felt to him, but I didn't know how to do so without sounding like I'd gone mad.

"I think that I... am about ready to stop for the night. If it's safe." I cringed. I shouldn't have chickened out, but without knowing what exactly I wanted to say, it was difficult to break through that barrier I'd put between us.

Or maybe he'd put it there.

Or we both had.

"I see a spot ahead we can use for the rest of the night," he replied.

With a sigh, I told myself it would be fine. This was exactly what I wanted. What I'd asked for. Nothing less, nothing more.

"Cass?"

"Yes?" My breath caught in my throat.

"If there's anything you ever want to discuss with me, you can. I know I make it hard when it's difficult for me to talk, but anything you want to know about my past or future? It's all yours. You are my best friend. Never forget that."

I turned away from his voice, knowing I wouldn't be able to hide my frown from him. "Best friends."

Too bad I wanted so much more.

CHAPTER TWENTY-SEVEN

The hours blurred together, as we continued downstream. We stuck to safer conversations that didn't leave me satisfied, yet I also didn't have to face feelings of wanting more from him.

Tewy grew bored with our journey, and played around the small boat like a crazed thing as we went down the path of the dead. It wasn't a path people travelled often when they were alive, except the high priest and perhaps those who lived in Madayah. They didn't tend to leave their dwellings often.

Because of this, we didn't pass many other people. The few we did cross paths with gave a brief *zaykai* as they headed up the river. I wanted to warn them of the chaos in Sirya and surrounding cities, but maybe it was just as bad where they came from.

Though the path of the dead was taken by all who finished their mortal life, save the rulers, no one knew what waited for them in the beyond. A similar chasm on the way to my old house at the waterfall awaited those who went to the end of the river. Once you went down, no one knew of a way to get back up, if there was one. Hence we only sent the dead and mummified.

As we headed out on the morning of the third day, I asked Nikon, "Do you think we'll reach Peka Tower today?"

"Yes. We won't go much farther before we'll have to find a place to stop."

Tewy hooted a happy note. Though he'd been a good travel companion, he had to be as sick of the boat as we were. "That's right, boy. We're almost done," I said. Then it would be on to greater danger. I turned to Nikon. "Is there going to be a spot to leave the boat safely? And a way for us to sneak up on Peka Tower?"

"It's surprisingly lusher here than other parts of Eppla are. Well, by the river, anyway. The rest of it is a sand desert, like most of Eppla. But the vegetation is thicker down here. From what I remember, we should have an easy time getting to Peka Tower, but getting in it will be another story."

"Warriors or more neczar there?"

"Both."

Not comforting in the slightest.

He added quickly, "With the high priest gone, though, it may be better than I remember."

"That might help." I hoped. "How is the inside? Is it very well guarded? And how big is it? I always imagined it to be a small tower, and no other houses."

"To answer your last question, it is a tower but a vast one. It's like a village in a single building. There are no other buildings around. I wish I knew more about how it was guarded in the high priest's absence, but every time I was here previously, it was to see him."

I had to interrupt, because we hadn't talked about this. "Would he remember you?"

The water splashed by for a moment, before he replied, "It's doubtful he'd recognize me on sight. I always went as a warrior or elite warrior. Because of that, I was in the background, as more of a listening ear for Theodore than anything else."

Tewy scampered around the boat, somehow finding more of an area to play about in than I thought he could.

"And inside of Peka Tower? What's it like? You said an entire village could fit in the building, but do you have any ideas where we would find any information?"

"I'm not going to lie, Cass. It's going to be hard." Nikon's voice was tight.

I expected as much, but it made me frown.

He continued. "Unlike in Sirya, when we went to the dungeon to rescue your parents, the places most likely to have information won't be easy to get to."

"You call Sirya's dungeon *easy*?"

"Eas*ier*. By far."

"Such a relief." I couldn't help the sarcastic bite to my words. "What are we dealing with?"

"A lot. Instead of being at the bottom of the tower, his main resources are toward the top levels. The only thing above them is an open roof with short walls, so the high priest can enjoy the nice view. I've never been there, but I passed by his area once, and the only access was through a narrow stairway, which is certain to be well guarded. I'm hoping it's easier to get inside, but we'll have to think of a way to get past the guards on that level, both going in and coming out."

"So if we'd brought the others with us, they wouldn't be of much use."

"Which is one reason why I didn't try to get more people to come with us. A death sentence on the two of us is bad enough; taking others down with us would be worse."

The realization hit me like a sphinx to the stomach. "You don't think we're going to make it." It was more statement than question, but he answered.

"No."

"Then why are we bothering?"

"Because it's important to attempt. Theodore believes in us, but if he didn't, the country deserves more than it is getting—even if this doesn't end up as well as we hope, we have to try."

I straightened. Wasn't that the truth? "We'll do our best." And possibly lose our lives in the process, but I wanted better for everyone. This was worth the risk.

Another thought occurred to me. "Can you tell if the water is tainted? I haven't noticed anything different with it, but I haven't thought to check."

"It's the same as it always was when I grew up, so if it's different, there's no way for me to tell."

Good point. The thought that I'd spent so much time in it made me shiver.

"We're almost to a spot that will work," Nikon said.

I hoped I wasn't taking Nikon to his death. I'd never forgive myself if I cost his life.

I had to do this, like he said. "We should have left Tewy with Zoe."

"Do you think he would have stayed with her?"

I sighed. "Probably not."

"He's a smart monkey. He'll be good. Won't you, boy?"

The shuffling around the boat stopped, and Tewy's pattering headed straight for me, as he *ooo oooo*ed.

"You are good," I said to him, his hand wrapping around my finger. "Just don't turn us in, this time."

He hooted, hopefully in agreement. Not that he could understand. Or maybe he could, but might not be able to help himself, should he feel the need to chatter.

It wasn't much longer until the boat bucked against the ground, causing me to shift on my seat.

Nikon slipped softly into the water and shoved the boat farther. He said, "Give me your hand, and I'll help you out."

I held my arm out toward his voice, letting him assist me out while I kept a hold of my cane. The warmth sparking from his touch raced up my arm, filling me. Whatever it was, it seemed to be happening more frequently. It made me want to touch him. To be near him.

I let go. He was in love with another, even if he hated her at the same time, and I couldn't forget that. I headed away from the boat, moving my cane before me. Tewy hooted softly from behind me. When I felt like I was a good distance from the boat without going too far so I would stay near Nikon, I stopped and turned back toward the river.

A faint scratching of something heavy being moved across the sand reached my ears. Nikon moving the boat, no doubt, hiding it in the vegetation he mentioned. As long as we didn't come back to it missing, or finding a bunch of scorpions in it, we'd be fine.

Though going up the river would be slower without it if we couldn't get back to it.

Nikon took my hand in his, shooting more warmth up my arm. "Are you ready?"

I wanted to shake my head. Only an insane person would be ready to storm the high priest's sanctuary. But I must be insane, because I wanted to help my country. As it was, breaking in was our only option. "As ready as ever," I said.

He squeezed my hand, and I took his elbow before he guided me away from the river. "Where's Tewy?" I asked.

"On my shoulder."

"Good. What are we going to do about the sunlight? Won't they see us?" I took care to keep my voice low.

"Not if we stick to the plants. They go most of the way around the tower, close to the building. We'll wait until dark to break in, but we should be able to figure out if there's a back way in."

"Do you think one exists?"

"I never saw one when I was here before, but there's a precedence for it."

Our steps were softened by the greenery beneath us. It was

more silent than sand, if nothing else. What was it? Would we leave tracks?

SOMEONE LIKE NIKON could probably follow us. Or worse, Valeriana or the neczar. Were they searching for us?

That led to another thought. What about Hupsheta? She wanted something from Nikon, and he'd promised it to her. Whatever she wanted couldn't be good. Though I'd tried to ask him about it, he'd never wanted to discuss it. I'd like to think she'd forget about it, but knowing her, she'd find a way to ask for more. She'd get every grain she could from him, no matter the cost.

I kept the thoughts to myself as we went on, and tried to shove them away. No sense in worrying about them now, when I had enough things on my mind. Besides, we likely wouldn't live to have to bother with Hupsheta's request.

Though there were a few sounds of animals—mostly the chirping of birds—it was otherwise silent of people. It was difficult to imagine Peka Tower loomed over us without human noises.

I kept my cane, not only out in front of me, searching for things I could bump into, but also ready to take it apart if needed. I wouldn't let the warriors capture us without a fight, which was what it would come to if we didn't figure out a way in that was safe from prying eyes.

That gave me an idea. "Can we climb to the top?" My muscles ached at the thought of more climbing, but I'd recovered enough I could manage.

"It wouldn't be as easy as climbing down the pyramid in Sirya." Though he sounded as if he was giving it some thought.

I couldn't imagine it going well, but we would have the advantage of arriving straight at the high priest's rooms at the top.

"How tall is the tower?" I asked.

"Taller than the pyramid." He sounded lost in thought.

And why not? That would be a lot of surface to travel up. If we could get to it from the top, that would possibly be the safest as far as running into warriors went. Yet, it'd be a long way to climb up. My arm twinged where I'd been cut, as if the pain was a response. It might be healed, but it might not be ready to climb up something that grand either.

"I don't think I can make it to the top," I said.

"It would be difficult, but if we can climb a ways, windows start about a quarter of the way up. High enough to discourage people from doing what we plan to, but low enough that we could make it."

Tewy gave a soft *oooo*.

Of course he'd agree. He was a monkey. For him, climbing was as easy as breathing. I rubbed my forehead. "Would we be seen before we made it to a window? Is there a safe way for us to climb up? Once we got there, would we be able to get in?"

"All good questions." Instead of answering, he led me farther down the path we'd trodden. I didn't stop to ask him more.

The breeze picked up, playing with my hair and bringing with it a foul stench. It was faint but made for an awful, nose-cringe-worthy wind.

Before I could comment on it, Nikon said, "We can do this. Most people would be discouraged by looking at it, but you don't have that problem. The fact that you came up with the idea proves you can think about things differently. That difference may help us get in with fewer problems."

"You said *fewer problems*, not *no problems*. What's the trouble going to be?"

"It *is* high."

I groaned inwardly.

"And—"

"Don't say *and* anything. I can't handle more than that height." I stopped, crossing my arm over my cane and gripping it tightly with both hands.

"It won't be easy, but it will be our best chance to get in and discover what is going on."

If the information was in there, to begin with. I hated that I thought it could be otherwise. "All right. Tell me."

"It's high, and there's a moat around it."

I harrumphed. "This is the best option? Sounds like it's not possible. It's not as if we have rope."

"There's many stones jutting out. We'll be careful not to fall. Honestly, I'm more worried about me than you and Tewy." And yet, he sounded so confident.

"This is really the best way in?" I didn't want to be skeptical, but I was. Didn't matter, though. If he thought this was the way to go, it probably was.

"It is."

"Then, let's try." And hope to all the sands neither of us got caught by the warriors in the process or fell to our deaths.

CHAPTER TWENTY-EIGHT

The wait for sunset annoyed me, but it gave Nikon a chance to scout out the best place for us to climb. Of course, the longer we took, the more my nerves rattled inside my chest.

Tewy had been surprisingly quiet on my shoulder. He didn't seem intent on giving us away, and he'd be able to climb on his own. That, or he'd stay here and we'd come for him when we were done. I had a feeling he'd create a fuss if he didn't come with us right away. Another thought hit me, leaving a tangle of worry tightening in my stomach. "What about my cane? How are we going to get it up there?"

"I'll strap it to my back."

Though relief filled me, I had to ask, "Can you climb like that? Not that long ago, you were worried about making it up there."

"It'll be fine."

And I believed him. The only nerves left now were those about getting up the side of the tower myself, and not getting hit by an arrow while doing it. I trusted Nikon to lead us. It wasn't because I couldn't see—that might actually give me an advantage in the dark. It was more because I'd never done anything like this before. Seemed like a horrible way to try it for the first time.

Nikon said, "It's pretty dark outside. Your dress is lightweight enough that we'll be fine in the water. Hopefully it doesn't weigh too much once we get out."

"And your clothes?" The question brought heat to my face, but I had to ask.

"I took off my armor and stashed it. The rest should be fine."

"Going without armor doesn't sound *fine*." Not when we were going into what was likely to turn into a fray.

"I'll be careful."

I grabbed a hold of his arm, the prick of worry mixed with the heat going through me. "Be more than careful."

"If I can, I will be. How about that? But if your life is in danger, I'll do what I have to."

I hated the thought of him giving his life or becoming seriously injured. I couldn't do this without him, but I also didn't want to lose him. There were no good options.

"See that you do," I said.

He moved so my hand was fixed more securely on his arm, and led me forward. "The moat won't be far. Take off your sandals. You ready for a swim?"

"As ready as I'll ever be."

"Good enough."

The stench from earlier wafted through the air, getting stronger the farther we went.

"What is that smell?" I asked.

"Erm... the moat."

I rolled my head back up to the sky. Why did the sands hate me so much? I didn't want to think about what we'd be swimming in.

"We'll have to keep quiet from here on out," he said.

He probably just didn't want to hear me gripe about it. Either way, I nodded—though I hadn't a clue if he saw—and went forward. We continued for a dozen and a half steps, before he stopped and whispered faintly in my ear, "Moat."

We were here, then. My eyes burned, but I took my next step as he guided me. Compared to the coolness of the night, the water wasn't bad—as long as there were no creatures hidden in it, waiting to snap us up. I stepped in further, handing my cane to Nikon. It'd do me no good here. He took it, adjusted for a moment with a shuffling, and returned to guiding me.

I slogged through the muck, attempting to move quietly while not breathing. Only a few steps, and I was in up to my chest, trying not to gag. Mud—*or something*—squished between my toes. It'd better not cause problems when I started climbing by making things slick.

The moat grew deeper. I wanted to ask Nikon how bad it was going to get and how wide it was, but I didn't dare speak. I soon had to start swimming instead of walking, while listening for the slight sounds Nikon gave, to guide me where we were going. I oh-so-carefully felt in front of me when I could, so I didn't bang my head on the tower. With everything about to happen, a head injury wouldn't help our problems.

The water grew colder the farther I went, chilling me, but more than that was the size of the moat. I'd expected it to be several body-lengths long, but it kept going. If the tower was as big as Nikon said, it made sense to have a huge moat around it.

And the smell of it... *Uck*. If we made it into the tower, the smell on us alone would give away our location. I was shocked Tewy wasn't putting up a fuss.

Nikon kept going, and I followed.

Many strokes later, he slowed and then stopped, to whisper, "Here."

I reached forward and came into contact with a man's chest, only thin cloth between us. My cheeks heated, as I brushed my hand away and treaded water. I might touch him a lot, but I usually didn't get this much into his personal space. It left me wanting to place my hand back on his chest and swim closer.

The stench cut off any more thoughts that tried to surface. As it should. I wanted to explore what was between us—but when our lives weren't in danger.

Nikon whispered, "You go first. I'll catch you if you need it. Just go straight up."

Straight was a relative term, but I'd try my best. He'd have to correct me if I went off kilter or overshot. I reached out, to find the wall I needed to go up. Nikon grabbed my hand and led it to my right a little, where there was a protrusion in the stony exterior.

Here went nothing.

I pulled myself up, water and gunk sluicing off me, as I felt around for another handhold. Below me, Tewy left out a soft *ooo*. That had better be all the noise he made, or we would be found.

Though I continued my ascent, my hands and arms shook, mostly out of worry someone might shoot us down with a bow and arrow or was waiting at the top with their sword. With any luck, it was a dark night and they wouldn't spot us. I had to get the shivering under control, though, or I'd never make it as far as I needed. I wished it was sunny and warm while dark and shadowed at the same time.

I reached up and found another stone, jutting out enough that I could grab on to it while feeling around with my foot for a place it could rest. I continued searching for handholds and footholds as I went.

It didn't take long, for my arms and legs to ache. Though I exercised often before my capture, my body had been through much. Despite the healing process, my muscles were exhausted. Still, I found the handholds fairly easily, which made the way up faster than it would have been otherwise.

As I pulled myself up, I reached out my other hand, searching for another jutting stone. This place was uneven. Sure, it was straight up and down, but there were more stones to grip onto than expected. Perhaps it was because the neczar and the high priest were usually here to stop unwanted visitors. That and the moat. Though the latter was disgusting, it'd only succeeded in making me cold and stinky. It hadn't hindered us much.

I shook from exhaustion but kept moving. I placed my hand on the next handhold and pulled myself up, when voices caught my attention. As soon as I was steady, I froze.

My heart beat faster, and I sucked in shallow breaths. The voices neared, but came from below. Though I couldn't make out what they were saying, I feared they were Peka Tower guards. If they were here protecting it, things could quickly go bad.

As best I could, I hugged the wall. Despite that, I was conspicuous, hanging here. They would find us at any moment. Assuming we were an *us*. There hadn't been a sound from Nikon since we started up. Tewy either. They had to be close by, though. Wherever he stood on the wall, he would be cautious about our next steps forward.

The voices grew louder, as I realized holding still was worse than moving forward. I didn't know how long I could hang here. Probably not long. I paused my thoughts as the words drifted up to me.

"We'll have to play our game of lin before the high priest gets back in."

"Tomorrow night is our last chance. You on guard then?"

What? The high priest was almost here? I thought he was going to stay in Sirya longer. If things went bad, we might be in Peka Tower when he returned. If they didn't go south, he'd be on the river, and we'd have to pass him on our way out of here.

"Nope. I'll spread the word."

"Just don't tell Kimput. He's such a sore loser."

The voices faded back out of comprehension, while they continued to murmur. I'd almost forgotten I was hanging on a wall while they drew my thoughts toward the high priest, but with them so close I couldn't move, my body grew heavier than ever.

I leaned into the wall, bracing myself against it. My foot slipped, sending a pebble or something like it tumbling to the moat below with a *splash*. It was a far longer drop than I thought.

It could have been me.

"Did you hear something?" a guard asked.

"I did," said the other.

Oh no. I'd drawn attention to us—exactly what I wanted to avoid.

Instead of trying to become one with the wall, I hung here, not moving a muscle.

"In the moat, maybe?" the first one asked.

"Maybe, but it wasn't a person. No one is stupid enough to go in that muck."

Ugh. What exactly was in there? No. I wouldn't think about it.

The guards went on.

"Sounded like it came from over here, though."

"It was probably an animal."

"I don't know..."

Couldn't they give up and move on? The longer they stayed around, the more likely they were to find us. If we were discovered here, we were in far too vulnerable a position to do anything about it.

My tense muscles shook. I could only hope they didn't knock something else off the wall. It'd been far too long a climb already, with a great chance of falling. The memory of how long it'd taken that pebble to splash was etched clearly into my mind. I couldn't let that be me.

"Come on," one of the guards finally said. "Let's finish our rounds."

"If someone's here, though, it'll be our heads on the line. You know how he's been, lately."

I winced at both the dedication and the fact that, if we succeeded, I would be the cause of someone else's trouble. It wasn't like everyone who served the high priest did it because they wanted to. Maybe some had to. That was what I kept telling myself.

With my body aching, I gritted my teeth, trying to stay put and not fall. As the two guards moved closer, thoughts of what I could do to throw them off the trail swarmed me. Nothing useful came to mind. I was unable to move, except to climb up, which would only create more noise and give us away.

With any luck, Nikon would think of something, though he seemed just as stuck as I was.

"I could have sworn I heard something right now."

"It's not worth it. No one would dare break into the place. The high priest would turn them into one of his experiments. It was your imagination."

What exactly were those experiments? The guards had to have a better idea than I did. It'd be nice if they mentioned something, though my arms wanted them to hurry along.

"Was not. You heard it too. You're just eager to see Belta."

I silently urged them to leave. The one appeared to want to.

A shuffling came from below. Maybe Nikon had knocked something off this time.

"See? There's something out here."

Blast the sands.

Tewy gave an angry screech from down below, far closer to the voices than I thought he'd be. What was he doing?

I clamped my jaw so tight it ached, but I didn't care. There had to be a way to get us out of this, but now they'd know for certain we were here.

"Look at that. It's just a crazed monkey."

Tewy shrieked again, his voice sounding farther away. I could have throttled the little guy if he was within arm's reach. Why did I bother to stay put, when he'd already given us away?

I tried to work past my pain, into more clear thoughts.

They hadn't found us. Didn't know we were above them. They thought it was Tewy. They could discover us, though, if they used their brains.

My little monkey's voice got farther and farther away. I didn't know whether to hope they chased after him or not. I didn't want him captured, but neither did I want them staying here. My heart thudded so hard against my ribcage, it would pound out at any moment.

"Let's go," the warrior said.

"I don't know. Something strange is going on. I've never seen a monkey here before. Have you?"

"Never thought much about it. We're going to miss check-in if we don't hurry. We shouldn't let an animal get us in trouble."

Yes, yes. Go check in. I hoped Nikon was managing well through all this.

"Fine, but we're bringing The Third here, to sniff around. Make sure there's nothing around."

"You're overreacting, but we'll do it if it makes you feel better. Come on. Let's go."

What was *The Third*, and should we be worried about it?

They were finally leaving.

I waited until a long moment had passed after they were gone from within hearing distance. It was probably time to get moving.

Nikon whispered from slightly below me. "Move. As fast as you safely can."

Clearly, we were in trouble.

CHAPTER TWENTY-NINE

I put on a burst of speed, while careful not to do something dumb, like falling. I didn't know how high up we were, but we'd scaled enough, and that pebble had dropped what sounded like a dangerous height.

And now we had *The Third* to deal with.

I reached up to find a handhold and pull myself up, and then did it all over again. Despite the cool night air, I was soon sweating, my hands feeling as if they wanted to slip from the stone.

Why, oh why, did I ever suggest going this way? What a bad move. I couldn't believe Nikon went for it.

Half a dozen more steps up like that, and Nikon said from far closer than I would have guessed, "There's a window just above us. I'll check it out and be back as soon as I can. Will you be all right?"

"Just hurry." And I'd do my best and hope it was good enough. If I failed, not only would I be taking a different path down the river of death, but Nikon would also never forgive himself.

I didn't hear a thing, as I worried about brave Tewy. No hint of him, moving up and over to the window. Nothing from the open space, either. I hoped that was a good sign, and didn't mean the warriors were quietly waiting for someone like us to come sliding in.

As the quiver in my arms grew stronger, I tried to lift all my weight on the left side of my body while holding on with my right hand, letting one side have more of a break. The rest didn't do anything except upset my balance.

Then a question hit me. We'd barely made it up here, with no little trouble. How would we ever make it back down?

We'd figure it out. Find a way. But if we discovered items like more papyrus we needed to take with us, it'd be difficult. We couldn't get them wet. Instead, we'd probably have to fight a horde of warriors.

I sagged. What would we do? And what about Tewy, who was out running wild? My sweet monkey probably saved our lives, but I hoped it wasn't at the expense of his own.

Would we meet up with him again? My stomach twisted, as worry gutted me. This had better be worth it.

"Cass, there's no one up here. Come straight toward my voice. There's a ledge not far up, and I'll help you." Nikon's words gave me something else to focus on.

I climbed up with drained arms, until I reached the ledge he'd mentioned.

Nikon wrapped his arms around my torso and pulled, as I hefted myself up. Once I was all the way in, I stumbled against him, arms and legs cramping. How had he managed to help me up after such a climb?

Bracing myself against him, his arms wrapped around me, I was safe. We both breathed heavily, my arms and legs feeling like they were full of water—heavy and liquid. But with his arms around me, I almost felt like we could do anything as long as we did so together.

"Where are we?" I whispered, trying not to think we abandoned Tewy.

"A storage room, from the look of things." His voice stayed low as well.

"What about Tewy?" I couldn't ignore his absence any longer.

There was a shuffle of movement, and I moved back to the window with Nikon.

Nikon said, "He's climbing up the wall now."

"Really?" Hope made my voice squeak.

Before he could respond, a scamper came from the window and toward me. Though my arms were tired, I let one down, for Tewy to climb. He hopped right up, as if it was no trouble. We weren't as used to climbing around and getting into things as he was. For him, this was just another day. Except he'd distracted those warriors from finding us.

"Thank you for your help, Tewy," I said.

He yanked on my hair, but I didn't mind.

"We have to go," Nikon said.

"Right. *The Third*. What is it?"

"A three-headed dog that's good at sniffing things out. I'm hoping it doesn't realize we've come here, but if it does and they bring it inside, we'll have all of Peka Tower on us in minutes."

"What about our pungent stench?"

"Nothing we can do about it at the moment."

I held out a hand. "Lead me. I'll keep silent."

He gave me my cane and his arm as Tewy rode on my shoulder, and we hurried forward. Weak, I continued along, anxious for us to do our job and be far from this place. A door squeaked, and as we rushed out, a new foul scent hit me. *Ugh*. What was that? It wasn't like the reek of the moat. It was almost like bad eggs. Really bad eggs.

It didn't seem to affect Nikon, who continued on. We went some distance down what I thought was a hallway, from the way my cane stopped on the edges and the air didn't circulate.

Nikon stopped, and I followed suit, blood pulsing in my ears to the point where I couldn't hear if someone was nearing. After a moment, we started up again and soon turned to the left. We made three more turns, going different directions, before he led me up a set of stairs. They weren't wide enough for us to go side by side, so I reached forward as he reached back, and managed a sort of awkward shuffle.

When the floor flattened out again, I was grateful—until we went up more. And higher and higher and higher.

My breathing came out heavy—so much so, it was a wonder all of Peka Tower didn't drop down on us. When Nikon had said it was huge, he'd been serious. This place was more massive than the biggest building I'd ever been in, the pyramid in Sirya. How had they managed such a feat?

A pain pierced my side when were partway up yet another flight of stairs. Voices sounded from behind us, footsteps approaching. Nikon put on a burst of speed that sent me racing to keep up. Tewy stayed wonderfully silent—more so than I could say for myself, since I made such a racket. Even my steps were loud. With any luck, if those below us heard us, they'd think it was someone who belonged in the tower. Unless The Third had already been let loose, and they were hunting us down.

I made like the sphinx was after me again. This was bad. As much as I wanted to keep going, I'd need a rest, sooner rather than later. Slowing down wouldn't be enough; I needed to stop. Yet here we were, going faster. It wasn't a pace I could keep up long, but if I wanted to stay alive, there was no other choice.

With only a little warning from Nikon's position, the stairs ended at a flat landing. Instead of continuing up, like we had been, Nikon burst to the side.

I followed him, wishing I knew a way to throw the guards off our trail. If I had some magic sand, maybe... Without it, and this being an unfamiliar place, it was not happening.

The stench was stronger on this floor. Like so many eggs had gone rotten that I hoped no one wanted to follow us. I didn't want to follow.

We whipped around a corner, and Nikon brought us to a halt.

I heaved a breath, trying to keep my gasps silent. It was near impossible, with the amount of exertion we'd just done. I put my hands to my sides and bent in half, attempting to slow my heart and get rid of the stitch in my side.

Though we'd gone some distance from the stairs, the voices could still be heard, and they were coming closer. I put my hand to my mouth, as Nikon grabbed the arm of the hand I was holding my cane in. He pulled me back farther, away from the sounds.

Despite my efforts to quiet my breathing, it came out loud. It was like I was blowing a horn, to let them know where we were. I softened my steps as much as I could, though I could faintly hear them while no sound came from Nikon. If he wasn't holding on to me, I'd think he'd abandoned me. Of course, he wouldn't do that, but with my other fears rising, I ruled nothing out.

The voices came closer, bringing with them an urgent need for us to be hidden. If there was a place to hide, I didn't know it, and Nikon might not either. We were going to be found out before we got any information that could stop the high priest and what he was doing to the water.

We turned another corner but only went a little farther before we stopped. Nikon took my free hand and held it to his chest. His breathing came out ragged, by the way his torso moved, but I couldn't hear it over my own.

I wanted to ask why we stopped, but didn't dare speak. The voices came closer, talking of things I didn't have a clue on or care about.

"Three-Five-Two is coming along. The high priest will be happy upon his return."

"We'll need that. He's been grumpier than usual, of late."

"You're telling me. Ever since Eight-Five was a loss, he's been extra terse."

That wasn't a kind way to talk about the intermediary between magic and the people, but knowing he wanted me for something to do with my blindness and wasn't asking nicely, I didn't feel bad for him.

These people had to be talking about the experiments he was doing. If only they'd say more.

"That's putting it lightly," one of them said.

They were so close now, sounding as if they needed to just round the corner to find us. Nikon moved our hands to the hilt of his sword. I braced myself to undo my cane into fighting sticks. If we had to take these two warriors down, it wouldn't be long until others realized they were missing and came after us. *Sand it.*

"Enough of a break, you two. Get in here," a new voice said.

"Coming."

Moments later there was the *click* of a door shutting, and then silence. I slumped against the wall, grateful we'd lucked out. Must have been a fairly thick door.

Nikon whispered in my ear, "You all right?"

I shook my head, my lungs burning from the exertion of getting up here. The stench didn't help. "Need break," I whispered back.

"Understood."

We could have kept going down the hall, but a door opened next to us. I braced for shouts of discovery, but Nikon led me away from our spot. He must have been the one to open the door, for one minute we were in the hall, and the next we were in a room the stink of which made my eyes burn.

We'd found a light reprieve, if no one else was in here, but it came at the expense of not being able to breathe because of the rotten-eggs air.

I coughed, unable to help myself. The fit didn't last long, but made me listen hard in case someone came running.

Nikon said in low tones, "We're alone."

"It stinks in here." Understatement. It was gag worthy.

"I'm not sure where we are exactly, other than this is the floor the high priest does his experiments on."

I shivered. "I heard a little about them at the pyramid. Do you know more?"

"Not much other than he tinkers around a lot."

"What could he be doing?" It was a puzzle we needed to solve, but I was shaky and worried for Tewy. "Where did Tewy go?

"He's exploring the room."

Good quiet monkey. "What should we do now?"

"Find a place to rest."

"Is it safe?"

"It'll have to be. Neither of us has the energy to fight, and Tewy can't take on all the warriors by himself."

That was true. "If that's the case, is there somewhere we can lie down or sit?"

"There are a couple of chairs. The only place to lie down is the floor, but I wouldn't do that. It's stained with... something."

Did he not know what it was, or not want to tell me? "Lead the way," I said.

With my hand on his arm, he took me farther into the room. It was larger than I originally thought, but not at all echoing.

Tewy let out an angry gibber, but it was thankfully on the quiet side.

I sat on the chair Nikon led me to, ready to take my cane apart, should someone come in and find us. "What happens after we rest?" I asked.

"I don't know, Cass. It's going to be hard."

If Nikon didn't know how we were going to get to the information we needed, I was next to clueless.

CHAPTER THIRTY

There had to be a way to get to the high priest's information. We might find something here, but I'd be shocked if what we needed was this easy to get—if you could call what we'd done so far *easy*.

"How many guards are typically around his quarters?" I asked.

"Hard to say. I don't know enough to give a good estimate. I just stumbled onto one of his experiment rooms," he whispered. "I could do some reconnaissance."

"No." The word was out of me before I could stop it. "It'd be better if we stayed together."

Tewy *ooo*ed in agreement.

"See?" I said. "Tewy knows."

"And I agree with you both. I just don't know what type of mess we're getting ourselves into, or if they're out searching for us already, with The Third."

As grateful as I was that we'd be resting, I was also worried about being caught here because we couldn't leave. "How far are we from the high priest's quarters?" I asked.

"Difficult to say. It feels as if we've come some distance, but as huge as the tower is, it could be many staircases yet. But knowing we've found the levels he uses for his experiments is good. When I came here before, that's where he kept his tests was near his personal rooms. I believe we're getting close, but that is a relative term."

Sand it all. The situation was beyond frustrating. I wanted to weep at the thought of continuing to climb, but for now, I could sleep.

"We'll figure it out." His voice was soft—not just quiet, but also gentle. "Try to get some rest now."

He was right. Whatever happened would happen, and stewing over it wouldn't help. I wished we'd brought some food and water with us to the tower and not left all our supplies in the boat, though neither would have made the trip through the mucky liquid.

I closed my eyes and sought a comfortable place to lay my head. Though I shifted many times, everything hurt. I had some time to rest despite the pain, and we were somewhat safe for the moment.

Relaxing was difficult. The longer we stayed, the more I worried we'd be found. Though this room stunk, perhaps it was rarely used. The thought left me relaxing more than before.

I closed my eyes, and the next thing I knew, sounds came from the hall outside.

I bolted upright, and Nikon gripped my upper arm. I went with him, as he led me deeper into the room. Hopefully to a stopping place that would hide us, should the people out there choose to come in.

The footsteps came closer as we moved. My palms grew clammy, as Nikon guided me under something and crouched down next to me, Tewy hanging on to my free hand. At least he was with us.

We could easily be found here. It didn't feel like we'd hidden ourselves well, but who was I to judge such a thing? Instead, the pounding came harder. So loudly, it could have been another set of galloping footsteps. And there wasn't a thing I could do about it.

The steps stopped, and the door opened with a whisper. Two people came in—one with a heavy stride, and the other with harder to hear, lighter steps. I told myself they couldn't see us—that Nikon had hidden us well—but it was difficult, crouching there and not being able to do anything. Not knowing how well we were covered.

Tewy tugged on my hand. I shook my head, internally pleading with him to not move or make a sound. He squeezed harder but didn't move. Yet.

"Is the high priest really going to be back early?" a woman asked.

"Tomorrow, if the forerunners are to be believed," a man responded.

Wait—what? That was earlier than they said previously. We were wasting time.

"And to think we've been able to avoid this room the whole time he's been gone. I'd be happy if he stayed away another month, like he originally planned."

"You'd better be glad I'm the only one who heard. Talk like that could get you sent to the dungeons—or worse."

"*Pish posh.* There's no point in beating around things with you."

Did her disdain for the high priest mean these two could be allies? It was something to consider, but unless they found us, I wouldn't be revealing myself. I couldn't chance missing knowledge that might help the country on such a whim.

"You know what the dungeons are like. I'd hate to see you go there," the man said.

"Are you turning me in?"

"No."

"Then I have nothing to worry about."

"Come on," the man said. "Let's finish up before you get any more *good* ideas."

A shuffling sounded.

"You're just sad they took The Third outside," she said.

Did that mean this man liked the three-headed dog the others didn't? It might be fun when it wasn't chasing after you, but I wasn't going to press my luck.

Tewy tugged on my hand again, harder than before. I wished I could comfort him or give him a reminder to stay silent. He was doing a great job—better than the pounding of my heart—but I couldn't tell him in that moment. I rubbed his chest, hoping that'd let him know.

"I don't know what you're talking about," the man replied.

How much longer would their cleaning take them? The longer it went, the less likely we'd get out of here unscathed, whether they had sympathetic leanings or not.

I bit the inside of my cheek.

The woman snorted, a rustle of footsteps approaching with her voice when she said, "We can pretend that, if it makes you feel better. I would lik— Come over here for a moment, would you?"

I stiffened. Did she see us? Catastrophe in the making.

But if that was the case, why didn't she come out and say there were intruders? Or scream for help? There were any number of things she could do if she'd seen us. I bit my cheek harder, my grip on my cane more awkward than I'd like if I was to fight, but I couldn't move it without attracting attention.

"What's that smell?" the man asked, coming over.

"You're joking, right?" she replied.

He made a loud sniffing sound. "Something stinks."

"Everything in here stinks."

The woman gave an exasperated sigh. Papyrus moved. Whatever was going on, it was good news for us. They weren't getting closer to Nikon and me. They were to our left, though their focus could change at any moment.

"Does the high priest mean to do this?" The woman's voice held a hint of fear.

"*Sands save us.* He's really trying."

What was he trying? This could be the information we needed. Or not. We were looking for something he'd already done or was doing. It could be a lead.

I wanted to growl in frustration. It was probably a mad scheme concerning the people he did experiments on. I wanted to help, if that was the case, but didn't know what to do.

"We'll be fine, though." She sounded more like she was trying to convince herself than him. "Just fine."

"Speak for yourself. I want a way out of this place."

"What will you do? Go down the south chasm? That's the only place the high priest can't touch. The rest of Eppla—all of it—is within his grasp. If we run, there'll be no hiding."

"Better dead there, than put through torture."

"He's not going to torture us. He doesn't know how we feel. It'll be fine."

This conversation grew more and more confusing. I wished them the best. I was less worried for myself at the moment than I was for their future. They were both clearly concerned about it, no matter what they said.

Nikon put a hand on my shoulder, steadying me. I was grateful for his presence, which calmed me and helped me keep quiet.

The rustling continued, like they were looking over papyri. I should have asked Nikon more about this room—what was in it and how everything was situated. I was stuck in a world I didn't know much about, wondering if I could fend for myself if I needed to.

These two didn't seem like much of a threat. No, the biggest threat was heading down the river toward us right now, but we'd be gone before he got here. If not, everything would be forfeit, because we couldn't escape this place with all the extra warriors and neczar he had with him.

"This only gets worse." The man finally broke the silence.

I bit my tongue, to keep from asking what.

The woman gasped. "This can't be right."

"But if it is..."

I gripped my cane harder. Of course they weren't going into more detail. They could at least have the decency to leave, though I suspected we were stuck with them for a while, given they only talked. If nothing else, I was growing accustomed to the stench.

Footsteps reverberated in the hall. Only one set, but they were thunderous. Whatever caused such a racket didn't sound like something I wanted to tangle with.

Nikon's grip on me tightened enough to let me know he was worried. Did he know what stomped down the hallway? It left me tense with his anxiety.

"Quick," the woman whispered. "Put them away."

There was a shuffling, before their footsteps hurried away. I almost relaxed, but Nikon's grip stayed tight. Though they were farther from us, he must believe we were in danger.

Before another word fell from their lips, the pounding steps stopped nearby and the door opened with a *bang*. A gravelly voice called out, "Why haven't you finished yet?"

"Sorry, sir," the man said. "There's much to do in here, but we'll get it completed soon."

"Don't be too much longer, or there will be consequences to pay."

"Understood."

There was a great sniffing sound, followed by a snuffling.

"Stinks in here. Can't smell a thing," the newcomer said.

The door slammed, as did the blood flow to my heart, as the pounding footsteps retreated. I bit my lip, to prevent myself from asking Nikon more about what or who came calling. It would have to wait until these other two left. At least the stench of the room covered the odor on our clothes.

"Let's hurry," the woman said.

"How can you be so calm?" the man asked her.

"Because you always talk to that thing, not me. Let's get going before it returns."

"Agreed. And you're welcome for speaking with that beast though I hate it."

They shuffled around, while I tried to puzzle out what *that thing* could have been. It must have been The Third.

They stayed silent as they worked; only the rustling and the occasional scruff on the floor gave any indication that they were continuing their task.

Time pressed on me. We needed to get moving. Despite our bodies' needing the break, with the high priest returning sooner than we thought, there wasn't much time to find the information we sought and get out of here.

When the door finally squeaked open and closed again, it surprised me. I hadn't expected them to go without another word. It was as if they were too afraid to speak, after whoever it was had spoken.

Nikon removed his hand, the blood flow in my arm restored. He shuffled forward next to me and said, "We've got to go."

Tewy gave a concerned hoot. He'd been well behaved—much better than I would have guessed he could be. Bless his little monkey heart. "You've been so good," I whispered. "Thank you."

"It's all going to be for naught if we don't get out of this part of the tower," Nikon said.

"What's going on?" I followed him, crawling forward on the floor, mindful he hadn't wanted me to lie on it previously.

Nikon's words made me forget all about the floor. "That was a neczar."

CHAPTER THIRTY-ONE

"I thought the neczar were all with the high priest," I said, fear and shock mixing together in a freezing conglomeration.

"Apparently not." Nikon ushered me forward, giving me a steadying hand to help me stand. He started again, but I didn't go with him.

"What were those notes they were talking about?" I asked. "The way they spoke of them, they seemed important."

"I don't know."

"We should take them," I said.

He'd have a hard time reading them, but if we could take them to someone who didn't struggle with it, they might help.

"The warriors will know we've been here."

I gave it a brief thought. "They'll know anyway. They've got The Third out already, and we'll likely cause a stir after we leave, whether we bump into anyone or not. Does it matter?"

He gave a half-growl, half-sigh. "No. I just don't want to get caught, though it's inevitable."

He let go of me, there was a rustling, and moments later, he settled my hand on his arm. "Got a bunch of them. We've got to move."

"Up we go." I tried not to let fear leak into my tone, but it was there anyway. Some of the neczar were here, and the high priest had previously wanted to capture me through them. Whatever came next, I wouldn't let them have me, Nikon, or Tewy. I wouldn't.

We slipped from the room, Nikon's steps as silent as ever and Tewy on my shoulder so quiet, I wondered what came over him. My monkey was never so silent and well behaved, but I'd take it while I could.

Though we stopped often, I assumed to listen for others, we wove our way back to the stairs without running into anyone. Sounds came from behind a few of the doors, which hadn't happened on the way up, but no one came out.

Much like before, we hurried up the stairs. Unlike before, though, it didn't take long for my thighs to burn from all the steps. One after another after another. We'd finish one level, only to go on to the next. The first few levels smelled similar to how the room had, though more faintly. It was easier to think about that, than process how much my body wanted to rebel.

The farther we went, the less it stunk, and the more another scent surfaced. It was more difficult to identify. Almost... coppery.

The higher we went, the more the tang filled the air. Along with the smell, noises drifted to us. At first, I paused. We were close to the end of the death river. A sign that the spirits lingered, perhaps?

Nikon tugged me forward. We couldn't afford the luxury of stopping. The more we climbed, the more I realized those voices weren't ghosts, but people.

Humans who were alive, but in a state of utter misery.

We were close to the high priest's quarters.

A noise like that would only come from an area that the high priest had full control over—even when he wasn't here. I sent a silent wave of hope to those we couldn't yet help. I wished we could save them from this place, but I didn't know if we could save ourselves. If we figured out how to undermine the high priest, though, and cause his downfall, it would lead to their release. What was he doing with them all, anyway? Was it because of the tainted water? I didn't know how exactly. Being here among it, despite not understanding it, left me ill.

My muscles trembled. It wasn't so much from exertion, though that was great, as from anticipation of what lay ahead. My thoughts tumbled around, jumping from those imprisoned here to the neczar and warriors, to whether we'd be able to escape. There was too much to worry about, and though I tried to push them away, the thoughts grew stubborn, sticking to me like the sewage I'd swam through.

A voice, clearer than the others, came from above, distant but definitely there if not something I could understand. It was a chance for me to come out of my morose thoughts.

Nikon pulled me to a stop and brought his mouth to my ear, making me shiver. "We're going to likely have to fight now, unless you have another plan."

"We could find someone who knows where the information is. Those two from before seemed knowledgeable, though probably not the right people to ask, unless we had a way to be sure they'd keep silent."

"We'll do our best, but no promises. You ready?"

Tewy shivered on my shoulder and hopped off. I asked, "Where did Tewy go?"

"He jumped on my shoulder. He'll be fine there, and he'll hop off if the fight gets too intense. He's done it before."

"All right. Let's go." Knowing what we were getting into, I wanted to run down the stairs, but I refrained. Too many people counted on us to find something up there.

"If it comes to a fight, I'm going to have to let you go. There are twelve stairs, before it levels out."

"Thank you," I said.

He squeezed my hand, leaving me wanting to thread my fingers through his. The snick of his sword being drawn, pulled me back. We continued up, my grip on him loose enough that I could grab hold of my cane and twist it into fighting sticks if needed. More like *when* needed.

I counted stairs as we went up. Eight. Nine. Why hadn't we heard anyone yet? Someone should have spotted us on the way, but it didn't seem to have happened. The voices were some distance off, near but garbled.

They hushed, and I gripped my cane.

Ten. Eleven. Twelve.

The floor leveled out. Being that we were at the top, I expected Nikon to let go and people to rush at us. Nothing happened.

I wanted to ask what was going on, but I kept the words to myself. The voices hadn't been far off enough that we'd go unnoticed, should I bring attention to us.

Nikon led us toward where the people seemed to be. Still nothing.

He jerked me to the side. Adrenaline pumped through me, as he pulled me into a tight alcove with him. His chest moved quickly, as if he was breathing fast. Despite the close quarters, Tewy remained quiet. If he could, then so could I, despite the questions burning my tongue.

Footsteps neared. People were coming. Nikon must have been hiding from them, though that didn't tell me how he knew they were coming. Perhaps he spotted them before they spotted us.

As they neared, I held my cane. If only I could maneuver, to get it into two pieces... But there was no room. The fight would come from behind me. Nikon would do what he could to protect me, but at this angle, it'd be a struggle for both of us.

Tewy stayed quiet, thank the sands. I tried to remain steady, to not give us away with a crazy movement or noise, but the need to move pulsed through me as the steps grew closer. I wanted to twist away from Nikon and face the challenge head-on, but there had to be a reason why he pulled us back here.

Trust. I needed to trust him.

As he continued to breathe hard, I calmed. If there was anyone who'd earned my trust, it was him. I attempted to keep that in mind, while I fought against the instinct to cover my back. The people came closer and closer. They were almost upon us. I didn't have a way to get to my fighting sticks.

As they came to us, I straightened, ready to whirl and pounce out. I waited for them to give some indication that they'd found us. There was no sense in giving us away, if Nikon thought we should be back here.

My muscles tensed, sending the ache of inaction through me. I wanted done. I steeled my limbs, to keep still despite the increasing desire to go. The fear of what could happen sent an acid-like feeling tumbling through me. It shocked, tensed, and pinched. Still, I held steady, as the people passed.

Wait. *They passed.* Why hadn't they stopped and attacked us?

We held still, and I did my best not to make a noise. Once their footsteps faded, Nikon whipped into action, moving back into the area they'd come from. I held on to him as he raced forward—he'd stop me from running into anything.

As we were running, a voice called out, "Where do you think you're going?"

I didn't wait for more of a warning. I let go of Nikon and untwisted my fighting sticks. I eased my knees so I could fight, but no threat reached my senses.

"We're here to make sure the high priest's rooms are prepared." Nikon sounded more commanding than I'd ever heard him before. He must have been pretending to be someone of import, probably at least as a distraction to get closer, but I hoped it didn't attract the attention of the neczar.

"You can't come in here and demand entry to the high priest's personal rooms. I'm goin— Fine, fine. No need to slit any throats. The high priest will have yours, though, should you go in there."

Nikon must have been showing them how serious his skills were.

"And yours," Nikon said. "Since we're going in there, no matter what you say or do, you might as well show us the way."

"Are you joking? He booby traps his door before he leaves." The man's voice shook with fear.

"There must be another way in, or a way to disarm the traps," Nikon said.

Tewy climbed onto my shoulder, though I wished he would have stayed with Nikon. It was dangerous out here, and we had a long way to go before it was secure. Despite that, having him near was comforting. I'd do what I could to keep him safe.

"I know of none." The man made a choking sound. "The high priest does sometimes appear in places we don't expect, so there must be secret passages, but I swear to you I don't know where they are."

Nikon mumbled something.

"What are you doing bringing a blind woman here anyway? Are you crazy?"

Nikon growled and the man squealed. "Sorry. It's just that it seems wrong with how the high priest treats the blind."

He wasn't wrong, but I also wasn't going to change my mind. We needed to find a way to get up to the next level where the high priest's rooms were. I couldn't think of anything. Well... except— "I don't relish the idea, but are his windows open? Are there windows here we could use, to climb to his window?"

"You're raving mad," the man said.

"No, she isn't," Nikon replied. "And you can go first and see if his window is open."

"I can't do that. Do you know how high up we are?'

I had a fairly good idea, from all the stairs we climbed.

"Where are the other guards?" Nikon asked, ignoring him.

"There are only three of us on this floor. The other two just left to do their rounds."

"Perfect," Nikon said. "To the window, and up you go."

"You're insane," the man said.

"Maybe, but all the more reason to listen, before we do something you can't come back from," Nikon replied.

Grumbling the whole way, the man walked away. I followed the sound of his voice and his steps, wondering if this plan would really work.

Moments later, there was a scuffing sound and a grunt. A gust of wind came my way. I was grateful for the fresh air. It was different up here. Cleaner. I stunk from the muck sewage, but this far away from it and somewhat used to my own smell, the scent of outside refreshed me. We'd climb up to the high priest's rooms, and then... Well, we'd figure it out when we got there.

Before long, Nikon whispered, "I'm following him. I'll call you when it's all clear. The window is almost straight up from here. If you climbed halfway up the tower, you can do this."

"I'm not worried about me; I'm more concerned with you," I said.

"I'll manage."

I felt the urge to pull him into a hug, but delaying him from following the guard could cost us, so I held back.

Nikon left in silence. The only reason I knew he was gone was the sudden loss of him next to me. Tewy jumped off my shoulder, and his scampering followed me. I carefully made my way to the window. There was a curtain that'd been pulled to the side. I ran my hand along the bumpy stone that made up the window, getting a feel for what I'd need to do, when I remembered I hadn't given Nikon my cane. I'd have to find a way to carry it.

"Cass, come up. It's clear," Nikon said.

That was faster than I expected. I ripped the bottom of my

dress, tearing off a strip of cloth, and made a makeshift sling, which I used to tie my cane around me well. The last thing I wanted was for it to fall and get lost. It was an extension of myself.

I carefully maneuvered it out the window, as I crouched through the opening and touched my hand to the outer wall next to me. The wind was brisker out here. It pushed against me with its cold fingers, daring me to tempt fate and come out onto the wall.

Though I didn't want to, I had little other choice. I heaved myself out, making certain I had good handholds along the way. It was as familiar as climbing before, but my muscles instantly ached. It was only one floor up this time, though. It couldn't be nearly as far as before. I could do it. I had to. My other choices were to get captured by the guards or fall to my death.

Death. Funny how that didn't scare me as much as it used to. I could deal with it, should it happen. I wasn't ready, but neither did I think it was as frightening as I once did. Perhaps going down the Death Path changed something in me.

I let my mind wander as I climbed, going through the motions without thinking about what I was doing.

"Almost there," Nikon said above me.

It wasn't so bad. I could do this. I'd make it easily enough. Then we'd be free to sift through the high priest's things and get answers. I reached up and pulled myself toward his voice. Halfway through, my fingers slipped, and I fell back.

A squeal of fear escaped me, as I struggled to hold on to the remaining one foot and hand. I flailed, seeking a grip I could stick with, hoping I hadn't called death upon me by being so cavalier toward it.

"You've got this, Cass," Nikon's voice curled around me, giving me strength.

My fingers found purchase, but the ledge was smaller than the others, and moments after I caught on, my fingers slipped again. My heart raced wildly, my breathing becoming erratic. I reached a second time and found a different jut that I was able to cling to.

I hung there, knowing I wasn't safe yet, but needing a moment to come to terms with the fact that I'd almost fallen off the top of Peka Tower. At least I couldn't see how long of a drop it was.

Once I caught my breath, I continued climbing, focusing more on my efforts. One. Two. More stones up. A hand wrapped around my wrist. Nikon. He hauled me up. Where did he get the strength?

When I made it through the opening—larger than below—he pulled me into a fierce hug.

"I thought you were going to fall," he said, an unusual quaver in his voice.

I hugged him back tight, unwilling to let go until my shaking subsided. Or never. I was good with that too. "I did as well."

Tewy chattered quietly, jumping on my shoulder that pressed against Nikon's chest, not seeming to care there wasn't much room for him. He put a hand on my cheek, his noises worried.

"I know, but I'm fine. We're all safe as we can be in this place."

Nikon lunged away from me with an, "Oh no, you don't."

Confused, I stayed there as the cold air nipped at me, leaving me alone without him for comfort.

"I can't be found, having helped you," the man said. "He'll do worse than torture me."

"Sorry, but we can't have you escaping to tell others what we're doing," Nikon said.

"They'll find out anyway, when I'm not at my post."

"But they won't know where we've gone for sure." For all the other guards knew, he'd run away. Besides, I wasn't feeling the most charitable toward him at the moment. He'd taken Nikon away from my arms. "Why don't we tie and gag him?" I asked. "Then we won't have to worry about him alarming others."

"Good idea," Nikon said. "Come here and hold the knife on him, so I can get him tied up. If he so much as breathes wrong, slice him through."

Not at all what I wanted to do, but I pretended like it was something I did all the time. "Consider it done."

I traced Nikon's arm to where it held the knife to the man's throat, and took it. As I stood there, Nikon ripped some items, before coming over and tying up the man.

"The high priest will find you. He won't let you get away with invading his space. He'll lock up the blind thing and kill you," the man said.

"I'm sure," Nikon replied.

All fell silent, save for the moaning in the distance. I hadn't paid much attention to it since we'd come up here, but it was louder than it'd been on the floor below.

Did I want to continue with this journey?

"Where do we start looking? What type of room is this?" I asked Nikon.

A heavy shifting sounded, as he replied, "Just moving our guard here, so he's harder to find. This is the final guard's room, the last protection for the high priest when he's in residence, I believe."

"Then we'd best get moving on, to where the high priest's private rooms are." Though I didn't relish the idea of going through his things, for fear of what might be lurking among them, we had to get answers.

CHAPTER THIRTY-TWO

Several rooms later, we were no closer to answers than before, though we were closer to the sounds of tormented people.

Since we weren't having much luck finding anything but rooms for cleaning supplies and storage of items such as blankets, we moved on.

The sounds from before—moaning and groaning—gained ground. It made me shiver. Whatever caused all these people to make these tortured noises had to be horrors beyond what I could imagine. We were getting ourselves into something we didn't understand. From the screams and moans, I could probably never understand.

The tormented voices followed us as we went further in the building, growing in both number and volume on all sides. The stench of unwashed bodies and urine stung my nose.

The anguished noises were so close, I should be able to reach out and touch them. I whispered, "Nikon, what do you see?"

Metal clinking sounded, like chains being dragged across stone.

"I'm not sure you want to know." His voice was soft.

I fisted my hand so tight on Nikon's arm, I worried I'd hurt him. "Tell me anyway."

He pulled me closer and put his arm around my shoulders, not breaking stride. "There are jail cells all around us, people mostly lying in them, though a few are milling about. All are not... Cass, it's the most horrid thing I've ever seen. They've been abused and abandoned in their own filth. They have food and water, but it doesn't look appetizing, though that appears to be the least of their worries. It's difficult to describe."

My stomach churned, trying to reconcile why the high priest would treat another human in such a way. What type of monster was he, using them to taint the water?

"Can we let them out? Save them?" I asked.

"To what end? First, I don't have a key. I could pick the lock, but we have no way of getting them out of here. Even with their numbers, there are more warriors and none are in good condition to fight their way out. Besides, I'm not sure *we'll* get out of here at this point."

"We can't leave them here." I brought us to a stop, as I tried to think of a solution. Nothing came to mind.

"I'm sorry. I don't know what to do. If I'd been the older brother and became ruler, things might be different, but I have no power over the high priest. I'm not sure anyone does."

"We have to tell your brother." The Reding could do something, if no one else could.

"It would probably lead to a civil war should my brother want to take him on. And the people, not knowing more about the high priest, might not want to take up arms against the intermediary for magic."

"Is that really what he is, though? I have my doubts," I said.

"As do I, but it's what the people think."

I rubbed the tension forming in my temples. "There has to be something to do now. People shouldn't be treated like this."

"No, we shouldn't." A woman's voice made me jump.

"Who are you?" I asked.

"That's the question I should be asking you. The man you're with looks like he could be a warrior, but you're clearly blind. If you're not in a cage or chains, the high priest doesn't know of your presence. Tell me, why did you come?"

"One of the prisoners," Nikon whispered into my ear.

We hadn't been found by the warriors—yet. "We're looking for answers as to what the high priest has done and what his plans are with his experiments. We know he's done something to the water, and that it has to do with magic." And with how I went blind, but the pieces of the puzzle weren't coming together.

I took a step closer, moving out of Nikon's grasp. Though he was near, he didn't interfere. I was grateful to have him at my back, but also glad he let me go. "Do you know what he wants? What he's doing with his experiments? We're hoping to find some proof we can take back to the Reding, so he can stop the high priest."

"How do you know he's done something to the water with magic?" the woman asked.

I wasn't certain how much to give away, but she was in a cell. What harm could she do? In fact, she could assist us. "We've put bits and pieces of information together. Some from his granddaughter."

Her voice turned suspicious, and with a note of something else in it. An emotion that almost sounded like longing. "You know the Vading?"

"Unfortunately. She was my caretaker for years an—"

"Cassandra?" She sounded shocked, but couldn't possibly be as shocked as I was that she knew my name.

"How do you know who I am?" I asked.

"You need to leave. The high priest thinks you're the key to getting his experiment right this time around."

I tensed. No matter how I felt, I couldn't let him scare me away. "We can't leave until we know what's going on."

She huffed, sounding like she had more energy than when she started speaking. "The high priest has been conducting experiments since he was spurned before the Govlin Wars. He used the new government with the aid of his neczar as a way to promote himself and have better access to what he needed, claiming to be a link between magic and the people. Instead, he's used his position to do horrible things. If he finds you, he'll do the same or worse to you."

"Spurned?" For some reason, that was what my mind caught on.

"By a woman."

I wrinkled my eyebrows, trying to follow what she meant. "He fell in love, but his other half didn't want to be with him?"

"He didn't fall in love at first sight, like people do now. He fell in love slowly, with a woman who didn't love him back. Because of that, he turned to experimenting, trying to ruin love for everyone. Instead, he accidentally made it so you only fall in love at first sight or not at all. He thinks you're the key to reversing that and getting rid of love altogether."

CHAPTER THIRTY-THREE

The high priest, spurned in love and bitter enough to stop everyone else from falling in love? I couldn't believe someone could be so hateful. There had to be a way to reverse it. And why was I involved?

Me, the key to stopping people from falling in love only at first sight? If only we'd solved this before Nikon fell in love with Lavti...

Ugh, I shouldn't be thinking of that at a time like this. "How could I possibly be the key? How did the high priest know about me before Antonia came along?"

The whimpering and calls to be released continued in the background.

"Something about a mole in the rebellion, years ago, when you first became blind. There isn't a way to find out much about it from the pieces I've been able to put together, because the high priest doesn't talk much, and in his rage, he killed the mole for not bringing enough information."

"That was rather short-sighted of him," I said.

Something clanked against the bars. "Which is why you need to escape this place," she said. "Now. The high priest's temper is not to be meddled with. Mixed with the fact that he wants you for his experiments, to somehow put back into the water what was taken, trust me, you want to be as far from this place as possible."

What was taken from the water? And the high priest thought I was somehow the key to it...

"Cass." Nikon's voice was filled with fear. "We've got to find proof and get you out of here."

I tried to ignore the fear bubbling up my throat. I didn't want to be a part of whatever those tests he was doing were. "Can't we free her first? She knows so much. We can take her with us." I turned back toward her. "You sound like just the well of knowledge we've been looking for." And to think I was going to be looking for scrolls or more papyri. "The Reding has to hear from you."

"There's only one key to my lock, and the high priest has it always." There was a wistful note to her voice.

"But if we can take you to the Reding and get his support, we can come back and rescue everyone." I didn't waste more time debating it with her. Instead, I turned to Nikon. "Can you pick it?"

"Maybe, but she also has manacles on. They'll both take time to get through."

Something we didn't have. But then, we didn't have the luxury of stealing the key off the high priest, either. "We've got to try," I said.

"Agreed, but we need to hurry." He brushed past me and must have got to work.

"Take me too," a weak voice called out.

"And me."

"Release us all."

The groans of the people pressed in on me, making me wish I could help them all. "We'll get you all out of here as soon as we can. We'll figure this out."

The voices cried out, louder but still weak from what they'd been through.

Tewy jabbered and jumped around the place, sounding ornery. I didn't blame him. I wanted to help them all, but there was only so much I could do.

"What's your name?" I asked the woman, frustrated there was nothing I could do to help.

"Japuta, if you must know, but this won't work. I'm not sure I could make it out of this place if I wanted to. The high priest keeps us from starving to death, but that's about it."

I strode over to the bars, careful not to bump into Nikon, and held out my hand, hoping to find her. She grasped onto me, her hands coarse and nails jagged. The body odor and smell of waste was worse this close, but I wasn't about to let that deter me. "Japuta, I'm sorry this happened to you and everyone else in here. We'll save you, no matter what it takes, and come back for the others as soon as we can."

Someone at my left stirred, presumably a person in the next cage over.

Japuta said, "If I leave, you have to promise that. Promise we'll rescue the others."

I tightened my grip on her. "I promise to do everything in my power to stop the high priest and help them."

"I'll take it. Do you know how to pick a lock as well?"

"No."

"Pity. We could be done with my cuffs sooner."

I bit my lip. I hoped Nikon could get through the door soon and free Japuta's wrists.

A creak sounded, and Nikon said, "Through the door."

Japuta sniffed. What was she thinking through all this? She pulled her hands away. Nikon must have been ready to pick the locks on her wrists.

I moved away from the cell and paced the floor, using my cane in the unfamiliar area. We were taking too long. The other warriors must have discovered the missing guard. I'd be shocked if they weren't looking for us.

"How's it going?" Though I shouldn't interrupt, I couldn't help but ask. Not knowing where we stood with getting out of here was driving me nuts.

"One moment." Nikon's voice was farther away, as if he had his back to me.

A noise sounded in the distance, different than the groaning around us. Like a door, maybe. And *there*. Footsteps. *Sand it all.*

Nikon cursed softly. I stopped my movements and gripped my cane. Should I take it apart, or get ready to whack someone with it?

How would we ever get out, with warriors blocking the way? Not to mention they'd soon be here, to imprison or kill us.

"Japuta is free," Nikon whispered, "but she's swaying on her feet. I think she's been drugged."

Sand it. "What do we do now? Is there another way out of here?"

"None that I know of."

"Through the high priest's room," Japuta said, coming nearer. "There's a hidden door."

"Wrap an arm around my shoulder. I'll help you," I told her.

She did so and was about my height. A little taller and bonier. Similar enough build that helping her walk should be fairly straightforward. For someone who was being fed, the woman seemed frailer than she ought to be.

We had to get moving. Those footsteps were coming closer.

Tewy sat on my shoulder and Japuta's arm, making a bed out of the two. I hoped he didn't fall off, with the jostling likely to come.

I took a step forward, though I didn't know where to go. Japuta followed, but her movements were stiffer than her words had been. I wanted to ask where we should go, but the footsteps of the warriors were so near, I feared they'd be able to hear me.

Nikon whispered, "Hold."

I did as he asked, wanting to know more of what was happening. The sound of warriors was far too close. Japuta swayed at my side, but I held her steady. Tewy patted my cheek, as a woman from the room behind us said, "Something's wrong."

"What is i—"

The clash of metal stopped whatever the man was about to say. Nikon's work, no doubt. The sound was close. He'd let me know if I needed to help, if the fight came toward us.

I shifted my weight from foot to foot, as the sounds continued mixed with the moans and cries of the prisoners along with grunts and the slapping of feet against the stone floor. Nikon would make it out of this. He'd made it out of far worse.

It was what I kept telling myself, but I ached to join him.

What seemed like too many minutes later but was probably only seconds, the woman yelled, "Go for help."

Footsteps ran from us but were quickly stopped with the *thud* of a body hitting the ground.

"If you want to live, you'll surrender," Nikon said, the sound of fighting exchanged for heavy breathing.

"I can't. The high priest will do far worse to me than you can," the female warrior said.

"Come with us," Nikon proposed.

"He'll hunt me down."

"I don't want to hurt you, but I will if I have to."

The silent moment stretched on, until Japuta said, "Spare her."

Nikon sighed and said, "And do what with her? She'll alert others to our presence."

"There's rope in the corner."

I gripped on to Japuta more tightly, wishing she was as strong as she sounded, and not swaying. If only there was hope that we would make it out of here now that the warriors were so aware of us.

The scuffle of someone moving closer reached me, and after a moment more, Nikon said, "She's tied up and gagged for the moment. It won't last long till someone finds her. We've got to get moving."

"Where? We're never going to make it out." I let the words slip through, and immediately regretted them.

"We aren't giving up now," he replied. "Japuta, are there any warriors in the high priest's room or on the way?"

"No."

"Then I'll protect our backs. Tell us where to go, and make sure Cassandra doesn't run into anything."

She gave directions, and I followed. We went straight for a while, before turning, and leaving some of the groans and smell behind. The more nervous I became, the harsher my breathing, the only sound besides our steps. If someone came along, they'd know right where we were.

"Getting close," Japuta said, making me think she knew this area very well or could see. But what use would the high priest have for someone sighted in his experiments?

I struggled on. Her weight wasn't a burden, but my fears were. Japuta had told us so much about the high priest—far more than I would have ever guessed I'd learn during this infiltration. The fact that he manipulated love and wanted to get rid of it altogether appalled me. There had to be a way to get out of here, so we could take this information to the Reding. Theodore must have done something about it.

Finally we stopped, and she said, "The door to his room will be booby trapped. To disarm it, he always did something to the top of his doorframe."

"I'll see if I can disarm it," Nikon said.

Silently, he brushed past me, and moments ticked by before a *click* sounded.

"That should do it," Japuta said. "You'll also need to pick the lock."

Faint voices came from the distance. The warriors would soon find out we were here, if they hadn't already. Nikon let out a curse, confirming my fears. The lock had better not be too hard to pick.

As Nikon worked on that, Tewy paced back and forth along my shoulders and Japuta's arm. It didn't take long for the door to click open and us to get in the room and bolt the lock.

"Now what?" Nikon asked. "There isn't much here. We were hoping to find information."

"We'll have all the information we can get with Japuta," I said. "The main thing we need to do now is escape. Unless there's some papyrus here I don't know about."

"There's not," Nikon replied.

"We have to go through a passage. Push on a stone on the left wall. Bottom row, third from the left." Japuta's directions were clear. She did have sight and must have paid close attention to what the high priest did when he spent time with her. The high priest probably thought she'd never escape.

The scraping of rock moving against rock filled the area with a rumble. It was far louder than I expected. All of the warriors searching for us must have heard ιτ.

A waft of that rotten eggs stench hit me, at the same time as Japuta stumbled. She pulled back with a whimper. I wrapped my arm around her waist, holding her tight, and said, "It's going to be fine."

She didn't respond.

I clenched my jaw, not sure if I was grateful for the chance to get out of here, if it was through such an awful-smelling place bringing memories of where she didn't want to go.

"The way's clear, as far as I can tell," Nikon said. "Lots of steps down, but dark. You'll do better than us two, Cass."

Perhaps, but we'd be slower than I'd like if we didn't light the way for them. We'd make it, though. I wouldn't allow anything else.

Nikon ushered us forward, and I carefully felt my way with my cane, urging Japuta on.

We'd gone down three steps, when the rumbling sound scraped behind us and the door banged closed. If the warriors didn't know how to get in, we might have a chance.

Though we continued down, the air was stifling, leaving little room to breathe without inhaling noxious odors that only grew stronger as we descended.

Japuta whimpered again.

I patted her back and tried my best to console her, in whispering tones. "It's all right. We just have to get out of Peka Tower, and we'll find somewhere safe for you."

"There's somewhere safe left?" Her voice was dull, compared to before.

"Yes, and if it doesn't seem that way, we'll make it so for you."

"If you're sure." She didn't sound hopeful.

I put an imaginary rod in my back, to deal with the emotional and mental weight pressing in on me. We would handle everything later, once we got out of here.

We'd climbed down twelve more stairs, when the way grew flat. There was another scraping of rock, and the stench grew strong enough to make my eyes water.

We didn't move forward. Instead, Japuta curled in around me with a moan, as Nikon cursed.

"What is it?" Only a room full of neczar and warriors would get that sort of reaction. My heart sped up.

Japuta mewled, as Nikon said, "It's a torture chamber."

CHAPTER THIRTY-FOUR

From Nikon's words and the way Japuta reacted to the chamber, she must have experienced the torture herself. But why? There had to be something the high priest wanted from Japuta without her being blind. If I was caught, I would join the blind and her in suffering through this. I shivered. What he wanted had to do with his getting rid of love altogether and my being blind. Just how the two fit together, I didn't yet know, but I'd find the answer.

"We've got to go," I said.

"Japuta? I'm sorry to bring you here, but do you know the way out?" Nikon asked.

She moved her arm and must have given Nikon the direction he needed, because we moved forward after that, with me helping her.

As my hip bumped into something blunt, I tried not to think about what it could be. I didn't want to know, with the way Japuta shrunk against me. My throat closed up, tight with fear and worry. This torture chamber could easily be the future of us all, if we didn't find a way home.

We had to get out.

As we navigated the room, making lots of sharp turns around what I thought were tables and bumping into more items, I couldn't help but think of all the different ways he must have had to torture a person. They had to be far more than I could imagine. None of those could explain the smell, though. Or perhaps that was part of the torture.

"Let me check the door," Nikon said, as Japuta pulled me to a stop.

I heard the *snick* of his blade, coming out of its sheath. He must have been worried about what he'd find, which left me biting my cheek and gripping my cane more tightly.

Tewy stirred on my shoulder but didn't leave. I couldn't believe I'd worried so much about taking him with us. For once, he'd not only been well behaved, but also helpful.

I listened into the silence. There was nothing other than Japuta's breathing. That had to be a good sign. If there were warriors around, they would have made a ruckus.

"Do you know a way out of the tower from here?" Nikon asked her.

She recoiled into me more but replied in a surprisingly clear voice. "*He* has a secret way. I went many times. Let me guide you."

He was the high priest, by how thoroughly disgusted she sounded. It made sense that he'd have a secret way in and out, but why would she have gone many times? I thought she'd been locked up or facing torture in here.

There had to be a way to get answers without letting her know I was suspicious of her. "What did he do when he took you out?" I asked.

She let out a strangled sob.

It'd been sickening. A person couldn't fake the terror in the sound she'd made.

"You don't have to tell me," I said.

"But I should. His experiments with me and the blind were sometimes done in the water."

I frowned. "With magic?"

"Yes."

There'd be time to ask more later, because we needed to get going. "Are there going to be warriors between here and there?" I asked instead.

Her shoulders sagged further against my arm. "I'm afraid so. The high priest always has guards around him. We're lucky we haven't run into them yet."

"He's gone. Supposed to be back tomorrow." Nikon's words were curt.

"Makes sense with how long it's been since he's taken me. But there'll be warriors about. Just not as many."

"How are we going to make it?" The question popped out. I needed answers, not more problems. There had to be a way I could fix not knowing how to get out of here. "Are there people who come and go that aren't warriors from the tower?"

"I didn't spend enough time around to know them, but there should be servants and washers and the like." Japuta's voice lost some of her confidence.

"What if we dressed as them? We could be the launderers, taking clothes or bedding or something to the river." The idea sparked a bit of hope inside me.

"It could work." Nikon sounded as if he was considering it.

We still stunk, but there were enough other odd stenches in this building, I'd have to hope it was enough to cover us. I turned my head toward Japuta. "Do you know where we could find the clothes to blend in? Preferably without running into others?"

"No."

I held in a growl. How would we pull this off if we couldn't get the clothes for it?

"And this man doesn't look like a servant or a laundry worker.

Too many muscles. He'd have to be disguised as a warrior, watching over us," she said.

Nikon snorted. He couldn't be happy about that with how much he'd hated what he'd once been, but maybe it was what he was doomed to be—always a soldier. "I can get an outfit for me from a guard if I knock him unconscious without spilling blood. Cass, let me borrow your fighting sticks."

If it was anyone other than Nikon, I'd hesitate, but I held them out and he took them. "Hope they work as well for you as they do for me."

"Doubtful, but they should do the job. Thank you."

"Can we go as prisoners, accompanied by a warrior?" I asked.

"No," she said. "If the high priest is really gone, there will be no prisoners moving in or out." Our stopping seemed to be giving her more strength, as she leaned on me less. She'd have to go by herself if we were disguised as washerwomen.

"Wait. What if Japuta and I dressed as warriors too?" It might be easier to get around that way.

"You could get away with it if people didn't realize you were blind, but Japuta doesn't have the muscle definition needed to pass for a soldier." His matter-of-fact response left the conundrum of finding the right clothes.

"We find a warrior with the right outfit for you, then," I said, and the rest of the thought hit me. "We can make him tell us where to find the washer servants we need and their outfits, and where to find things to pretend to launder."

"We'll make it happen," he said. "Come on. We've got to move."

I didn't know where he was taking us, but with a plan in place, I felt more confident. As Japuta moved forward, I tried to support her but let her guide me. Without the use of my cane, the world was blank around me. I hoped we found someone soon and knocked them out, so I could get my cane back.

There were no voices on this floor or the next two. Where

were all the warriors? With any luck, all but a few were searching for us above. After dodging them all, it felt as they were purposefully hiding from us. Or worse, they knew we were looking for a way out, and stationed all the warriors at the exits. We'd never make it out if that was the case. With The Third on their side, we could easily be gobbled up.

Squashing the thought, I continued forward, pausing only when we came to a landing another three flights down, as the sound of voices came to me. I held steady, as did Japuta, not sure what Nikon had in mind.

Within moments, the voices were closer than ever, and there was a *thud*, followed by calls of distress. It wasn't long before they were silenced. Had Nikon killed them? I winced. It would be fine. We had to get out of here, no matter the cost.

Though that cost was higher than I liked.

Japuta wobbled beneath my grip. How much longer would she hold up? She had to keep going. I didn't know if there would be a chance to rest, like there had been on the way up.

Worry pressed in on me, tightening my headache into a mass of pain.

Far too many moments later, Nikon whispered, "Got the clothes and information."

He was becoming an expert thief. "You're a warrior?" I asked.

"Dressed as one, anyway." He handed me my cane, back in one piece. Or maybe he never untwisted it in the first place.

"We're about five floors up from where the laundry is gathered. Higher than I thought the room would be, but as long as we get there, we'll be fine."

The unspoken *might get there* was what had me concerned. I didn't know what would come, but it had to be better than staying up in the torture chamber or jail cells.

We hurried down the flights of stairs so fast, I might tumble down them. Luckily, I stayed on my feet, probably more due to helping Japuta, though it was easier with my cane back in hand.

As we turned away from the stairs five stories down, I steadied myself. It didn't take long for voices of more people than we wanted to deal with to drift to us.

As much as I wished to ask what to do, I couldn't bring more attention to us. Thankfully, Nikon was on it. "In here."

We turned, and the air closed in around us.

"Are we in a closet?" I asked.

"Yes. I'll get you both what you need and be back."

I opened my mouth to protest—splitting up made my heart race—but he added, "It'll be safer and faster."

He was correct. I needed to wait with Japuta. Even if separating from him for the second time in a matter of minutes left me scowling.

A door closed, and there was nothing but the sound of our breathing. Nothing of the outside world got in. Not the voices we'd heard before. I strained to see if I'd hear Nikon's gathering of outfits, to figure out how he was going about it. Still, no sound came.

Japuta's breathing came heavier and heavier.

I whispered, "Are you well?"

"I have to be."

Giving her a side hug, I said, "Hang on. We'll get you out of here."

We had to, not only for her sake and ours, but also to take her to the Reding. He was the one we relied on now, to help us with the answers and the papyri we'd gotten for him. We just had to get her there.

The confined area closed in on me. I needed a distraction. Maybe I could get answers at the same time. "Why does the high priest have you locked up for experiments if you're not blind?"

"Because he's cruel." While her words were true, it felt as though there was something she held back. What wasn't she telling me? I wanted to ask, but she already sounded on edge and I didn't want to push her off.

Nikon must have run into trouble, or maybe he needed time to get what we needed. It felt as though it'd been too long, and at any moment, a warrior would discover us. It left me gritting my teeth against the emotions warring within me. I couldn't let myself grab hold of any of them. We were in too much peril, for there to be hope we'd all make it out of here without a problem.

The door burst open. I jumped.

"Put these on as quickly as you can. I don't know how much time we'll have." Nikon's words were laced with a warning. I was simply grateful he'd returned. Perhaps he was as concerned as I was about our escape. If we did make it, we had to deal with the fact that the high priest would soon be coming down the river. I shoved the thought down for later, as I put on the washerwoman clothes, grabbing my original ones to leave no sign of our escape.

Japuta asked, "Ready?"

"Yes. Can you make it on your own?"

"I'll do my best."

The door opened, and instead of telling me to leave my clothes behind like I was loathe to do, Nikon said, "Put your dresses in this basket. I'll cover your clothes, so Cassandra can keep them for later, though they'll need to be washed. Sorry, Japuta, I don't think yours are worth keeping, but we'll hide them at the bottom of the basket so as not to give a clue where we are."

"I don't want them on again, anyway," she said.

I held out my cane. "Should I trade this with you for the basket?"

"Yes." Nikon took my cane and handed me the basket of clothes. It was heavier than expected, weighing me down for a moment before I pulled it closer and rested it against my chest for support.

"Tewy, you hide under the clothes," he said. "No washerwoman or warrior would have a monkey here, I'm afraid."

Though he quietly griped, Tewy balanced himself on my arm and hopped off, his weight making the basket dip. It shifted, as I assumed Nikon covered him up. It was a sad state of things that I didn't know how long we'd be able to keep him covered.

"Stay there, Tewy. And quiet, if you can. It's imperative that we get through this," I said.

"We'll make it." Japuta's words, not Nikon's, which surprised me.

Why did she have more confidence in our escape than the two of us? Probably because we lived through having to sneak in here. Or perhaps she was more desperate to be out of this place. She'd dealt with torture; she had to be chaffing to get out.

"Hold on to Japuta," Nikon said. "It'll be hard to get through some narrower spots, but we'll make it if we're careful. I'll lead the way."

I hoped he knew the way out. He made his steps noisier than usual, as he moved down a hall. It had to be for my benefit. I held the basket close, linking arms with Japuta. The clothes and Tewy felt awkward, but as long as I didn't drop Tewy, it would be all right.

We followed Nikon until we came to some stairs where I slowed us on the way down. I tried to keep up with Japuta's steps, but the uncertainty clung to me, bringing us to a crawl as she pulled me faster.

She stopped. "Sorry. I'm not used to this. I just want out of here." She sounded upset, though I suspected at herself and not me.

"It's fine. Just an adjustment."

Once she slowed, my steps became a little more confident and our overall speed crept up. I didn't go as fast as I wanted on the stairs, but we made progress. As we came to more than ten different floors, sometimes we heard voices in the distance, but only a handful. I whispered, "I thought there'd be more people on the stairs."

"Probably not with *him* gone," she whispered back.

"Get to the side," Nikon demanded, voice sharp.

I hastened to do what he asked, Japuta disengaging from me. I stayed very still, alone on my step, hoping I didn't have to go the rest of the way to the ground floor floundering by myself.

Footsteps came up the opposite direction with... Was that panting? Lots of panting. And sniffing.

I gulped.

"Seen anyone who doesn't belong?" a woman asked.

"Just The Third." Nikon's words were easy and sure. "What's he doing out?"

"Some patrol thought they had indications of people trying to get in through the moat. Can you imagine someone going through that? And to get in here? Who'd want to bother?"

"No one smart."

"My thoughts exactly. All of you heading out?"

"Yup. Cleaning."

"Good. That clothing stinks. Don't take too long, though. The high priest is supposed to be closer than they thought. He'll want everything where it ought to be within the hour."

Blast the sands.

"Good to know. Thank you," Nikon replied.

As the sniffing passed, I thought for certain The Third would growl or bark at us. He hovered close to me, breath hot on my shoulder. Just how big was he? I shook despite not wanting to give away my fear. Any second now, the creature would clamp its jaws around me.

"Do I know these two servants?"

My heart pounded in my chest, struggling to keep terror in check.

"I brought them in myself a couple of weeks ago."

Did the woman believe the lie? Please let her believe the lie. Drool dripped onto my hand holding the basket. I grimaced, waiting for barking or biting.

The snuffling went by.

"The Third doesn't seem to mind them, so I suppose you're

right," the woman said. "But get going, that stench is something foul."

I stepped forward at the dismissal, unbelieving that The Third hadn't barked at us. Perhaps the odor was covering our unique smells. Whatever the case, relief blossomed in my stomach. It would have left me at ease if we hadn't heard the news about the high priest.

We continued on. We had to get out of here fast, but the stairs were seemingly endless. Who wanted to live like this? Then again, most didn't go out much once they were in here.

Though Japuta had said the high priest took her out sometimes. There had to be something to that. Japuta huffed beside me, gasping for air. I might have been through much, but she'd been through added strain. She needed a break far more than I did. But with the high priest almost here, we couldn't delay.

We went down, down, down, and down. Sometimes we moved over for others, and sometimes they did for us, but we had no more chats like with The Third's handler. The closer we got to the bottom, the greater a hurry everyone seemed to be in.

I couldn't get over the shock that The Third hadn't barked at us. Voices drifted up to us again, more plentiful than before. We had to be close to the end, with all the stairs we'd gone through and the amount of people gathered down there.

We stopped. The voices weren't close, but Nikon whispered, "Hide your faces as best you can."

He cursed, as Japuta fussed with a cloth over my head, adjusting it some way, to do as Nikon asked. People didn't often wear fabric over their face, so if he was asking us to do so, something bad must be coming.

We continued down, and I tried to walk as nonchalantly as possible while linked with Japuta. When the ground flattened out, the voices were louder.

"Quick."

"Get a move on."

"There's a spot of dirt just there."

"Don't forget to bow deep enough."

"Fix that tapestry."

I held in a gasp, because their urgency could only mean one thing. The high priest had arrived.

CHAPTER THIRTY-FIVE

Japuta pulled me forward, and I went with her, not letting fear tamper with my expression, like Nikon had taught me.

We only took a couple more steps toward the chaos, when a woman called out, "What are the washers doing here? Get them outside and out of sight."

"You heard her. Get a move on. We can't have you seen when the high priest gets here. Out now." Nikon's sharp tone was directed at me.

Japuta increased her pace, and I tucked my chin down to appear meek. I didn't know if it would work, but I'd try anything to get us past the gathered crowd.

"Move it," Nikon hissed at us. "He doesn't want to see who cleans his underthings."

We hurried along, and a waft of fresh air hit me. Fresh and clear. We were going to make it. My heart lifted, and then fell as Japuta stopped.

A man asked, "Where are you going?"

"Got to get this clean," Japuta said.

"This time of night?"

We were caught for sure. I wished I had my cane, so I could help Nikon fight our way out, but there'd be nothing for it.

Japuta responded. "With the high priest coming, we don't have any other choice."

"Get on with you, quick like. He's bound to come into view at any moment. Make sure you're in the trees before he comes."

My plan and hers both. I quickened my steps, trying not to drop my shoulders in relief.

Behind us, the same man asked, "And you, warrior? You have clothes to wash as well?"

I forced myself to keep going and not give away my fear. If Nikon couldn't come out with us, I didn't know how long he'd last without being captured, or how long we'd last without him.

"I was told to keep an eye on these two, as they weren't working fast enough earlier," Nikon said.

"Lazy servants. Move it, then."

I held in a relieved sigh and continued forward at a fast pace. We were going to make it. All of us. The sands were blessedly on our side, though I didn't understand why.

I tripped, and the basket tumbled forward.

Magic save us. We were going to be back to the tower for sure.

"Pick up that mess and get moving," Nikon snapped. "The high priest doesn't have time for clumsy, lazy servants."

I clenched my teeth, as I pulled myself up. I didn't want to sit here, but I couldn't grope around for clothes and give away my blindness, either.

Thankfully, the basket was handed to me, and I held it as items were tossed in.

Japuta pulled me up, and I tucked the basket in close. Why was it lighter? Did Tewy jump out? Where was he? Whatever the case, I had to hope he'd make it to the trees without anyone the wiser.

We went on at as fast a pace as I dared.

I didn't know exactly when we hit the trees, but there was more vegetation around than I expected, sooner than I thought it should appear. The ground grew bumpier, and branches smacked into me. The plants weren't a lot, but it would give me some peace, though we didn't slow. If there were trees this close, Tewy must have found them.

Behind us was the silence, but Nikon whispered, "We need to get away from here as soon as possible."

"Where to?" Japuta asked.

"We've got a boat stashed a ways up. If you two let me pass, I'll lead you to it."

We halted briefly enough for him to rush past, handing me my cane as he did so.

"What about Tewy?" I asked.

The monkey in question jumped on my shoulder, chattering softly. Apparently, he hadn't gone far.

"I know," I whispered to him. "You did good."

There wasn't any more time to praise him as we were on the move again. With my cane in hand, my movements grew more confident. I didn't have to rely solely on Japuta, who took the clothes basket from me so we wouldn't leave evidence behind. Let them work for answers.

We rushed through the vegetation, a clamor coming behind us. I sped up, despite not believing they were coming for us—yet.

It sounded more as if the people we'd left behind at the tower were making a big hubbub. The high priest had arrived.

I didn't want to think what would have happened if we'd been only a few minutes later. The high priest wouldn't recognize me on sight, but would he know Nikon?

Japuta was an entirely different story. He'd know her instantly.

We kept as silent as possible, combing through the undergrowth for some distance. The noises behind us grew fainter, the farther we went, but the presence of Peka Tower, the high priest, and likely more neczar made my back itch with the knowledge they could come after us at any moment.

I wouldn't feel comfortable until we were far from here. The marauders camp for Japuta, most likely, once she'd talked to the Reding. Unless he had somewhere he could keep her safe, but I wasn't positive of anything at this point.

Despite not feeling the threat of the high priest growing, the worry and tension had me moving more quickly. Something poked my foot, and I sucked in a breath. I hobbled on as fast as I could, but it was a slower pace than before.

Knowing I was what kept us from going faster gnawed at me. There'd be nothing left to help them with escaping, should the fear and anxiety continue, but what else could I do? They thrummed in my ears, urging me out of this place.

I did what I could, to focus on each step and sweep of my cane. To find precision in my step, despite the fear of every rustle that met my ears.

Moments later, we came to a standstill. We must have arrived at the boat, but no one said anything. I heard the loud scratching of something heavy dragged across the sand. It likely was the boat, with Nikon doing all the work. I was certain he didn't mind, as long as we got out of here.

"Get in," Nikon said ahead of me.

Japuta hurried me over to the river, the splash of its familiar warmth brushing my toes. I shivered at the thought of the high priest tampering with its source, using sighted or the blind or some combination of them.

Nikon's familiar grip closed around my hand, and he helped me into the boat. I crouched to one side, Japuta next to me. We were squished, since we hadn't planned for another person on the way out, but it would work. The boat rocked, and soon I heard the faint dipping of a paddle. Relief flooded me.

Japuta slumped against me, shoulders shaking. Was she crying? She seemed like the strong sort through the entire escape, but after everything she must have been through, the strongest would have cried.

Wanting to comfort her, I put my arm around her, as Tewy climbed into my lap. I whispered, "You'll be safe now."

Her voice cracked, as she said, "We'll never be safe from the high priest."

I wrapped my arm more tightly around her, not sure how else to ease her worries. There was nothing I could do to erase past hurts, other than being there for her now.

The steady dip of the paddle in the water brought me a sense of calm and tranquility. As I held on to the crying woman, I let the tension ease out of my body and relaxed into a bit of a slump. Nikon would need help at some point. But for now, I could rest.

Japuta's sobs slowed as the dipping of the oars continued on a steady rhythm that made me feel safe. The wind smacking against me told me we were going at a good speed, but also that we might have to fight our way upstream.

"Nikon, do you need help?" I asked.

"Not yet."

"Why did the two of you come to Peka Tower?" Japuta asked.

"We're trying to stop the high priest, like we told you before. He has too much power and has hurt too many people for it to stay that way." The Vading would have to go down with him, but hopefully not Theodore. Nikon's brother deserved the chance to show if he was trustworthy. I hoped he'd prove work with the rebellion to make Eppla a better country for everyone. But if he let the high priest return so soon, was he really on our side?

"He can never be stopped. His influence is too vast," she said.

I didn't disagree, but I wanted there to be hope. "There ha—"

Horrendous howls echoed through the chilling air, bringing goose bumps to my skin, as Japuta stiffened.

"What was that?" I asked.

"The neczar," she responded.

Nikon added, "They're on the hunt."

And there was only one thing they'd be on the hunt for. They wanted us.

CHAPTER THIRTY-SIX

Panic thrummed in my chest. "Can we go faster? Should I row? What can I do?"

"There's only one set of oars." Nikon ground out the words as if he was personally affronted that he couldn't do more. "I've got them."

"We'll make it away from them." I added more confidence to my voice than I felt, despite my frustration that I couldn't help.

"They're smart, and their senses are more heightened than ours." Japuta's words echoed with fear and strain.

I didn't want to think about why she knew that about them, but thoughts of them coming in with the high priest to help torture her arrived anyway. We needed to figure out a faster way out of this place. "The river is probably the safest bet against them, yes?"

"True. On land they would catch our scent and find us rapidly. Unfortunately, there aren't many places to go on the river," Nikon said. "On water, we stand some chance, but they'll know we went this way. The only other option is down the chasm, which is more a death sentence than facing them is."

"It would be over quickly," Japuta muttered.

"They're going to catch up to us, aren't they?" I asked.

The grim silence told me all I needed to know. Unless something changed, and drastically, we were doomed.

Another idea came to me. "Can we block the river, somehow? Keep them from following us for a time?"

"No," Japuta said.

"Any attempts to block it here, where it's so wide, would only slow us down," Nikon stated, kinder than she had but disheartened.

"What if we did a disguise spell, like we tried before, Nikon? Then, when they catch up, they won't know it's us."

"There's no one else on the river. They'd know." His tone was like a desired caress that couldn't happen, frustrated and upset.

I bit my lip. Fear and pressure built inside me. They swirled and railed like the sandstorm Nikon and I had been in what felt like ages ago. The memories of it stayed strong and currently thrashed about inside me. How much could I do? None of my ideas would work against the neczar. They had to be on the river after us already, though our boat had been hidden. Whether the creatures took boats of their own or swam, I didn't want to think about what they'd do when they caught up to us.

I shook my head, to clear it of my thoughts. Nothing would make a difference.

Tewy stirred in my lap, giving a hoot that sounded encouraging.

Unfortunately, I couldn't understand monkey, so there was no way to know for certain and no way for him to help.

His continuing babble did bring to mind an idea that'd worked before.

"What about the sand?" I asked.

"What about it?" Nikon asked.

Japuta didn't sound enthusiastic when she replied with, "It'll do no good. "

"This will work. I know it will. We can use the sand on the boat and the paddles. It might make them go faster."

"Or it could slow us down. Plus stopping to do so would help the neczar catch up to us sooner." The negative words from her were resigned. She hadn't had much of a reason to hope, lately, but I'd show her hope that brightened.

"Nikon? What do you think?" I asked. "If the neczar are going to catch up to us anyway, isn't it worth a try?"

"Already headed to shore," he replied.

My heart leaped in my chest. He trusted me and the magic, probably more than I did. I had to believe it would make a difference. Since the loss of my sight, the sand had aided me. I had to wonder if, when I'd lost my sight, it'd been trying to help.

"Japuta, maybe you shouldn't use the sand on the boat, if you're unsure if it's going to work," I said.

"You think that'll make a difference?"

"I don't know, but I do know that its power grows when you have faith in it."

Her shoulder that brushed mine slumped. "Nothing else will work. This probably won't, either, but you're correct. It's worth a try."

A few more dips of oars splashing water, and the boat bumped into something solid. I didn't wait for him to say anything. I bent over, reached into the water, and found the sand wet with magic. The high priest hadn't taken that away when he ripped away the people's ability to fall in love on their own. I gripped a handful and smeared it along the side of the boat, hoping to the sands it would make us fast enough to escape.

Working as quickly as I could, I continued moving around different areas of the boat.

Tewy jumped from my lap, his little *ooo*s coming from the other side.

"Why is the monkey putting sand on the boat?" Japuta sounded surprised.

If the situation hadn't been so serious, I would have laughed. "Because he's making a difference. It will hopefully aid us. Thank you, Tewy."

He hooted back at me, as someone—probably Nikon—splashed nearby. We worked like that for what felt like hours until my arms ached, before Japuta gasped.

"What is it?" I asked.

"A boat headed this way fast, from downstream."

"The neczar," Nikon added.

Icy fear plummeted through my heart and into my stomach. I slathered the last bit of wet sand in my palm on the boat as Nikon said, "We've got to move."

I didn't bother washing off my hand. "Tewy? Where are you, boy?"

There was a scamper as the boat rocked, and he jumped on my lap, making a wet, sandy mess of me. I'd do whatever it took to keep him near and keep us safe, like he'd attempted to do for us.

The splash of the oars came faster than before, a slip of wind picking up against my face.

"Are we gaining speed?" I asked, hoping and fearing at the same time. It might not be enough.

"We are." Japuta's voice was full of wonder.

My plan worked, in part. We'd slowed down to execute it, and the neczar might be able to reach us before we pulled away. "What's happening? Where is the other boat?" I asked.

She shifted beside me, voice wavering. 'There are three of them within sight now. They're not gaining on us anymore, but are too close for us to be safe."

"Let's hope to the sands we put distance between us soon." As soon as I said the words, a whistling sounded across the water.

"*Duck*," Nikon yelled.

Without thinking, I did as he asked, crouching down into the smallest space I could make myself fit. Several more twangs of arrows flew, but nothing caught, as splashes sounded in the water.

Or so I thought, until Nikon hissed.

"What happened? Did it get you?" My voice came out frantic to my own ears.

"I'm fine," he gritted out.

"He's hit." Japuta confirmed my fears.

"Switch places with me and give me the oars." I didn't waste time, giving Tewy to Japuta as I shifted toward Nikon.

"I've got it." But his voice grew more strained through the few words he said.

"Let me help." I tried to imitate his tone when he commanded people.

He grunted, which I took as assent because he crept near me. The boat swayed but stayed upright, as we switched places. I found the oars, put them in the water, and pushed with all my might. As another whipping of air from an arrow went past, I said, "Guide me, so I don't take us back or run into shore." Though I could feel the water moving through the oars around us, I didn't want to risk any problems.

"I'll let you know if you go off course," Japuta said, with greater confidence than before.

Nikon hadn't replied. How badly was he hurt? I couldn't stop to think about it. If I did, I might fall apart. I continued rowing, putting everything I had into it. Japuta's daintier hands occasionally touched mine, adjusting the direction of my rowing, but mostly I was left to myself.

The whistling of arrows continued, but they slowly sounded farther and farther behind. I could only hope that meant our plan was working, as my muscles strained to keep going.

Finally, I couldn't wait any more. Gasping for breath, I asked, "Are we losing them?"

"It appears so," she replied.

"Then why is your voice so strained?"

"Nikon is bleeding a lot. He passed out. No, don't stop. I'm trying to contain it."

I went back to rowing, but worry cascaded through me, washing me in icy waves. "What do you need?"

"Just row. That's the best thing for him now. I took the arrow out, but that might have been the wrong thing to do. Don't worry. I'm applying pressure. Hopefully, he just passed out from the pain."

That didn't sound like him. The Nikon I knew was tough and wouldn't succumb to any type of pain. If he was hit with the worst sort of torture, I imagined he'd grit his teeth through it all. That he could be taken out by an arrow meant it had done a lot of damage and shock had likely set in.

"Where's he hit?" I asked.

"The shoulder," Japuta said. "You're slowing down."

"Sorry." I couldn't focus on Nikon for the time being. All I could do was trust Japuta to keep an eye on things. I rowed, trying my best to keep steady.

Tewy gave an *ooo aaa ooo* which sounded far too sad.

"What's going on, boy?" I asked.

"He's looking at Nikon," Japuta said.

Fear pierced my heart, as I scowled. "We need to get magic on his wound. Can we stop long enough to do that?"

"The boats are far behind us but within sight."

"So no." I pushed myself harder. I wouldn't let something bad happen to Nikon because I didn't get us to where we could use magic soon enough. My shoulders and body throbbed, but I pressed on. How much farther did we need to go?

The rhythmic gliding of oars dipping in and out of the water soon became all I focused on. I did my best to keep steady and even, ignoring the aches stretching across my body.

Because of my anguish and worry for Nikon, it felt like hours and hours passed before the boat thudded to a stop. I hadn't a clue how much time had actually gone by.

"What happened?" I asked.

"We're caught on a bank. Sorry, I wasn't paying attention," Japuta said.

Or maybe she was, but not to what I was doing.

I didn't wait for her to say anything else. I leaned over and scooped my hand down in the water, searching for the sand Nikon so desperately needed. The wet sand glopped between my fingers, and as I pulled it up, I said, "Put my hand on his wound."

Japuta didn't waste words, but moved my hand forward, as Tewy let out a sad *oooo oo oooooo*. Hoping this would close his wound, so the bleeding would stop, I gently pressed it onto him. I waited only a moment, before reaching down and grabbing more as I knelt on the bottom of the boat.

I went back to his shoulder and placed the fresh handful over the other sand. We probably couldn't linger, but I wanted him to be well. "Did the arrow go all the way through?" I asked. "Does he need sand on the opposite side, too?"

"Yes."

The boat rocked, as Japuta grabbed my wrist and helped me to the other side of his shoulder, where I pressed the rest of the sand. I packed a few more handfuls on, trying not to think of the fact that he wasn't moving or talking. I couldn't think of it. Not now. We were being chased. I only wanted to stay at his side and concentrate solely on him, but that wouldn't be helpful for any of us.

I asked her, "Can you push us off the bank and help me get headed straight again, before they catch up to us?"

The boat tilted, something splashed, and the boat moved.

Once we were clear of the bank, Japuta jumped back in with a *thud*. She grabbed my arms, helping me row for a moment, before saying, "You're heading the correct direction now. We need to keep moving."

"Are the other boats in sight?"

A pause. "No."

We'd fallen back, but not so much as to put us in danger. Good. "And Nikon? Is he waking? Did the bleeding stop?"

A longer pause. "The bleeding stopped, but he's not stirring."

Panic blossomed inside me. I tried to force it into boosting my rowing, but stress and anxiety were crashing into me so hard, I could think of nothing else. "Are you certain?"

"He's out cold."

"Is he breathing?"

"Yes."

"Maybe he needs more time." Or maybe, like when my parents had blinded me, I had been wrong to use magic on him at all.

CHAPTER THIRTY-SEVEN

I rowed for some time, putting my back into it, though my heart was left behind, to bleed out in the river somewhere. Nikon—my dearest friend, the man I wanted to be more than a friend—was unconscious, despite the hours that had gone by. It was my fault he was here in the first place. It'd been my suggestion. I should have done something to keep him safe.

But I hadn't.

Japuta and I hadn't spoken. She'd readjusted my angle for rowing every once and a while. I didn't want to ignore her, but I also had little energy left in me to talk. What strength I had remaining was all going toward getting us somewhere safe, and I didn't yet know where that would be.

We hadn't passed anyone on the river yet. Or nobody I'd heard. Maybe Japuta saw someone but didn't tell me. Tewy bounced on my lap, then away from me and back again for a long time, but eventually settled at my feet.

I didn't know how long I kept going, but I pressed on well into the night. It was exhausting—more so emotionally, when I worried about Nikon and whether he'd ever wake up again.

Japuta only spoke when I asked how he was doing, to tell me there'd been no change in his breathing or status.

If he never woke up...

I choked. No. I couldn't think like that. The magic had worked on closing the wound. Maybe he needed time to recuperate. But it made me nervous. I couldn't handle the strain much longer.

"Lights in the distance," Japuta said. "I believe Sirya is up ahead."

It was a miracle we got here so fast, considering it should have been days away—longer even, since we were going upstream.

"We should get out of here, then. I hate to leave the boat, but we'll be too conspicuous in it. Is there any vegetation we could hide it and ourselves in?"

"It's hard to tell in the dark, but I believe there is some on the right. Here. Let me take over, and I'll get us there."

As I swapped places with her, I held in a groan from my tender body. Moving across the boat without tipping it or stepping on Nikon was more difficult than I thought. I wanted to lie down and sleep for ages, but I had to figure out how to get help for Nikon, safety for all of us, and knowledge to the Reding. I knew more about the world and what was going on in it right now than Japuta did. With Nikon out, everything was up to me.

Before long, the boat bumped to a stop. A massive problem hit me. A Nikon-sized one, to be exact. "How are we going to get him out of here and hidden?" I asked. "The boat we can probably do, but I'm not sure about him."

"I don't know." Worry crept into her voice.

The situation put more strain on her than she wanted to admit. I had to remind myself that she was imprisoned earlier in the day, and had been, for some time.

I tapped my hand on my leg. What to do?

Tewy hopped up on my lap with a hoot.

I wanted to assure him we'd be all right, but it felt more like he was reassuring me.

He jumped onto my shoulder and gave my hair a good yank. That was more like it.

He climbed back down and shoved something at me. It was thin and long. Its calling to me and the rightness in my hand reminded me it was my cane. I must have been too exhausted, to not realize.

I picked it up with a "Thank you," and ran my hand across it. Though it couldn't help with our current situation, having it in my grasp again made me feel more confident. As I curled my hand around it, feeling how smooth it was against my skin, an idea came to me. "We could put sand on our hands and try to lift Nikon. The magic might help us go where we need to hide him."

"I don't know..." The uncertainty in Japuta's voice was more pronounced than before.

"What harm could it do? It's either try and hope for the best, or have those following us find us and take us back to the high priest."

Her response was to jostle the boat. At first, I thought she was uncomfortable, but she said, "I'll do it. I'm getting sand out of the river now."

Sure enough, I heard the soft splash of water moving. Relief relaxed out of me, though not enough to pull the tension fully away. We might have a chance. I'd feel much better if he was awake, but this would have to be sufficient for the moment.

Dipping my hands past the side of the boat again, I let my cane roll off my lap, to be retrieved later. The sand's soft texture was familiar, as I filled my hands and rubbed my palms together. This had to assist us in lifting Nikon.

"Ready?" Japuta asked.

"Yes." I moved my hands over to find Nikon. As I touched his shoulder, where the stolen armor clipped together, a strange feeling grew, starting from my fingers, and going up my arms and through my whole body. It was warm and comforting, but also left me feeling stronger than I had since before being taken to the Vading.

This would work.

I pushed both hands and part of my arms beneath him, and grasped him around his chest. "Do you have his feet?"

"I do."

"On the count of *three*. One. Two. Three." I lifted, expecting to strain, but it was like carrying Tewy. The only difference was that Nikon was more awkward, due to his size, but he weighed hardly anything. I didn't know how it worked, but I sang silent praises to the sands. If I could have sang them aloud without worrying about someone from Sirya hearing and coming to investigate, I would have.

The tricky part didn't end up being carrying him, but my lack of sight and not having anything or anyone to guide me, though Japuta tried. "Lift your legs now and step over the side. That's right. You've got this. Walk toward the way I'm pulling him now," she said.

The water was surprisingly warm when I jumped in. And welcoming. So welcoming. I loved it. My heart gave a twist of longing for my simple life when I'd spent more time with it.

But then I hadn't known Nikon or that the water was tainted.

I went forward slowly, especially once we got on land and the ground slipped beneath me as the grains of sand shifted. I followed her lead when something whacked me in the face. Shock made me almost drop Nikon, but I kept a firm grip on him, grateful I couldn't feel his weight. It'd be a bad trade to drop him, after all he'd done for me.

"Sorry." Japuta kept her voice low. "We are coming up on more trees and some tall bushes."

Within a few steps, leaves and twigs cracked against my side, jostling me but not so I couldn't continue on.

We rustled through a short distance, before she said, "Put him down here."

I did as she asked, careful to feel beneath him before setting him down, to make certain I wasn't laying him on a rock. "We've got to get the boat," I said. "Can we leave him here? Is it safe?"

"It'll have to be."

I didn't like that answer, but she was correct. We couldn't let any evidence we'd landed be left around. "Tewy, stay with Nikon, please."

He gave an oddly solemn *coo.*

Once we got to the boat, she guided me to the opposite side, where I latched on to it. She splashed through the water, before saying, "Follow my lead again."

I picked up the boat. The wood weighed heavy in my grasp, surprising me, after carrying Nikon and hardly feeling it. Despite the strain in my muscles, I waded through the water, breathing hard but not like the huffs that came out of Japuta.

I wanted to ask if she was well, but didn't have the air for it, nor did I want to stop. We had to get this out of sight. There was no question of that.

My arms wobbled, legs pushing on. I followed the boat and carried it at the same time, until the other half clunked to the ground.

"Sorry," she said between panted breaths.

"It's fine. How far are we with respect to vegetation? Can we cover it here?" There were enough bumps beneath me and branches tickling my thighs that we might make it.

"I can cover it." She heaved for breath.

"Hand me my cane, and I'll get some sand to help." I hoped the magic would hide the boat and our tracks.

"Here you are." She gave it to me, the familiar call comforting as it fell into my hands.

I headed back toward the river, keeping careful track of my steps and sweeping my cane before me. When its tip dipped into water, I bent down and grabbed a scoop full of wet sand. Though it dripped from my hand, I made it back with most of it and smeared it over the boat.

It had been a long time since I used magic this much in such a short amount of time. I didn't mind it nearly as much as I thought. Instead of struggling with the fact that it might do harm, I was more concerned that what the high priest did to the water would affect the magic in the sand.

"Japuta, if I go back to Nikon, can you hide the rest of the boat and our tracks with magic? Just scatter it across everything."

"I will. Go to him and see if you can figure anything out."

I wanted to run there but had to stop and say, "Point me in the right direction, and I'll whisper for Tewy so I can find him."

"It's that way." She turned me toward the left.

I went forward carefully, determined to find him without being slowed down by falling or tripping. I swept my cane in front of me, finding more of the vegetation. "Tewy? I need to find you and Nikon. Talk to me."

No response.

I walked and asked again, trying to ignore the creeping fear. "Tewy? Where are you and Nikon? I need to help him."

Quiet persisted, except for faint splashing from the river. Japuta, perhaps. Given her first reaction to using magic, I was grateful she was willing to help.

Something jumped on my arm, and I held in a scream. It climbed up my arm, pulling the fear from me, as Tewy settled in his usual position on my shoulder.

"You scared the sand out of me," I said.

He gave a monkey laugh, hooting at me in his way.

"I'm grateful you have a sense of humor, but where's Nikon? He needs me." Though I didn't wait for a response, instead carrying my cane more carefully, in case I was getting close.

Tewy *ooo oooo*ed at me but didn't give any further hints.

I shook my head, and moments later, my cane thudded against something firm, near the ground.

I fell to my knees, reaching out. "Nikon?" Skimming my fingers across his familiar shoulder, I found the not-so-familiar clasp, holding together his armor. "Can you hear me?" I asked.

Moving closer, I ran my hand down his arm and shoulder, searching for the wound. A hole in the cloth just above where his armor started on his shoulder was where the wound must have been. It was either a lucky shot, or far too close for comfort. As I prodded gently, my fingers found a bump of skin where a ridge like a scar remained, but no wound.

If we'd healed him, why hadn't he woken?

I rested my hand on his chest, grateful to find it moving steadily up and down beneath the armor. My heart ached for him. There had to be something I could do to help. To wake him.

"Nikon, please. I need you." More than words could say. I took his hand in mine. The unfamiliar bump where his amant marking was made me stiffen for a brief moment. *Lavti.* Forget her—I was the one here for him now, and would do everything in my power to take care of him. I loved him too much to do otherwise.

And it might just be the romantic sort of love.

The thought made heat pour through my chest. I'd have to deal with the realization that I was in love with him later, though I didn't understand how it was even possible when I couldn't see him. I wanted to discover the answer, but shoved all thoughts of it aside for if he recovered. No, *when*. He had to.

"Nikon?" I said again.

Tewy climbed off my arm and sat on my hand, and there was a series of small smacking sounds.

"*No, Tewy.* Don't hit Nikon." The rascal seemed to be trying his own way of waking Nikon.

My monkey replied in curious tones.

"I know you're trying to help, but that's only going to hurt him," I said. "We need to figure out what the problem is, so we can fix it, not slap him."

Oooo oooo, was all Tewy said.

I *pffted* at him.

Footsteps eased closer from the direction of the water. "Japuta?"

"It's me." Her voice assured me I wasn't being snuck up on by someone nefarious. Moments later, she sat down beside me, the sand and plants crinkling. "Any better?" she asked.

"The same." I tried not to sound worried but failed completely.

"I'm so sorry."

I jerked away from the sound of pity in her voice. "No. He'll be fine. He needs a healer or time, or something. He'll wake up."

"You seem very attached to him." Her voice was soft.

I contemplated her word. "He and Tewy mean everything to me. Tewy is the best of friends, and Nikon... Well, I..." Couldn't bring myself to say it aloud. It was crazy. Unrealistic. So very true.

"You're in love with him."

I gasped. "How do you know? I mean, it's not possible."

"It's why the high priest is searching for you. He knows something happened to you that broke through the change he made so you can only fall in love at first sight. A spy told him that an event took place, but he was never able to find out what. He wants to figure out how you are different and why, so he can reverse it."

It was all so much to think about. "But I didn't know I could fall in love, and the high priest has been wanting information about me since his granddaughter took me from my parents. It doesn't make sense."

"It's why he's been searching for the blind. Experimenting on them. He believes there's a link between them and no longer falling in love at first sight—or at all, if he has his way. Rumors of your becoming blind must have gotten to him, and he wanted to use you."

"But why the blind? And why me? I'm not the only blind person."

The pause had me both wanting to lean in closer and cower away. Whatever was coming felt important but dangerous. When she finally spoke, her words were flat, as if she'd leeched all emotion away from them. "My mother loved my father who was a blind man."

I wanted to ask what this had to do with her becoming an experiment for the high priest, but I had a feeling she was working up the courage to tell her story.

"Before my parents met, there was a man who wanted to marry my mother back when you could fall in love however it happened. She scorned him. Saw too many evil, greedy things inside him. The man swore if he couldn't have her, no one would. Love was a terrible, awful thing he would ban from the world."

"The high priest," I whisper, chills crawling across my skin.

"Yes. You know what he did from there. He did experiments until he thought he'd made a potion that would get rid of love. He used it at the waterfall, the source of water for all Eppla, but to his dismay, people still fell in love, except now they only fell in love at first sight or never."

"But you said your father was blind. Did your mother and him fall in love before the experiment?"

"They fell in love after."

A jolt hummed through me so hard it took me a moment to realize what it was. Hope mixed with the feeling of not being alone. "How? Is he still alive? Where are your parents?" So much I needed to know.

"They're dead." Her tone was wistful. "But I'm getting ahead of myself. My mother met my father after he'd become blind. No one ever knew how exactly, only that it hadn't been natural. He thought he would never be able to love, but my parents fell for each other anyway. Whatever happened allowed him to break through what the high priest had done to the water."

I was not as alone as I'd always thought I was. Or wouldn't have been if her father was still alive. "What happened?"

"The high priest found out."

"And I'm guessing that ended badly." It was only too easy to tell where the story was going.

"He killed my father and my mother died soon after, whether at his hand or because of her grief I don't know. I managed to escape and stay hidden from him, but I heard about him. Everyone did. How he grew stronger in power, an intermediary between magic and humans, but I knew better. Knew how he manipulated things to his will from my mother's stories from before the Govlin Wars.

"A couple of years later, I became an amant. I was so happy when I discovered I was pregnant, but then the high priest found me. He tried to convince me of my mother's wrongdoing. Of my needing to tell him everything I knew about my father and how he'd managed to fall in love despite being blind. I refused to tell him anything." She gave a mirthless laugh. "I didn't know most of the answers anyway."

"What happened to you, your husband, and child?" Though I didn't want to know, I needed to. It was going to be something horrific, so I steeled myself for it.

Her voice went flatter than ever. "He killed my husband and captured me. Tried to convince me to join his side. Though I feared for my baby's life with the rage stewing within him, I couldn't lie to him any more than I could myself. I rejected all of his words. Perhaps I should have tried to pretend because when I had the baby, he took her from me and added me to his tower of experiments."

Bile rose in my throat. I give a harsh whisper. "Your daughter?"

"You know her as Vading Antonia."

"He stole her and claimed her as his own granddaughter." The realization of just how deep his depravity went grew stronger with every word I heard about him. I gripped Nikon's shoulder, probably far too tightly, but couldn't bring myself to let him go despite his unconscious state.

"The high priest brainwashed my daughter. I tried to counter his claims whenever I saw her, but he always laughed it away as the ramblings of a crazy woman. He raised her with stories that her parents had been murdered by the blind, not some useless experiment he kept in his tower. He contributed to Eppla's growing hatred of the blind and did everything he could to lay hands on them so he could discover how my father fell in love in order to prevent it from happening again. He worked even harder to find someone who became blind by unconventional means. Someone like you."

I gulped down my fear of his cruelty. At least I knew why he wanted me.

"It would have been a good goal at least, despite how he tries to go about it, but he only wants to fix it so he can do what he wanted to in the first place."

"Banish love from the world." My heart was cold.

"He's close to doing so; all he needs is you."

If she was right—if I was the only thing between the high priest and getting rid of all love—I had to stop him. I'd stop him anyway, but being the key meant I had a more vested interest. It might have been too late for me, but I would help others enjoy what I never could.

CHAPTER THIRTY-EIGHT

"How can I stop the high priest?" I asked Japuta.

She sighed, sounding tired. "I don't know. I only know he believes you're the key to reversing things. He's done everything he can to me to figure out what happened to my father, but since I never knew exactly what it had been, I couldn't tell him."

But I suspected I knew. It was magic, just like had been done with me.

"When he does get his hands on you and fix things, he'll taint the water more than ever with his latest experiment, like he did with his latest potion he used on me."

I hesitated to ask, but it felt like a critical piece of information. "You can't fall in love?"

"Who knows? Maybe I can, maybe I can't. My amant mark from my late husband disappeared though. Could I love another? Perhaps, but I believe there's a possibility not. If he gets his hands on you, there'll be no hope at all." Her voice was matter of fact but with an underlying sadness.

"How will I make the difference?" If he knew, maybe I could stop him.

"I'm sorry, I don't know."

I wanted to find out, but Nikon still wasn't moving. In order to do what I could against the high priest, I'd need Nikon as much as possible. "We'll figure this out, but first I need your help," I said.

"Tell me what to do. I'm in both of your debt, for rescuing me."

Grateful she was willing, I said, "The most important thing we need to do is tell Reding Theodore all you know, but before we do that, we need to help Nikon. Since I can't be wandering around Sirya, I need you to go to my friends and tell them where we are. They'll know what to do."

"But will they trust me?" She didn't sound certain.

The truth was I didn't know, but I had to hope. "If you tell them I sent you—that we rescued you from Peka Tower—but Nikon was injured on the way, they will. We need help, and fast."

"I'll do my best. Where can I find them?"

Her courage gave me hope. I gave her instructions to Hupsheta's the best I could, and explained that Zoe and Kaius should be there. That they'd know what to do if she led them back here.

"Just promise you'll be careful," I added.

"I will. And I will come back to you and Nikon."

Tewy gave an angry hoot.

"And you too, monkey."

"Tewy," I corrected without thinking. I wished I could go instead, but this was for the best. "Any questions before you leave?"

"None. I'll be back as soon as I can."

"Be safe." I pushed down the growing fear inside me, and pleaded with the sands that this would work.

Her footsteps faded away. I clung to my cane with one hand and rested the other on Nikon. Tewy crawled onto my lap and curled up. It didn't take long for his breathing to become steady like Nikon's.

The world was desolate and cold. As I sat here, I tried to hope Japuta wouldn't be captured, and that she found Zoe and Kaius. Those two would bring help. I knew it.

So much damage had been done at the hands of the high priest. The world had been changed for the worse under his hand. I might only be one person and didn't know how much I could do, but he was only one person too. He'd accomplished many things, albeit terrible ones, but many things nevertheless. I didn't have to do as much as he had, only enough to stop him.

As time passed, the cool night air fluttered against my skin. The rush of the river was the only sound. My eyelids grew heavy, and I wanted to rest them, but I should stay awake and listen for trouble. Nikon had done it often for me; it was time to return the favor.

Japuta's words about Nikon echoed in my mind. I loved him. Not as a friend or a stand-in brother, but as a woman loves the man she marries.

Yet it was impossible for him to love me back. He had Lavti, though he despised her as much as he loved her. There was no changing that. The thing I'd wanted most had happened—I had fallen in love.

But he didn't love me back.

I didn't know whether to be joyous about having the impossible happen, or dismayed that it had happened after he was already committed to another, even if the high priest was right and I was the key to breaking the unnatural problem he'd created with the water.

Sitting straighter, I steadied myself with Nikon's soft breaths. Didn't matter if he'd never return my love; he'd always be my best friend.

The faint sound of people walking and talking came to me. I

went rigid, clinging onto my cane. Should I stand, so I could fight them off if they weren't here to help?

The soft tones continued, but the female voices sounded familiar. Zoe and Japuta.

The latter said, "We're here."

Her words eased some of my immediate concerns, but I didn't loosen my grip on Nikon. I wouldn't feel better until he was back to himself. "You found them," I said.

"She did." Zoe's footsteps rushed toward me, before she wrapped her arms around me. "And we brought a healer. This is Burnetpo."

I didn't care about formalities as I put a hand on the healer's arm, beyond grateful he was here. "Is there anything you can do for him? He got hit by an arrow. We tried to heal him with sand, and it did stop the bleeding and close the wound, but he hasn't woken since it happened."

"Let's have a look." Burnetpo's voice was deep and rough.

Zoe backed away, though she kept close, and there was a shifting at my side.

I pointed to Nikon's shoulder, about where I thought the arrow had gone through. "He was hit here."

I moved my hand and scooted to the side to allow the man to work, but stayed near enough to touch Nikon.

Tewy scampered off my lap, and Zoe made welcoming noises, but I focused on what was happening before me. "Have you been a healer long?" I asked.

"Long enough."

With that as the only response, I had to make myself patient, as he did what he needed to. I drummed my fingers on my leg, wishing the results would come faster, but good ones seemed to always take time. I had to believe this would be such an occasion, and not that the results were poor.

"You put sand on it, you say?" the healer finally asked.

"I did. Was it the wrong thing to do? Is he not going to wake?" I gulped down my fear, so I could hear his reply.

"I don't know yet. What were you thinking when you put the magic on him?"

I paused. What had I been thinking? It'd all happened so fast, and we were trying to get away from those chasing us. "That I wanted the wound to close and the bleeding to stop. Something like that."

"Ah. I see." There was movement beside me. Burnetpo moving away from Nikon?

Either I'd done something really wrong, and it was already too late, or there was nothing more the healer could do. "What do you see?" I asked.

"Though it's not well known, my theory and that of my former masters, is that the magic contained within the sand and water responds to people. Most believe it has a will of its own, and it does, but it often takes in mind the notions of the user. That's what our studies led us to believe."

I tried to think of all the implications of that, but I only wanted to focus on Nikon. "Does that mean he's never waking up, because I didn't wish for him to as I put the sand on his wound?" My chin quivered, but I wouldn't allow myself to think on it any more.

"Let me ask more, before I decide. Why is he dressed as a warrior? Is he working with the rebellion?" Burnetpo's words bore down at me.

It must have been safe to reply, or Zoe wouldn't have brought him. "No. Well, yes. Or rather, he was a warrior, but hasn't been for some time. He dressed this way in order to help us escape Peka Tower." It was strange, telling him so much, but I wanted him to know Nikon wasn't a threat.

"And he got injured how?"

"In the escape." I wished he would hurry things along.

Nikon's suffering must have been great, for him to not wake, and I wanted him better. There had to be a way for him to be healed.

The healer sniffed and shifted around again. "His pulse is steady, and his breathing looks good. My guess is there was something on the arrow, to cause this sort of reaction. Something you didn't know to direct the magic to fix, and the magic didn't know what to do with, so the problem was left alone."

My heart dove past the depths of my soul. There had to be something we could do. "Is it dangerous? Will it kill him?" I clenched my hands together, willing myself to be strong, but I was about to crumple. "Can you fix it?"

"Without opening a new wound, it's unlikely."

My hopes deflated with my shoulders. But he hadn't answered my first question.

Zoe's familiar movements came toward me, and she knelt, putting an arm around me.

Burnetpo said, "He will recover, given time. There's no reason to fret—not yet. As long as you stay safely hidden, I'd say he should wake sometime between the coming dawn and dusk."

"Unless the neczar find us before then." The sour answer came out of me before I could stop it. I'd turned bitter with worries over him not being safe. But why should I bother keeping my fears inside? The way our luck was going, it was true they'd find us. There was little we could do to dispute the fact; we might as well face it head-on. Though I could have been gentler in how I brought it up, as Japuta hissed in a breath.

Zoe gave my shoulders a squeeze. "We'll get through this. We've been through worse. As long as we stick together, they won't find you."

I was glad someone believed that. I didn't feel as hopeful. "There are things you don't know. Answers we've gotten."

"I'll take my leave of you, then, so you can discuss such things," the healer said. "I brought some food for you, though I'm afraid not enough. I must get back to my family, before I'm discovered missing."

Zoe withdrew from beside me. "Thank you for coming to our aid."

"May the rebellion fix what has been broken," was his reply. "If there's any change for the worse or he doesn't wake, come for me again, but I don't think it'll happen, and it's better not to risk yourself unless absolutely needed."

Tewy yammered something at that. The man gave his good-byes, and Zoe crouched back down beside me. I told her, "It's good to have you here. Thank you for getting the healer. I know it must have put you in danger, but I'm grateful for your help."

"No problem. I would have done so for any member of the rebellion, but with you two coming back so soon with information, it carries more weight. More importantly, we are friends. I owe you both a great debt. Who is this woman you sent for me?"

"I'm Japuta," she said, not far off. "Nikon and Cassandra saved me from Peka Tower, to bring news of what the high priest is doing."

"He saved her," I corrected, resting my hand back on Nikon's shoulder.

"No, you both got me out of there," she insisted.

I sat back, stunned. She was right. I had helped. I knew it, of course, but to hear her say it left me feeling a bit rattled. This was a stark reminder that during the worst of times when I felt useless, there was still more to me than I believed.

"I know you need rest," Zoe said, "but answers would be helpful. I'll deliver them back to Kaius, and we can figure out our best move, going forward."

"There's a mole though," I said. "Or at least there was at one point when I became blind. The high priest killed the one I heard of, but where there's one there could be others."

Quiet was followed by Zoe's hesitant response. "I'll keep

things between Kaius and me for now, unless it's something that we can share to give hope without giving away too much."

"Thank you. There's something more you can take to Kaius. Nikon and I stumbled across something that may be of significance. We grabbed some papyri that should have important information. If Kaius can read them, perhaps we'll have another clue as to what's going on. Though Japuta should be all we need."

"Where are they? I'll take them to Kaius," Zoe said.

Leaning forward, I slipped my hand next to Nikon's collarbone and down between his armor and his clothes. "Sorry, Nikon. I need to intrude in your space, to get the papyri."

He didn't answer, though his chest continued to move with his breaths.

I couldn't handle him staying like this. I wanted it all to be so different.

Shoving the thoughts aside as hard as I could, I found the papyri, pulled them out, and handed them over. "Please let me know what they say when you return. Unless Nikon wakes soon and we can come to you."

"I will." Zoe took them from me. "I'll be eager to hear more, but I should get moving. I'll be back as soon as I can. I'll see about bringing a fighter to protect you, but with a possible spy in our ranks, I don't dare take Japuta with me. I'll hurry."

"Thank you, Zoe."

She pulled me into a hug and whispered, "It's going to be all right. He'll get well again."

I bit my lip but could only nod and hope she was right.

Soon after Zoe left, Japuta said, "We need some rest."

"Should we set guard, though?" I asked, hand on Nikon's chest.

"I'll take first watch," she said.

I argued a moment but finally consented. I lay down next to Nikon, my monkey squished between us. He gave a contented *hoot*, though, and was soon breathing deeply.

I eased into comfort, knowing Nikon was alive and not letting worry overwhelm me on other things. He would live through this.

I woke to someone touching my arm. I jolted awake, Nikon's scent and the familiar callouses of his hand calming my worries. *He was awake.*

My heart fluttered. I wanted to whisper I loved him, but instead I said, "Thank the sands you're awake. How are you feeling?"

"Not myself. What happened?" His voice was groggy.

I wiggled closer. "After you were shot, Japuta and I put sand on your wound, but I had the wrong intentions. Or not the full intentions. I only partially healed you, and afterward you didn't wake. I thought you never would."

He groaned softly. "I feel like I was in a dark trap, until I slowly became aware of you next to me. I wouldn't have survived without you—my best friend through all of this."

My hopes for us dimmed. *Friend.* That was all I was to him. All I ever could be. He loved another, and there was nothing I could say or do to change that. I sagged against him, both grateful he was there and angry at the high priest. He'd ruined everything before I was born. Not just for me, but for everyone.

"We have to stop the high priest," I said, giving Nikon a quick rundown of all that Japuta had told me.

Nikon sighed, the weight on him sounding heavy. "I know. I wish we had a better idea of how."

"That makes two of us. Your brother should know a way. And maybe the papyri or Japuta will have more answers. I haven't had near enough time to talk to her and find out all she overheard or went through."

"Doubtful it will be easy for her." His hand left my arm, leaving me cold. "I can't believe all that the high priest has done. It hasn't had time to sink in," he said.

"I can't believe it either. It makes me wonder about the woman who didn't like his advances, Japuta's mother. What was she like? What must she have suffered? Plus, I've been thinking about his experiments. I can't imagine what all those people must have gone through." I shivered.

"When I think he wants you to be one of them—" He gave an angry growl, deep in his throat, but the effect was lost in a yawn.

"I'm fine, though." For the moment. "Besides, I have you to protect me." And I did feel safe here, in his arms.

"I wish there was more I could do." His words were sleepy.

Didn't we all?

We fell silent, his breathing steady. Since he'd woken, I was at ease. I'd helped him back to health.

Comforted, I sleepily said, "I don't know what I'd do without you."

He didn't respond.

Rest. It was what he needed, but I wanted to wake him and make sure he could return to consciousness again. I refrained, letting my body relax besides his, and soon drifted off.

I woke to his hand, covering my mouth. Confused, I wanted to take it off and ask what was going on, until I heard voices indistinctly speaking nearby. Not Japuta; where was she? The strangers were coming closer, and they were searching for us.

CHAPTER THIRTY-NINE

I shifted slightly, and Nikon tightened his grip. I brushed my hand across his wrist, to let him know I understood. Did he get the message?

Whoever searched for us crunched in the sand, coming closer. I wished I knew where Japuta was—if she was awake and on her guard.

"Don't know why we have to keep looking for runaways," a woman said. "There are so many people in Sirya; we're not going to find them."

"The monkey will give them away," the man replied.

She scoffed. "It'd rather be home sleeping. It's too early for this."

"You want to tell that to the neczar?"

My rigid pose grew stiller, heart thumping rapidly.

"We'll search, but I don't have any hope of finding them," she said.

Nikon's hand eased but didn't leave. I patted the ground around me softly, in an attempt to find my cane. It called out to me from my right, as the two continued to talk about the neczar, nearing us as they did so. Through the sand and some sort of plant, I finally moved my fingers across the familiar wood. Curling my hand around it brought the comforting belief I could face what was to come, especially if there were only two guards after us.

What was more, Nikon was awake. That had to mean he was well or on the mend. That was a reason to celebrate, right there.

The two people were almost right on top of us. I loosened my muscles, seeking a way to get them ready to fight without alerting the warriors to our presence. I wanted to jump up, but the noise would draw attention to us if they hadn't already seen us.

As they crowded in, thoughts of last night came to me. Japuta, hiding our tracks and boat with the magic. Perhaps she hid us better than I thought. If the healer was correct, Japuta's intention to not be found would have been strong indeed. She knew better than anyone the horrors of the high priest's hospitality.

The footsteps ceased. My heart beat a wild pattern, like a ride down the rapids.

Without warning, Nikon's hand disappeared and he jumped into action. He didn't know we were hidden. To my left, came the sounds of fighting and jostling around. I didn't know what spurred him on, but it must have been safe for me to move, if he did so.

I got to my feet. Where were Tewy and Japuta? There wasn't time to contemplate it, as a flashing sensation of a sword coming at me flickered through my awareness.

In one fluid movement, I batted the sword aside and twisted my canes apart. I set my knees to bend slightly, and burst into action. The fighting sticks were natural extensions of my arms, helping me know when to strike and when to fall back.

The fight continued, more weapons coming at me like there were two attackers and not only one. Nikon fought at least one opponent to my left. Were there more people than I thought?

I'd worry about it later.

I jolted to the side, wind whipping across the skin of my arm, as a sword flicked past. This was a fight I didn't want to continue long. Whoever I fought against, they were stronger and better trained than the average warrior. They must have been elite warriors. Blast Antonia and the high priest.

I ducked and *whooshed* my stick up, getting between their defenses and slamming it against someone's chest. A cry of pain came from their direction—a sharp, breathless sound. The second person I fought against growled deep, sounding like a man, and came at me more fiercely than before.

"No one hurts my partner," he called out, his rage evident, as his weapon came flying at me repeatedly, making it so I had to move faster than I was used to.

With the strain of the past few days—weeks—I wouldn't be able to continue on long, despite my fighting sticks. He'd get the upper hand, which would mean wound me at best and capture me at worst. I couldn't let that happen.

Though fear sprayed shards in my stomach, at the thought of Nikon being weakened and me failing, I ducked and slammed my stick against the man's legs. He howled, and the feeling of a sword coming for my chest had me falling back.

We went back and forth a few times. Had I met my match? And where was Japuta?

I should end the fight. Now.

Giving it one last effort, I struggled against the inclination I had to dodge his next attack, instead letting his sword sink into my bad arm just enough to leave him open. I whacked him in the head as hard as I could, pushing past the pain.

The sharpness on my arm disappeared as the man fell with a *thud.*

"Nikon?" I called out, hoping his fight wasn't going badly for him.

"*Sands. The* Nikon?" the woman's voice spat out between huffs of air.

The words were followed by a quick brush of footsteps,

fleeing from us. I expected Nikon to follow, catch her, and keep her from spilling our location or our return to the city to her superiors. Instead, his breath came in labored gasps.

I rushed to him as liquid dripped down my arm from my wound. "Are you hurt?"

"You said my name. They know it's us. We have to move." He sounded worried. "Where are we?"

"The outskirts of Sirya," Japuta replied from behind us.

"Did they hurt you or Tewy?" I asked, fear bubbling inside me in a frothy mess.

"We're fine. You're the one bleeding," she said.

Something sounded like cloth being ripped.

"It's nothing," I said.

"I'm going to get sand, to heal you. Just a moment." Her steps hurried off.

"Nikon? Are you angry?" I had a mad desire to tell him my discovery—that I loved him and wanted to spend the rest of forever proving it to him. I clamped down on the urge.

"You shouldn't have said my name." His words were gruff.

I went rigid. "I'm sorry. I wasn't thinking."

"I know."

With the accusation in his tone, I clenched my jaw. If only I'd been able to keep my mouth shut.

"Sorry," he said. "I'm confused about what's going on and—honestly—weak."

I went to him and put my hand out until I found his arm. "We'll steady each other."

"I still shouldn't have said that."

"I forgive you." I was just happy that he was alive. I gave him a quick rundown of what had happened while he slept—minus my revelation that I loved him.

While I was talking, Japuta returned and tied a cloth covered in wet sand on my arm.

When I'd caught Nikon up, I added, "Whatever we do, we

have to stop the high priest. His experiments already went too far when he changed the way we love. If he gets rid of the emotion altogether, the world will suffer."

"I agree. We have to get to Theodore," Nikon said. "The sooner the better."

"We'll send word. Should we go through town? The desert?"

"Not through town. We'll have to send word to Zoe and Kaius, but we can't stay here, and we're too recognizable to go to town."

"I'll go," Japuta said. "Take us where you're going to hide, and I'll take the message. No one will recognize me, except the neczar, and I'll avoid them."

"It's going to have to be that way." Nikon took my hand and rested it on his arm as he moved forward. We walked for so long, my legs wanted to give in to the temptation to take a break for a while. Though it would be nice, there was too much as stake, for us to stop.

When Nikon came to a stop, he said to Japuta, "Do you remember the way here, and how to get back to Zoe and Kaius?"

"I do. I'll be back as soon as I can."

"You should rest first." She'd had little chance to, since we took her from Peka Tower.

She hesitated. "I can rest after the high priest is dead."

Her hatred was venomous, but I didn't blame her. She gave a quick goodbye and left. Tewy pattered quietly about. He'd gotten more sleep than any of us except Nikon, and I was jealous of the monkey.

"Rest, Cass," Nikon said.

I relished hearing my nickname from his mouth.

"We have much to deal with yet ahead, and you will need the strength," he added.

I didn't have to be told twice, until I remembered the state he was in. "Are you well enough?"

"To watch, yes. I'll wake you if there are problems."

"Thank you." I wanted to curl up next to him again, but I stretched out on a patch of greenery and fell asleep.

When I woke, all was quiet. I whispered, "Nikon?"

He gave a deep sigh. "Here." His response sounded weary.

I crawled over a few steps to him. "I can keep watch now, you rest."

"I already rested for a whole day."

"When? When you were knocked unconscious by the arrow? That's why you need to take a break—your body must recover." It would be hard for him. He wasn't one to sit and rest when things needed done and danger lurked. "Come lie down here next to me. I'll wake you right away at the sign of others," I said.

"Fine. I'm sorry I can't do more, though." He must really be feeling ill.

"Don't worry over it."

It didn't take long for him to stretch out next to me and fall asleep. I rested a hand on his shoulder, like I'd done when he was injured, wishing he'd recover soon. We should have gone to the river and gotten him more magic, to help his stamina if nothing else.

Time trickled by more slowly than I wanted, in utter silence. At some point, something pressed heavy on my senses. It was difficult to tell what, exactly. Not a person—I didn't think. And no threat, or we would have already been in trouble.

Nikon rolled closer to me, and the presence jolted away, a soft padding the only hint that I hadn't been imagining things.

I bit my lip. Should I wake him? No. More sleep would be better for him than chasing after things that might not be real.

The heat increased, and then decreased. It wasn't fully gone yet, when several sets of footsteps approached us.

I shook Nikon's shoulder, and was grateful when we woke quickly but quietly, and put his hand over mine.

We drew apart, and Tewy climbed on my lap, settling down like he hadn't any plans to go anywhere for a while. Dratted monkey picked the worst time to relax. I needed to prepare, in case trouble was heading our way.

With my cane in hand, I scooted Tewy out of my lap. I got ready to jump up and lash out.

The footsteps closed in, but before they were within striking range, Zoe called out, "It's us."

I relaxed, until she said, "We've brought the Reding with us."

It was time to explain all we had learned on our journey.

CHAPTER FORTY

"Are you well, Nikon?" Reding Theodore asked. "I've never seen you so pale."

"Just tired."

"Having a neczar arrow shot through you will do that." The Reding had clearly been talking with Japuta, thank the sands.

I got to my feet, Tewy hooting at me for disrupting him. I didn't bother apologizing, instead telling the Reding, "Did Japuta tell you what the high priest has done, how he took something from the water, and what he plans to do?"

"She did, on the way over." His voice was guarded.

"How do we move forward from here? We have to stop him," I said. "That is, if you believe her."

"I don't want to, but her appearance certainly adds credibility to her story. She... She shares features with Antonia." He cleared his throat. "Plus, the high priest does have his strange experiments, though I never knew they involved people. If I had, well I hope I would have figured out how to act sooner."

Relief flooded me. He would take us seriously, then. I'd hoped, but it was hard to know what meddling Antonia would do, as his wife. Apparently, not enough to get in the way of our plans.

Theodore took his time replying. "It is a problem I'm not certain what to do with. I want it fixed, though. It'd go a long way toward helping the people of Eppla be more united—less broken by distinctions that they can't control."

It was near impossible to believe this was the same man who claimed we needed to root out the odiosom pretending to be amant months ago.

Nikon said, "It will take time to heal Eppla, no matter how quickly we figure out how to fix things."

I stood straighter. I wasn't the only one who wanted change, though my shoulders wished to sloop at the thought of how long it would take. I wouldn't let them.

"That may be, but the sooner we get rid of this falling-in-love-only-at-first-sight business, the sooner we can work toward recovery. Any ideas how we should accomplish that?" Theodore asked.

No one said a word.

"I'm the key, aren't I?" I said, though I didn't like it. Whatever needed to be put back in the water, it would be related to me. I didn't know what it would take, but if it meant restoring things to the way they should be, I'd do whatever was necessary to make that happen. My stomach roiled, and my chest hurt. "We need to do something with me in order to restore things to their natural order."

Tewy's monkey noises grew more and more animated. Too bad no one knew what he was saying. It probably wouldn't have made a difference, but it would make me feel better if I understood him.

"Whatever we decide, we should focus on the waterfall," Japuta said.

"Why?" Nikon asked.

"Because the high priest talked about it so often. He

mumbled something once about it being *the source.* He said himself that it was where he poured the first potion. That was where something was taken from the water to cause the taint. Something that he believes Cassandra is the key to," she said.

Just as I suspected, which didn't give me much satisfaction. It was hard to feel anything but sorrow over him ruining the water source for the entire country. And if I was the key to putting things back, how much would I have to give to make things right?

When no one else spoke, I said, "I'm willing to go to the waterfall. That's where all the trouble started. From there I'll figure out how to fix it." Horridly, I had no idea how to go about it, but I'd do whatever it took.

"I will go with," Nikon said.

Concern raced through me, even as part of me jumped at the thought of having him stick around. I knew he kept near me out of friendship, but it was heartening to hear him volunteer.

"Are you well enough?" I asked.

"Yes."

I had a feeling he was holding back his lingering injury, but I also couldn't refuse his company. I was far too selfish for that. Plus, I would take all the help I could.

"I can arrange for others to aid you," Zoe said. "It will take some time though."

"We'll go as soon as we can and start guarding it and figuring out what we can while you make arrangements," I said.

Nikon said, "What else?"

"Kaius read the papyri. We gave them to the Reding, but I can tell you what they said." Yet, Zoe didn't go on.

I grew more agitated. What it said had to do with the high priest, so I needed to know it. It might give us a clue what to do at the waterfall, but if it didn't, it'd still help us know more of what was going on with him. All the better to fight him.

When Zoe spoke again, her words were soft but clear. "The

high priest is making an army of enhanced neczar to ensure the Reding has no power."

Fear slammed into me. There was nothing we could possibly do against a group of neczar treated with extra magic.

"I have little power anyway, but still enough to appear a threat to him," Theodore said.

"Where's he getting neczar to turn enhanced, and what enhancements are they getting?" I asked.

It was the Reding who replied, "It appears he's been creating them in Peka Tower. As part of his experiments. They're stronger, faster, and more lethal than before."

Someone—Japuta?—shuddered.

I couldn't blame her. I was disgusted, and I hadn't been through the experimenting she had. I wanted to do more for her, but first, the country needed to be set right. After that, I would help one person at a time, as I could.

The way wouldn't be easy though. The neczar were already such a force without being enhanced.

"Do we need to worry about enhanced neczar following us to the waterfall?" I asked.

"We don't believe so," Zoe said. "It appears his work is not yet complete according to the papyri you brought us."

I straightened my shoulders, showing greater confidence than I felt. "Then we get rid of him before he can do the damage."

"It's not that simple." The Reding spoke this time. "I have only so much power over him. Being the Reding doesn't mean what it used to. My wife and the high priest have been conspiring against any movements I've made in the past. After I spoke with you, I've only taken small steps. If I tried to oust the high priest, they would imprison or kill me, and claim it was the rebellion, in order to accomplish what they want."

There was only so much any of us could do, though I wanted to fix it all. My loved ones could help—not to mention the rebellion—but with my being the key to things, I felt responsible. In part.

"Zoe and Kaius, you can help here in the city, while Nikon and I go to the waterfall, yes?" I said. "And then, once we figure out how to stop the high priest's meddling with the water, we'll come back and do what we can. If people fall in love naturally, and not just at first sight, we may make more headway."

I turned toward where Japuta should be standing. "Do you have any idea what exactly the high priest has done to the water, so we can undo it?"

"I don't know any more."

Disappointment clung to me, but I couldn't let it override my desire to make a difference. "Thank you for your help. What you've told us is more than we knew previously."

"Do you want to start out now?" Nikon asked.

"As soon as we can get the supplies together. People are suffering under Antonia and the high priest." Though I didn't know how we would make a difference or get there without being caught. It'd been a dangerous journey down the river near the chasm, last time. Going up it would be just as dangerous, but going around would take too long.

We'd figure something out.

"Already have supplies," Zoe said. "Kaius thought you'd want to leave right away, so we gathered some things together."

"What would we do without you two?" Leo's making them our housemates had been one of the best choices for us. They were as dear to me as if they were my siblings.

"You'd be lost; that's what," she teased, coming closer. She handed me a bag, and in a lower voice, said, "We'll keep an eye on your parents and Japuta while you're gone. Please, be safe."

"Thank you. I'm more concerned with your safety. The biggest danger to us will be falling in the chasm," I said.

"Japuta told me what you did with the boat on the way here

from Peka Tower. Why don't you do that again? You can spell it to go faster, and to not fall down the chasm."

And hope that the sand listened to our intentions and didn't have its own. "It's a good idea. We'll try it." I pulled her into a hug. "Thank you for all you've done. The rebellion is lucky to have you both as The Jackal."

"We're luckier to have you. Be safe."

"You too."

Nikon and I gave our goodbyes to everyone else.

He surprised me when he lingered over the parting from his brother. He said to Theodore, "With this new understanding you've gained, you've also gained more enemies."

"Your warriors have done a good job, watching out for me. I'd feel more comfortable, though, if you took some with you."

"There's nothing but monkeys and birds, once we get back to the waterfall," he replied. "We'll be fine."

"I hope that's the case." Theodore's voice came toward me, as he said, "Take good care of my brother."

Surprised he'd say that to me, I could only answer with, "I will."

"I know you and those sticks of yours are capable of it. Heard enough complaints from beaten warriors to discern that."

I didn't know whether to laugh or feel bad. "What can I say, except *they were in my way*?"

"Which is why I know Nikon will be in good hands. I'll see you both when you finish. I hope by then to have my wife and the high priest under control, if not dealt with."

"Be careful, brother." Nikon's voice was firm, but softened to let me know he cared far more for his brother than he usually let on.

After a few more hugs and well-wishes, Zoe led us away from the scene, to the river. There, she had a boat waiting for us.

We rubbed it down with sand, as she suggested, intending to make the boat fast enough to get to the waterfall in less than a day, but without causing any problems, and specifically without falling down the chasm.

"This is it, then," Zoe said.

I smiled. "We'll be together again, soon." Just perhaps not as soon as we all wished.

Nikon, Tewy, and I settled in the boat, and off we went.

CHAPTER FORTY-ONE

Under the cover of darkness, we traveled faster than before. It appeared the magic saw our intentions of hurrying to aid the people of Eppla, and did what it could to help.

While Nikon rowed rapidly, judging by the way the wind surged around me, I kept silent.

He wasn't at his peak condition, and I wished there was more I could do to assist. I bit my cheek. How bad was his health at this point?

"What is it?" Nikon asked, as Tewy rummaged about the boat and through our things. With the way the monkey carried on with his jabber, he might know where we were headed and was excited to be returning. It was more his home than mine, after all.

"What is what?" I asked back.

"You look worried. Are you stressed about what's going to happen at the waterfall? We'll figure it out."

So much for keeping my worries from him. I should have known better than to attempt it, but I couldn't help wanting to protect the one I loved. "That's a concern, but I'm more thinking about you," I said.

"Me?"

"With everything you've been through, I'm not sure it was wise of you to come. I know you want to—and I want you here, don't get me wrong—but I also want you safe." Which was probably more honest than I should have been when I needed all the assistance I could get, but if I couldn't be honest with him, who could I be honest with?

A soft noise, like a rumble, grew in the distance as he said, "You're my best friend. It doesn't matter what condition I'm in; I will always do what I can to help. The fact that it affects so many people means I want to help even more."

My heart fluttered at the same time as my eyes stung. Though part of me knew it was huge to have this sort of friendly love, I still wanted more, impossible as it was. Despite that, he was right. He was my best friend. And so, he deserved to know the sweeping sensation that came through me because of him.

"The thing is, Nikon, there's more going on." How did I tell him I loved him? It wasn't something he'd understand. Or maybe he would, but he couldn't love me back—not with Lavti pulling on his thoughts and emotions. His connection to her meant there would never be room for me. I'd have to learn to live with that.

The distant roaring grew louder. "What is that noise?" I asked.

"The chasm." Nikon sounded weary. "We're almost there."

"Already?"

"The magic intention seemed to work well, and it explains a lot about the past."

I leaned forward, resting my elbows on my knees. "Do you think we'll be safe? From the chasm?"

"I believe, and that should be enough."

As much as I wanted to agree, the *should* made me hesitate. "As long as we don't get swallowed down the hole."

The roar grew louder and louder.

"We'll make it," he yelled over the sound.

I gripped the sides of the boat, willing us to live through this. Without being able to see what was going on, I had no idea how close to the edge we were. All I could do was hope to the sands it wasn't close at all.

Tewy jumped on my lap and clung to me. Though I worried about not having enough to grasp on to, while I continued to hang on to one side of the boat with one hand, I gripped him with the other.

"We're coming up to it," Nikon called. "Hang on."

We bounced up and down, flashes of going under the water when I'd last crossed this area coming to me. The fright had been bad. Almost losing Tewy had been worse.

Holding my monkey more tightly, I made sure he wasn't going to fall out of the boat as the waves grew wilder, bouncing me on my seat. We bucked up in the air and back down, hard. I gritted my teeth.

We'd make it through. All of Eppla was counting on us.

We jutted up again, before slamming back down so hard, I thought the boat would break beneath me. It shuddered, but somehow stayed together.

The crazy jolting about eased some, and Nikon said, "Almost through."

Seconds later, the roaring remained loud, but it was behind us. The noise made me shiver. The boat had held true, and we were all well—that was what I needed to focus on. "You did well," I said.

"Thanks to the boat," Nikon countered.

"I was talking to Tewy."

"Oh."

I laughed. "I'm only teasing you, Nikon. Though he did good as well. I'm sure the magic on the boat helped, but it took someone skilled with oars to get us through. I'm glad the crossing was quicker and safer than last time."

He didn't respond.

I furrowed my eyebrows. "Is everything all right?"

"No." The word came in a whisper. "There are a dozen boats pulled up onto the sand ahead."

I ducked, like that would somehow hide us, before realizing what I was doing. "Do we turn back? Fight? Hide? I don't know."

"There are no people around, but there are two decent-size boats. If they're neczar, fighting them would be hard. We should leave."

"But who knows if we can make it back? Or worse, if it's the high priest, what he could be doing here?" Could he have had time to make it up here? If he used magic, it was entirely possible.

"Exactly what I'm worried about." Nikon leaned closer, his hand brushing my knee. "I'll stand by you, whatever you think we should do."

"You're leaving it up to me?"

"Yes. If it is the high priest here, you're the most at risk."

And with me, love.

I squirmed in my seat. I didn't want to be the reason we left. Fear shouldn't drive me away. Yet I also didn't want to stay and have the high priest use me. If he was here, though, he had a plan. If he wasn't, we should figure out what was going on and how to move forward.

"I think we take the chance, but stay hidden," I said.

"Got it."

"Can they see us?"

"No. There's too much vegetation between us and wherever they are. I'll pull in away from them and hide our boat." He squeezed my knee, sending tingles through me. "And, Cass, I think you're brave."

Not nearly as brave as I wanted to be, but some courage was better than none.

The soft splashing of his paddles barely made any sound over the distant roar. I said, "Who do you think could be here?"

"Who else, but someone who has a connection to Antonia

and the high priest?"

I felt queasy. I didn't want to deal with either of them, especially at this place I used to consider home. "Do you think they, themselves, are here?"

"I don't know."

I wished we did somehow have the answers, but it might be good that we didn't. If Antonia or the high priest were here, I didn't want to be involved in any of it.

But we had to.

"Do you remember much about around here? We should find a way to the waterfall that we won't be visible to anyone who might be there," Nikon said.

"If you get me to territory I'm familiar with, yes, I can take you there. It'll be slow going, with the bushes and trees, but we can make it," I whispered.

"Understood." Which mean he thought we could do this, but we needed to be careful about talking, going forward.

I lowered my face close to Tewy. "Quiet, little monkey. I know you'll be excited when we're back by the waterfall, but others may be listening."

Ooo oo, was his reply. Whatever that meant. One monkey in an area with lots of them shouldn't make a difference to whoever was here.

Only a few strokes of Nikon's oars dipping in the water later, the boat bumped against solid ground, and we came to a stop. Tewy jumped off my lap and hurried away, his scampering audible. So much for him sticking with us.

The loss was sharp in my chest, but he had to be excited to get back to his own kind.

Fishing my cane out of the bottom of the boat, I held my hand out, and Nikon immediately took it.

He'd been waiting for me.

Together, we left the boat and pulled it onto shore, and he hid it.

Going deeper into the vegetation, it was impossible for me to know where we were. I hadn't ventured far down the river when I lived here before, plus I had nothing to orient me.

Nikon did a good job of leading me forward, though, my hand on his arm growing warm from touching him. The heat moved through me and to my heart. I didn't want to end our contact. I should have told him about my feelings toward him. Now, it was so quiet except for a few birds and the soft rush of the river, that I didn't dare speak and notify others of our presence.

We quietly made our way through the tangled vegetation. It snarled at me, branches whipping at me. I might have turned me back if I didn't know there were other people around we needed to avoid. The trees and shrubs whacked against me, getting in my face and hair.

We shifted through them, continuing on, the sound of excited monkeys coming in the distance. Perhaps Tewy had found some of his friends. Further down, I heard a different sort of roaring. We were getting close to the waterfall.

Nikon whispered in my ear, "Your house is ahead and to the left. I don't dare take us there, because coming out of the bushes could prove to be trouble, should someone be watching. Do you know how to get to the waterfall from here?"

It would take some doing, but I could figure it out, so I nodded. He took hold of my hand, and I wished he wanted to hold it for more than to simply keep us together.

Shoving my feelings aside, I skirted the area where my old house was, the way growing more and more familiar as I went, despite the passage of time and the fact that I didn't usually walk among the plants.

Strange memories and impressions came to me. Fragmented and painful. The loss of my parents I'd felt the first time I came here. Being with Antonia. Her disappearance. The lonely period that followed. Tewy, as my only company.

As grateful as I was to have had him by my side for so long, a pang went through me. With all the monkey chatter going on, I'd be surprised if he wanted to leave here after this. I didn't know if my place was there or here, but it likely wouldn't be here. As much as I loved the solitude, the waterfall, and Tewy, I needed to be around people. Those I cared about.

I blinked back tears. What was it with the sudden emotion? There wasn't time for it, and yet, here it was.

As we walked, I focused on the wisps of plants brushing against my arms and bringing me back to the present and all the things I needed to do. I wished I knew more about what made me the key. What I could do, to reverse the problem with the water.

The thought stopped me cold in my tracks. Icy pricks went down my spine, and I shuddered.

Nikon pulled back toward me, giving my hand a squeeze. I squeezed back and worked to steady myself. If only we'd thought of that sooner...

But we were here, and there had to be something we could do or learn. I'd spent many years in and out of this water at its very source. Being here now couldn't change anything for the worse.

I took a step to let Nikon know I was ready, and pressed forward, stretching my arm back so our hands could stay connected. The waterfall grew louder, drowning out much of the chirping of birds, though, if anything, the monkey squeals had grown louder.

My mind set the way for me, the steps so familiar, I didn't have to think about them. In no time at all, I crouched down behind some bushes and whispered toward Nikon, "We should be here."

"The waterfall is ahead, and I don't see any people."

"Then why is there a tightness to your voice?" And his grip was strong, almost enough to hurt.

"The sphinx is here."

CHAPTER FORTY-TWO

The sphinx. If she was on the side of the people I suspected were here on behalf of Antonia and the high priest, we were in for a bad surprise. If she was here of her own accord... Well, that wasn't much better. At least she'd already given me her riddle, to which I'd discovered the answer.

What was it she'd said? *Heart*—I would need it more than ever, in the time to come. But I'd already done that, which she'd mentioned. Hadn't I?

Either way, I didn't dare speak as we crouched. I didn't know how long we stayed, but my thighs burned. I slowly lowered myself to the ground. When the sphinx didn't pounce on me and the people didn't come running, I counted myself lucky. Keeping us alive was good enough for the time being.

My pulse thrummed in my ears, as Nikon settled next to me. Though he was silent, I felt him move by my side. It was near impossible not to feel him by me and know what he was doing. His proximity caused an innate sense of wonder and excitement, despite a dangerous creature hovering near.

I reached for Nikon, and was grateful when he took my hand. I clung to him and to my cane. Was there going to be a way out of this? Some way to get the sphinx away from the waterfall, so we could figure out what was going on with it? There had to be some evidence of the taint and a way to counteract it.

Time passed slowly. The sphinx might have realized we were here, but if so, she could have taken us out. Nikon and I had both answered questions from her riddles in the past, so maybe she didn't want to bother us anymore.

Whatever the case, waiting for the sphinx to make a move left me annoyed. We had other things to deal with that only got harder with her here.

When voices sounded in the distance, coming closer, Nikon went still a moment before whispering in a hushed tone, "The sphinx left."

Odd that she was here in the first place, but more, curious that she seemed scared off by whoever was coming. I doubted there was anyone she couldn't take on, if she wished it.

Nikon had never described her to me, other than she was big. She'd swiped me with a paw once. Though all I'd felt was the *whoosh* of being hit, it impressed upon me how massive she really was. She could take down a few people.

The voices grew closer, until I could make out what they were saying. Nothing of interest, just general teasing of one another. I picked out at least seven distinct voices, though it easily could have been more.

That changed when a man said, "It's just this way, high priest."

Panic drove through me harder than when I knew the sphinx had been here. There were a lot of horrific things that could come of his being here. My safety was in question, though it wasn't nearly as important as all of Eppla's ability to love being at risk.

Did he need me to counteract his original spell, or create his new spell that precluded everyone from falling in love? Either was trouble.

Nikon rested a hand on my knee. I took a steadying breath, to clear my mind. It was good the high priest and his people were here—as long as we didn't get captured. We could get more answers from their actions.

"He's been here before, you idiot," Antonia said.

I tensed back up. I didn't want to think what I'd have to deal with if she was here. She put me through far too much, and I'd had enough.

A person hurried back, as the others came closer.

The high priest said, "Not much has changed here. It should work the same as before, though without that blind woman, it's difficult to know how my experiments work."

"We can wait for the warriors and neczar to find her," Antonia said in a soft, meek voice I'd never expect from her, even back when I thought we were friends.

"I'm sick of waiting. We need to attempt the next trial now. Besides, we had her for years, and there was nothing that led me to believe we can't try this out. It may not work like we expect, but I've refined it enough over the years. Bring my portable lab."

"You heard the high priest," Valeriana called out. "Get his things, so we can put them together."

I froze at her voice, Nikon's fingers digging into me. She was a problem, but we'd deal with her the same way we'd deal with everyone who got in our way.

There was some stomping about, and one man muttered, "We could get some sleep first."

"I've not slept well in years; you can handle a night." The high priest's voice was low but deadly. I wouldn't want anything to do with him when he sounded like that. Coming here had been a mistake.

Except, it sounded like he was going to go ahead with his plan to rid the world of love altogether—with or without me. I couldn't let that happen. I loved Nikon too dearly, even if he didn't love me back, and the emotion caused so much wonder. We couldn't let that be taken from Eppla.

I didn't know what to do, but that wouldn't stop me from acting.

As I stayed hidden, with Nikon's hand on my knee, the sound of monkeys chattering and calling out came closer. Soon, they were all around us, and a scampering headed straight for us. *Tewy.* He returned with an animated chatter I hoped none of the people closer to the water realized was directed at us. It was certainly loud enough to catch attention, but with all the other monkeys, perhaps it blended in.

"Someone shut those creatures up," Antonia barked.

"Vading, forgive the noise," Valeriana said, before her voice echoed around the area. "Kill the monkeys."

Fear clamored through my heart. Tewy had no problem continuing on, making more noise than one monkey should be allowed to, and from the sound of things, he wasn't the only excited little chirper. The other monkeys grew louder too, making enough sound to rival that of the waterfall. They were putting themselves far more at risk than I liked. I pleaded with the sands that none of the little creatures would be hurt.

Nikon gave my free hand a tug, then moved away. Taking the hint, I crouched as low as I could and kept my steps silent, as I followed his guiding hand. Those invading the area probably couldn't hear us over the din, anyway, but I remained cautious.

We went some ways, going faster the farther we went. Tewy rode on my shoulder, growing quiet after a few hoots. The monkeys behind us grew louder, somehow, making all the noise they seemingly could.

Nikon pulled me close, making my heart thump excitedly in my chest, until he whispered, "Can you lead us away from here? It's not safe. We've got to find a place to wait them out."

I shook my head and raised my face up toward him. "We can't let them do this without a fight."

He wrapped his arms around me, my pulse more rapid than ever. He said, "I know you want to help, but even though there's only two warriors, the neczar change everything. We don't stand a chance."

I thrummed my fingers on my leg. I had to think of a solution that wouldn't involve us getting hurt, but couldn't think of anything that would keep us safe and allow us to stop the high priest and Antonia.

"We have to try," I whispered.

He sighed, but the tension in his hold increased. "Let me scout a few things out, and we'll come up with a plan together when I get back."

"I could come with you."

"I know, but I'd feel better if I didn't drag you closer to them sooner than I have to. Is that all right?"

"I know the area well though."

"I'm just going back to where we were. It will be fine. If you're comfortable waiting here for me where the high priest won't find you?"

I wanted to go, but he was correct. It would only make our capture twice as likely Maybe more so. "What about the sphinx?" I asked.

He hesitated. "You answered her riddle. I don't think she'll bother you."

It was the *think* part that had me nervous, but I nodded. "Go, then. But come back whole as soon as you can."

His grip tightened around me for a brief moment, emotions flooding through me, and he said, "Anything for you."

It was said lightly, but I detected a seriousness in his tone. He'd do whatever he could to make it.

"Take Tewy." I turned toward my monkey. "And boy, you return to me if anything happens to Nikon." I didn't know that he would, but he was a smart little guy. I could hope he understood and would help.

Tewy jabbered at me and hopped off my shoulder.

Nikon whispered, "We'll be back when we can."

I nodded, and his warmth left me. The night air was cold without him. Despite not hearing him leave, I felt his presence was no longer there. I was alone.

I found a spot to sit in the area and got myself ready to wait. By the time night had stretched into coldness, worry ate at me. I tapped my fingers against the wood of my cane.

The night deepened, and as tired as my body felt, I couldn't bring myself to doze off. One of the warriors could come upon me, and I wouldn't have any idea. Besides, my worry was too tightly wound.

A familiar screech was the first clue that my worries over Nikon might be well founded. Tewy came hurtling toward me and jumped in my lap, his chatter quieter but more insistent.

"Shush, boy. Calm down. Where's Nikon?"

It wasn't like him to get caught. What could have happened? The panic in my chest thrummed uselessly inside me. What now?

If Nikon got caught, I'd be of no use. Yes, I'd learned much since meeting him, but I wasn't as capable as him at sneaking around. If I did make it through the vegetation without getting caught, I wouldn't have any idea of how to move forward.

Didn't matter. Nikon was in danger, and so was the rest of Eppla.

I grabbed my cane and oriented myself from the distant sound of the waterfall. The monkeys were no longer making a fuss, from what I could tell, and I knew the area well. I'd make it there, if no further.

"We're going to find and rescue him," I whispered to Tewy.

Tewy jumped on my shoulder, giving a reassuring *ooo*. I hurried forward as fast as I could without making noise. I didn't want to draw attention to me, but I was afraid I'd be seen. The trees in the area were familiar to me. I'd have to stick close to them.

I went from one to another to the next, slipping closer to the waterfall. Though Nikon might be at the house or elsewhere, my gut said to check here first. As I approached, the sound of voices slowed me. Voices, steps, and rustling.

The high priest could have already poisoned the water against love. Perhaps that was why there was moving about.

I bit my lip. If Nikon was here, I would find him.

Regardless of my desire to march forward, I continued my silent creeping through the trees. The sounds of people moving grew louder, and I eased behind a tree to listen to them. No one came my way, so they must not have seen me.

"Are you certain she's here?" the high priest said.

"Positive," Antonia replied. "If Nikon's here, so is she."

I shivered. Japuta seemed sweet despite all she'd been through, but it was clear those traits didn't carry on to her daughter. The high priest's words had influenced Antonia more than anyone or anything else.

"If your dimwitted warriors had followed him around, instead of capturing him, we could have found her too," he said.

"Yes, Grandfather. My apologies. We could send the enhanced neczar after her."

My body went icy cold with fear. Enhanced neczar were here.

"No. I don't want them wandering about."

I pressed my back against the tree, and Tewy hopped off my shoulder.

Warriors—probably elite ones—and enhanced neczar.

I didn't stand a chance.

CHAPTER FORTY-THREE

I stayed extra still, trying to determine the next path forward. I didn't know where Nikon was, but they had him. If I moved forward, they'd have power over me, because they knew I wouldn't let harm come to him.

Gritting my teeth, I searched for another option.

Tewy's chatter sounded a ways to my left. The little rascal was going to get caught. The thought of something happening to him made me more ill.

More monkeys joined the chorus.

"Someone shut those blasted things up again," the high priest shouted.

"Sorry, Grandfather. There's nothing we can do about them. Our warriors haven't been able to kill them, but they quieted on their own last time." Antonia sounded as agitated as he did.

Tewy's hooting went farther away and closer to the other monkeys, distinct from their sounds. I couldn't have said why, but I was grateful I could tell him apart. His sounds soon stopped, but the other monkeys continued in full force.

Sneaky monkey was up to something, but there wasn't time to dwell on what. I needed a plan.

"What's that monkey doing?" Valeriana called out.

"Get the creature before it releases the prisoner," Antonia belted out.

Tewy was trying to free Nikon. That had to be it. Several people rushed toward the monkey commotion, and I took the chance to sneak a couple trees closer.

Voices reached me more clearly.

"I told you, Cassandra isn't here," Nikon said. "I set off on my own."

Hearing his voice again made my heart thrum back to life. He was alive and well enough to talk, sounding like his usual self. That was something.

Someone gave a heavy sigh. The high priest said, "Tie his mouth back up, before he goes off on the subject again. I weary of hearing it."

And though Nikon didn't say another word, he'd accomplished what I needed him to. I now knew where he was. The question was—what to do about it? If Tewy couldn't sneak up to him, I wouldn't be able to.

I rested the back of my head against the tree trunk. What I needed was a distraction, so I could untie Nikon and— What? Leaving was an option, but we'd be no better off than we were now. Plus, they'd come after us. Fighting might help, but we were outmanned.

No. What we needed was a way to fix the water and oust the high priest and Antonia. If I had the entire rebellion and Reding Theodore with his people at my back, it would be a manageable task.

Tewy landed on my shoulder, making me jump. Little monkey had almost scared me into a mummy.

I petted him and whispered, "Good job."

He didn't respond with words but did give my hair a good yank. In truth, he'd done a very good job. Maybe he could continue to help. "Can you cause a distraction? I'm going to get Nikon out of here." It was the least I could do.

Ooo oo. Tewy leaped off me and scampered away.

There was enough other-monkey chatter that I didn't think he'd be caught. Now that I thought about it, there were more monkey noises since we'd arrived than there had been when we arrived. It might just be that Tewy was gathering them together. It wouldn't surprise me.

I curled my toes and relaxed them, trying to be patient. Time ticked by, and Tewy did nothing. The warriors continued to move about, but I heard nothing from my little monkey. Maybe I'd overestimated how much he understood.

Nikon needed rescuing. There had to be some plan I could come up with.

Not knowing what else to do, I untwisted my cane into fighting sticks. I could get Nikon out of his bounds, but I doubted they'd make it out of the clearing.

I wished I knew more about what the high priest and Antonia had planned. How long would the high priest's plan take, to put into action? If I did have a part to play in it, maybe the best thing I could do for Nikon was leave him here alone and go for help. The boat would hopefully keep me from the chasm, but otherwise, I might keep running into the bank, though the sand would help. If I miraculously made it downstream to Sirya, Zoe, Kaius, and my parents would all be difficult if not impossible to reach before I was captured and brought back here.

If I was going to do something about this, it needed to be now.

"She's not coming," Antonia said. "She's brighter than I thought. We'll have to send the warriors and neczar out, to look for her."

"If you think that's the best course of action. I'll keep some of the neczar here though." The high priest sounded distracted. "I've got to finish my experiment. Do what you will, to bring me the blind one."

He'd better not be close to finishing.

What would they do if they knew I was listening in? Capture me and run experiments, no doubt. Find ways to use me. I couldn't let him infect the waterfall with something worse than he already had.

"We'll get her," Antonia said.

"She may or may not be the key. Either way, I have plans for her," the high priest said.

I shivered. I wanted nothing to do with his plans.

"Valeriana, you stay. The rest of you spread out and find the blind woman," Antonia said.

"And half of you beasts go with," the high priest said, still sounding distracted.

Sands blast it. The footsteps hurried this way and that. I scrunched into as small a ball as I could silently make myself, while they approached. My pulse grew rapid, the pounding in my ears fiercer, the closer they came. How would I keep them from finding me?

Only one person headed my way, but it'd be that one to alert the group to my presence. It didn't sound heavy enough to be a neczar; still, it was difficult to tell. I gripped my sticks. I'd need them at any moment.

Preparing to pounce, I eased my muscles while the person passed me by.

No call came up. I stayed as I was. Somehow, they hadn't seen me. Not yet. As the steps faded, I took a deep, shuddering breath and let it ease the thrumming in my chest.

I leaned the back of my head against the tree. Who was left between me and Nikon? The high priest, Antonia, Valeriana. Those first two shouldn't be a problem for my skills, though I knew little about the high priest.

Valeriana and half of the neczar would cause problems, though.

I needed something. A distraction. Where was Tewy with it? The wait continued, leaving me gnawing at my lip, until the high priest called out, "It's ready."

My heart sped up. I had to do something. I couldn't let his newest experiment get in the water.

"What do you need me to do?" Antonia asked, sounding far too obedient.

"Take this, but be careful. I want to pour it in myself, but feel the power of holding it."

The high priest's words left me chilled.

Tewy's distraction wasn't coming. I had to act.

I jumped out, and, screaming, ran for where his and Antonia's voices had come from. If nothing else, I could delay the inevitable. Expecting to be stopped any moment, I untwisted my cane and readied it into fighting sticks. They wouldn't do much good against a neczar, but they'd buy me more time.

"It's her," Antonia said. "Quickly, get her."

"I can't leave Nikon," Valeriana said. "He'll find a way to escape. She's just a blind girl."

"She's more than that. Neczar, capture her." The Vading sounded desperate.

But I heard none of them coming at me, and couldn't feel anyone from my sticks, so I pummeled on.

"Get her, neczar," Antonia screeched, far closer this time.

I was going to do it. I'd attack them, and do what I could to steal the vial. After that, I'd deal with whatever I had to.

"You heard my granddaughter. Stop that woman." The high priest didn't raise his voice, but the effect was a thumping, running toward me from four different directions. The neczar.

I barely had time to register the attack, when one of them slammed into me.

I hurtled through the air and smacked into the water and down onto the sandy riverbed. My grip loosened, as I struggled to right myself under the water. I had to get to safety. My sticks floated one way, as I washed another. If I got control of myself, I could fetch them through their call, but the water flipped me about.

The coldness shocked through me, compounding the problems of lack of air. Though the waterfall should have pushed me away, the water felt as if it surrounded me and attacked from all sides. Where were the neczar? They should have attacked. I had other problems to worry about. Each stroke of my arms seemed to find me more turned about in the water than before, but I pushed on, desperate for air.

As I tried to ignore the burning in my lungs from not being able to take a breath before I sank, I righted myself.

The water pounded above me, as I thrashed through the fall itself. My hand hit rock. I pulled myself up. I popped out of the water with a gasp, the roaring water covering the noise. The waterfall flowed behind me, giving me space between the curtain of water and where my enemies were by the side. Oxygen filled my lungs, giving its power back, clearing my thoughts.

I was outnumbered and had no idea what to do next. I clung to the rock behind the rush of water, sharp bits poking into me.

"Where did she go?" Antonia's voice was difficult to discern through the falls. "Did she drown?"

I scowled at how happy she sounded, but it was the least of my worries.

"Doesn't matter. I think I figured how to get rid of romantic love that ruins everything with this potion. This vial will change everything, Antonia."

Thunderous footsteps headed away from the water. It had to be the neczar; no one else was big enough to be that loud. Maybe the one who charged me.

The high priest's plan was *worse* than having the amant and odiosom. Falling in love only at first sight might not have been right, but love disappearing entirely was downright wrong. Too many problems awaited with no recourse. It would end our people, slowly dying as we aged with no more children to continue our legacies.

I had to stop this.

No cane. No Nikon. No Tewy. Just me.

CHAPTER FORTY-FOUR

Better to go down the river after a fight for love, than keep on living without it.

I didn't wait a second more. I slipped back into the water, brushing against the bottom. I needed to reach the high priest and Antonia before they ruined Eppla and possibly the world beyond.

I slid through the water with a grace and ease that surprised me, jetting toward the other side of the river, like it was helping me. As the water grew shallower, I jumped to my feet and ran ahead.

"She's alive," Valeriana shouted.

Antonia screeched and the high priest grunted. I ran directly for them and rammed into someone. I bowled them over, gratified when the high priest groaned.

We fell to the ground with a *thump*, the old man bonier and smaller than I expected. I recovered before he did, as Antonia shouted, "*Grandfather*."

Valeriana swore, but was still far off. Neczar hurtled toward me, but there was time to make a difference. I jumped to my feet and kicked. It was the only chance I hand. My foot landed, harsh and jolting, forcing him back with a splash. I must have kicked him in the water, the impact still thrumming up my legs.

The thumping steps of at least three neczar thundered toward me. I turned back toward Antonia's screech, putting on a burst of speed. If she still had it, I couldn't let the concoction get in the water and ruin love for Eppla.

I wouldn't make it to Antonia before the neczar reached me. My body ached, and I knew this would never work. Despite that, I carried on, though neczar or Valeriana would take me down at any moment. The running boomed past me, heading toward the high priest. Shock burst through me.

Whatever was going on, I wouldn't waste the opportunity. I continued toward Antonia.

Tewy let out a crazed screech, followed by a huge explosion.

"How dare you touch my grandfather's lab, you stupid monkey," Antonia called. "I'll kill you."

Inside, I shuddered. What had he done? The explosion must have been his distraction, with the lab if I had to guess.

Before I reached her, Antonia said in seething tones, "Give up now or I kill the monkey."

I stopped, perhaps an arm's length away from her. *Tewy*. My dear, sweet monkey. I loved him, but I couldn't let the whole world suffer because his life was in danger.

Tewy gibbered, twisting my heart into pieces.

Valeriana chuckled darkly.

"Please, Antonia, leave him be." I couldn't listen to her torture him, but neither could I sit by, as she poured the contents of the vial into the river.

Instead of answering, she called out, "Where are you going?"

Confusion flowed through me, until I realized the neczar hadn't stopped at the high priest. They'd kept on running, their footsteps becoming faint. They were leading away from us.

"Get them, Valeriana," Antonia demanded.

"But "

"Go after them. Now."

"Yes, Vading."

Lighter footfalls followed the deeper ones that were quickly fading. Without warning, Antonia screamed.

"What have you done?" Antonia shrieked and ran past me, to where I'd left the high priest. I turned toward the sound of her steps, not wanting my back to her.

Tewy let out a painful chirp and Antonia screamed. "Don't bite me, you stupid thing."

Seconds later, I heard him running toward me, and then he jumped up my arm and to my shoulder.

I hesitated, wanting to both comfort him and figure out what was going on.

"*Grandfather*." Antonia sobbed.

Tewy yanked on my hair, away from the direction she was at, and hopped away. Where was he going? He squeaked again, and I followed. There had to be one place he was going. Nikon. Less than a second later, there was a grumble from Nikon.

I bumbled to a stop in front of him and got to my knees, reaching out. My hands found his shoulder, following it down until I located the ropes and untied him. I reached for his mouth to get the scrap of cloth there so he could talk, but he said under his breath, "Tewy got it, I'll get my feet. Get Antonia before she does something rash."

I wanted to linger, to feel his skin, his pulse, to know he hadn't been injured, but he was right. She had the vial. I had to get it from her. I stood and headed where I last remembered her at.

"*You*." Antonia's voice grew clearer. "You killed him, Cassandra."

I took a step back from the venom in her tone. I killed the high priest? "It was an accident. I only wanted to stop you both from ruining Eppla," I said.

"You're a murderer," she hissed.

Crashing came through the underbrush toward us. The neczar returning?

"They're not coming back," Valeriana called back.

"Grandfather's hold on them is no more with his death." Antonia's voice seethed with anger. "Kill them both."

"Yes, Vading."

Despite the threat behind me, I headed for Antonia, knowing I had to get to her before Valeriana reached me. A couple of steps toward her, and Nikon's voice rumbled behind me. "You have to get through me before you can get Cassandra."

"My pleasure," Valeriana practically purred.

There was only an instant to send him good wishes for defeating her before I was back at Antonia. The woman in question had to be close, but I didn't know where exactly. I said the thing I knew would provoke the strongest reaction. "I'm glad the high priest is dead."

She growled deep in her throat, far louder than a human should be capable of. Wait, was that her? It had come from my right.

"You will pay for this," Antonia said, coming closer in front of me and not to my side. "I'll throw this vial in the water to make my grandfather's wish come true, and then I'll take great pleasure in killing you, your Nikon and Tewy dead by Valeriana's hand."

I took a step back, as my heart dropped. Without my fighting sticks, she'd have the upper hand. Plus, she had Valeriana close by if something happened to Nikon. There were also those two warriors who had to be on their way after hearing that ruckus, whatever Tewy had done. I took a second step back, as I heard her come toward me. I had to figure out how to fix this, to sacrifice myself if need be, to fix the water before I was killed.

The fighting behind me in grunts and ringing of metal intensified, Nikon clearly in trouble of his own.

"Antonia, please. Think this through. Why rid the world of

love? The high priest is gone now. Let him and his ideas be put to rest."

"You have no clue. If his idea had worked the first time, I wouldn't be married to and in love with a weak man I despise. I let Grandfather use one of his experiments on me, but only because it would let us take power and stop love from plaguing anyone else. I could have lived my life without him in peace."

The high priest had made her fall in love with the Reding. That's what some of his experiments had done. The thought of just how much had been manipulated made me shake with horror.

A realization smacked me and plunged into me so suddenly and deeply, I wondered why I hadn't thought of it before. "If he'd succeeded the first time, you would never have been born."

She stood still and didn't speak.

The clangs rose and Nikon's deep voice came out in a groan. I wanted to help him, but I didn't have a chance yet with Antonia still holding the vial in front of me. Maybe I was getting through to her. "There's time to stop this. Your parents only had you because they loved one another. If we reverse the original spell, the rest of Eppla that hasn't already fallen in love at first sight won't have to. No one else has to be tied to a spouse they despise." Nikon flashed through my mind. I wanted to go rescue him, but I had to convince Antonia to hand over the vial first.

"You know nothing. My parents were killed by the likes of you, horrible, blind girl." The attack of her words was as sharp as any sword, but I had a shield of knowledge.

"No, they weren't. The high priest killed your father, but your mother has been alive this entire time. We rescued Japuta from Peka Tower and she told us everything. You still have her. There's time to make amends and relish company from her."

She laughed, the sound pitched high. "That woman is nothing but an experiment gone wrong. She's mad with all the things Grandfather did to her."

It was unlikely that I would be able to convince her of her true parentage. "The Reding won't stand for this. He and the country deserve better."

The sounds of fighting intensified, but I kept focused on her, inching closer.

"He's a weak man with a weak heart. I'll get rid of love forever and won't ever have to deal with him again, except to have him killed and take his place as sole ruler of Eppla."

"Antonia, no. You may not care for me or him, but think of what you're doing. Humanity will cease to exist if you do this. Please."

A moment's pause was followed by a ragged noise, deep from her throat. "No. My grandfather was right. He could have saved us all this pain."

"No, he didn't care about anyone's pain. He wanted to punish the world."

She growled. "I will do what he wanted."

Her words were registering in my mind as she headed toward my right. I pivoted toward her, as if everything had slowed.

I wouldn't make it to her before she got to the water.

I ran like I'd never run before as behind me Valeriana screamed. As the river's edge lapped at my feet, I bowled into her, knocking us both to the ground. I grabbed a hunk of sand and threw it at her face. She screamed. "My eyes!"

Good. It'd done something more than just served as a distraction. I pushed against her.

"No. No, no, no." Antonia's cries grew more desperate. "I have to do this. I have to."

I grasped her shoulder and followed it down to her flailing arm, only too grateful when I found a stoppered vial in her hand. She alternated clawing at me and smacking me with her free hand. Ignoring the pain, I took it from her and held it tight. What should I do with it? I couldn't just discard it; it might get into the water.

A heavy thud came from where Nikon and Valeriana fought. I winced, but there wasn't time to worry over Nikon. I stood and took a couple steps backward, when a loud *whoosh* came from behind me.

I whirled around in time for the sphinx to say, "Vading of the land, you have done us all wrong. Answer my riddle, and your life will be given another chance."

"You." The word spat out of Antonia. I didn't know if it was more dangerous to have my back to her or to the sphinx, so I tilted slightly, putting them on either side of me as she continued. "My grandfather told me all about your kind and how you became one. It's your fault everything is ruined."

What was Antonia talking about? The sphinx didn't use to be such a creature? And how had the sphinx ruined everyone?

"All that was done was done for the best. Now I wander, looking to test those whom I wish."

I'd responded to her, and it wasn't my life on the line. But Antonia's was.

"You pay too much mind, Cassandra, to the one who's done so wrong." The sphinx could read minds. I'd forgotten about that. The sphinx was lethal and intelligent.

I had to respond with, "That may be, but I won't be the one to condemn her."

"Perhaps I shall. Vading, answer me this. I happen only once, quick as a flash. Those who don't find me are left out like trash. I may be wrong, I may be right, but I was never meant to be."

My mind scurried about for an answer, but before I could come up with one, Antonia spat out, "I won't ever answer the creature that shouldn't exist."

"Then, you shall die."

I scrambled backward, hoping to stay out of the way, but before I'd gone far, wind rushed over my head.

The sphinx had jumped over me and landed with a soft grace I could barely hear.

Antonia's shriek that followed made me slam the palms of my hands with a wince, almost dropping the vial.

The sound stopped, and there was no doubt in my mind that Antonia had found her end.

I straightened, wishing I had my cane. The sphinx might be here and a possible threat, but I couldn't leave Nikon. If it'd been him that'd fallen instead of Valeriana... No. I wouldn't think like that. But if he was alive, where was he?

"Where are you, Nikon? Can you make a sound?" My heart thudded in my chest when there was no response. The area had grown quiet. Too much so. All I could hear was the rush of the waterfall. No screams or chiding from Antonia. No mocking Valeriana. None of the warriors, running to their aid. No sphinx, giving riddles, or monkeys, chattering about.

But also no hint to where Nikon was. I'd search the whole area until I found him, no matter what it took. He and Tewy couldn't be far, and they were both still alive, they had to be. I would find him, and we would leave this hateful place.

"Nikon, I'm coming." And maybe then, I'd be brave enough to tell him how I felt.

Something felt off, but wanting to get started, I reached out my hand. My fingers brushed against something wholly familiar, and yet completely off. Was that grains of wet sand, smoothed together to form something? That didn't make any sense.

"Because that is me, Cassandra," the sphinx said, making me jerk back. She went on like I hadn't reacted. "Your little man is to your right, alive, but there's something going on with you. Something I feel from you that reminds me of myself."

I wanted to puzzle this out, but wanted to get to Nikon more. Hoping she wasn't lying to me about his location, I turned to the right and stepped forward one foot at a time, feeling my way forward. Only a few strides in, and Tewy's familiar squawk came hurtling toward me. No, not toward me. In front of me and to the right a bit.

"Tewy, you're back." I was grateful my little friend survived everything we'd gone through.

I continued on my way, and had almost reached the area where Tewy's hoots came from, when Nikon said, "Cass."

My nickname coming from his lips halted me for half a second. "Nikon, I..." Had so much I wanted to say. The thoughts and feelings inside me warmed me to the point of burning, yet it was a pleasant sensation I wanted more of.

I'd find him and convey my feelings for him.

But first, I wanted to touch him.

Clutching the vial in one hand, I walked on.

"She loves you." The sphinx's voice stopped me cold with fear, but the wonder and awe in her statement surprised me. "Truly, the blind has seen the truth of love and broken through my absence."

Despite my fear and my desire to get to Nikon, her presence kept me from going. "*Your* absence?"

"You feel for the man what you should not, since I was taken from the water." The sphinx's voice was as soft as I'd ever heard it.

"Is that true, Cass?" Nikon's question made me flush with worry.

This wasn't the way I wanted to tell him, but knowing our lives, there wouldn't be a perfect time. "It is. I love you, Nikon. If things were different, and you didn't have to fall in love at first sight, maybe you could have been with me, instead. Regardless of what happens, I love you and will always do so. I would give everything for you."

It was the sphinx who responded first. "The gift of love will come back to Eppla, for all to find."

"What do you mean?"

"Like the riddle I gave the angry one. The answer was love at first sight. It never should have been. The experiment man did his tricks to the water at its source here, pulling me out. I am the embodiment of falling in love the way people were meant to. This shape I took so I could spill anger onto the land of people who rejected love. Instead of love, I became power over others. Magic fueled by love turned sour. I believed the path was right, but now I wonder. Staying away might have been a blunder."

She, the sphinx, wasn't a sphinx at all. She was love who turned into a sphinx when the high priest forced one of his experiments on the natural way of things. But it also sounded like there might be a chance to change things. "I'm not the key to changing things back to the way they were. You are."

"And I chose not to."

"Why?" My word was soft, but she still heard.

"The hate of the man who turned me made me forget that there were those who still deserve."

"There are bad people," I conceded. "But there are many out there that try their best. People are entitled to the chance to fall in love as they should. They need to know the way real love brings joy. It doesn't mean heartache won't come. People will still do horrid things, but with love, *real* love, there's hope there too. A chance to break through the anger, hurt, and sadness people feel."

I turned to where Nikon was. "Like I love this man. I wouldn't be the person I am, wouldn't want to fight as hard as I do for things that are right, if I hadn't fallen in love with him." I turned back toward her. "That feeling healed me. Yes, it also brought pain, but the light it brings makes me want to be a better person. People deserve that chance."

It was so quiet, she could have left and I would have never known.

"I understand," she finally said. "I will put things right. Goodbye, Cassandra and her little man. Remember love is worth more than might."

There was a soft dip into the water, followed by a loud splash. Water rained down on me for a moment.

What just happened?

I wouldn't let whatever it was keep me from Nikon any longer. I hurried toward where I last heard his voice.

"She disappeared." Nikon's voice was filled with the wonder I felt.

The sphinx had been love, giving herself back to the water, restoring the natural way of things. At least I hoped all of Eppla could go back to falling in love how they should.

I stumbled to the ground, felt around until I found Nikon. He was on the ground, breaths coming heavy. "Are you injured?"

"Just winded. Valeriana is dead."

The death blow must have cost him. She was no friend, but I also knew he hated to have more blood on his hands. I reached out to him before hesitating halfway. He grabbed my hand with both of his. The pounding of my heart felt uneven and skittish.

"You really love me?" There was a strange note to his voice, but I couldn't tell what it was.

"I do. The sands did what my parents asked. They made me able to fall in love."

Though things would never be perfect or like I wanted, my heart soared. I carefully set the dangerous vial to the side, knowing I'd have to find a way to destroy it. I threaded the fingers of my other hand through Nikon's. I shouldn't push, when he loved another, but I was content to have this moment.

Until the strange smoothness I felt registered in my thoughts. "The amant marking. The ridge isn't there," I said.

"It's gone, Cass." There was a hint of hope in his words. Hope I wanted to explore.

My heart beat faster, my palms growing sweaty and my chest tight. Could he...? Was it possible...? Was he really free of love for her—Lavti? I licked my lips. How could I ask? It didn't feel like the right time, though I ached to know. Instead, I let my fingers thread through his, content when they curled around mine.

Tewy jumped onto my shoulder and squawked triumphantly,

doing monkey jumps at the same time. I didn't know how he managed to stay on. "You did good, boy. Really good," I told him.

The distraction had come too late, but he'd helped me find Nikon, which was all I wanted.

He chattered happily. I grinned and untied Nikon's feet, ready to head down a familiar, yet somehow new, path.

CHAPTER FORTY-FIVE

The rebels and the government worked together. Peka Tower burned down. The amant and odiosom no longer existed. All amant bonds had disintegrated and people were free to love who they chose.

Things were in chaos but getting better. It'd be some time before everything calmed down and found a new normal.

It had been over a month since I'd defeated the high priest, and there were times I didn't believe it.

Nikon had told me the high priest had hit his head on a rock when I kicked him. That was how he died. Though his death was on my hands, I hadn't meant to kill him, and I couldn't feel guilty about it.

Together, Nikon and I had burned the contents of the vial. No one would ever get the chance to take away love. We'd seen to that.

The neczar, whether enhanced or not, had rarely been spotted since the high priest died and lost control over them. The vicious beasts people might still want to kill, but they were no longer murdering under orders. They rarely came to settlements, which was a gift of its own. Instead, they stuck to the desert where they naturally came from.

Sirya thrived with sound, far below my perch at the top of the pyramid. Now that I could walk around freely, I longed to be down among the people. Some former amant were struggling with the changes, though, and it wasn't safe for me to go out without someone to watch my back.

It was just as well, for at the moment, Theodore was getting ready to address the crowds.

Nikon stood near enough I could feel the warmth coming off him, though he wasn't touching me. Tewy sat on my shoulder—a hero for certain.

Though I'd expected him to stay back by the waterfall with all his monkey friends, when I'd tried to say goodbye, he'd squawked and climbed up my side. Maybe it was selfish, but I was happy.

I would have been more so, had Nikon been closer to me. He hadn't been distant, but with the loss of his connection to Lavti, I expected he'd warm up to me a little. Instead, things were strange. Though he stayed in my company and helped with what was needed, he never made the move to hold my hand or touch me unless he was guiding me. If he cared about me, I would have thought he'd make a move toward becoming a couple or speak with me about it.

On my other side, Zoe and Kaius stood, the leaders of the rebellion coming to terms with a new form of government that would benefit all people, no matter their situation in love. My parents were here also, but more in the background behind us, as support to me.

Thankfully, both of their relationships were about more than instant love—they were about care, friendship, and respect. The loss of amant status hadn't affected them.

Not all who'd been amant felt the same. Some had called for

an immediate divorce of their spouse, something not heard of since the Govlin Wars.

"Hupsheta looks smugger than a cat that caught a fish," Zoe whispered to me. "I still say we should have convinced Theodore to imprison her."

I wanted to agree. The woman wasn't my favorite person, but I said, "Nikon did give his word to do what he could to establish her in whatever government was left." It'd been her price over him for helping us. "I might not like it, but she is very useful."

"You mean good at getting what she wants." Zoe snorted.

I shrugged. "At least here, we'll be able to keep an eye on what she's doing."

"True."

We were lucky Nikon had convinced her that being an advisor to Theodore was the coveted position she wanted and that she hadn't insisted on more. Theodore had been warned that she was pushy, but she really did get things done.

"My people," Theodore called out, loud enough for his voice to quiet the chatter below, "it is with pleasure I come before you today. As you are aware, the amant markings have faded. There will be no more distinction between those who are in love and those who are not.

"In the past, I have directed you to shun the odiosom. For that, I am sorry. I've seen the error of my ways and know we all should move forward. We need to march ahead with a new presence of mind that takes everyone into consideration. We can go forward and help each other, instead of dragging down those who don't meet our ideas of perfection. There will be many challenging times ahead for us and our country, but we can make the best happen. We can bring Eppla together."

I straightened as he spoke, feeling new life within me. I didn't know what the future held, but I wanted to be part of it. I wanted to help heal our country and make it a better place for all. Already, I was supporting the blind who'd been enslaved, with

Elata's help. They knew and trusted her, and we were making strides in helping them find their place in this new normal.

Theodore continued for a while, before wrapping up to cheers and some booing. It wasn't perfect, but it was headed in a good direction.

The Reding strode toward us, footsteps so different than his brother's silent steps. Instead of stopping or passing us by, he surprised me by taking my hand and placing it on his arm.

I followed him toward a private receiving room, grateful it wasn't where Antonia had me beaten. Though I'd come somewhat to terms with my time as her slave, I didn't want to have to relive it.

Japuta had been jubilant when we told her of the high priest's death but stoic when we told her of Antonia's. Zoe was working with her to help her integrate back into society with the rest of the blind prisoners and slaves who'd been rescued from the pyramid and Peka Tower. It would take a lot of time and work, but she'd already proven to be strong.

Familiar steps followed us—Zoe, Kaius, and my parents.

We gathered together, Tewy scampering about the room once I sat down.

"Thank you for joining me today, and for all you've done for Eppla," Theodore said. "I appreciate your help in seeing what Antonia was doing to my country and its people. We'll make progress with them; I know it. Zoe and Kaius, I believe the Jackal could be of great use to the entirety of the kingdom. Edita and Dorian, I would like to take you on as advisors. While I have some from the former upper crust, your wisdom and insights will be of great value to the country.

"Cassandra, I would have you be a representative for the blind, if you are willing. There is much to be done, to help with the damage that was done. Much for me to atone for. Having your help and your words of advice would give me peace of mind.

"Nikon, what does one say, as a brother who wronged you?

I'm sorry, and if you'd like to come back as my personal, elite warrior, I would rejoice in your skill and your judgment. It would be different than before. I'd like the warriors to take on a more protective role, instead of policing."

He concluded with, "Each of you may take as much time to think about this as you wish, but please do let me know when you have an answer."

Though I hadn't expected anything of the kind, I didn't need any time at all to think on my answer. "It would be a pleasure to help you, Reding."

"Just *Theodore*, if you please."

I nodded. "Yes, Theodore. It would be my honor to assist you."

Everyone else gave a similar statement—except Nikon, who said nothing. I couldn't blame him. Though things were changing for the better, he'd been through a lot, and done things as an elite warrior that he never wanted to repeat. All the same, it was something he could do. Whatever he chose, I hoped he'd let me support him.

"What about Lavti?" my mother asked. We hadn't spoken of her much, but my mother must have known how much damage she'd done.

"We lock her up again," Nikon said. "She should never have done what she did to Cassandra."

"No," Theodore replied. "What she did was despicable, but so are acts I've performed."

At least he'd had the wherewithal to change his mind once he was presented with the facts. The same information given to Lavti seemed to make her worse.

Theodore continued. "Regardless of how wrong it was, at the time it was still within the law. We have no grounds to punish her. Now that she's no longer in love with Nikon, there's no threat she'll lash out at Cassandra again. She's agreed to move away from Sirya and leave things alone, and as long as she sticks to that and the law, we'll leave her alone too."

Nikon said, "I don't like it, but she did the most damage to you, Cassandra. What do you think?"

I wasn't certain of that. It felt like she'd done far more damage to Nikon than me. "I can't say she's a person I ever want to be friends with, but I'm no longer angry with her. If she leaves us alone and follows the law, I don't see her being a problem."

With a long-suffering sigh, Nikon said, "Very well then. I won't press the matter, and I'll work to forgive as Cassandra has done."

I supposed it would take some time even though he wasn't in love with her anymore. She'd been someone he thought he could trust, but in the end only ended up being a traitor. That kind of betrayal took effort and patience to work through.

The others spoke to Theodore for a while, but I had a hard time concentrating. I wanted to be with Nikon—that didn't change—but the fact that it may be a possibility raised my hopes. How much time did I want to spend with a man I loved, who didn't love me back?

Who was I kidding? I'd be happy to torture myself. Anything he needed, I would get for him, because I cared so deeply. Even if it meant we'd only ever be the best of friends.

The room dispersed into smaller groups talking among themselves, but I didn't have anything to add.

I stood. "If you'll excuse me, I'm going to wander around the pyramid for a while."

"Please, make yourself at home here," Theodore said.

"Thank you."

Tewy chattered from the corner, clearly happy with what he'd discovered. I had no doubt he'd find me when he was ready.

Zoe came over and gave me a hug. "I'll join you later. Kaius and I want to spend some time together alone for a while, but I'd like to see you after."

"That'd be wonderful." I hugged her tight. "I'm grateful to have you for a friend."

"I'm the lucky one."

Before I could refute that, she snuck off, likely to Kaius. With a shake of my head, I grabbed my cane and headed back toward the door. I wasn't surprised when my parents came with.

Mom said, "We'll walk with you for a bit."

"That'd be nice." Now that we weren't on the run, we had much to catch up on after years of being apart, but I found myself wanting to develop a new relationship, going forward. As we walked down the hall, I said, "Where are you planning on settling?"

"If we're honest," Mother said, "close to wherever you are."

"We may be the Reding's consultants, but we'll change that if we have to. We can't find another you," Dad added.

It was a good thing that they wanted to be with me, but I was also looking forward to growing on my own, in a world that was more accepting of me.

"We've been talking..." Dad hesitated.

I stopped and asked, "What is it?"

"Your mother and I were thinking that maybe..."

She jumped in to help. "Would you like us to put magic on your eyes again, to see if it gives you back your sight?"

I leaned back a moment, before continuing down the hall. My thoughts on the matter were far clearer than I'd expect. "No."

"Really?" Mother sounded surprised.

"Now, Edita. She can make her own choices," Dad told her.

"I know," she said. "It's only that I didn't expect this choice. May I ask why?"

I sighed, trying to put my thoughts and feelings into words. "There's always a chance that it won't work, unlikely given what we know of magic now, but still a possibility. More than that, though, while it would be nice to see again, all the growth I've experienced in my life has been because of my blindness.

It doesn't take away from my quality of life. I enjoy how I live, and have adjusted to the change. I feel like I can help others like me. Not to say that I couldn't if I could see, but I understand them better as I am." I shrugged. "The magic would know my heart, and see all this, so I don't know that it would do anything, except perhaps something I'd rather not deal with."

"Fair enough." My dad sounded content with my decision.

Mom wasn't, but I knew she felt the guilt of making me blind in the first place, despite what it led to. She said, "If you ever change your mind, we'd be happy to help."

"Thank you," I said. "But if I change my mind, I'll probably do it myself."

"You have grown," Dad said.

We continued on, walking through the pyramid, while I became more acquainted with the area, a different space than I had cleaned. Dad grew tired after a while, and they left me with hugs and plans to see me soon.

I wandered, letting the time roll by, before I realized I was heading to Nikon's old room. I didn't hesitate to go in when I found the door open. The room was as bare of furniture as the last time I was here, but had tapestries on the walls. Ones that had saved my life twice.

"I finally found you," Nikon said from the doorway.

Tewy hooted his excitement and hurried over to me, quickly making his way to my shoulder.

"I didn't know you were looking for me," I said.

"I thought we might talk. Would you like to go down to the river with me?"

I wouldn't hesitate at that offer, especially now that I knew the water wasn't tainted. "Let's go."

We comfortably made our way through the pyramid and out onto the streets with my hand on his arm, before he led me down an unfamiliar path.

Soon the voices of others were gone, replaced by the soft peace of the river.

I let him go and treaded down into the water, enjoying its cool embrace. Tewy jumped off my shoulder, going back toward Nikon, and splashing me while doing so.

"Tewy, you scamp." I laughed.

I splashed back, and Nikon called out, "You got me, not the monkey."

Laughing harder, I spun in a circle and settled in place with a sigh. Nikon moved toward me, his usual quiet movements made louder by the river. He came up behind me. I wanted to lean back into him, but overly aware I wasn't in that sort of a relationship with him, I turned and smiled instead.

My grin felt forced.

"Cass." He said my name so seriously, I let the smile drop.

"What do you need?" I asked.

"I don't know how to say this. It's different for me. So different. How I felt when I loved Lavti... Well, that wasn't love. It was a strange pull that made me want to be with her and be affectionate, but it's not at all what I feel when I'm with you."

My throat closed, making it difficult to get out an, "I understand."

"No, Cass. What I'm trying to say is that I wasn't certain what to do when the sphinx told me of your feelings. I didn't know how to act or where I should go in our relationship from there. Everything was different, and yet there was that feeling I've always had toward you. You became my best friend. With love returned, it's given me a chance. Us a chance. It's been slow. I don't even know when it fully crept up on me, but I no longer want to be parted from you.

"Everything we've been through, everything about you, the more I think on it, the more it makes this emotion grow inside me. It makes me want to hold you dear. To be close. To care about you before I care about myself. And maybe that's what love really is."

He cleared his throat. "After thinking about it, if you're all right with it, I would like to... That is to say— Can I court you?"

I didn't bother holding in my squeal of delight, as a pressure lifted off my chest. *He wanted to court me.* I never thought this could be, and yet, here he was, asking. I longed to bask in the way his words made me feel, but I didn't want to leave him hanging longer than I already had.

"I would enjoy that," I said. "I love you too, Nikon. I've loved you for a long time. It grew on me so slowly as well and seemed to be impossible, so I don't know when it rightly began. I'd like to let it keep growing."

Slowly, he moved his hands around my waist and pulled me toward him as the water flowed downstream.

I gave in to my feelings and placed my hands on his shoulders, pulling myself up. "If it's all right with you, I'd like a kiss now."

"More than happy to oblige."

I tilted my head up, and he pressed his lips against mine. The warmth flowing through me was immediate and intimate. As the magic flowed in the water around me and through the sand beneath my feet, it felt like a good omen.

My nose bumped against his, and I pulled back with a laugh.

He rested his forehead against mine, his breath sweet. "Ready to try that again."

"And again and again."

We came together once more, this time with more excitement and eagerness. He kissed me until I wanted to melt into him. I parted my lips, and he deepened the kiss into something greater than I ever expected could be.

I pulled his shoulders closer to me, as he threaded his fingers through my hair.

Tewy hooted, right before water splashed me again, getting us both wet.

Nikon and I came apart, but Nikon kept his arms tight around me, as I held him close.

To Tewy, I said, "You'd better get used to this."

For as long as I could remember, I'd wanted someone to care about me more than anything else in all of Eppla. It had finally happened. I was blind, but had fallen in love, just like anyone else could. Slowly or quickly—it didn't matter.

With Tewy and Nikon at my side, I'd stopped the poisoning of the water, and Eppla was now the home of my heart and my life.

THE END

If you enjoyed this book, please consider leaving an honest review.
Looking for new releases and a free novella from Janeal Falor?
Sign up for her newsletter on her website: janealfalor.com

Enjoyed the Sands of Eppla series? Look for more of Janeal's books!

OTHER BOOKS BY JANEAL FALOR

Mine Series

Mine to Tarnish (Mine Prequel Novella)

You Are Mine (Mine #1)

Mine to Spell (Mine #2)

Mine to Fear (Mine #3)

Sacrifice of Mine (Mine #4)

Mine to Defy (Mine #4.5)

Death's Queen

Death's Queen (Death's Queen #1)

Death's Betrayal (Death's Queen #2)

Death's Embrace (Death's Queen #3)

Death's Assassin (Death's Queen #4)

Darkening Light

Ever Darkening (Darkening Light #1)

Savage Light (Darkening Light #2)

Elven Princess

Bound by Birthright (Elven Princess #1)

Bound to Endure (Elven Princess #2)

Bound by Love (Elven Princess #3)

Standalone

Goddess Ascending

A Genie's Heart

Adult Fantasy

Mother of the Chosen (Mother of the Chosen #1)

Protector of the Chosen (Mother of the Chosen #2)

Guardian of the Chosen (Mother of the Chosen #3)

Sacrifice for the Chosen (Mother of the Chosen #4)

Anthology with Other Authors

In the Valley

ABOUT THE AUTHOR

Janeal Falor lives in Utah with her husband and three children. In her non-writing time she teaches her kids to make silly faces, cooks whatever strikes her fancy, and attempts to cultivate a garden even when half the things she plants die. When it's time for a break she can be found taking a scenic drive with her family or drinking hot chocolate.